Leeanne M. Krecic

Layout assists by **Nicholas Hogge**

Color assists by **MeliZbeauty**

Rocketship Entertainment, LLC

Tom Akel, CEO & Publisher

Rob Feldman, CTO

Jeanmarie McNeely, CFO

Brandon Freeberg, Dir. of Campaign Mgmt.

Phil Smith, Art Director

Aram Alekyan, Designer

Jimmy Deoquino, Designer

Ted Keith, Social Media

Jerrod Clark, Publicity

rocketshipent.com

LET'S PLAY VOLUME 4

Softcover ISBN: 978-1-962298-29-2 | 978-1-962298-25-4 (GAMER Ed.)

Hardcover ISBN: 978-1-962298-24-7 | 978-1-962298-26-1 (GAMER Ed.)

First printing. January 2024. Copyright © Leeanne M. Krecic. All rights
reserved. Published by Rocketship Entertainment, LLC. 136 Westbury
Ct., Doylestown, PA 18901. "Let's Play", the Let's Play logo,
and the likenesses of all characters herein are trademarks of Leeanne M.
Krecic. "Rocketship" and the Rocketship logo are trademarks of
Rocketship Entertainment, LLC. No part of this publication may be
reproduced or transmitted, in any form or by any means, without the
express written consent of Leeanne M. Krecic or Rocketship Entertainment,
LLC. All names, characters, events, and locales in this publication are
entirely fictional. Any resemblance to actual persons (living or dead), events,
or places, without satiric intent, is coincidental. Printed in China.

Previously on
Let's Play.

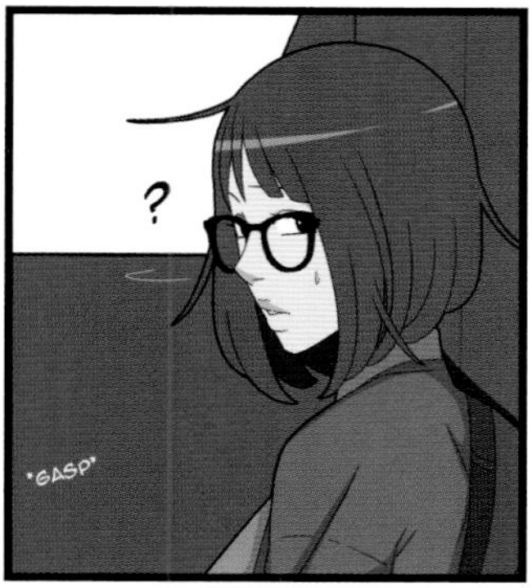
?
GASP

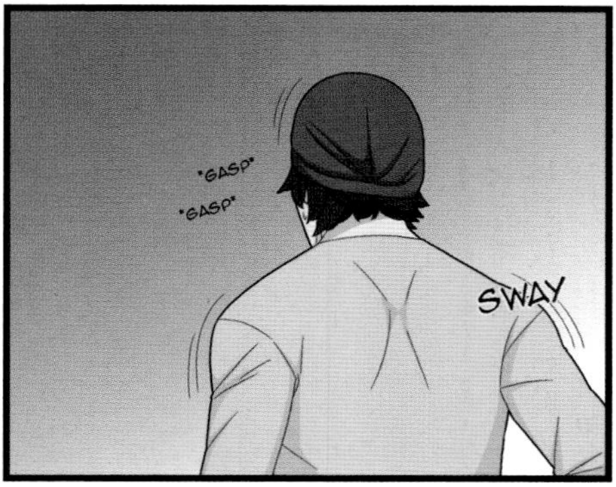
GASP
GASP
SWAY

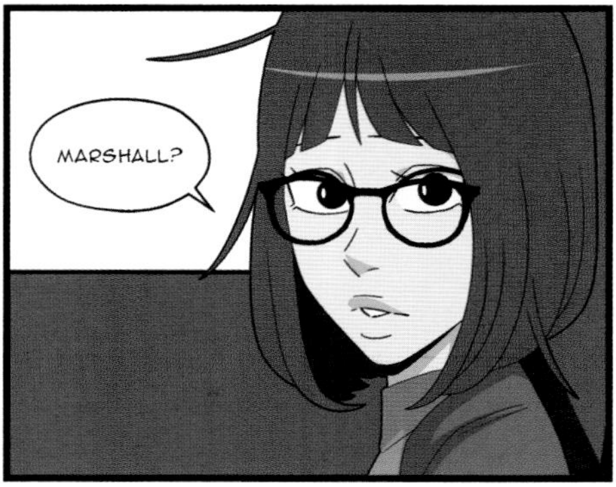
MARSHALL?

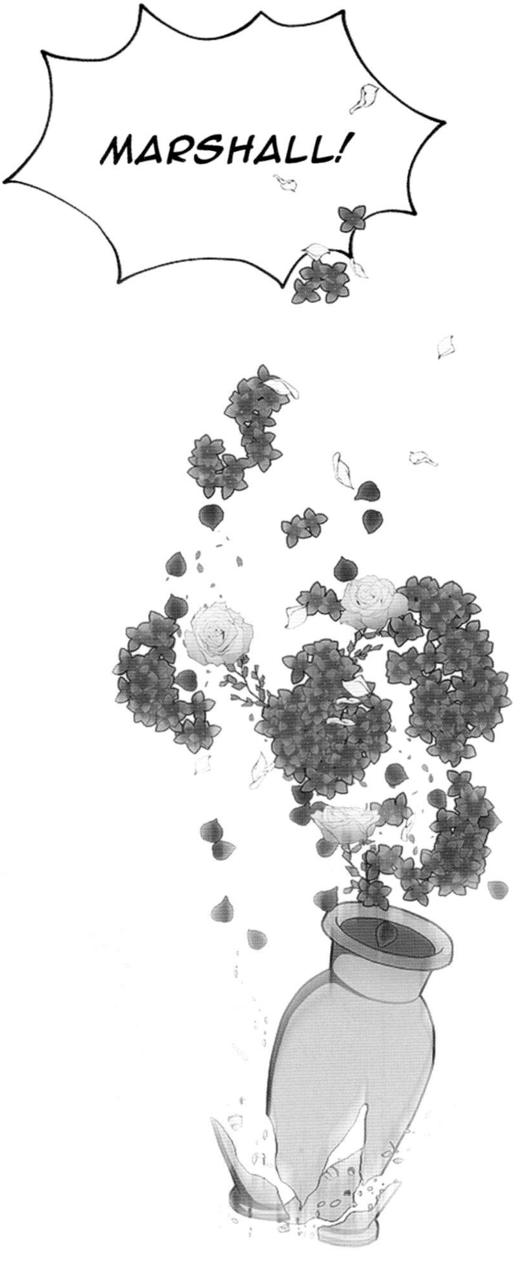
MARSHALL!

We continue.

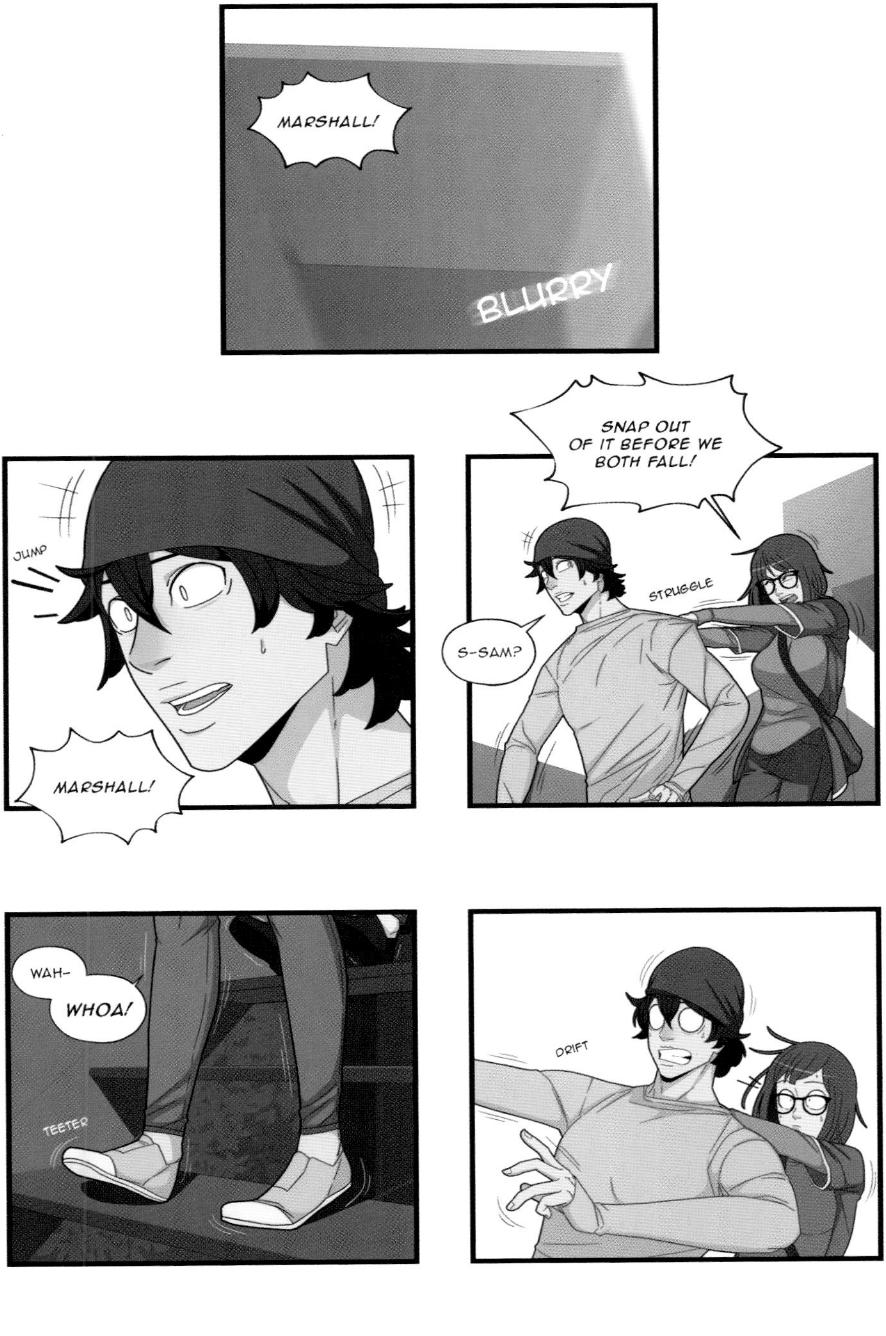
MARSHALL!
BLURRY
JUMP
MARSHALL!
SNAP OUT OF IT BEFORE WE BOTH FALL!
S-SAM?
STRUGGLE
WAH-
WHOA!
TEETER
DRIFT

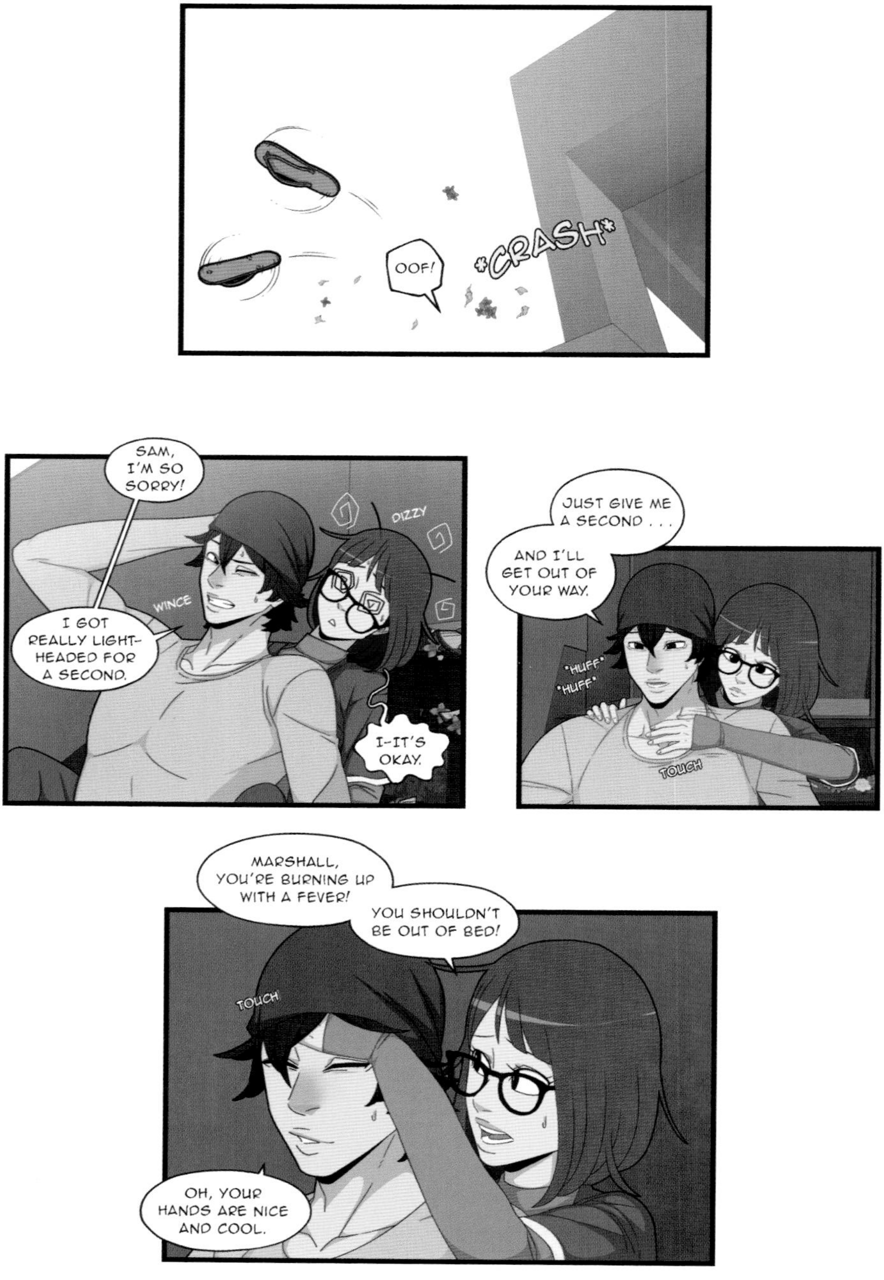
OOF!
CRASH
SAM, I'M SO SORRY!
WINCE
I GOT REALLY LIGHT-HEADED FOR A SECOND.
DIZZY
I-IT'S OKAY.
JUST GIVE ME A SECOND . . .
AND I'LL GET OUT OF YOUR WAY.
HUFF
HUFF
TOUCH
MARSHALL, YOU'RE BURNING UP WITH A FEVER!
YOU SHOULDN'T BE OUT OF BED!
TOUCH
OH, YOUR HANDS ARE NICE AND COOL.

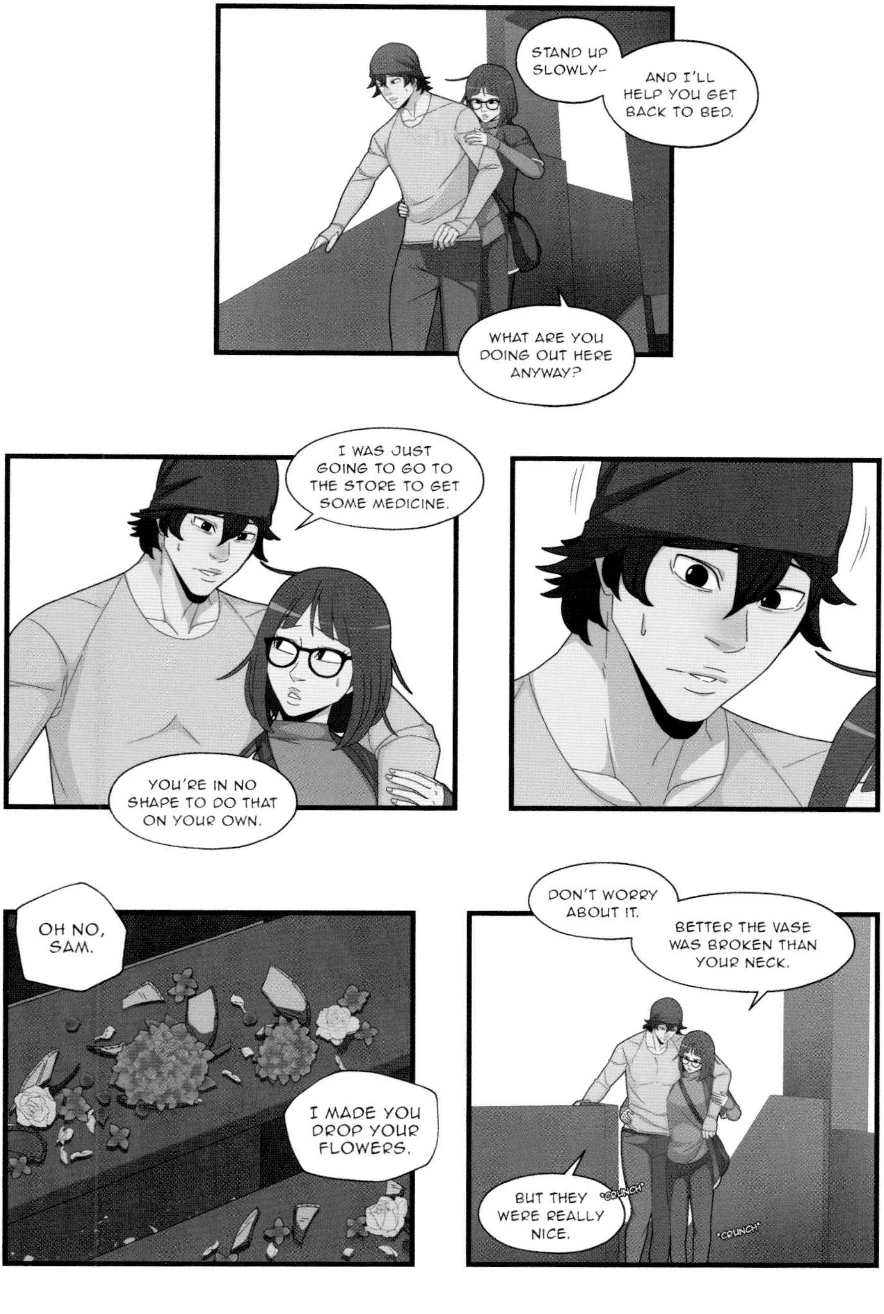
STAND UP SLOWLY-
AND I'LL HELP YOU GET BACK TO BED.
WHAT ARE YOU DOING OUT HERE ANYWAY?
I WAS JUST GOING TO GO TO THE STORE TO GET SOME MEDICINE.
YOU'RE IN NO SHAPE TO DO THAT ON YOUR OWN.
OH NO, SAM.
I MADE YOU DROP YOUR FLOWERS.
DON'T WORRY ABOUT IT.
BETTER THE VASE WAS BROKEN THAN YOUR NECK.
BUT THEY WERE REALLY NICE.
CRUNCH
CRUNCH

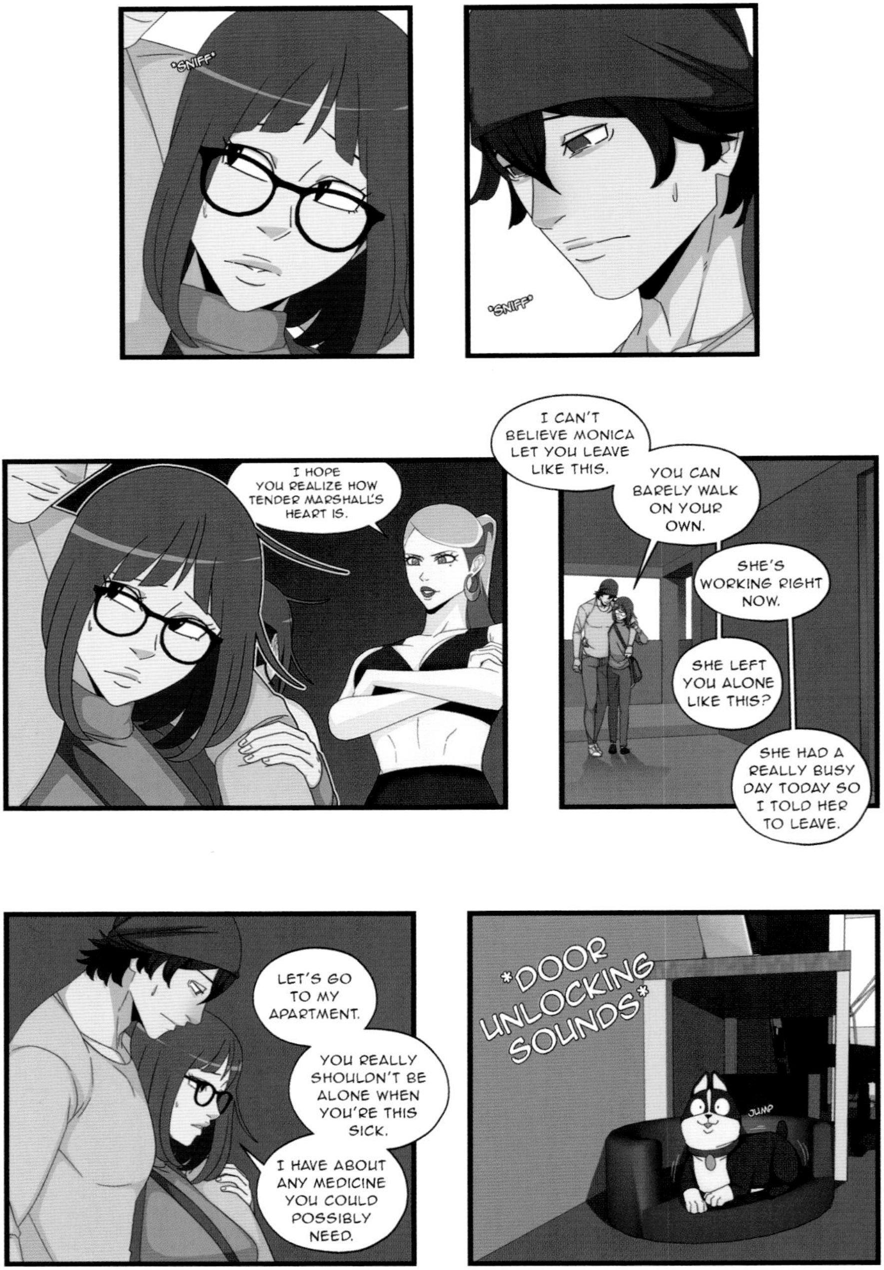
SNIFF
SNIFF
I HOPE YOU REALIZE HOW TENDER MARSHALL'S HEART IS.
I CAN'T BELIEVE MONICA LET YOU LEAVE LIKE THIS.
YOU CAN BARELY WALK ON YOUR OWN.
SHE'S WORKING RIGHT NOW.
SHE LEFT YOU ALONE LIKE THIS?
SHE HAD A REALLY BUSY DAY TODAY SO I TOLD HER TO LEAVE.
LET'S GO TO MY APARTMENT.
YOU REALLY SHOULDN'T BE ALONE WHEN YOU'RE THIS SICK.
I HAVE ABOUT ANY MEDICINE YOU COULD POSSIBLY NEED.
DOOR UNLOCKING SOUNDS
JUMP

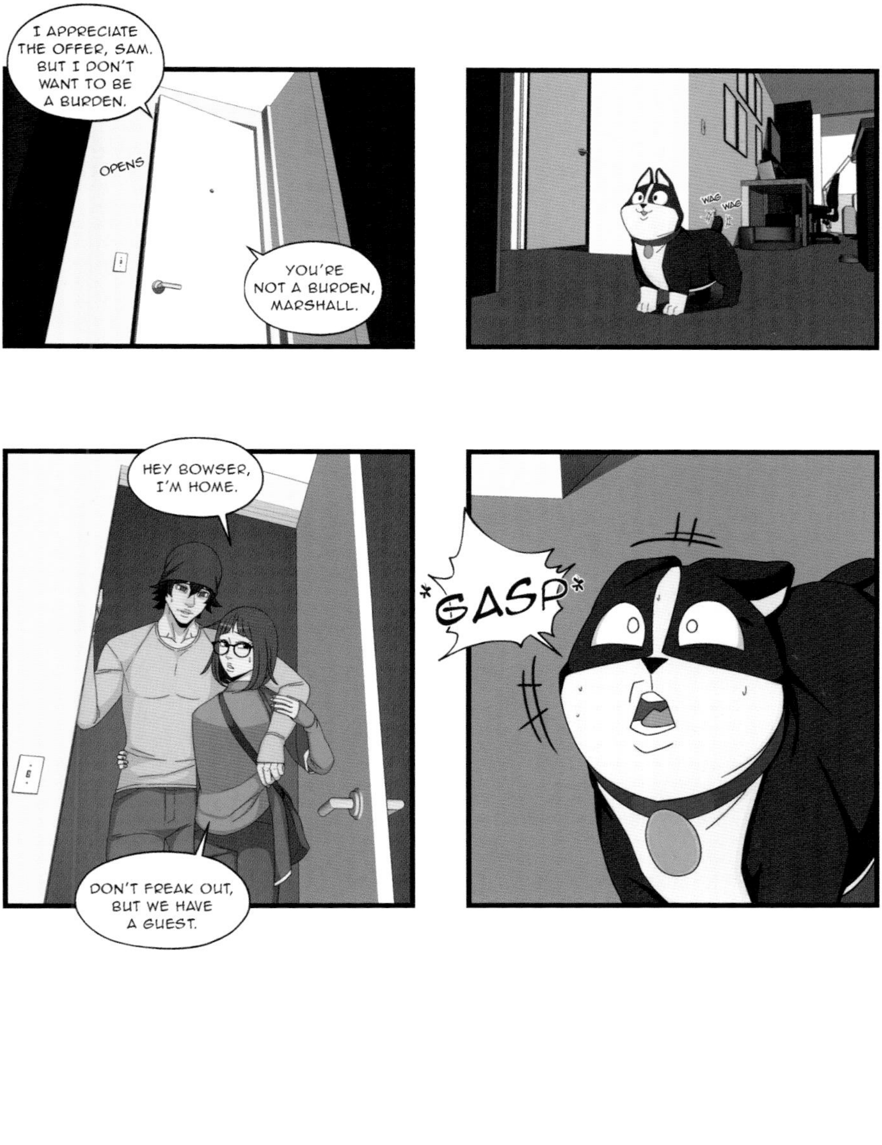
I APPRECIATE THE OFFER, SAM. BUT I DON'T WANT TO BE A BURDEN.
OPENS
YOU'RE NOT A BURDEN, MARSHALL.
WAG
WAG
HEY BOWSER, I'M HOME.
DON'T FREAK OUT, BUT WE HAVE A GUEST.
GASP

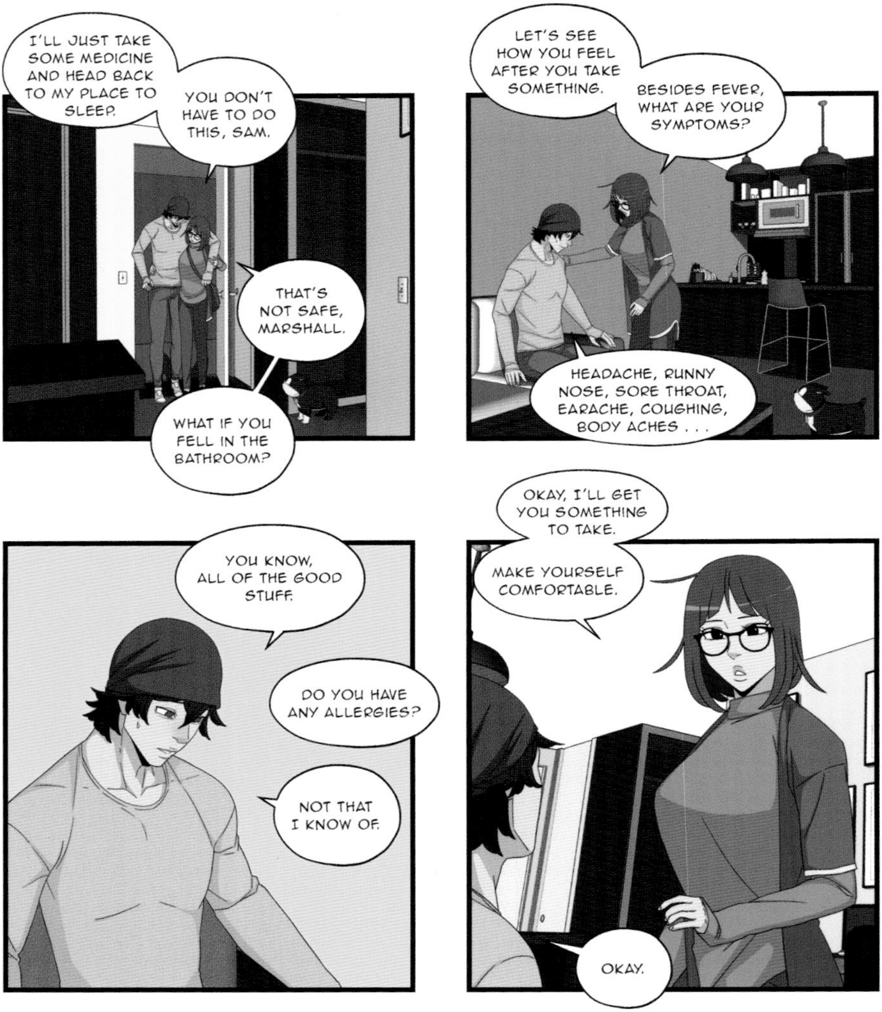
I'LL JUST TAKE SOME MEDICINE AND HEAD BACK TO MY PLACE TO SLEEP.
YOU DON'T HAVE TO DO THIS, SAM.
THAT'S NOT SAFE, MARSHALL.
WHAT IF YOU FELL IN THE BATHROOM?
LET'S SEE HOW YOU FEEL AFTER YOU TAKE SOMETHING.
BESIDES FEVER, WHAT ARE YOUR SYMPTOMS?
HEADACHE, RUNNY NOSE, SORE THROAT, EARACHE, COUGHING, BODY ACHES . . .
YOU KNOW, ALL OF THE GOOD STUFF.
DO YOU HAVE ANY ALLERGIES?
NOT THAT I KNOW OF.
OKAY, I'LL GET YOU SOMETHING TO TAKE.
MAKE YOURSELF COMFORTABLE.
OKAY.

. . .
GLANCE
GLARE
CHUCKLES
I DON'T BLAME YOU, PUPPY.
I DON'T LIKE ME MUCH EITHER.

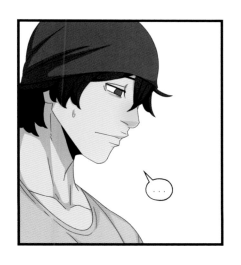

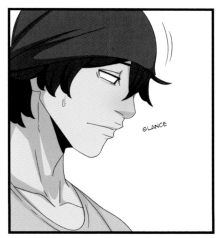

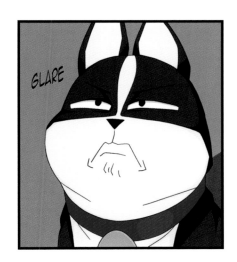

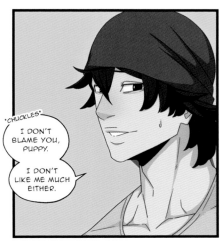

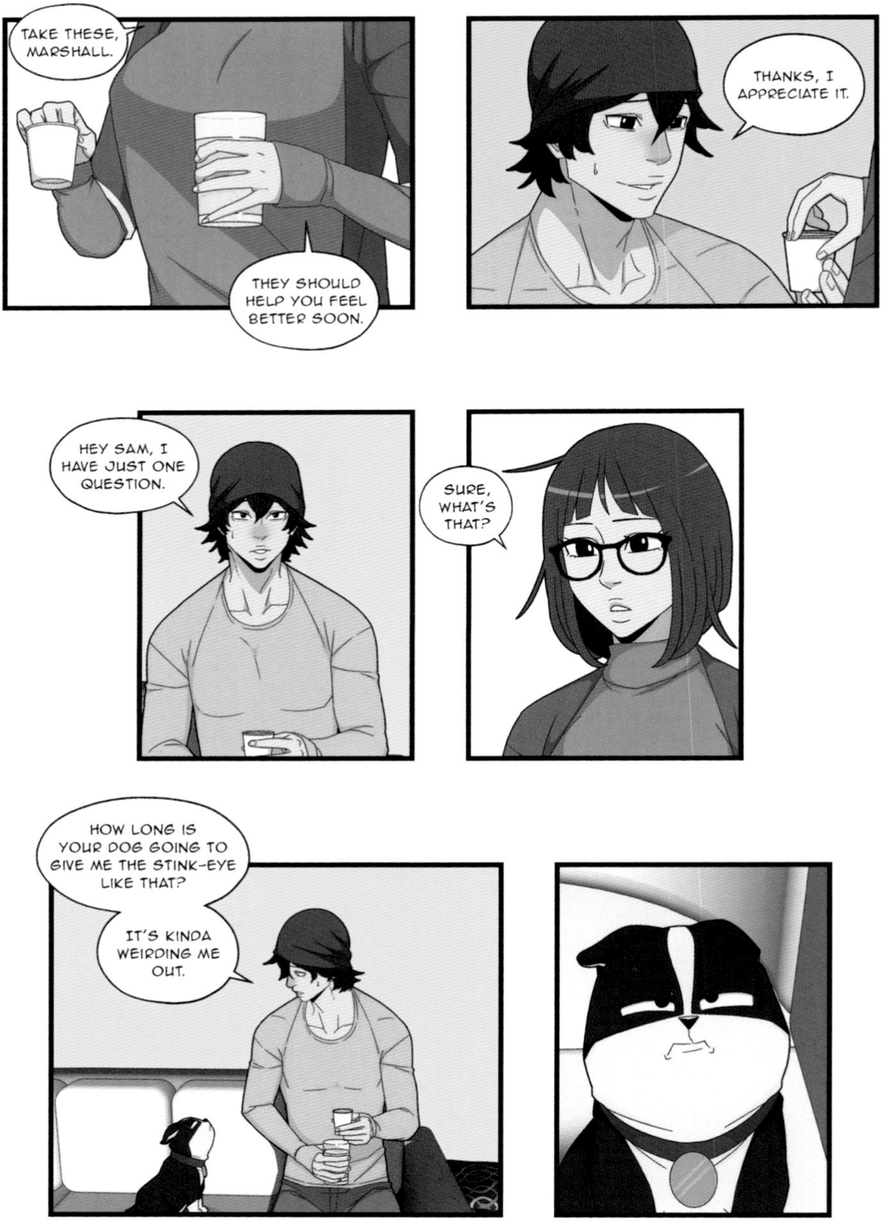
TAKE THESE, MARSHALL.
THEY SHOULD HELP YOU FEEL BETTER SOON.
THANKS, I APPRECIATE IT.
HEY SAM, I HAVE JUST ONE QUESTION.
SURE, WHAT'S THAT?
HOW LONG IS YOUR DOG GOING TO GIVE ME THE STINK-EYE LIKE THAT?
IT'S KINDA WEIRDING ME OUT.

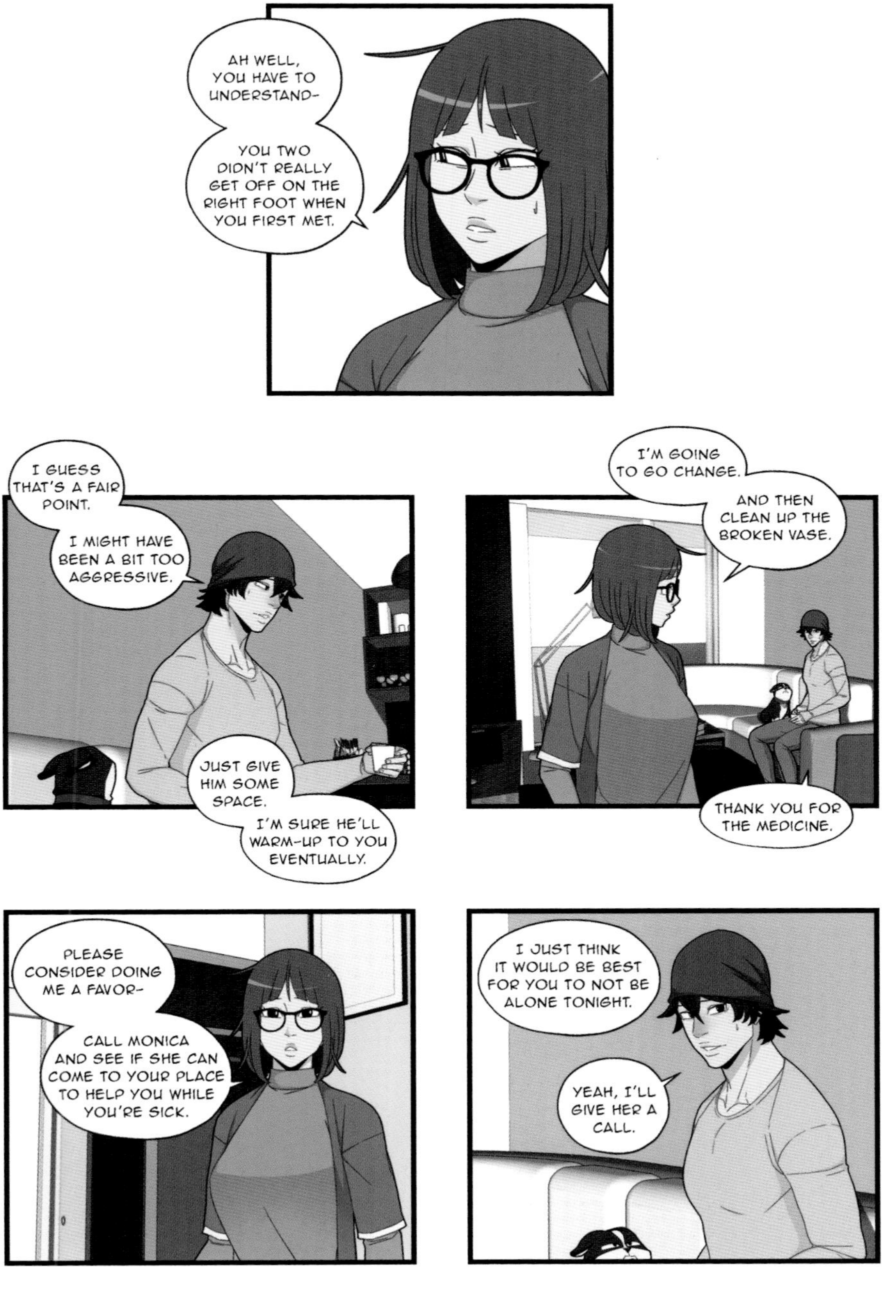
AH WELL, YOU HAVE TO UNDERSTAND-
YOU TWO DIDN'T REALLY GET OFF ON THE RIGHT FOOT WHEN YOU FIRST MET.
I GUESS THAT'S A FAIR POINT.
I MIGHT HAVE BEEN A BIT TOO AGGRESSIVE.
JUST GIVE HIM SOME SPACE.
I'M SURE HE'LL WARM-UP TO YOU EVENTUALLY.
I'M GOING TO GO CHANGE.
AND THEN CLEAN UP THE BROKEN VASE.
THANK YOU FOR THE MEDICINE.
PLEASE CONSIDER DOING ME A FAVOR-
CALL MONICA AND SEE IF SHE CAN COME TO YOUR PLACE TO HELP YOU WHILE YOU'RE SICK.
I JUST THINK IT WOULD BE BEST FOR YOU TO NOT BE ALONE TONIGHT.
YEAH, I'LL GIVE HER A CALL.

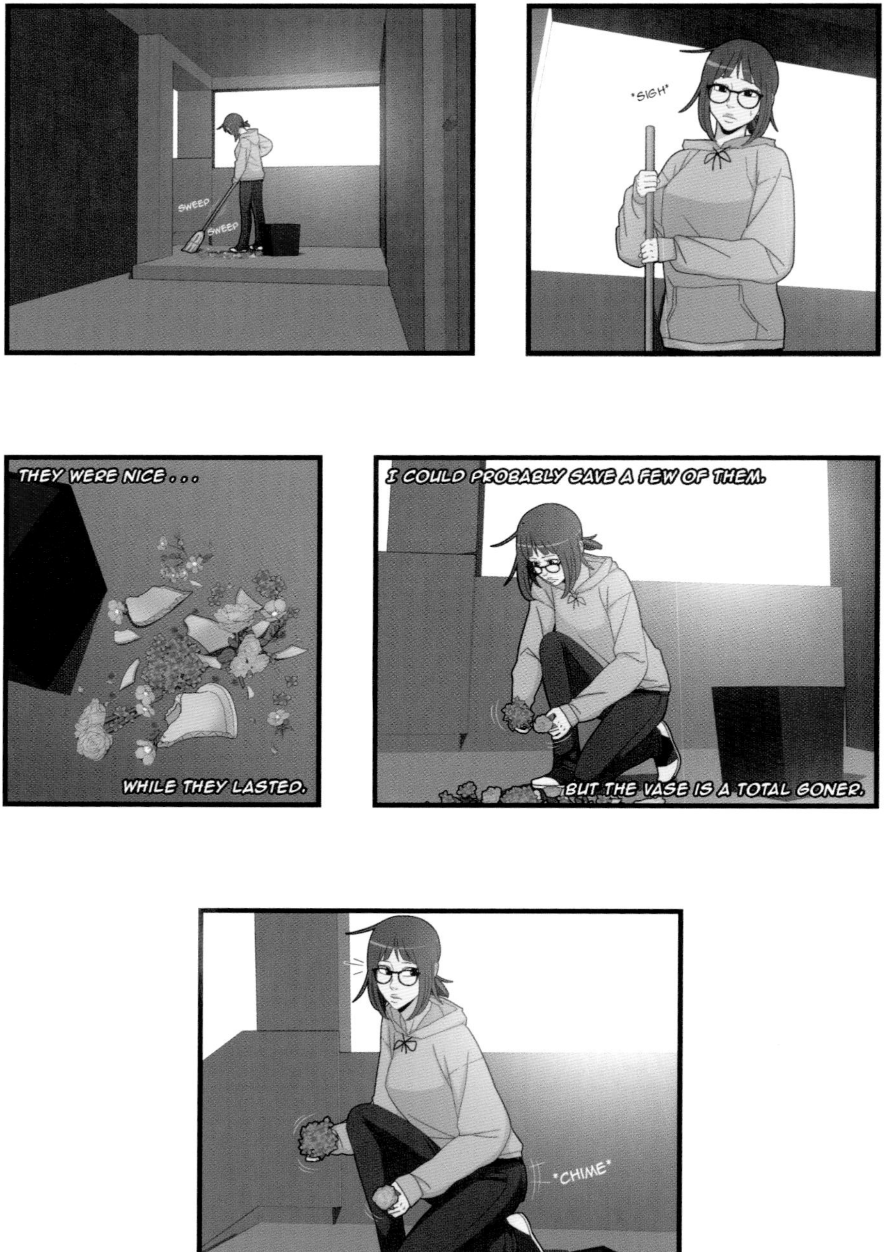
SWEEP
SWEEP
SIGH
THEY WERE NICE . . .
WHILE THEY LASTED.
I COULD PROBABLY SAVE A FEW OF THEM.
BUT THE VASE IS A TOTAL GONER.
CHIME

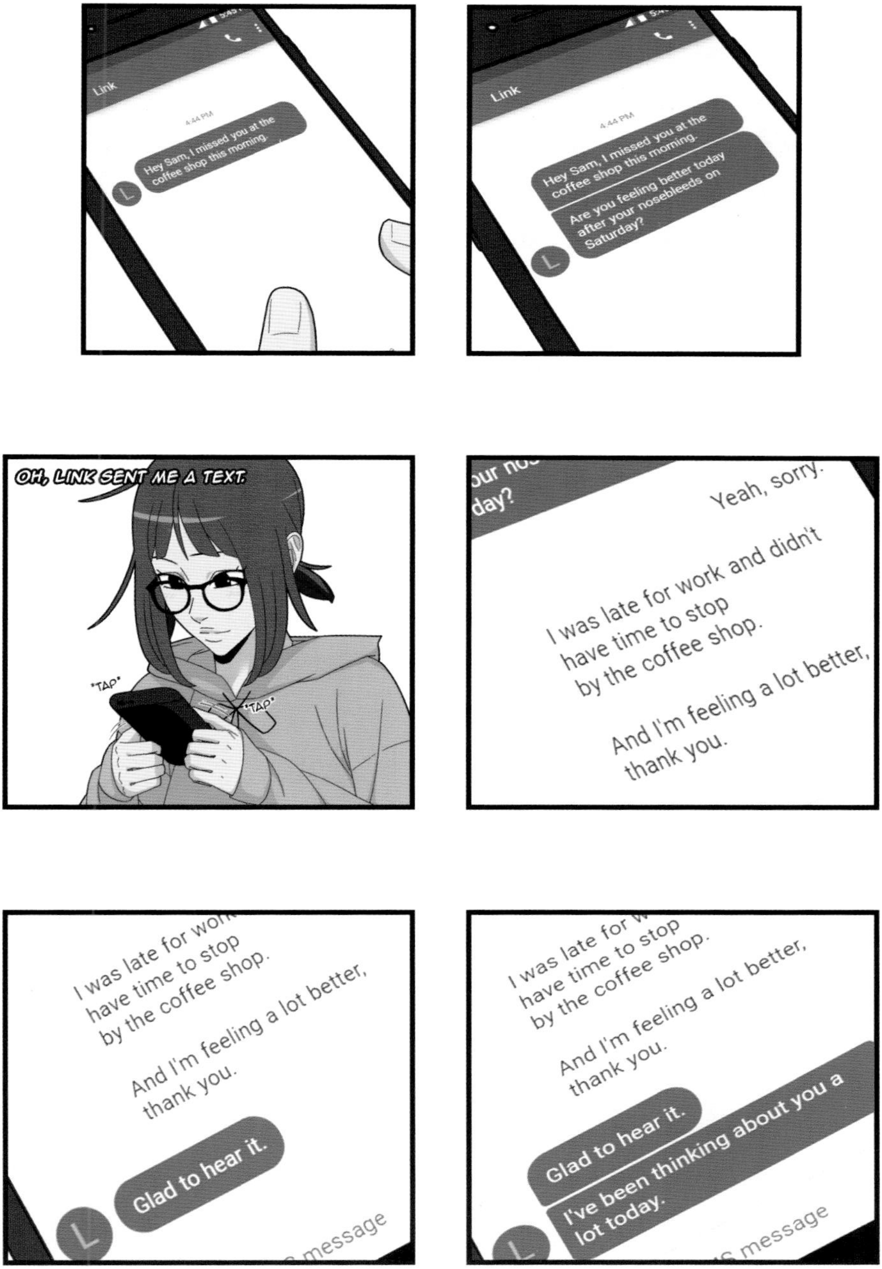
Link
4:44 PM
Hey Sam, I missed you at the coffee shop this morning.
Link
4:44 PM
Hey Sam, I missed you at the coffee shop this morning.
Are you feeling better today after your nosebleeds on Saturday?
OH, LINK SENT ME A TEXT.
TAP
TAP
Yeah, sorry.
I was late for work and didn't have time to stop by the coffee shop.
And I'm feeling a lot better, thank you.
And I'm feeling a lot better, thank you.
Glad to hear it.
And I'm feeling a lot better, thank you.
Glad to hear it.
I've been thinking about you a lot today.

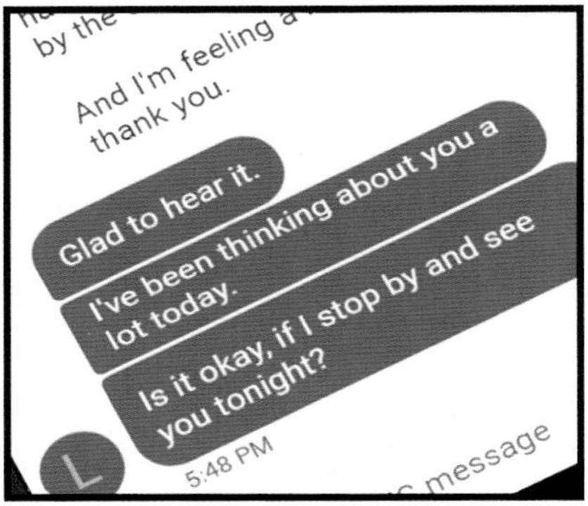
by the
And I'm feeling
thank you.
Glad to hear it.
I've been thinking about you a lot today.
Is it okay, if I stop by and see you tonight?
L
5:48 PM
message

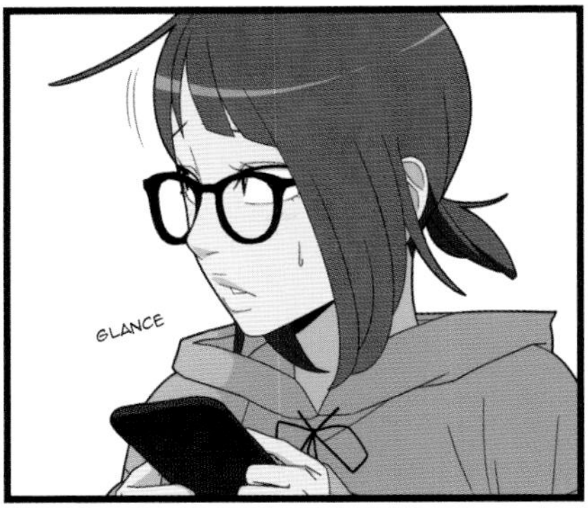
GLANCE

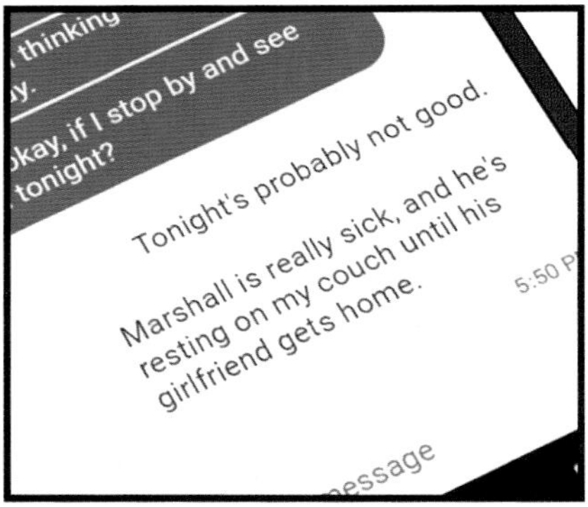
thinking
okay, if I stop by and see
tonight?
Tonight's probably not good.
Marshall is really sick, and he's resting on my couch until his girlfriend gets home.
5:50
message

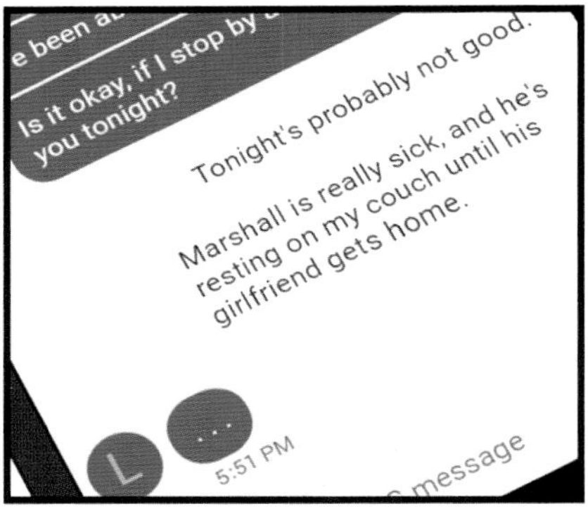
Is it okay, if I stop by
you tonight?
Tonight's probably not good.
Marshall is really sick, and he's resting on my couch until his girlfriend gets home.
L
...
5:51 PM
message

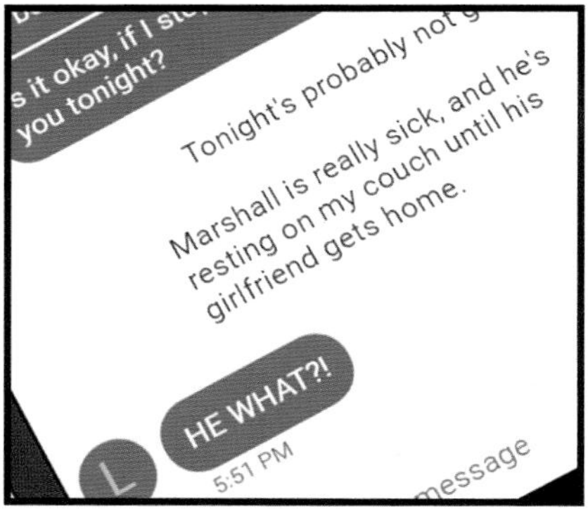
s it okay, if I
you tonight?
Tonight's probably not
Marshall is really sick, and he's resting on my couch until his girlfriend gets home.
L
HE WHAT?!
5:51 PM
message

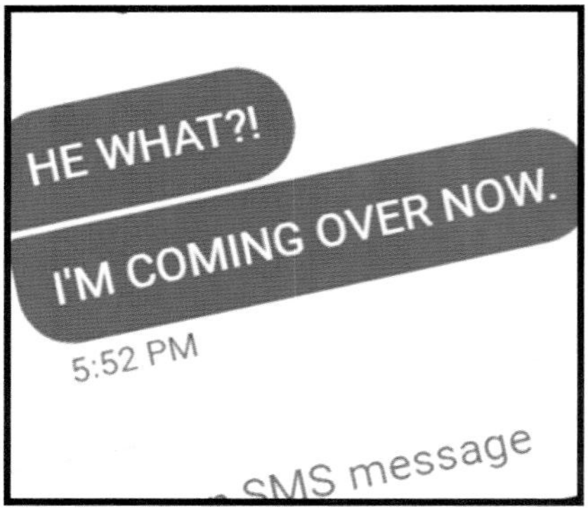
HE WHAT?!
I'M COMING OVER NOW.
5:52 PM
SMS message

UH HO, THAT MIGHT BE A PROBLEM.

HE DOESN'T SOUND HAPPY.

SPARKLE

REACH

SLICE

FLINCH

OWW!!

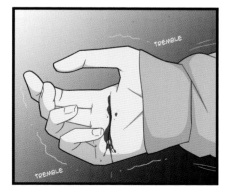

TREMBLE

TREMBLE

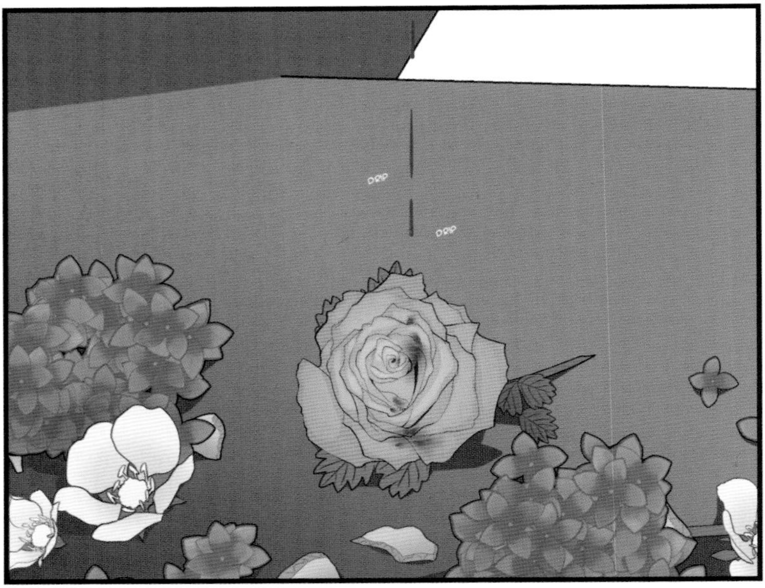
DRIP
DRIP
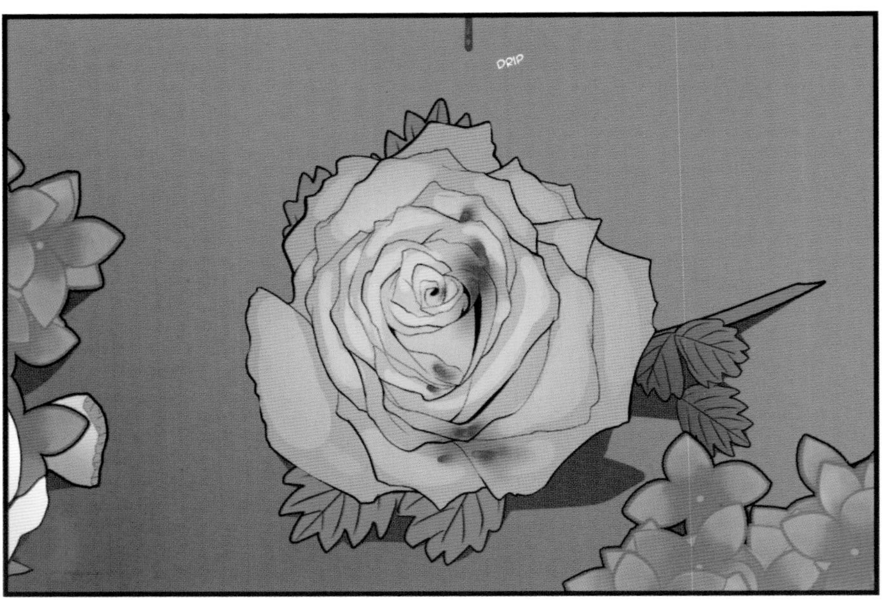
DRIP

HEY, MONICA!
YOU'VE GOT A PHONE CALL.
TURN
HEY BABE, IS EVERYTHING OKAY?
HI MONICA, SORRY TO BOTHER YOU, BUT IT LOOKS LIKE I MIGHT BE PRETTY SICK.
I WAS WONDERING IF YOU COULD COME TO MY PLACE AND KEEP AN EYE ON ME.
OF COURSE!
BUT WE ARE JUST ABOUT TO GET STARTED OVER HERE.
AND WE WON'T BE WRAPPING UP FOR A FEW HOURS.
WILL YOU BE OKAY UNTIL THEN?

YEAH, NO PROBLEM, MONICA.
I KNOW YOU'RE REALLY BUSY TONIGHT.
HOW IS THE SHOOT GOING?
IT'S GOING REALLY WELL.
BUT THERE ARE A BUNCH OF GUYS HITTING ON ME HERE.
YOU NEED TO GET BETTER SO YOU CAN BE HERE TO FEND THEM OFF.
HAHA, THEY'VE GOT GREAT TASTES.
YOU BET YOUR ASS THEY DO.

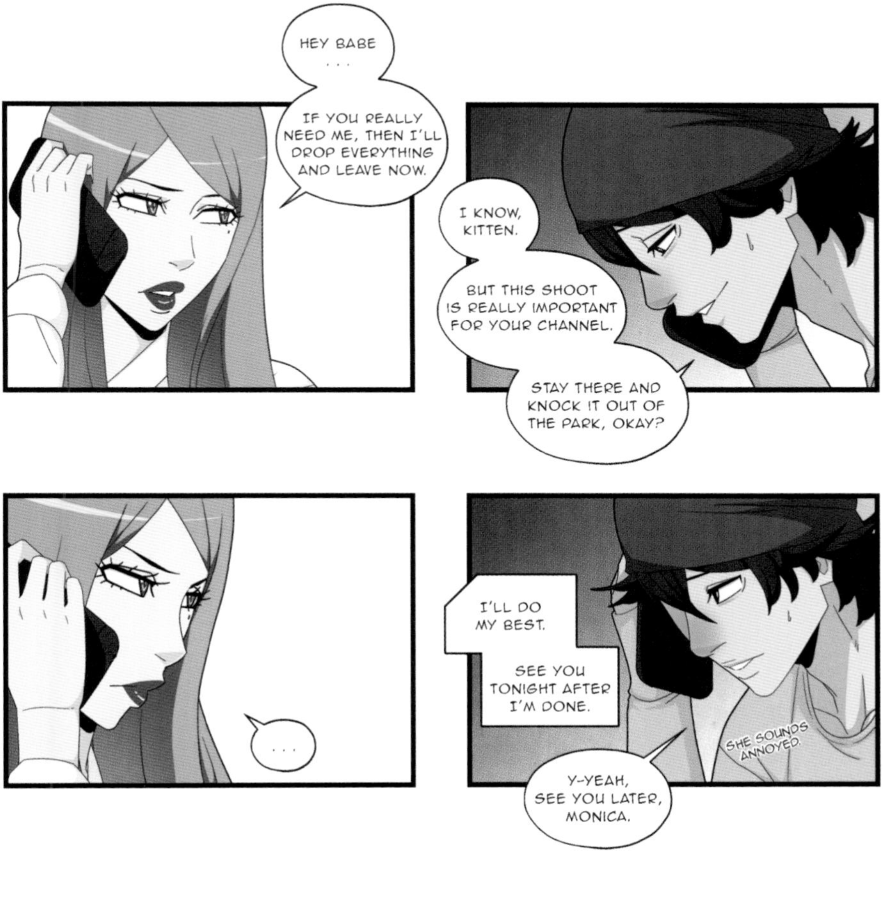
HEY BABE
. . .
IF YOU REALLY NEED ME, THEN I'LL DROP EVERYTHING AND LEAVE NOW.
I KNOW, KITTEN.
BUT THIS SHOOT IS REALLY IMPORTANT FOR YOUR CHANNEL.
STAY THERE AND KNOCK IT OUT OF THE PARK, OKAY?
. . .
I'LL DO MY BEST.
SEE YOU TONIGHT AFTER I'M DONE.
SHE SOUNDS ANNOYED.
Y-YEAH, SEE YOU LATER, MONICA.

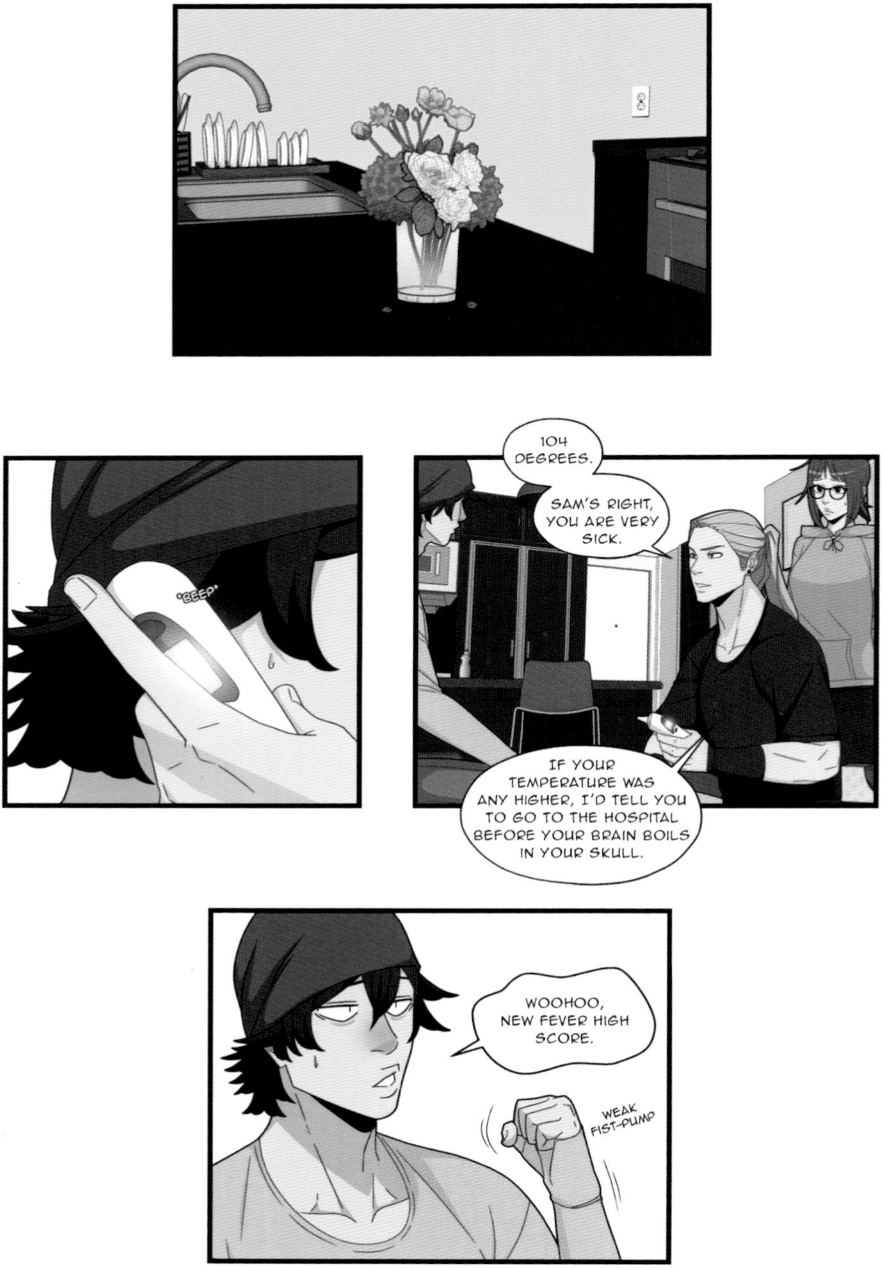
BEEP
104 DEGREES.
SAM'S RIGHT, YOU ARE VERY SICK.
IF YOUR TEMPERATURE WAS ANY HIGHER, I'D TELL YOU TO GO TO THE HOSPITAL BEFORE YOUR BRAIN BOILS IN YOUR SKULL.
WOOHOO, NEW FEVER HIGH SCORE.
WEAK FIST-PUMP

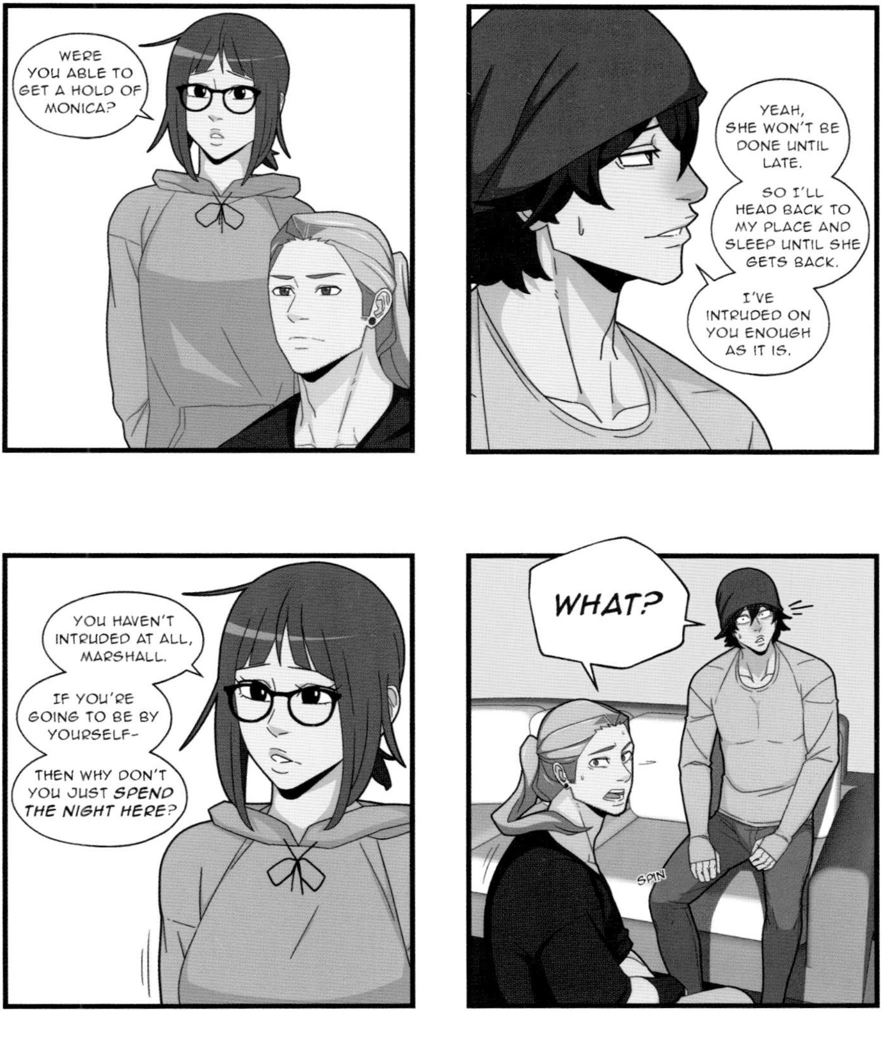
WERE YOU ABLE TO GET A HOLD OF MONICA?
YEAH, SHE WON'T BE DONE UNTIL LATE.
SO I'LL HEAD BACK TO MY PLACE AND SLEEP UNTIL SHE GETS BACK.
I'VE INTRUDED ON YOU ENOUGH AS IT IS.
YOU HAVEN'T INTRUDED AT ALL, MARSHALL.
IF YOU'RE GOING TO BE BY YOURSELF-
THEN WHY DON'T YOU JUST *SPEND THE NIGHT HERE*?
WHAT?
SPIN

BE SURE TO WORK ON YOUR EXERCISES.

A LARGE PART OF FENCING IS MUSCLE MEMORY.

YES, MR. JONES.

GOOD, YOU ARE DONE FOR TODAY.

I BELIEVE YOUR MOTHER IS WAITING FOR YOU IN THE LOBBY.

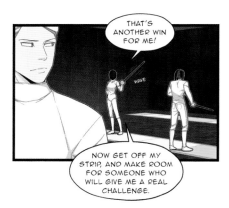

THAT'S ANOTHER WIN FOR ME!

WAVE

NOW GET OFF MY STRIP, AND MAKE ROOM FOR SOMEONE WHO WILL GIVE ME A REAL CHALLENGE.

SPEAKING OF WHICH . . .

IF YOU'RE DONE WITH YOUR LITTLE LESSONS, CHUCK—

THEN MAYBE YOU'D LIKE TO TRY TO REDEEM YOURSELF?

UNLESS YOUR BODY AND EGO ARE STILL TOO SORE?

. . .

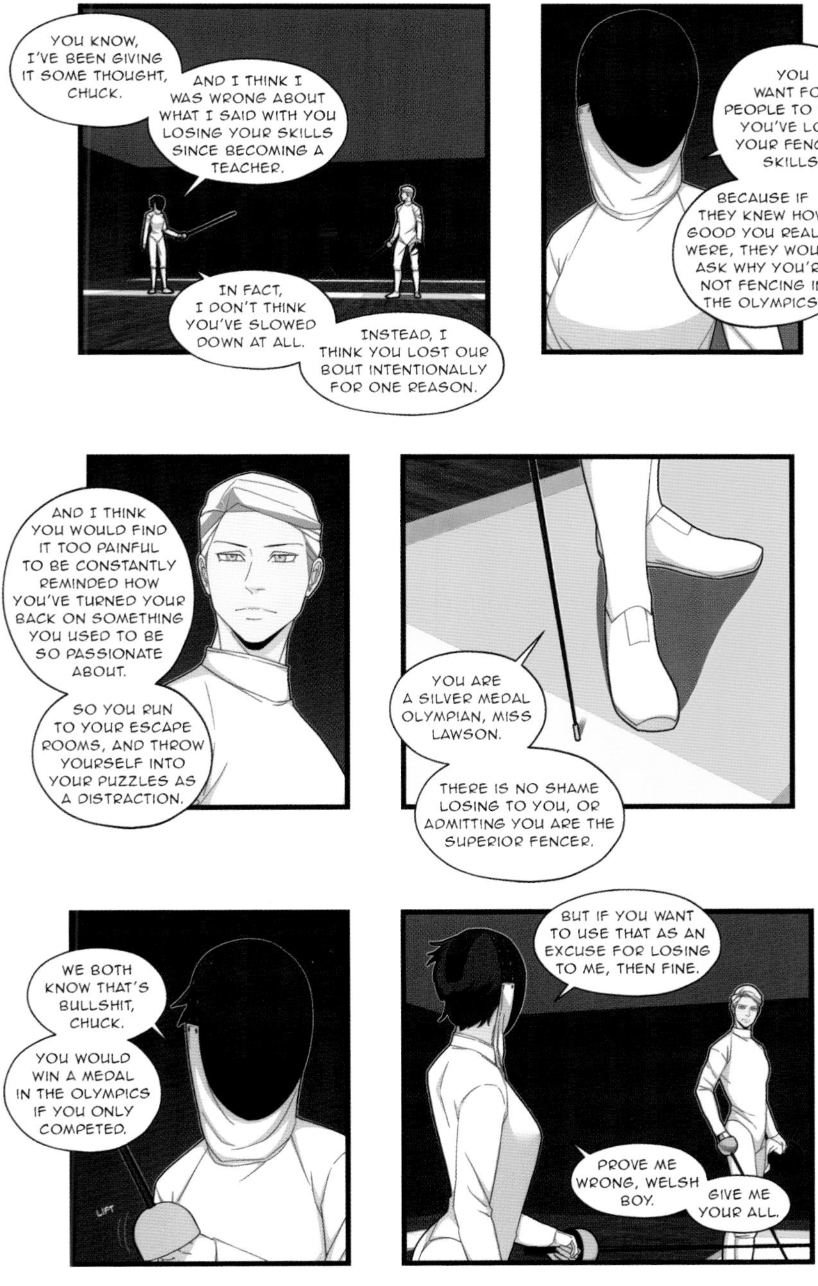
YOU KNOW, I'VE BEEN GIVING IT SOME THOUGHT, CHUCK.
AND I THINK I WAS WRONG ABOUT WHAT I SAID WITH YOU LOSING YOUR SKILLS SINCE BECOMING A TEACHER.
IN FACT, I DON'T THINK YOU'VE SLOWED DOWN AT ALL.
INSTEAD, I THINK YOU LOST OUR BOUT INTENTIONALLY FOR ONE REASON.
YOU WANT FOR PEOPLE TO THINK YOU'VE LOST YOUR FENCING SKILLS.
BECAUSE IF THEY KNEW HOW GOOD YOU REALLY WERE, THEY WOULD ASK WHY YOU'RE NOT FENCING IN THE OLYMPICS.
AND I THINK YOU WOULD FIND IT TOO PAINFUL TO BE CONSTANTLY REMINDED HOW YOU'VE TURNED YOUR BACK ON SOMETHING YOU USED TO BE SO PASSIONATE ABOUT.
SO YOU RUN TO YOUR ESCAPE ROOMS, AND THROW YOURSELF INTO YOUR PUZZLES AS A DISTRACTION.
YOU ARE A SILVER MEDAL OLYMPIAN, MISS LAWSON.
THERE IS NO SHAME LOSING TO YOU, OR ADMITTING YOU ARE THE SUPERIOR FENCER.
WE BOTH KNOW THAT'S BULLSHIT, CHUCK.
YOU WOULD WIN A MEDAL IN THE OLYMPICS IF YOU ONLY COMPETED.
LIFT
BUT IF YOU WANT TO USE THAT AS AN EXCUSE FOR LOSING TO ME, THEN FINE.
PROVE ME WRONG, WELSH BOY.
GIVE ME YOUR ALL.

SALUTE

SALUTE

LUNGE

STEP

CHING
JAB
GAH!

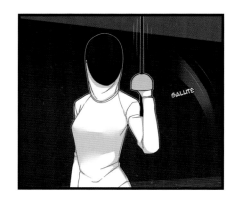

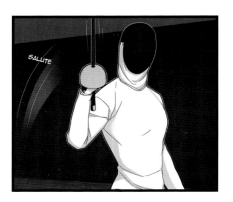

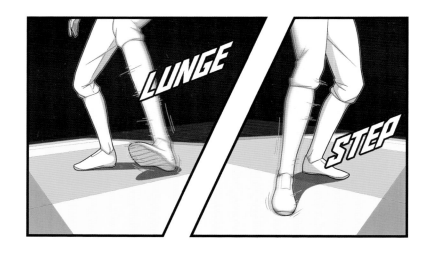

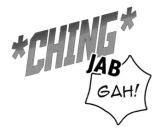

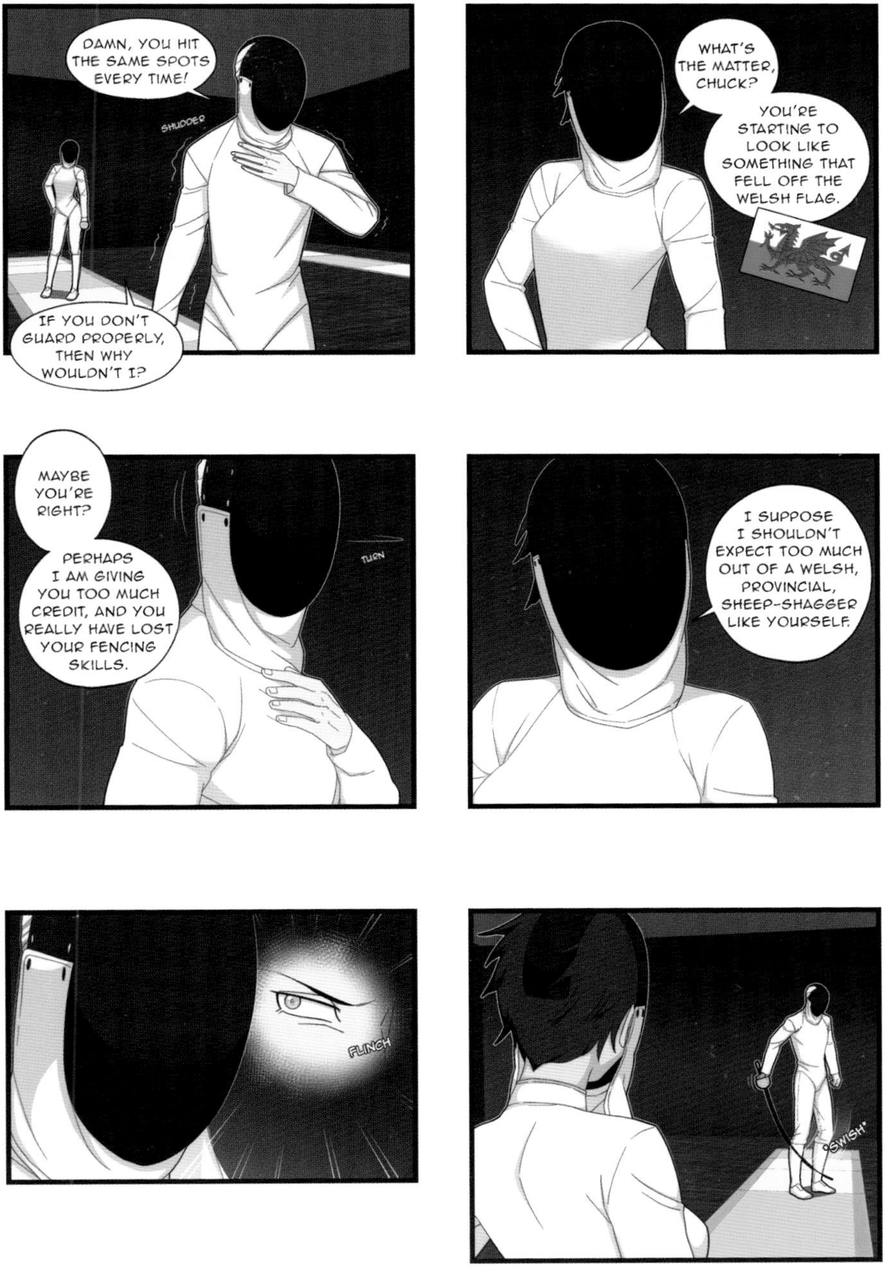
DAMN, YOU HIT THE SAME SPOTS EVERY TIME!
SHUDDER
IF YOU DON'T GUARD PROPERLY, THEN WHY WOULDN'T I?
WHAT'S THE MATTER, CHUCK?
YOU'RE STARTING TO LOOK LIKE SOMETHING THAT FELL OFF THE WELSH FLAG.
MAYBE YOU'RE RIGHT?
PERHAPS I AM GIVING YOU TOO MUCH CREDIT, AND YOU REALLY HAVE LOST YOUR FENCING SKILLS.
TURN
I SUPPOSE I SHOULDN'T EXPECT TOO MUCH OUT OF A WELSH, PROVINCIAL, SHEEP-SHAGGER LIKE YOURSELF.
FLINCH
SWISH

BEND
BEND
CHUCKLES
SALUTE
PANT
PANT
POISED
DASH

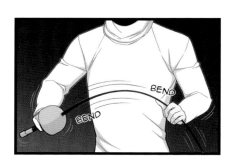

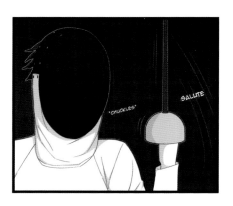

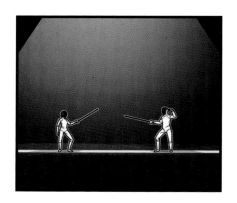

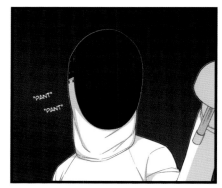

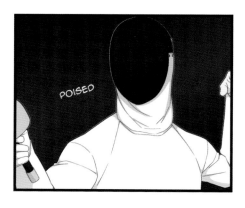

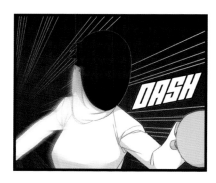

CHARGE

BLURRED MOVEMENT
TING

THRUST
SCRAPE
SCRAPE

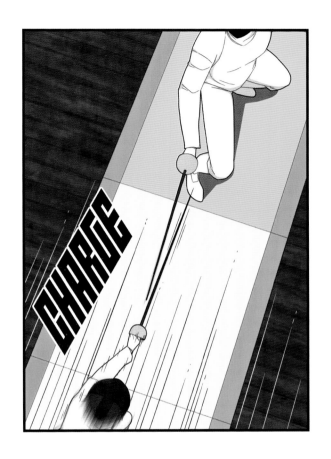

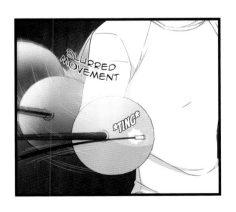

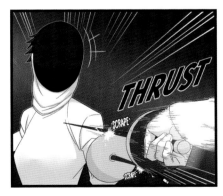

IT'S TOO FAST!

SCRAPE

JAB
BEND
PROTECTED
SNAP
STUMBLE
DROP
SLAM
OOF!
STEP

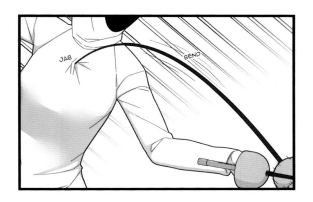

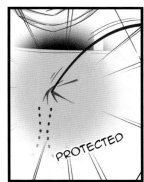

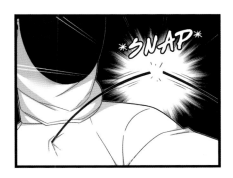

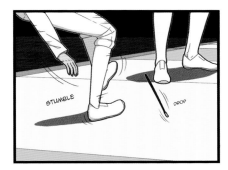

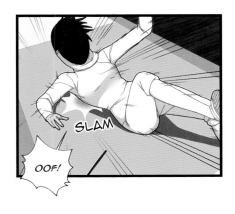

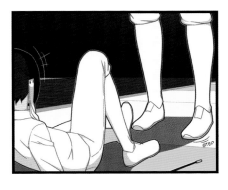

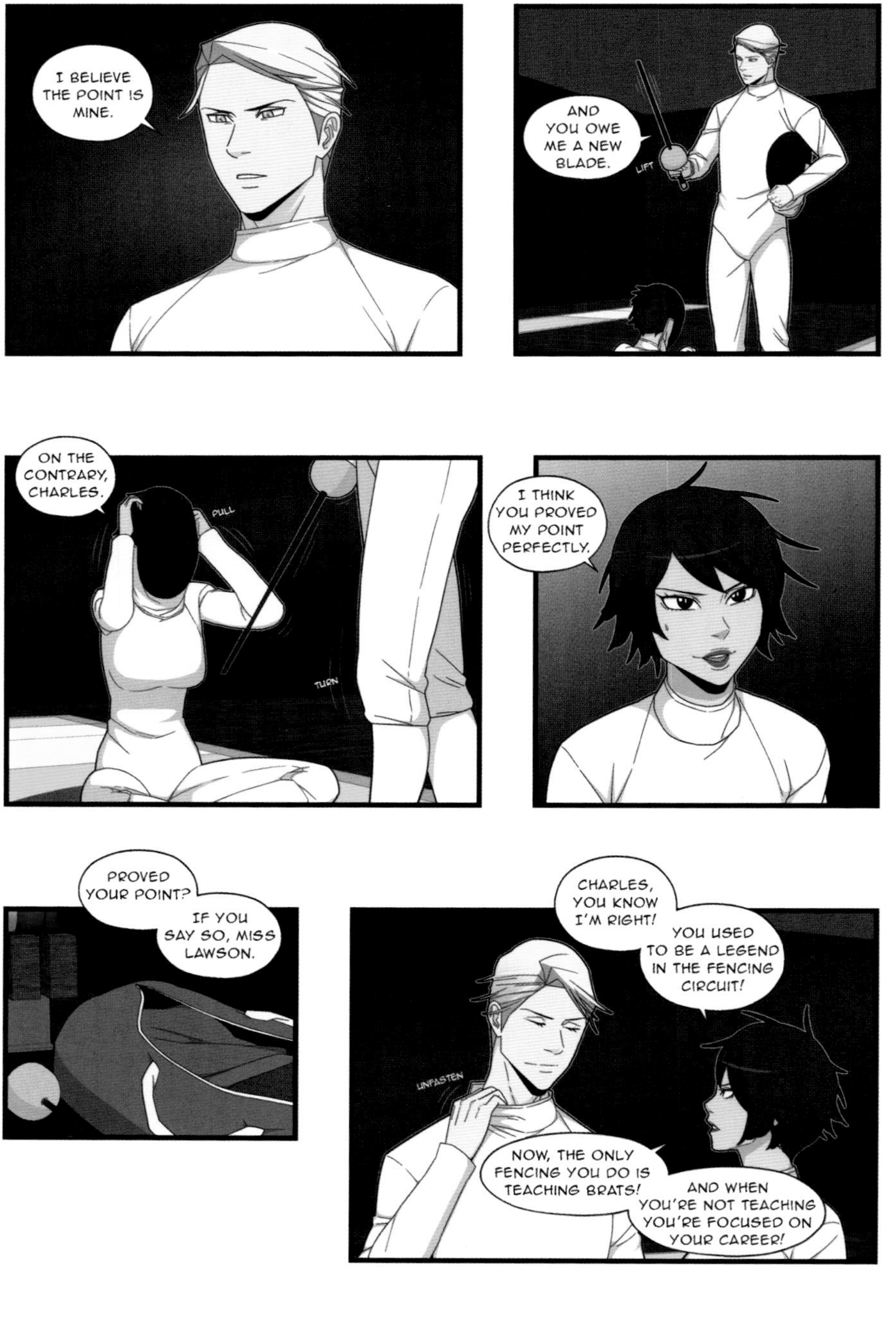
I BELIEVE THE POINT IS MINE.
AND YOU OWE ME A NEW BLADE.
LIFT
ON THE CONTRARY, CHARLES.
PULL
TURN
I THINK YOU PROVED MY POINT PERFECTLY.
PROVED YOUR POINT?
IF YOU SAY SO, MISS LAWSON.
CHARLES, YOU KNOW I'M RIGHT!
YOU USED TO BE A LEGEND IN THE FENCING CIRCUIT!
UNFASTEN
NOW, THE ONLY FENCING YOU DO IS TEACHING BRATS!
AND WHEN YOU'RE NOT TEACHING YOU'RE FOCUSED ON YOUR CAREER!

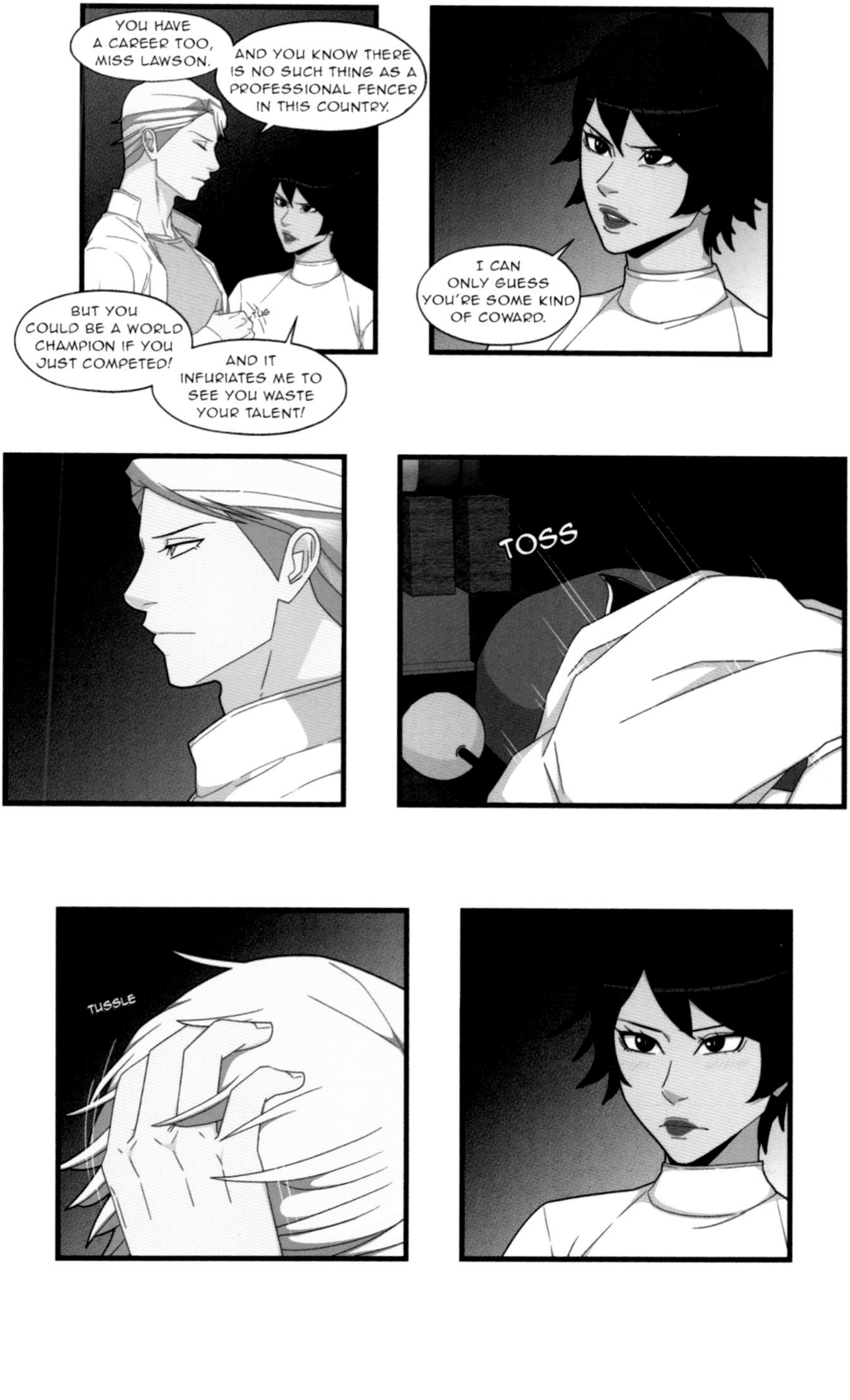
YOU HAVE A CAREER TOO, MISS LAWSON.
AND YOU KNOW THERE IS NO SUCH THING AS A PROFESSIONAL FENCER IN THIS COUNTRY.
TUG
BUT YOU COULD BE A WORLD CHAMPION IF YOU JUST COMPETED!
AND IT INFURIATES ME TO SEE YOU WASTE YOUR TALENT!
I CAN ONLY GUESS YOU'RE SOME KIND OF COWARD.
TOSS
TUSSLE

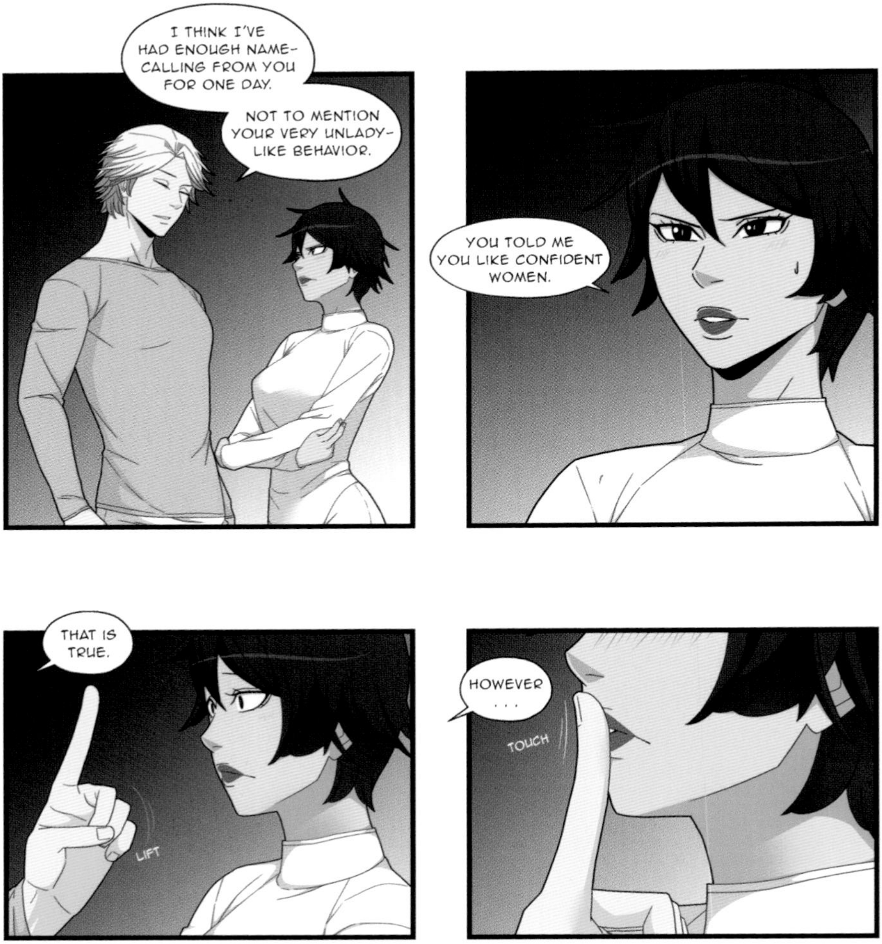
I THINK I'VE HAD ENOUGH NAME-CALLING FROM YOU FOR ONE DAY.
NOT TO MENTION YOUR VERY UNLADY-LIKE BEHAVIOR.
YOU TOLD ME YOU LIKE CONFIDENT WOMEN.
THAT IS TRUE.
LIFT
HOWEVER . . .
TOUCH

LIFT

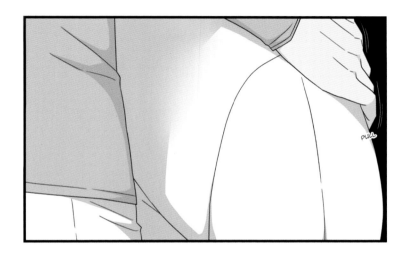

PULL

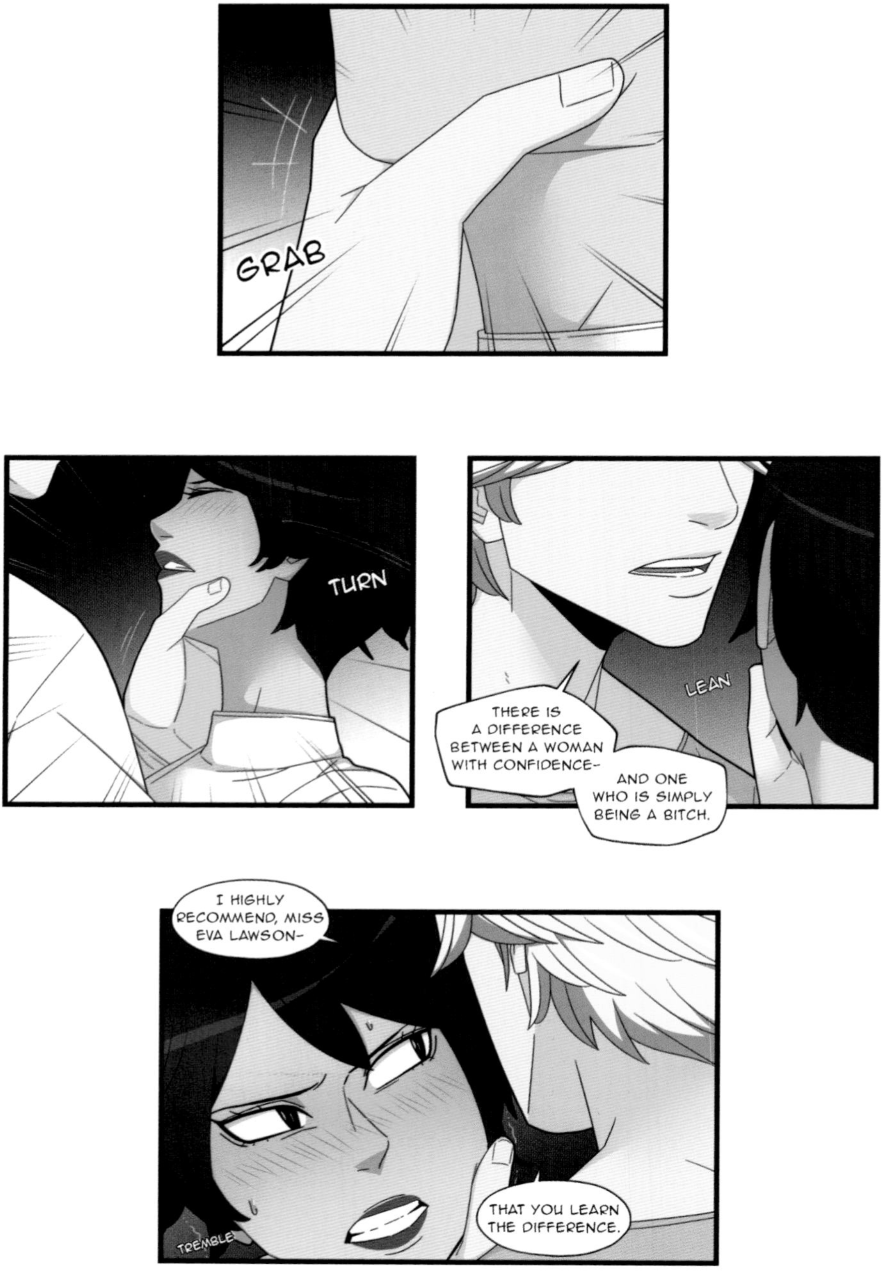
GRAB
TURN
LEAN
THERE IS A DIFFERENCE BETWEEN A WOMAN WITH CONFIDENCE-
AND ONE WHO IS SIMPLY BEING A BITCH.
I HIGHLY RECOMMEND, MISS EVA LAWSON-
TREMBLE
THAT YOU LEARN THE DIFFERENCE.

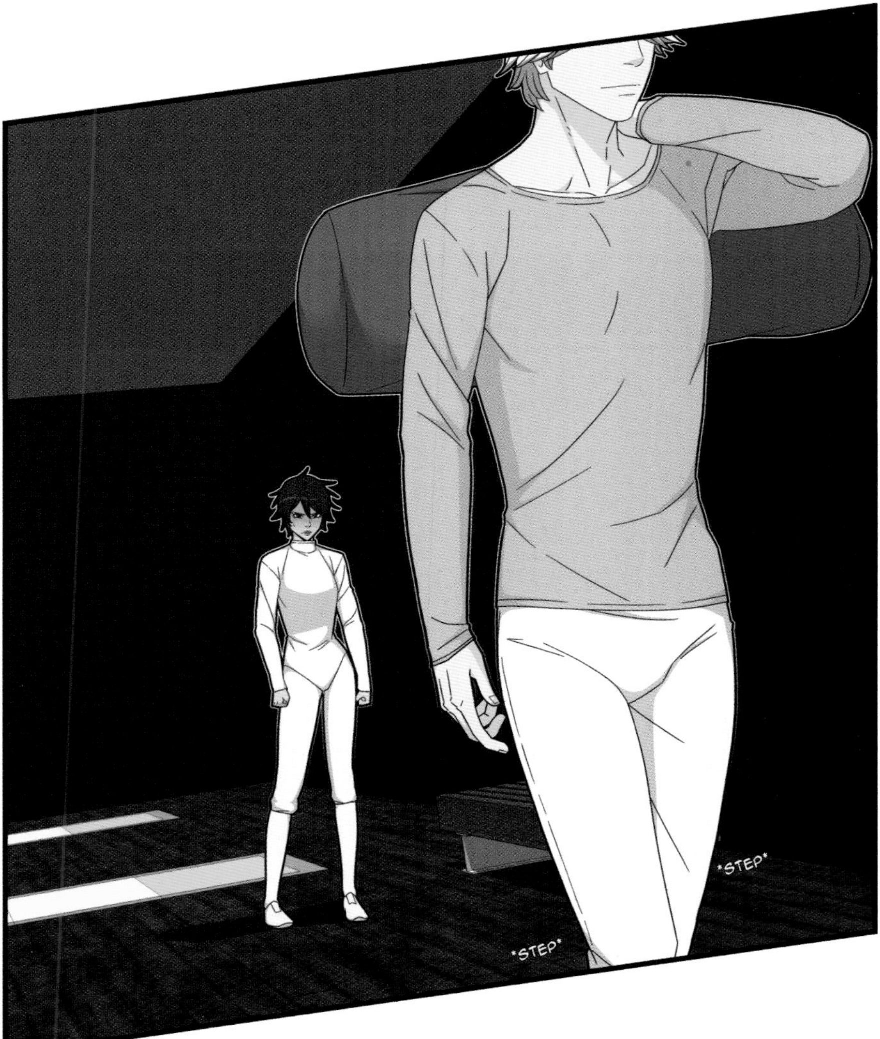
STEP
STEP

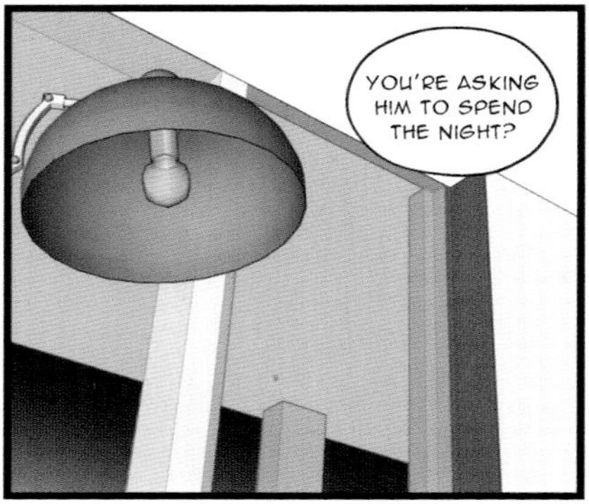
YOU'RE ASKING HIM TO SPEND THE NIGHT?

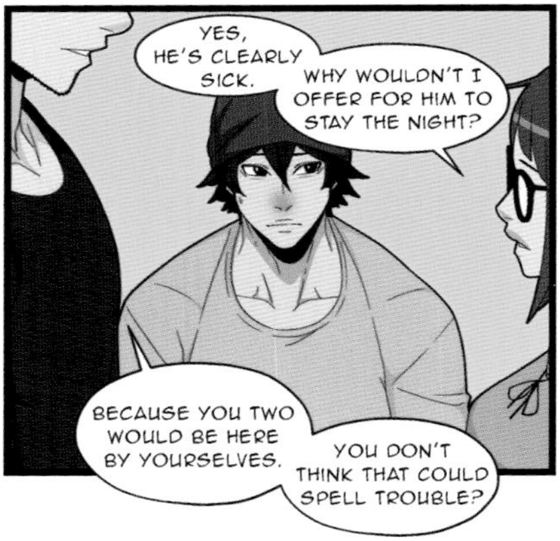
YES, HE'S CLEARLY SICK.
WHY WOULDN'T I OFFER FOR HIM TO STAY THE NIGHT?
BECAUSE YOU TWO WOULD BE HERE BY YOURSELVES.
YOU DON'T THINK THAT COULD SPELL TROUBLE?

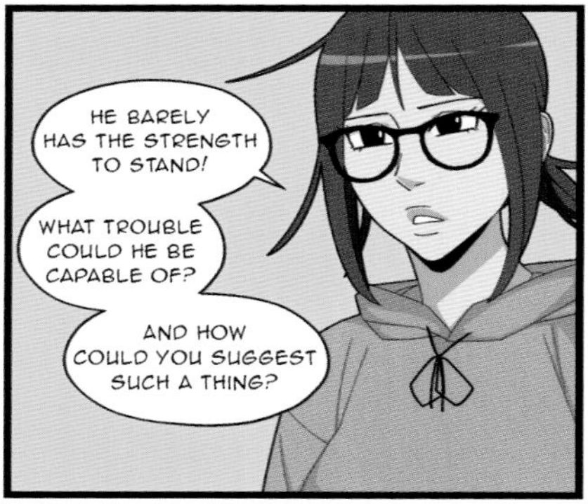
HE BARELY HAS THE STRENGTH TO STAND!
WHAT TROUBLE COULD HE BE CAPABLE OF?
AND HOW COULD YOU SUGGEST SUCH A THING?

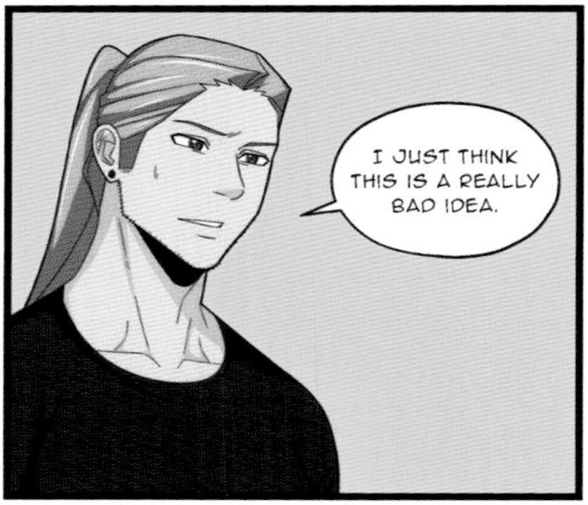
I JUST THINK THIS IS A REALLY BAD IDEA.

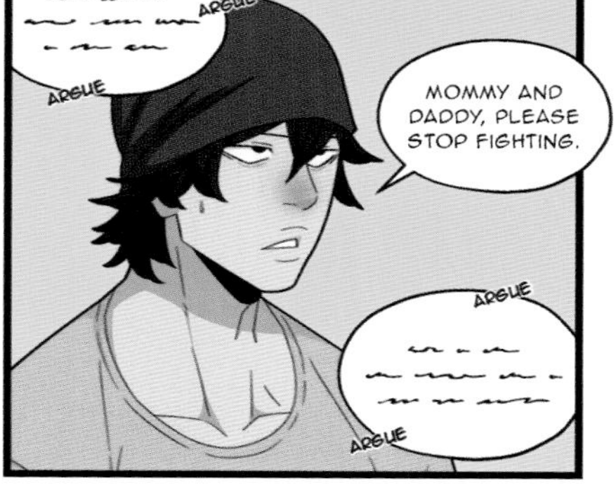
ARGUE
ARGUE
MOMMY AND DADDY, PLEASE STOP FIGHTING.
ARGUE
ARGUE

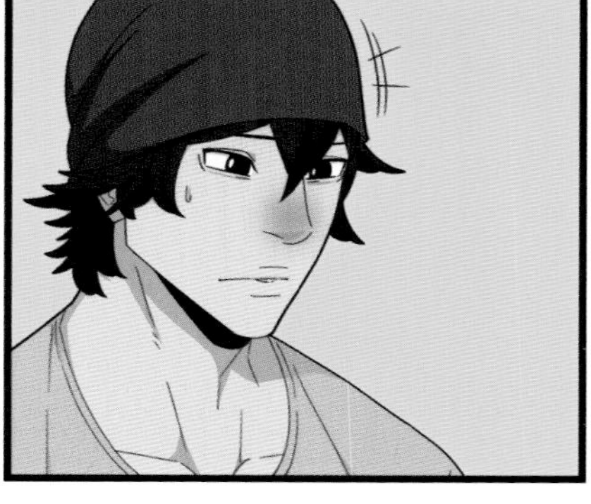

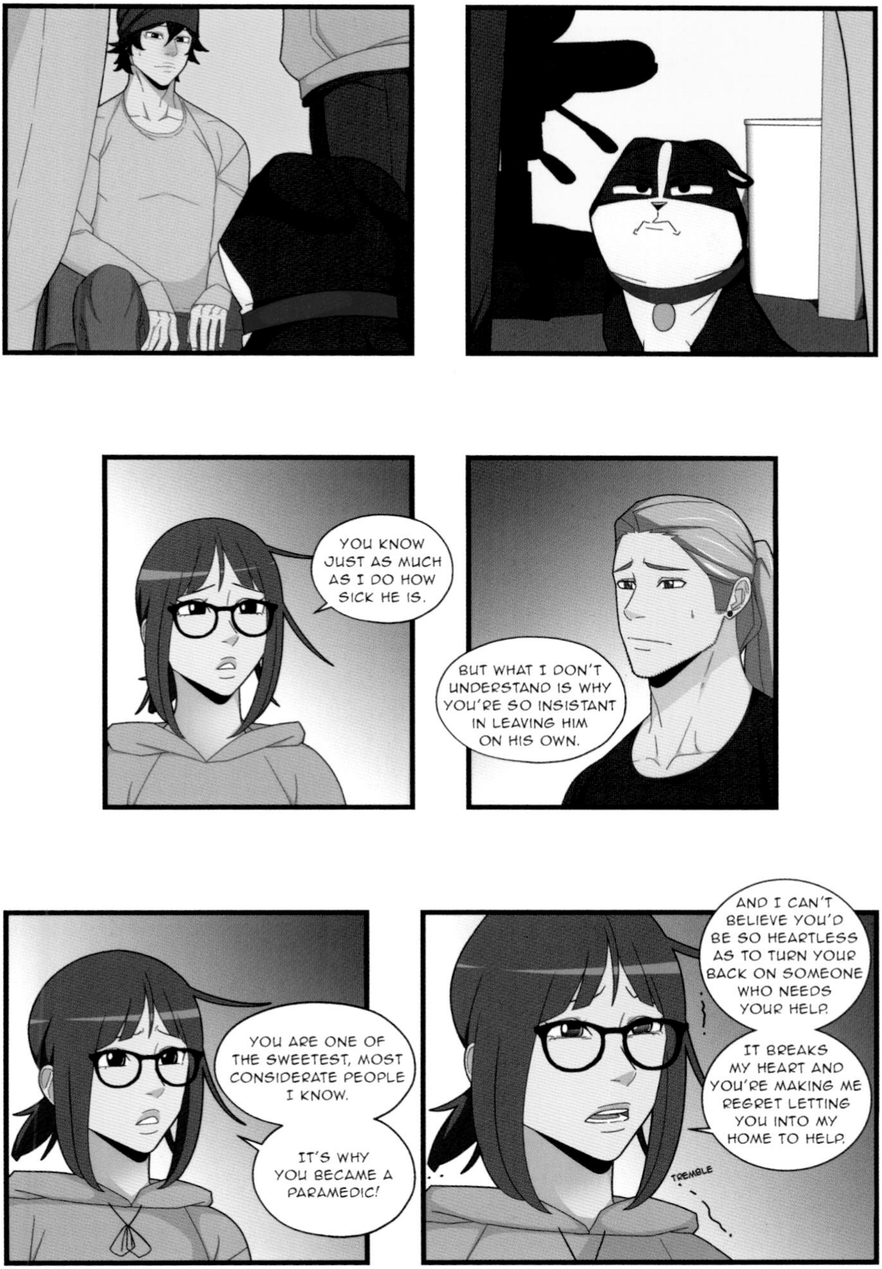
YOU KNOW JUST AS MUCH AS I DO HOW SICK HE IS.
BUT WHAT I DON'T UNDERSTAND IS WHY YOU'RE SO INSISTANT IN LEAVING HIM ON HIS OWN.
YOU ARE ONE OF THE SWEETEST, MOST CONSIDERATE PEOPLE I KNOW.
IT'S WHY YOU BECAME A PARAMEDIC!
AND I CAN'T BELIEVE YOU'D BE SO HEARTLESS AS TO TURN YOUR BACK ON SOMEONE WHO NEEDS YOUR HELP.
IT BREAKS MY HEART AND YOU'RE MAKING ME REGRET LETTING YOU INTO MY HOME TO HELP.
TREMBLE

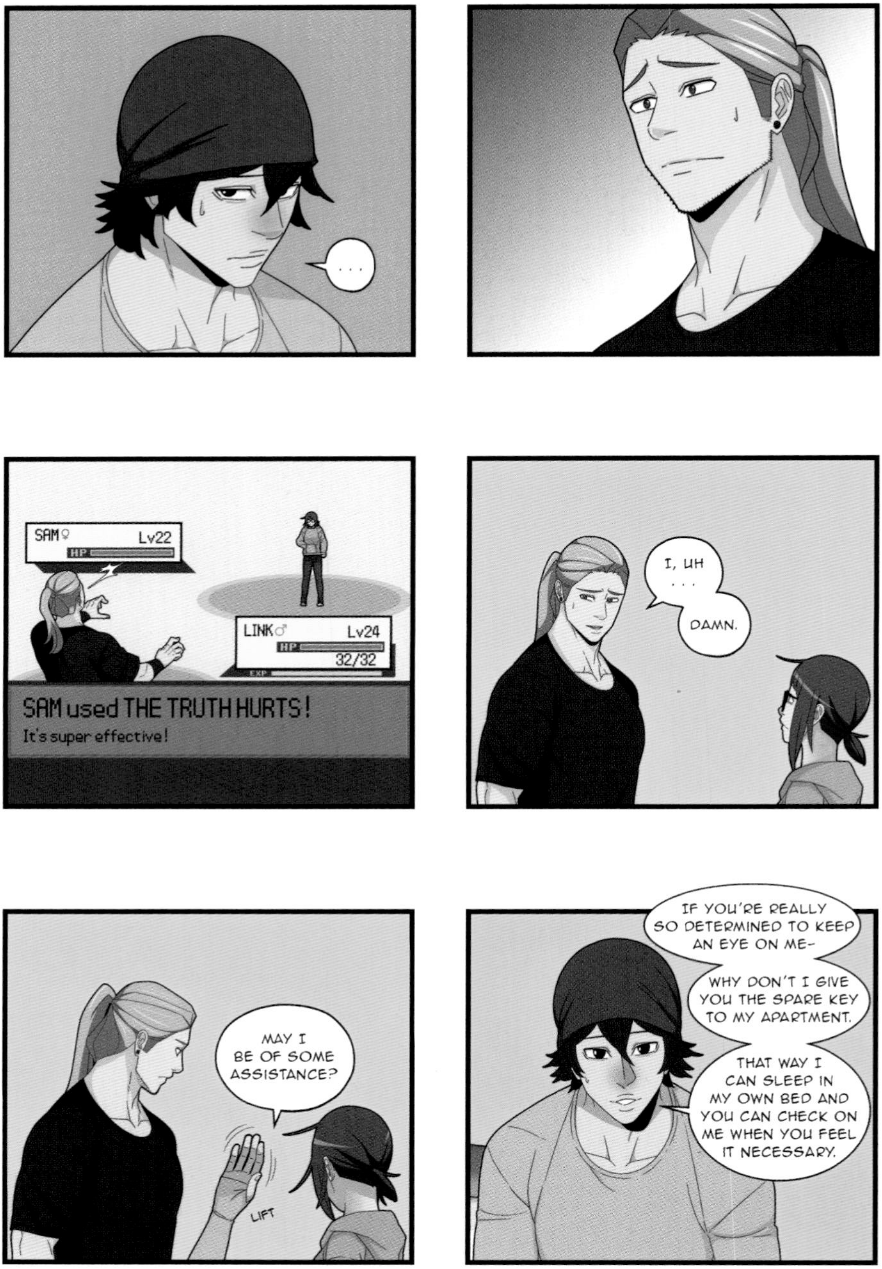
. . .
SAM♀ Lv22
HP
LINK♂ Lv24
HP 32/32
EXP
SAM used THE TRUTH HURTS!
It's super effective!
I, UH . . .
DAMN.
MAY I BE OF SOME ASSISTANCE?
LIFT
IF YOU'RE REALLY SO DETERMINED TO KEEP AN EYE ON ME-
WHY DON'T I GIVE YOU THE SPARE KEY TO MY APARTMENT.
THAT WAY I CAN SLEEP IN MY OWN BED AND YOU CAN CHECK ON ME WHEN YOU FEEL IT NECESSARY.

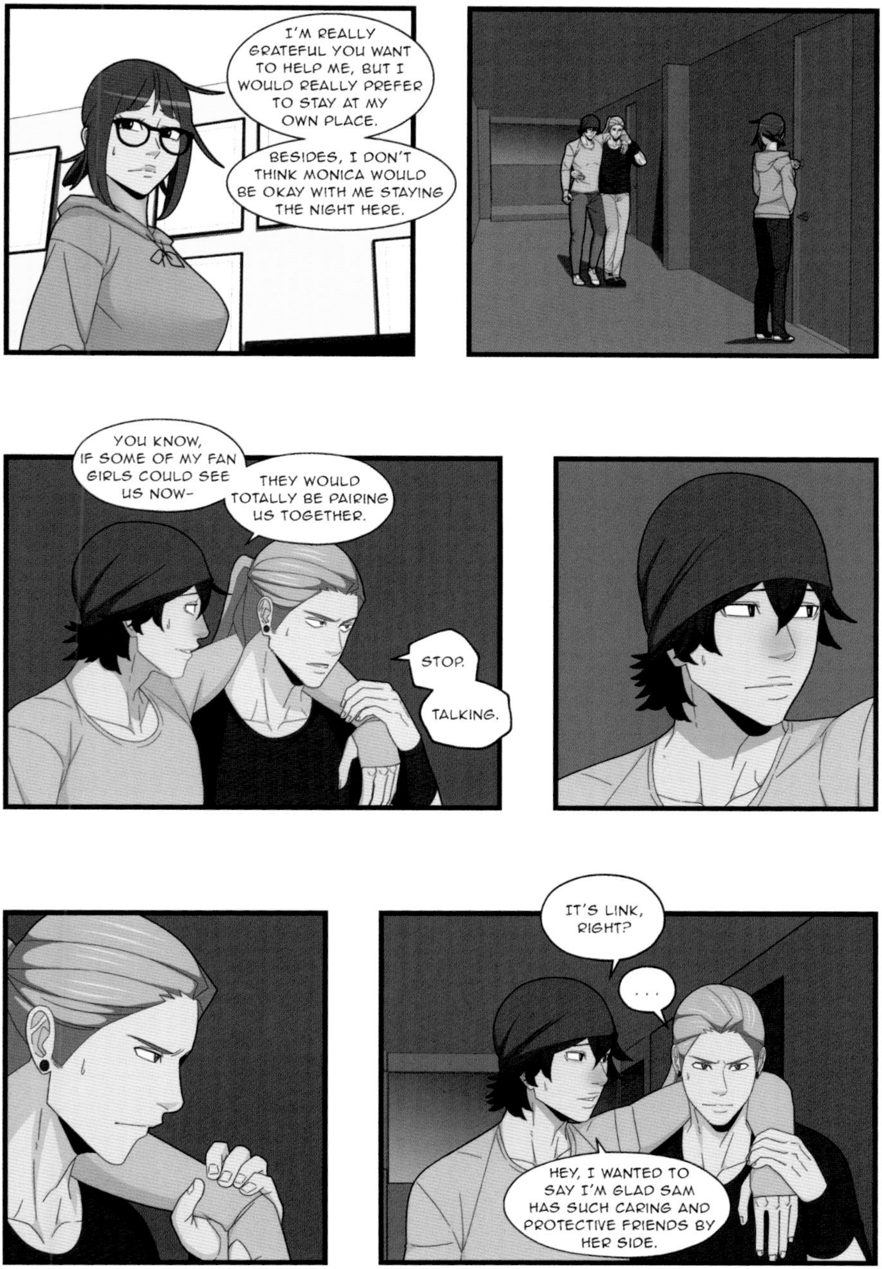
I'M REALLY GRATEFUL YOU WANT TO HELP ME, BUT I WOULD REALLY PREFER TO STAY AT MY OWN PLACE.
BESIDES, I DON'T THINK MONICA WOULD BE OKAY WITH ME STAYING THE NIGHT HERE.
YOU KNOW, IF SOME OF MY FAN GIRLS COULD SEE US NOW-
THEY WOULD TOTALLY BE PAIRING US TOGETHER.
STOP.
TALKING.
IT'S LINK, RIGHT?
. . .
HEY, I WANTED TO SAY I'M GLAD SAM HAS SUCH CARING AND PROTECTIVE FRIENDS BY HER SIDE.

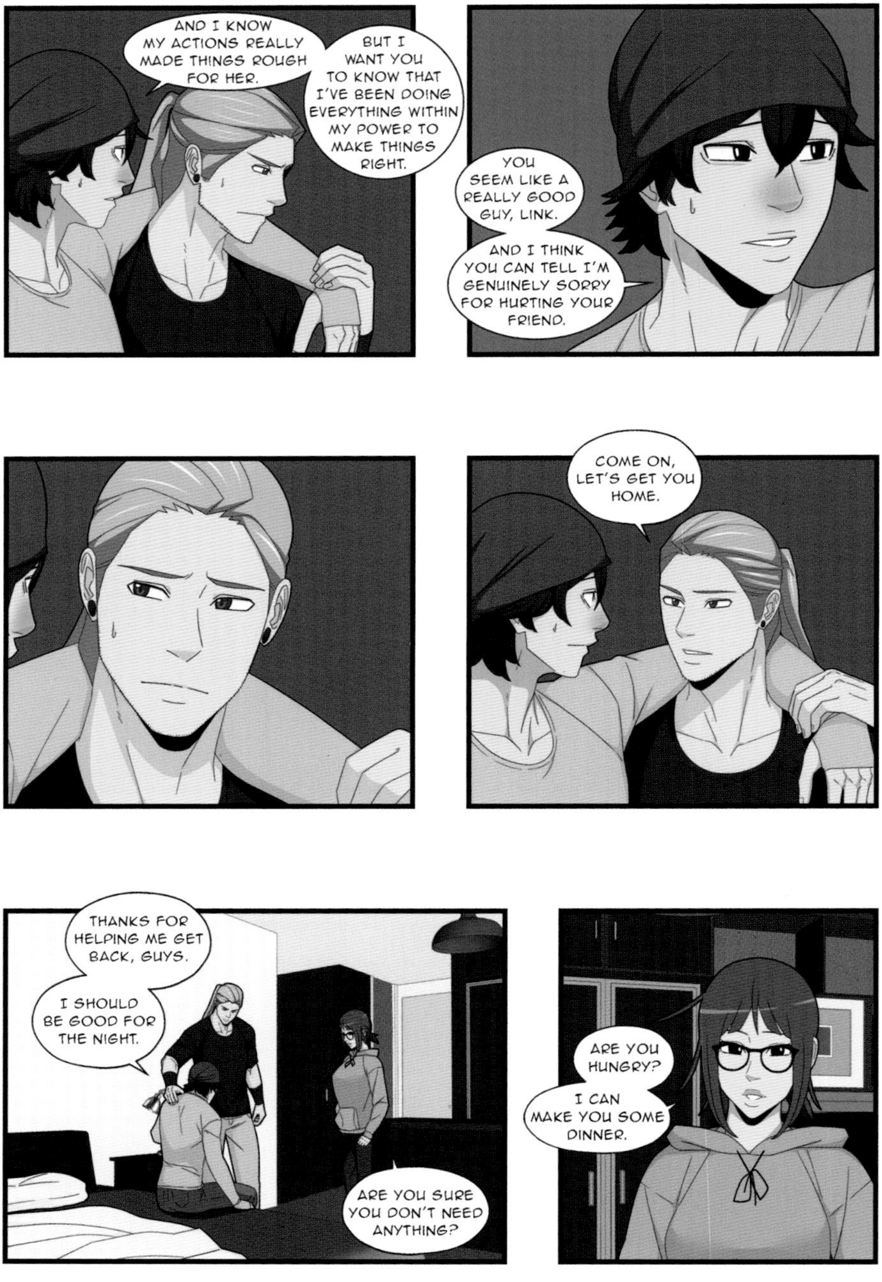
AND I KNOW MY ACTIONS REALLY MADE THINGS ROUGH FOR HER.
BUT I WANT YOU TO KNOW THAT I'VE BEEN DOING EVERYTHING WITHIN MY POWER TO MAKE THINGS RIGHT.
YOU SEEM LIKE A REALLY GOOD GUY, LINK.
AND I THINK YOU CAN TELL I'M GENUINELY SORRY FOR HURTING YOUR FRIEND.
COME ON, LET'S GET YOU HOME.
THANKS FOR HELPING ME GET BACK, GUYS.
I SHOULD BE GOOD FOR THE NIGHT.
ARE YOU SURE YOU DON'T NEED ANYTHING?
ARE YOU HUNGRY?
I CAN MAKE YOU SOME DINNER.

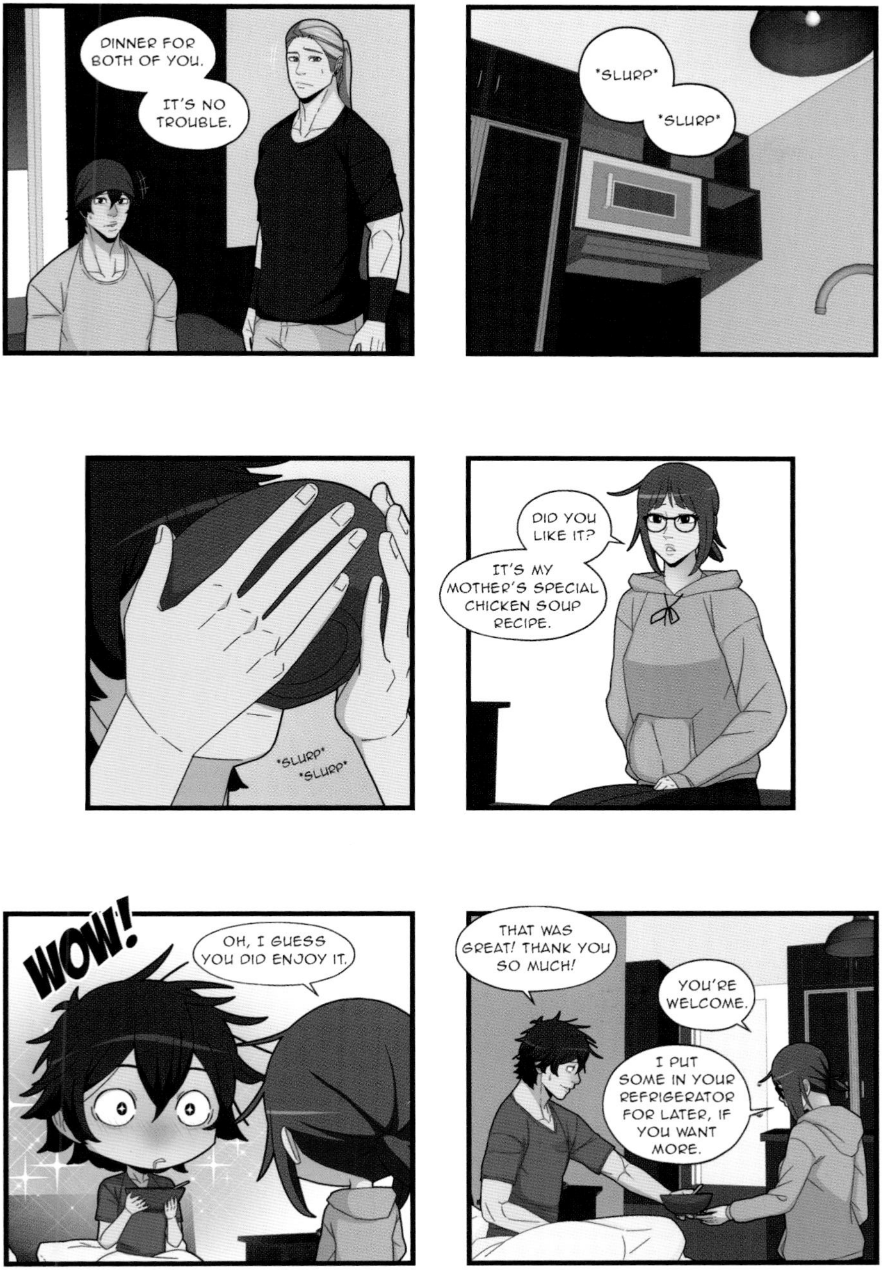
DINNER FOR BOTH OF YOU.
IT'S NO TROUBLE.
SLURP
SLURP
SLURP
SLURP
DID YOU LIKE IT?
IT'S MY MOTHER'S SPECIAL CHICKEN SOUP RECIPE.
WOW!
OH, I GUESS YOU DID ENJOY IT.
THAT WAS GREAT! THANK YOU SO MUCH!
YOU'RE WELCOME.
I PUT SOME IN YOUR REFRIGERATOR FOR LATER, IF YOU WANT MORE.

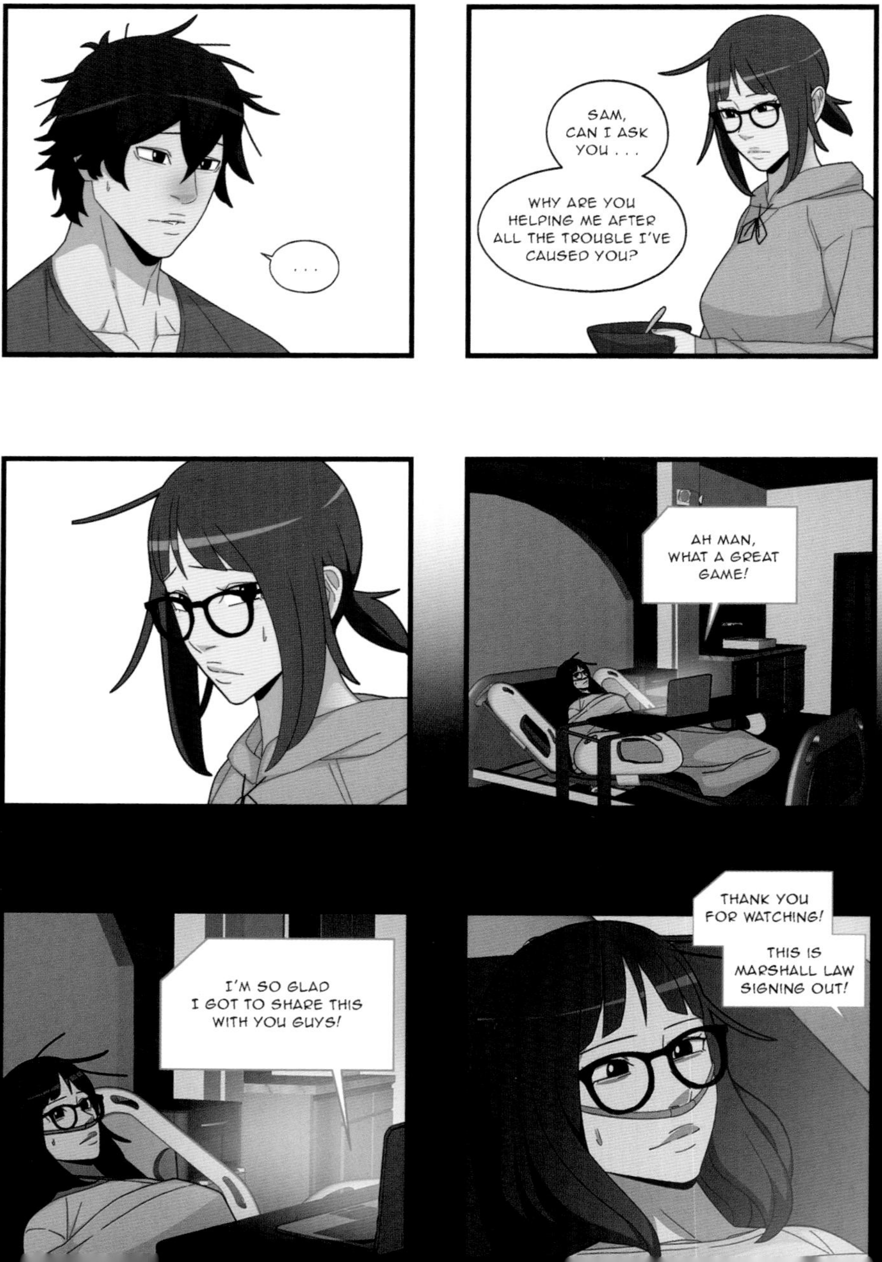
. . .
SAM, CAN I ASK YOU . . .
WHY ARE YOU HELPING ME AFTER ALL THE TROUBLE I'VE CAUSED YOU?
AH MAN, WHAT A GREAT GAME!
I'M SO GLAD I GOT TO SHARE THIS WITH YOU GUYS!
THANK YOU FOR WATCHING!
THIS IS MARSHALL LAW SIGNING OUT!

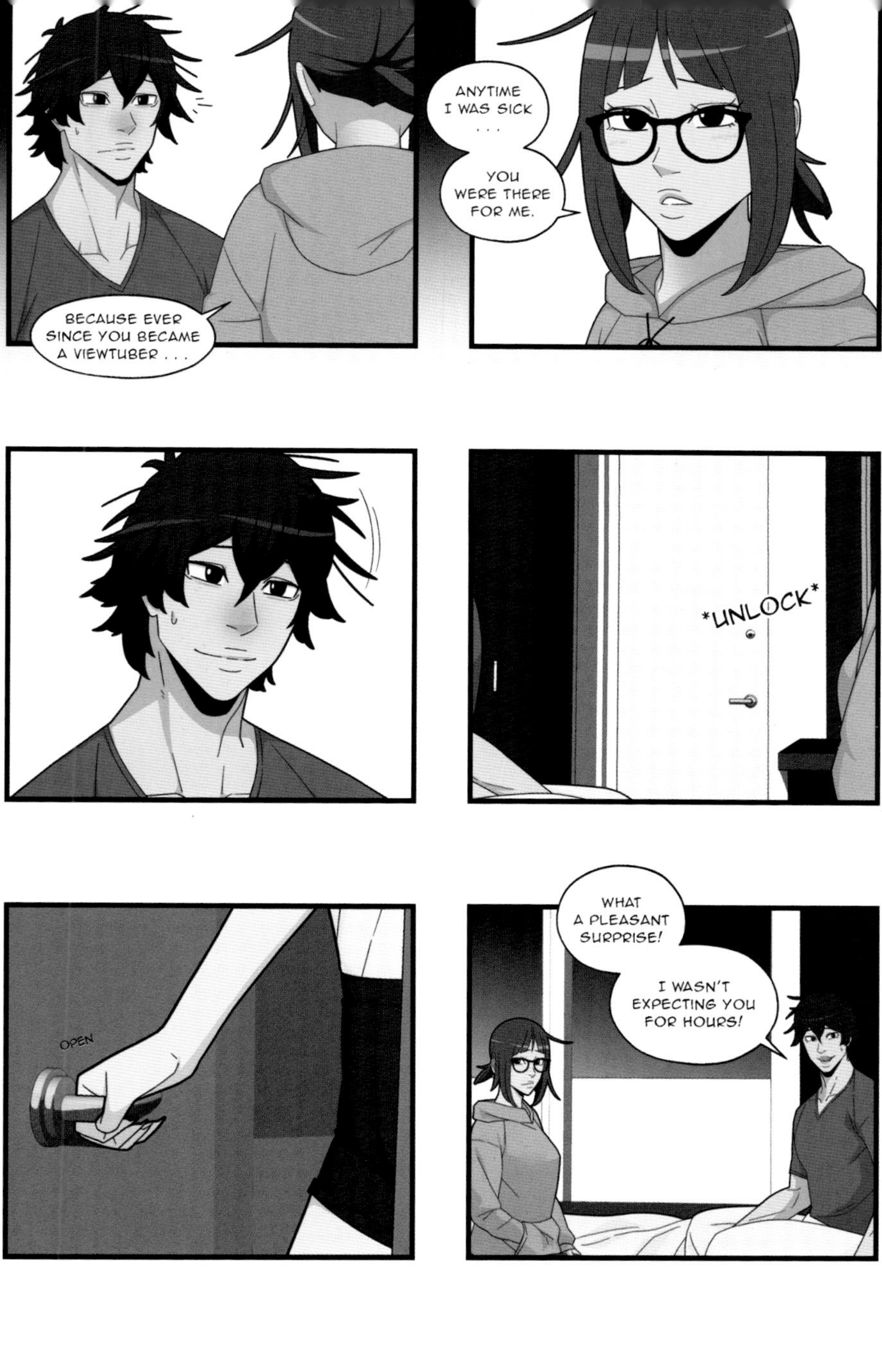
BECAUSE EVER SINCE YOU BECAME A VIEWTUBER . . .
ANYTIME I WAS SICK . . .
YOU WERE THERE FOR ME.
UNLOCK
OPEN
WHAT A PLEASANT SURPRISE!
I WASN'T EXPECTING YOU FOR HOURS!

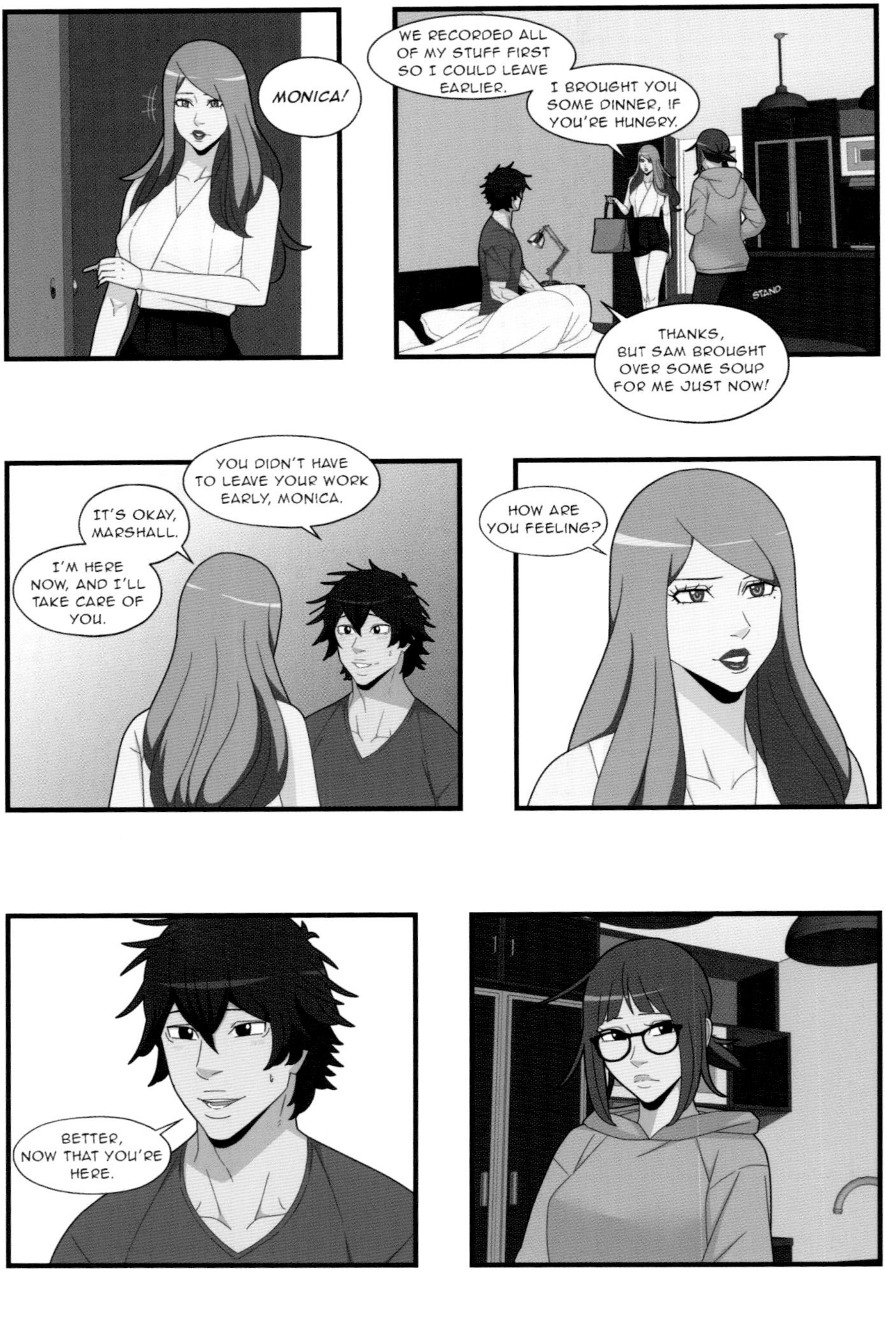
MONICA!
WE RECORDED ALL OF MY STUFF FIRST SO I COULD LEAVE EARLIER.
I BROUGHT YOU SOME DINNER, IF YOU'RE HUNGRY.
STAND
THANKS, BUT SAM BROUGHT OVER SOME SOUP FOR ME JUST NOW!
YOU DIDN'T HAVE TO LEAVE YOUR WORK EARLY, MONICA.
IT'S OKAY, MARSHALL.
I'M HERE NOW, AND I'LL TAKE CARE OF YOU.
HOW ARE YOU FEELING?
BETTER, NOW THAT YOU'RE HERE.

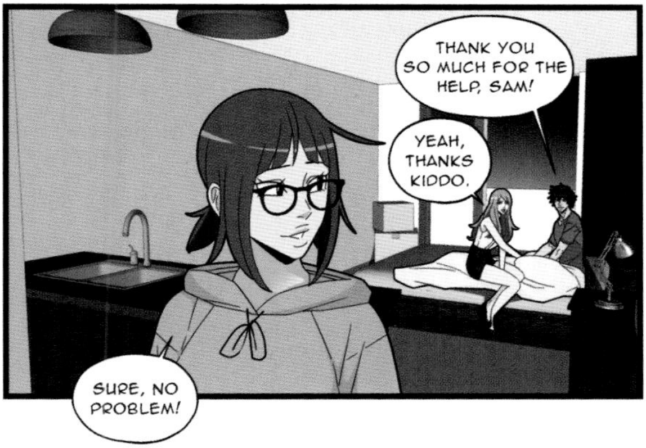
THANK YOU SO MUCH FOR THE HELP, SAM!
YEAH, THANKS KIDDO.
SURE, NO PROBLEM!

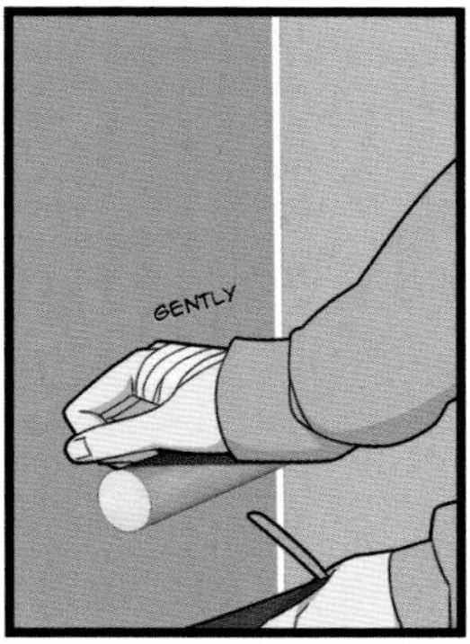
GENTLY

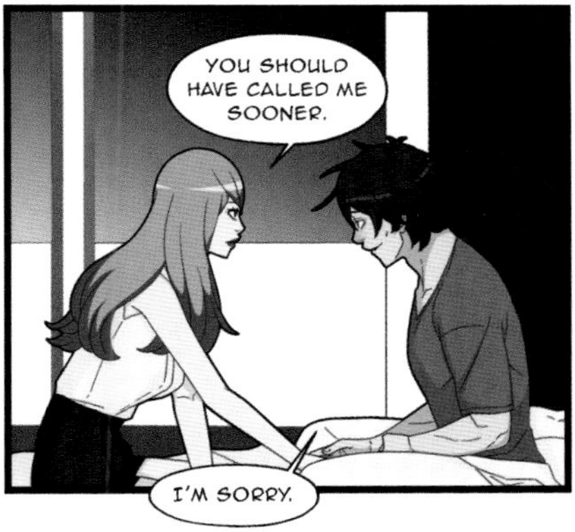
YOU SHOULD HAVE CALLED ME SOONER.
I'M SORRY.

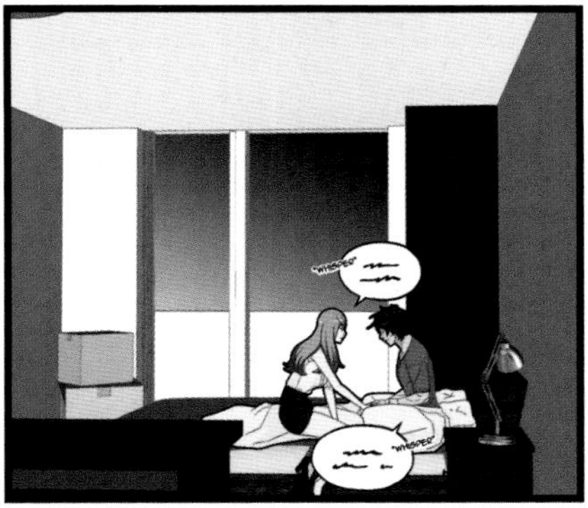
WHISPER
WHISPER

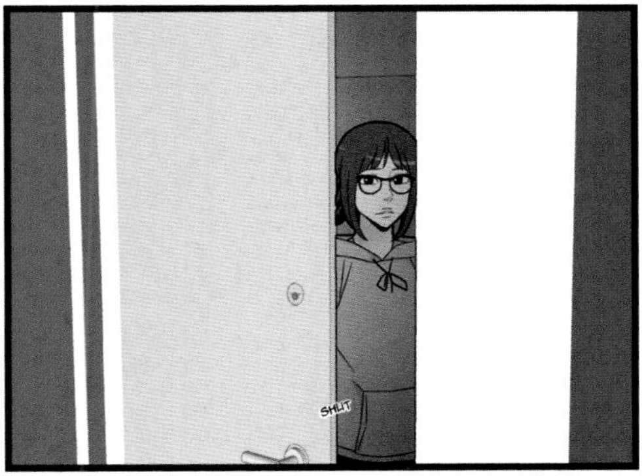
SHUT

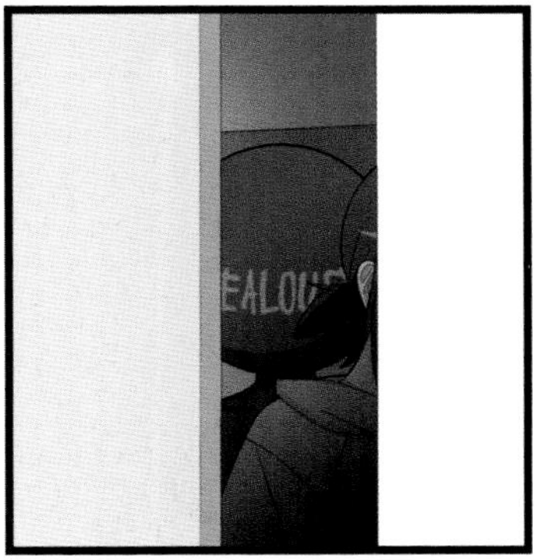

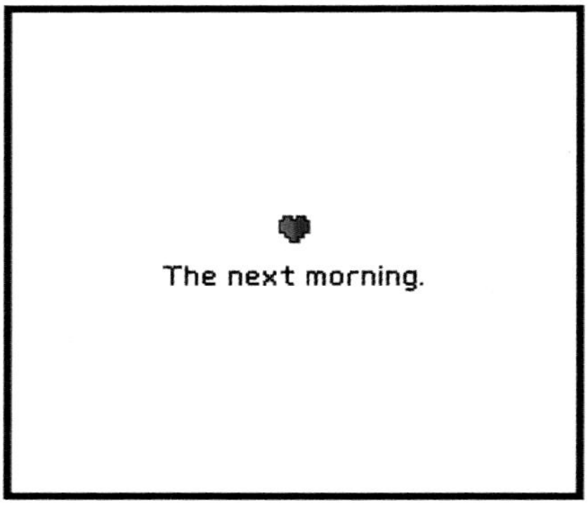
The next morning.
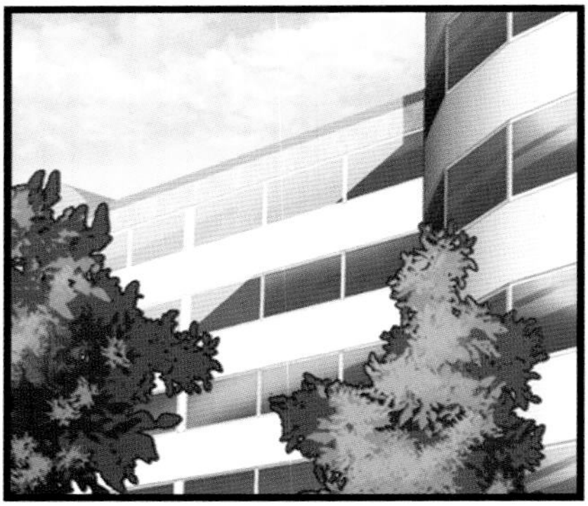
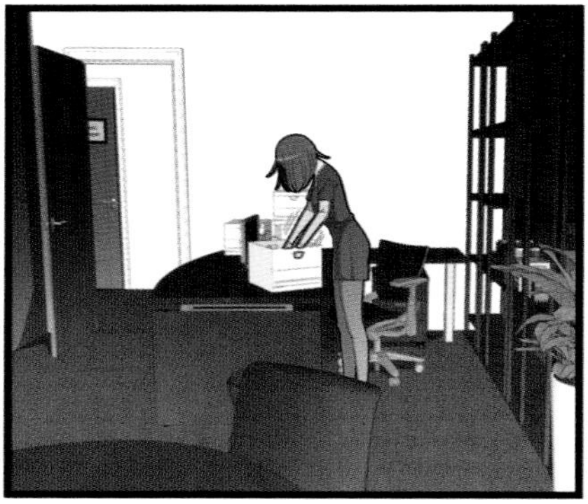
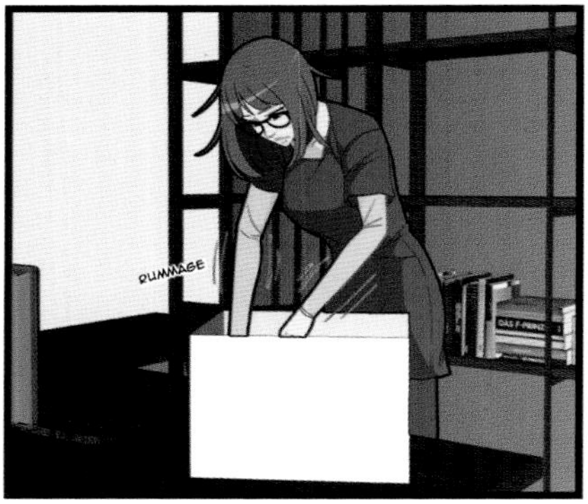
RUMMAGE
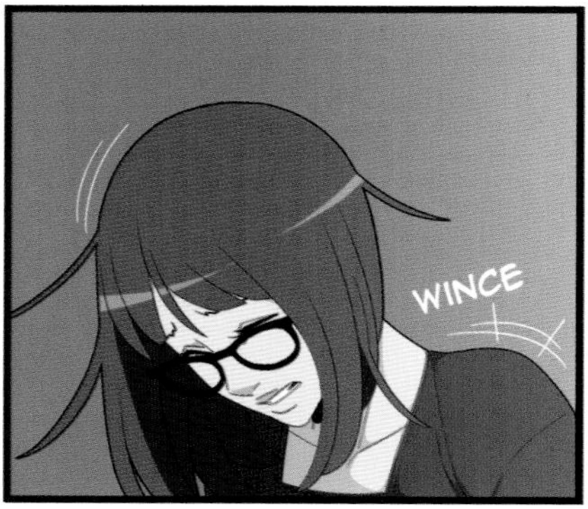
WINCE
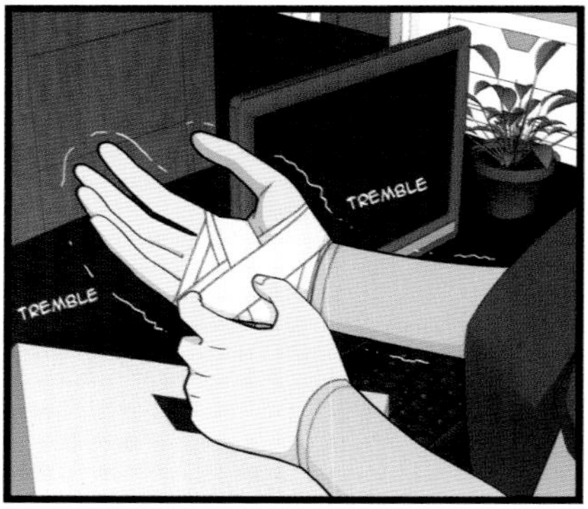
TREMBLE
TREMBLE

MONICA IS WITH MARSHALL NOW.

HE SHOULD BE SAFE FOR THE NIGHT.

HOW WAS THE SOUP?

DID YOU LIKE IT?

OH, I GUESS YOU LIKE IT.

WOW!

DO YOU WANT SOME MORE?

GRUNTS

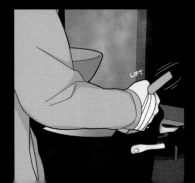

LIFT

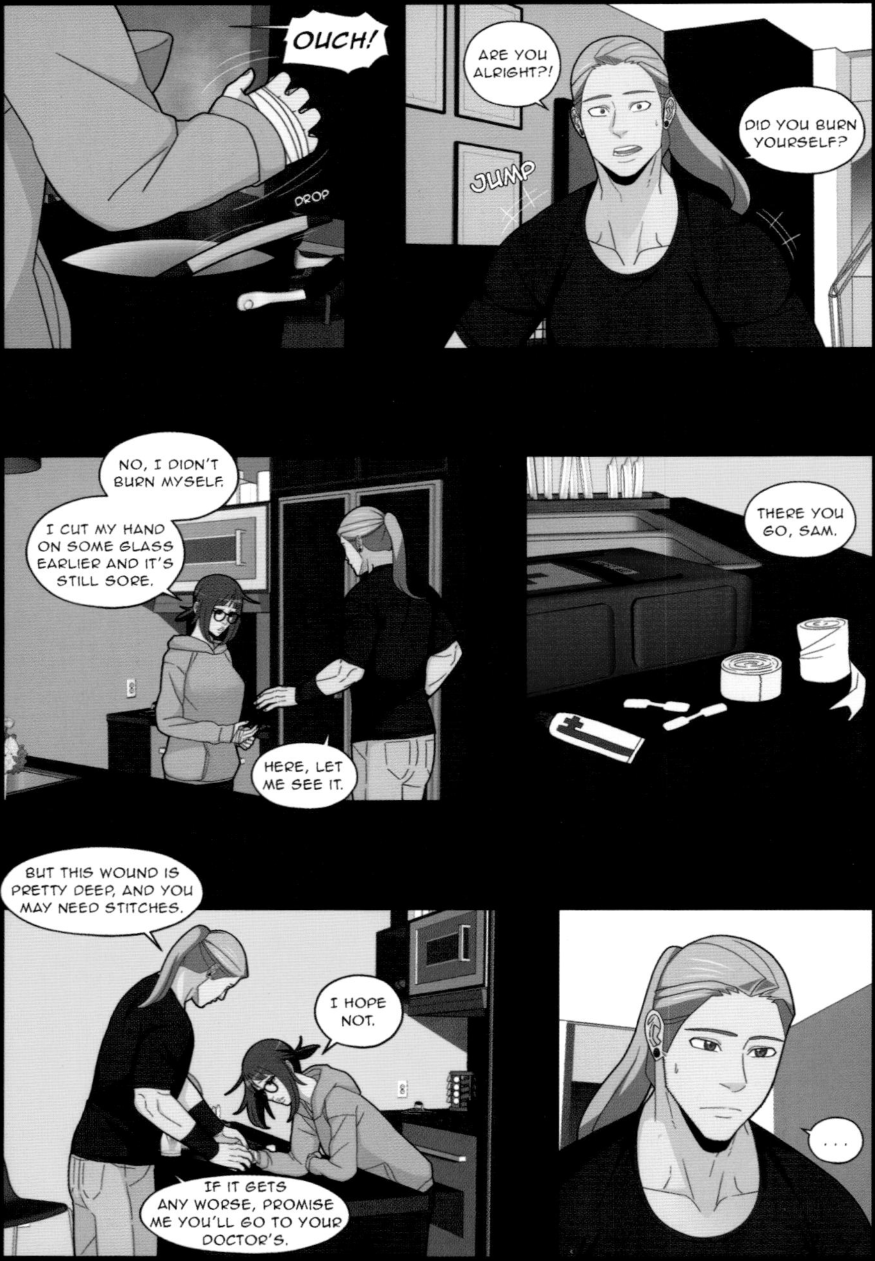
OUCH!
DROP
ARE YOU ALRIGHT?!
JUMP
DID YOU BURN YOURSELF?
NO, I DIDN'T BURN MYSELF.
I CUT MY HAND ON SOME GLASS EARLIER AND IT'S STILL SORE.
HERE, LET ME SEE IT.
THERE YOU GO, SAM.
BUT THIS WOUND IS PRETTY DEEP, AND YOU MAY NEED STITCHES.
I HOPE NOT.
IF IT GETS ANY WORSE, PROMISE ME YOU'LL GO TO YOUR DOCTOR'S.
...

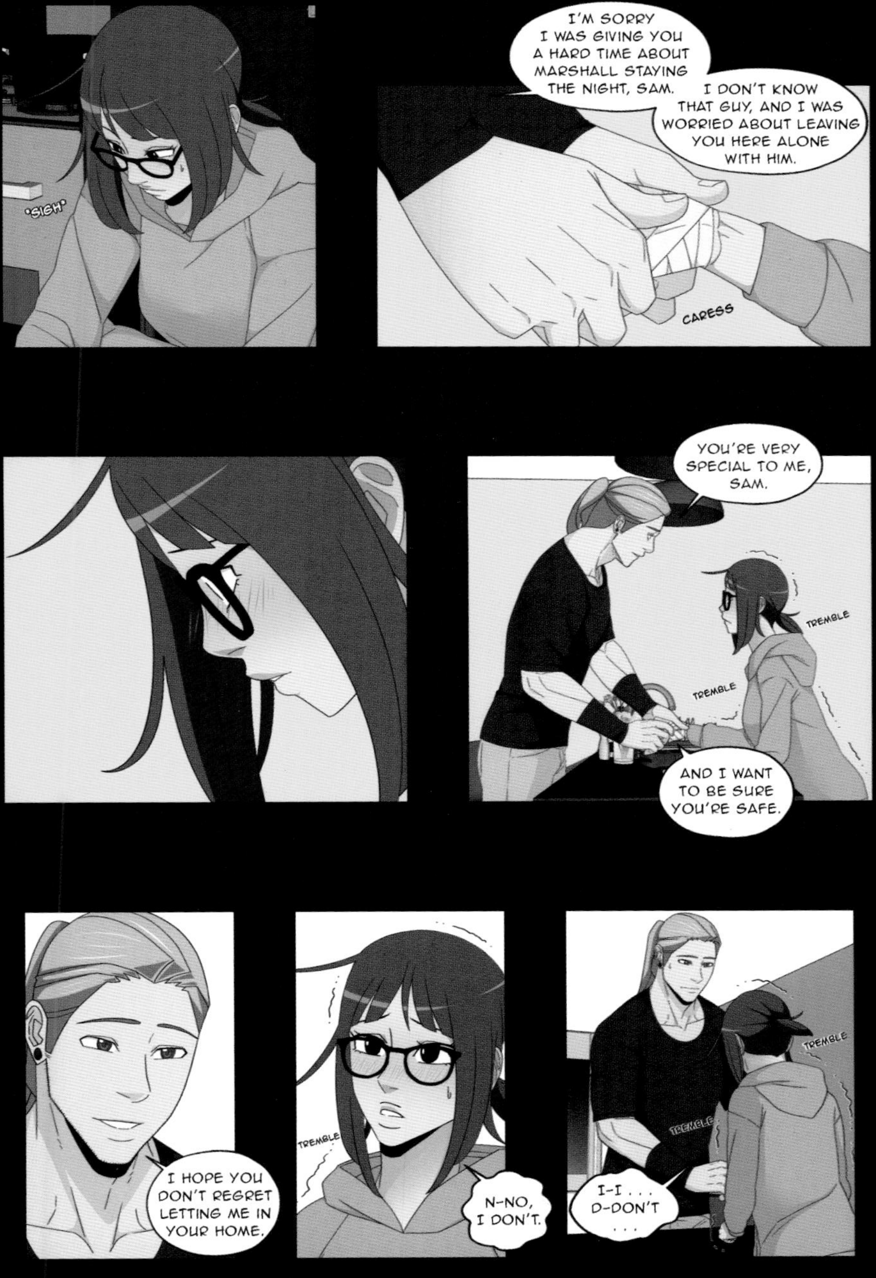
SIGH
I'M SORRY I WAS GIVING YOU A HARD TIME ABOUT MARSHALL STAYING THE NIGHT, SAM.
I DON'T KNOW THAT GUY, AND I WAS WORRIED ABOUT LEAVING YOU HERE ALONE WITH HIM.
CARESS
YOU'RE VERY SPECIAL TO ME, SAM.
TREMBLE
TREMBLE
AND I WANT TO BE SURE YOU'RE SAFE.
I HOPE YOU DON'T REGRET LETTING ME IN YOUR HOME.
TREMBLE
N-NO, I DON'T.
TREMBLE
TREMBLE
I-I . . . D-DON'T . . .

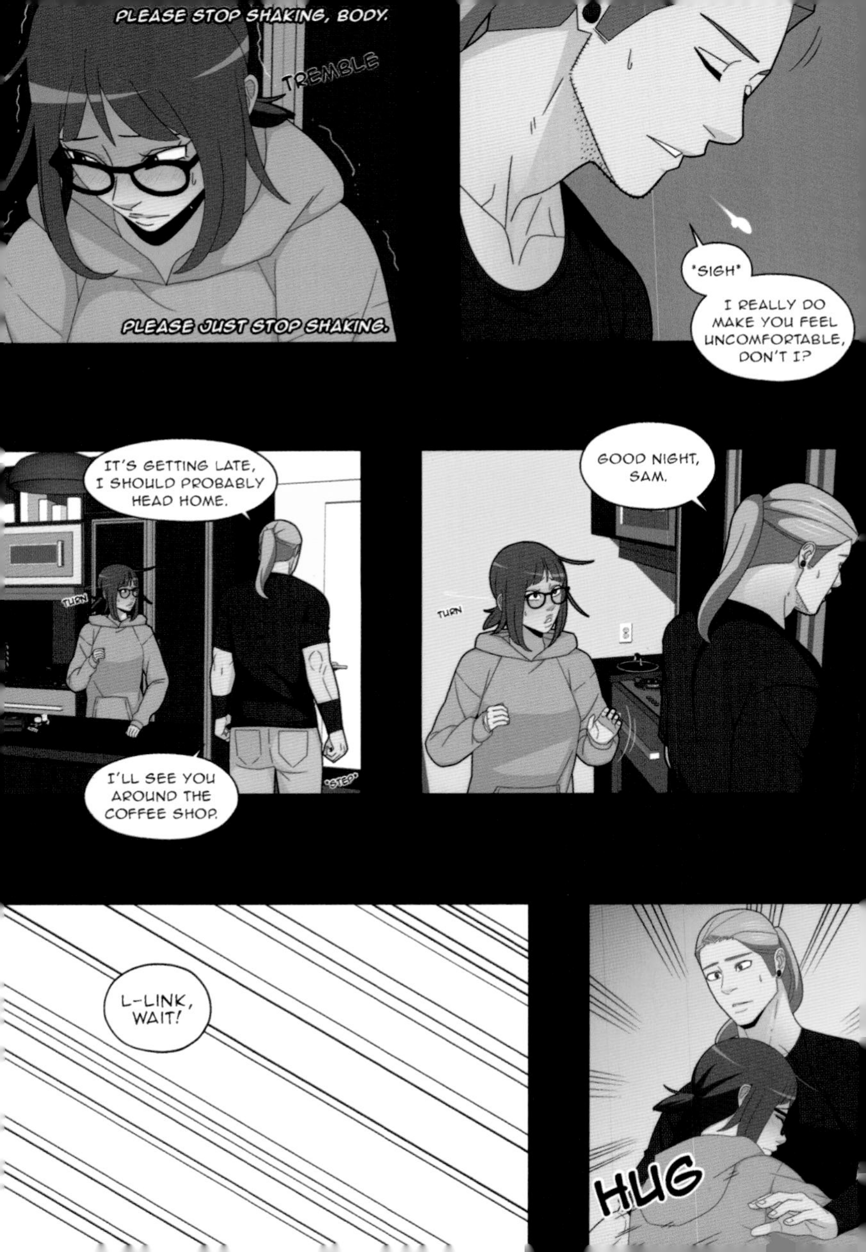
PLEASE STOP SHAKING, BODY.
TREMBLE
PLEASE JUST STOP SHAKING.
SIGH
I REALLY DO MAKE YOU FEEL UNCOMFORTABLE, DON'T I?
IT'S GETTING LATE, I SHOULD PROBABLY HEAD HOME.
TURN
I'LL SEE YOU AROUND THE COFFEE SHOP.
STEP
GOOD NIGHT, SAM.
TURN
L-LINK, WAIT!
HUG

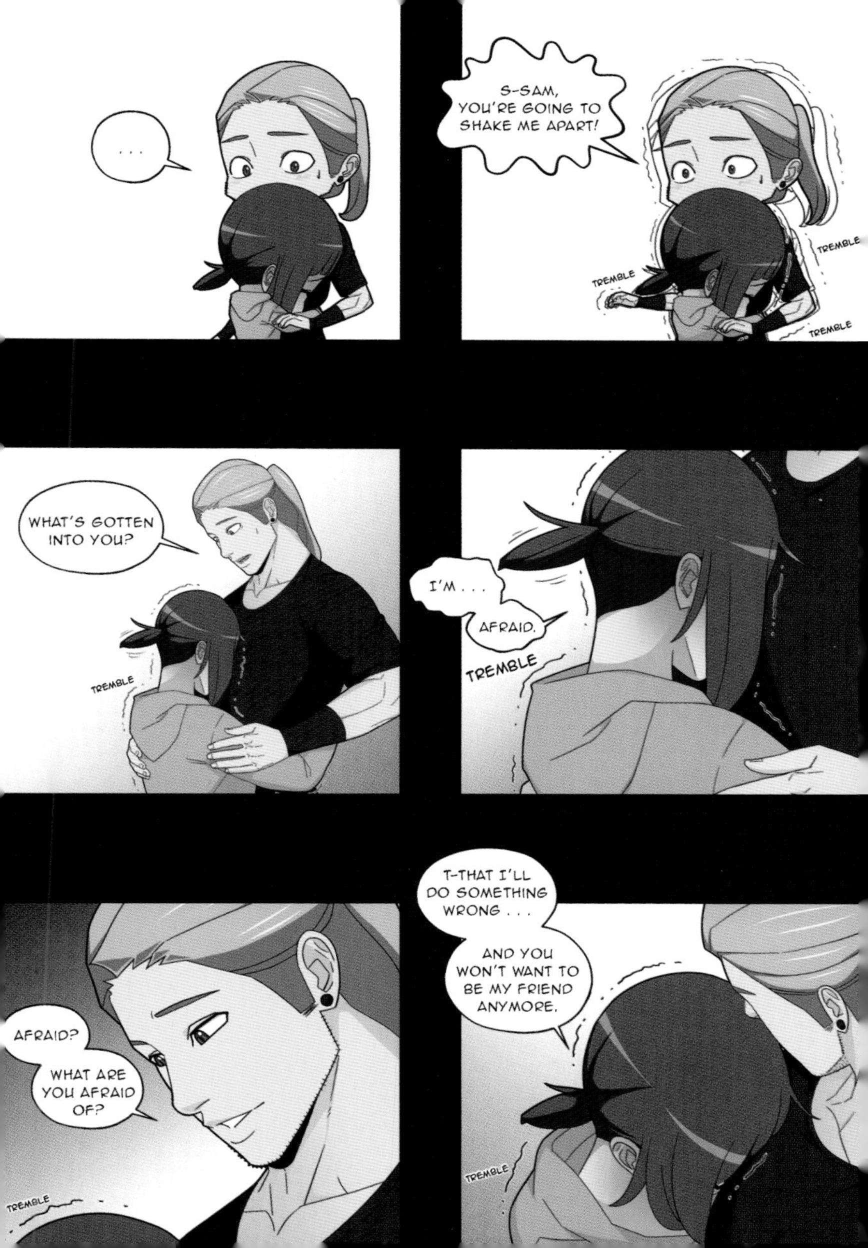
. . .
S-SAM, YOU'RE GOING TO SHAKE ME APART!
TREMBLE
TREMBLE
TREMBLE
WHAT'S GOTTEN INTO YOU?
TREMBLE
I'M . . .
AFRAID.
TREMBLE
AFRAID?
WHAT ARE YOU AFRAID OF?
TREMBLE
T-THAT I'LL DO SOMETHING WRONG . . .
AND YOU WON'T WANT TO BE MY FRIEND ANYMORE.
TREMBLE

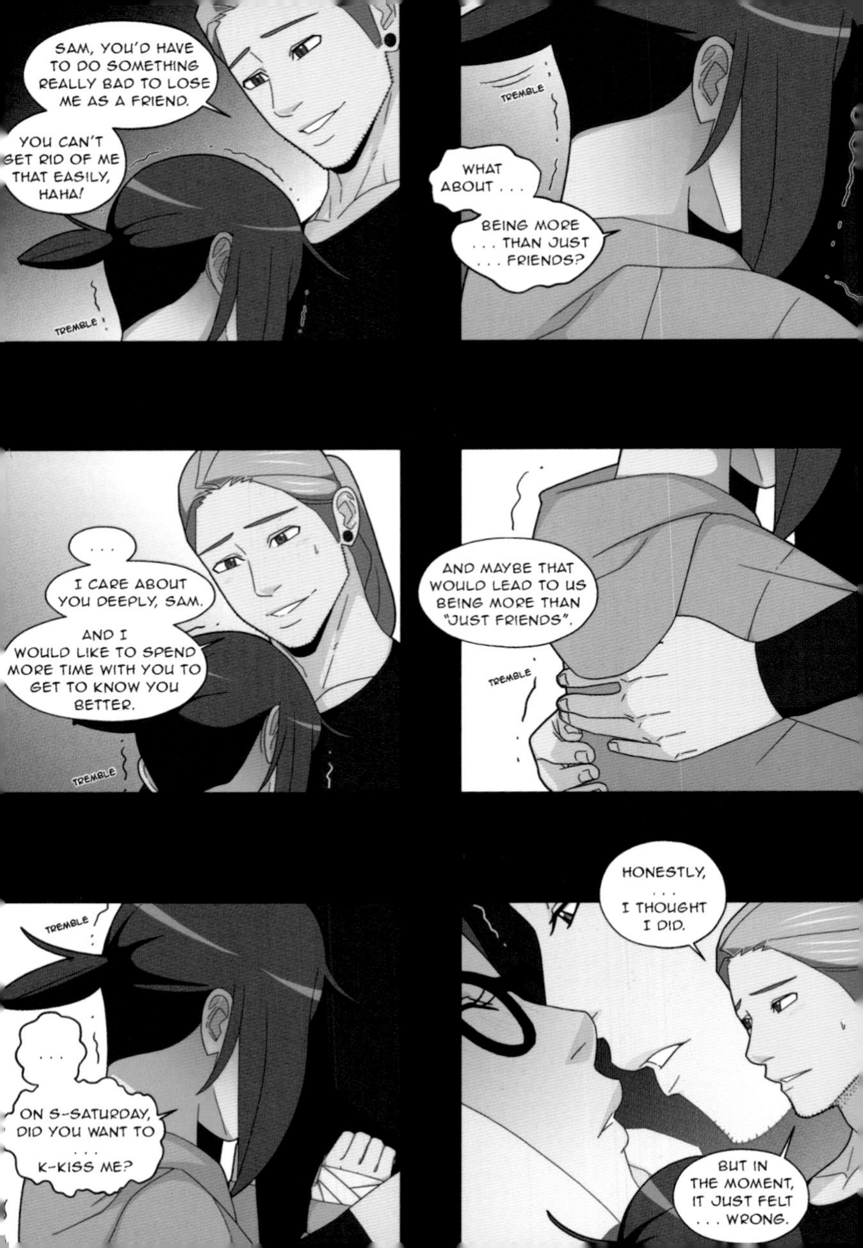
SAM, YOU'D HAVE TO DO SOMETHING REALLY BAD TO LOSE ME AS A FRIEND.
YOU CAN'T GET RID OF ME THAT EASILY, HAHA!
TREMBLE
TREMBLE
WHAT ABOUT . . .
BEING MORE . . . THAN JUST . . . FRIENDS?
. . .
I CARE ABOUT YOU DEEPLY, SAM.
AND I WOULD LIKE TO SPEND MORE TIME WITH YOU TO GET TO KNOW YOU BETTER.
TREMBLE
AND MAYBE THAT WOULD LEAD TO US BEING MORE THAN "JUST FRIENDS".
TREMBLE
TREMBLE
. . .
ON S-SATURDAY, DID YOU WANT TO . . . K-KISS ME?
HONESTLY, . . . I THOUGHT I DID.
BUT IN THE MOMENT, IT JUST FELT . . . WRONG.

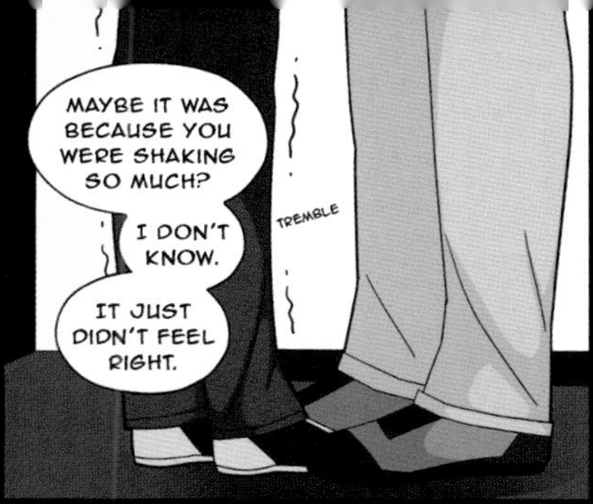
MAYBE IT WAS BECAUSE YOU WERE SHAKING SO MUCH?
TREMBLE
I DON'T KNOW.
IT JUST DIDN'T FEEL RIGHT.

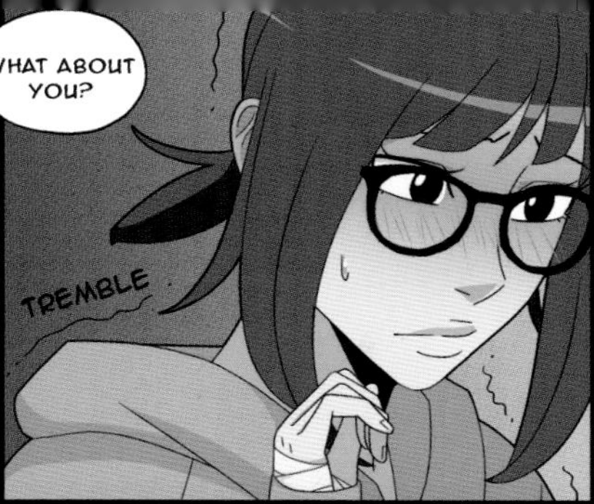
WHAT ABOUT YOU?
TREMBLE

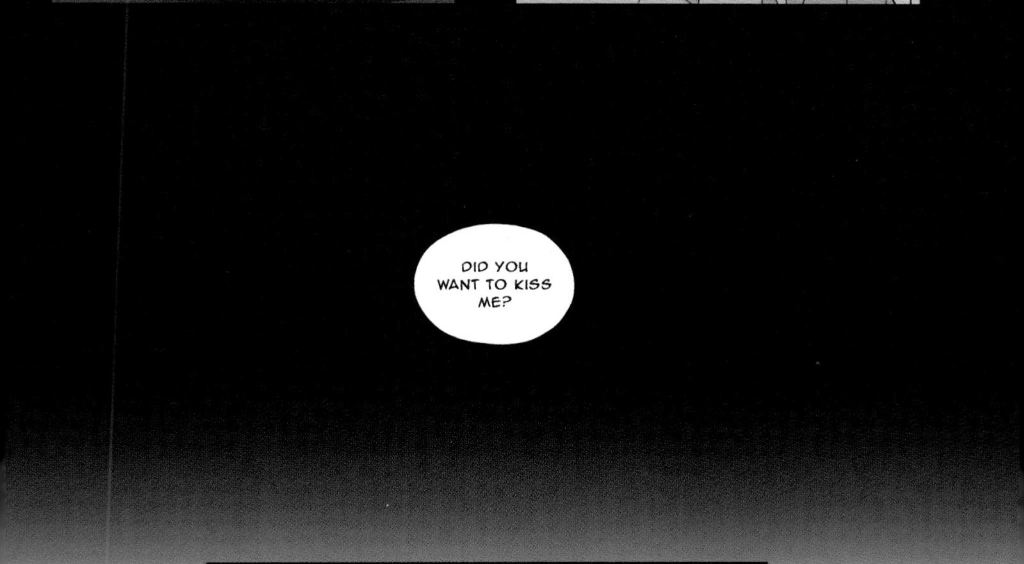
DID YOU WANT TO KISS ME?

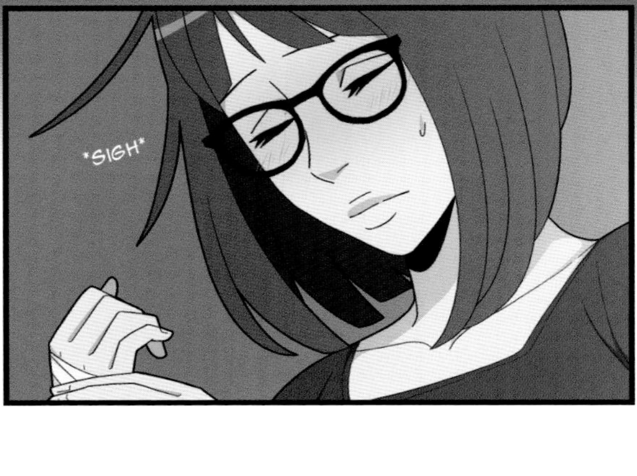
SIGH

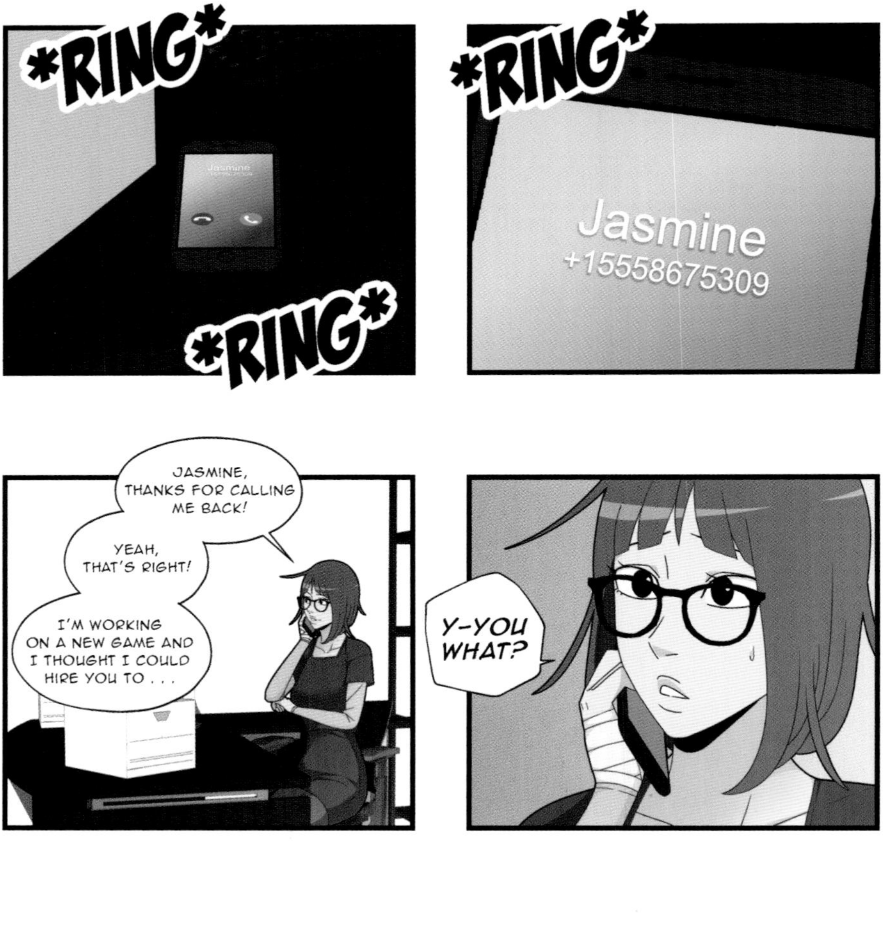
RING
RING
RING
Jasmine
+15558675309
JASMINE, THANKS FOR CALLING ME BACK!
YEAH, THAT'S RIGHT!
I'M WORKING ON A NEW GAME AND I THOUGHT I COULD HIRE YOU TO . . .
Y-YOU WHAT?

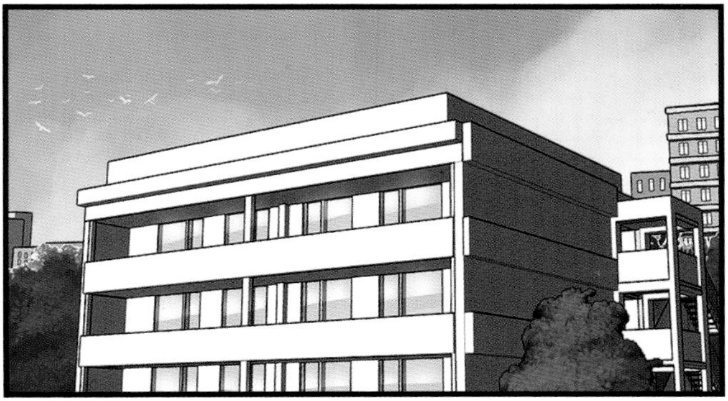
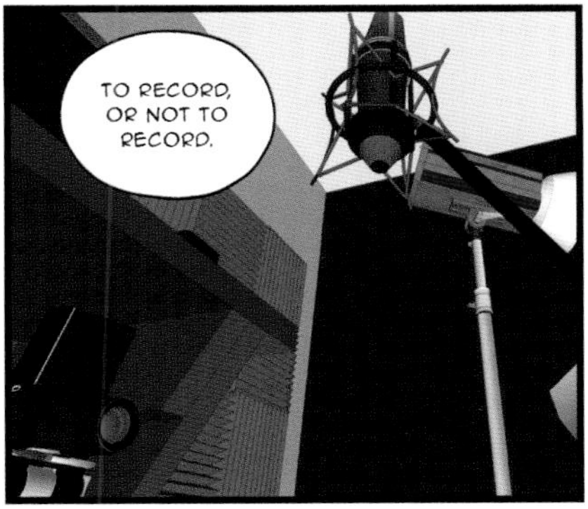
TO RECORD, OR NOT TO RECORD.
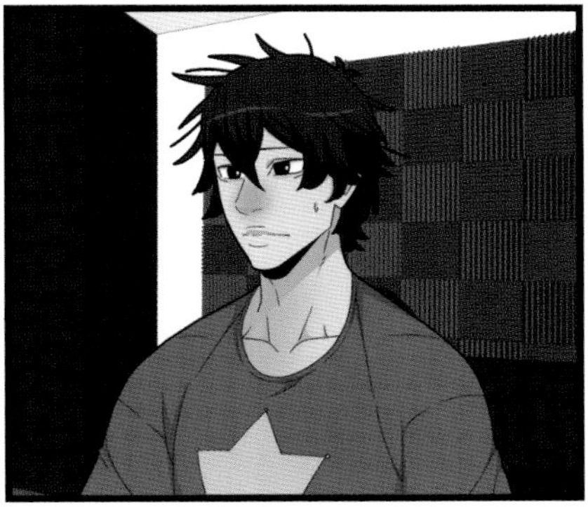
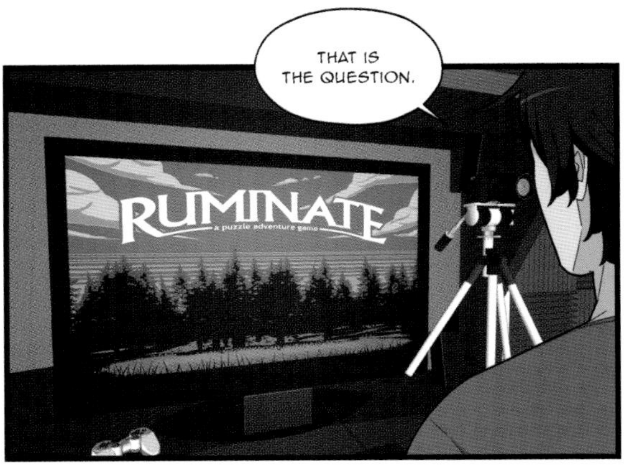
THAT IS THE QUESTION.
RUMINATE
a puzzle adventure game

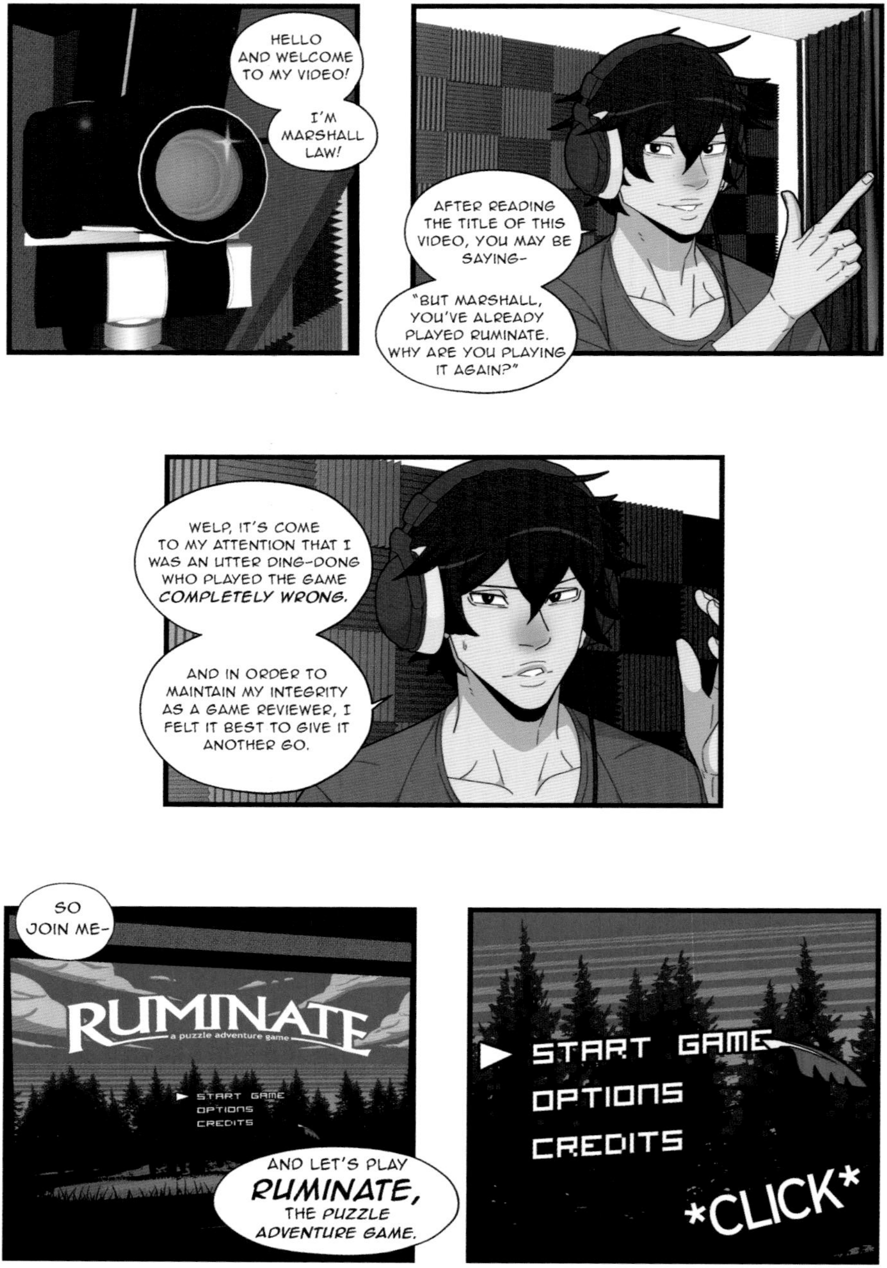
HELLO AND WELCOME TO MY VIDEO!
I'M MARSHALL LAW!
AFTER READING THE TITLE OF THIS VIDEO, YOU MAY BE SAYING-
"BUT MARSHALL, YOU'VE ALREADY PLAYED RUMINATE. WHY ARE YOU PLAYING IT AGAIN?"
WELP, IT'S COME TO MY ATTENTION THAT I WAS AN UTTER DING-DONG WHO PLAYED THE GAME COMPLETELY WRONG.
AND IN ORDER TO MAINTAIN MY INTEGRITY AS A GAME REVIEWER, I FELT IT BEST TO GIVE IT ANOTHER GO.
SO JOIN ME-
RUMINATE
a puzzle adventure game
START GAME
OPTIONS
CREDITS
AND LET'S PLAY RUMINATE, THE PUZZLE ADVENTURE GAME.
START GAME
OPTIONS
CREDITS
CLICK

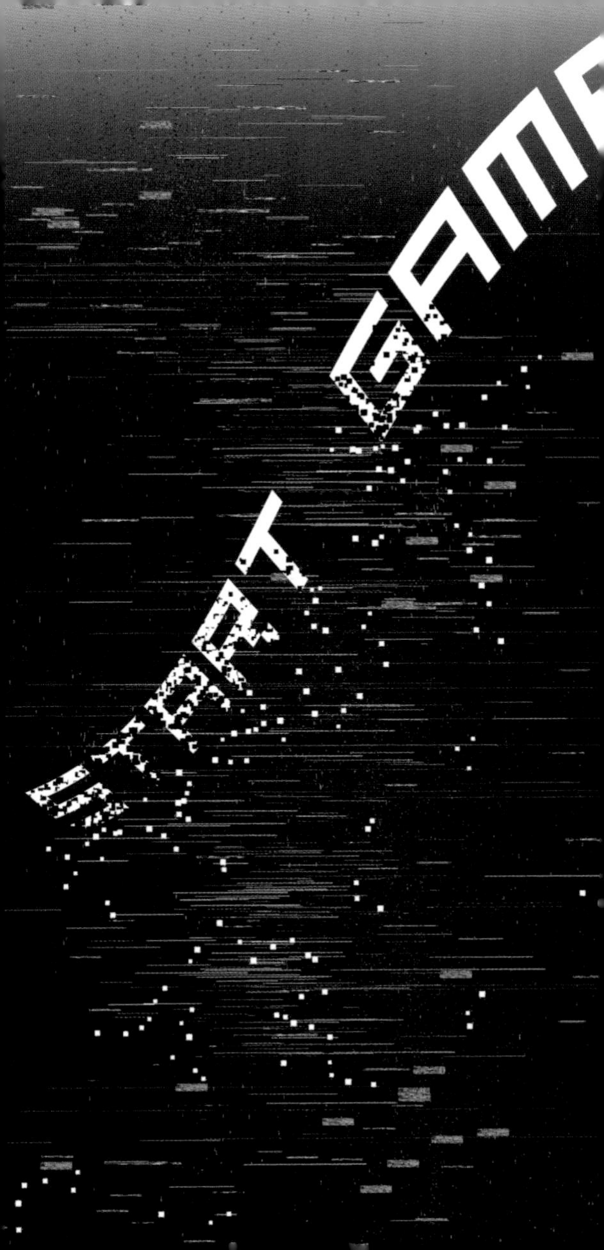

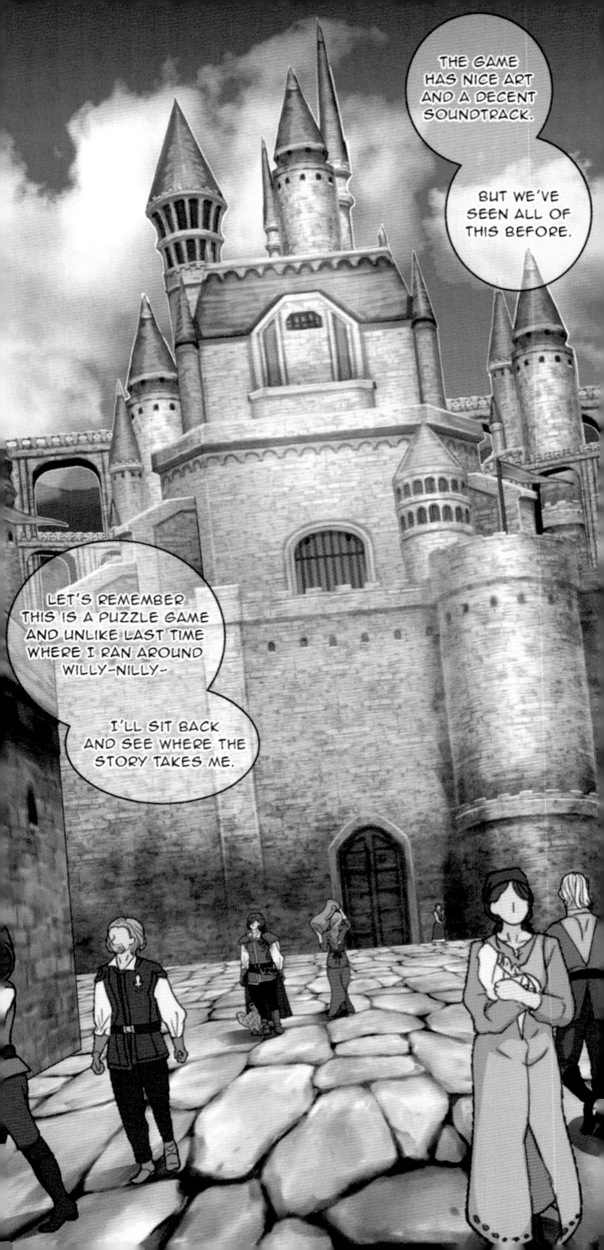
THE GAME HAS NICE ART AND A DECENT SOUNDTRACK.
BUT WE'VE SEEN ALL OF THIS BEFORE.
LET'S REMEMBER THIS IS A PUZZLE GAME AND UNLIKE LAST TIME WHERE I RAN AROUND WILLY-NILLY-
I'LL SIT BACK AND SEE WHERE THE STORY TAKES ME.

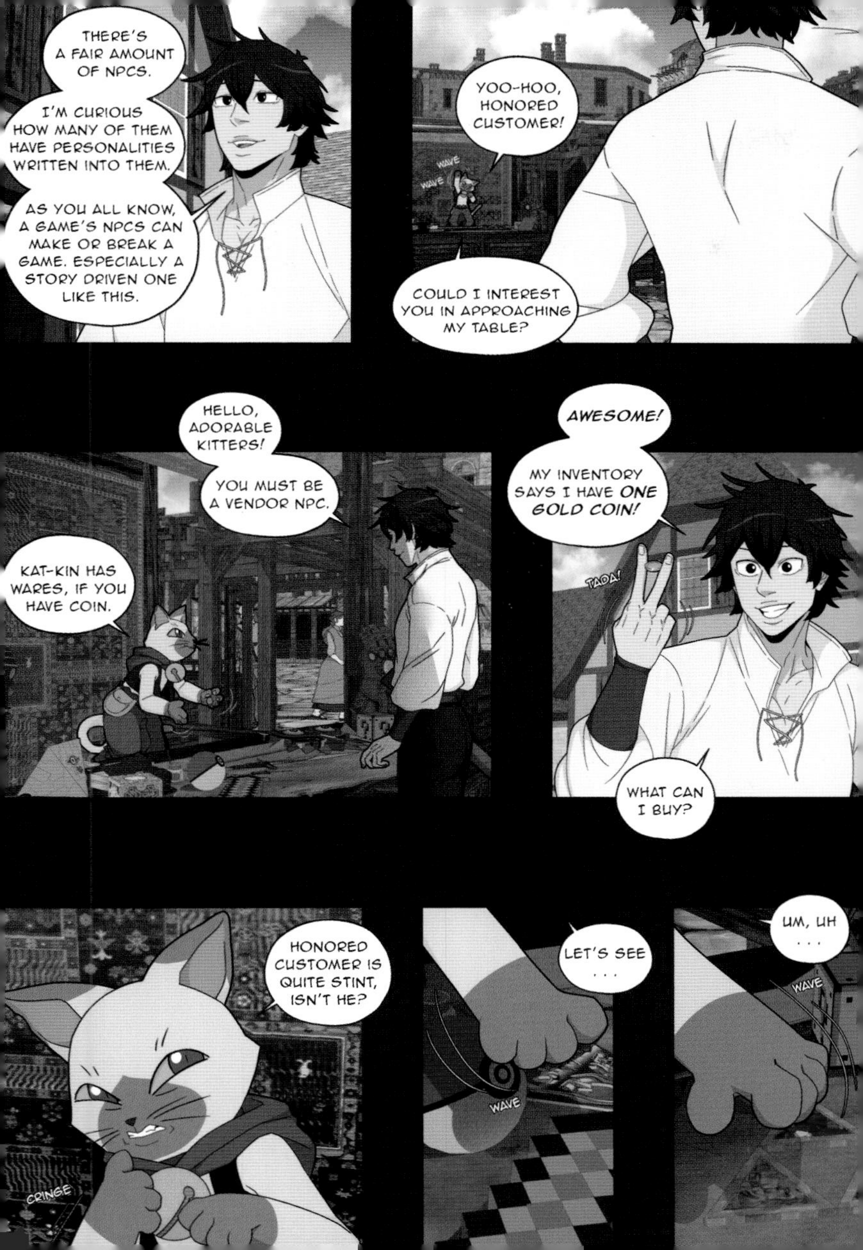
THERE'S A FAIR AMOUNT OF NPCS.
I'M CURIOUS HOW MANY OF THEM HAVE PERSONALITIES WRITTEN INTO THEM.
AS YOU ALL KNOW, A GAME'S NPCS CAN MAKE OR BREAK A GAME. ESPECIALLY A STORY DRIVEN ONE LIKE THIS.
YOO-HOO, HONORED CUSTOMER!
WAVE
WAVE
COULD I INTEREST YOU IN APPROACHING MY TABLE?
HELLO, ADORABLE KITTERS!
YOU MUST BE A VENDOR NPC.
KAT-KIN HAS WARES, IF YOU HAVE COIN.
AWESOME!
MY INVENTORY SAYS I HAVE ONE GOLD COIN!
TADA!
WHAT CAN I BUY?
HONORED CUSTOMER IS QUITE STINT, ISN'T HE?
CRINGE
LET'S SEE . . .
WAVE
UM, UH . . .
WAVE

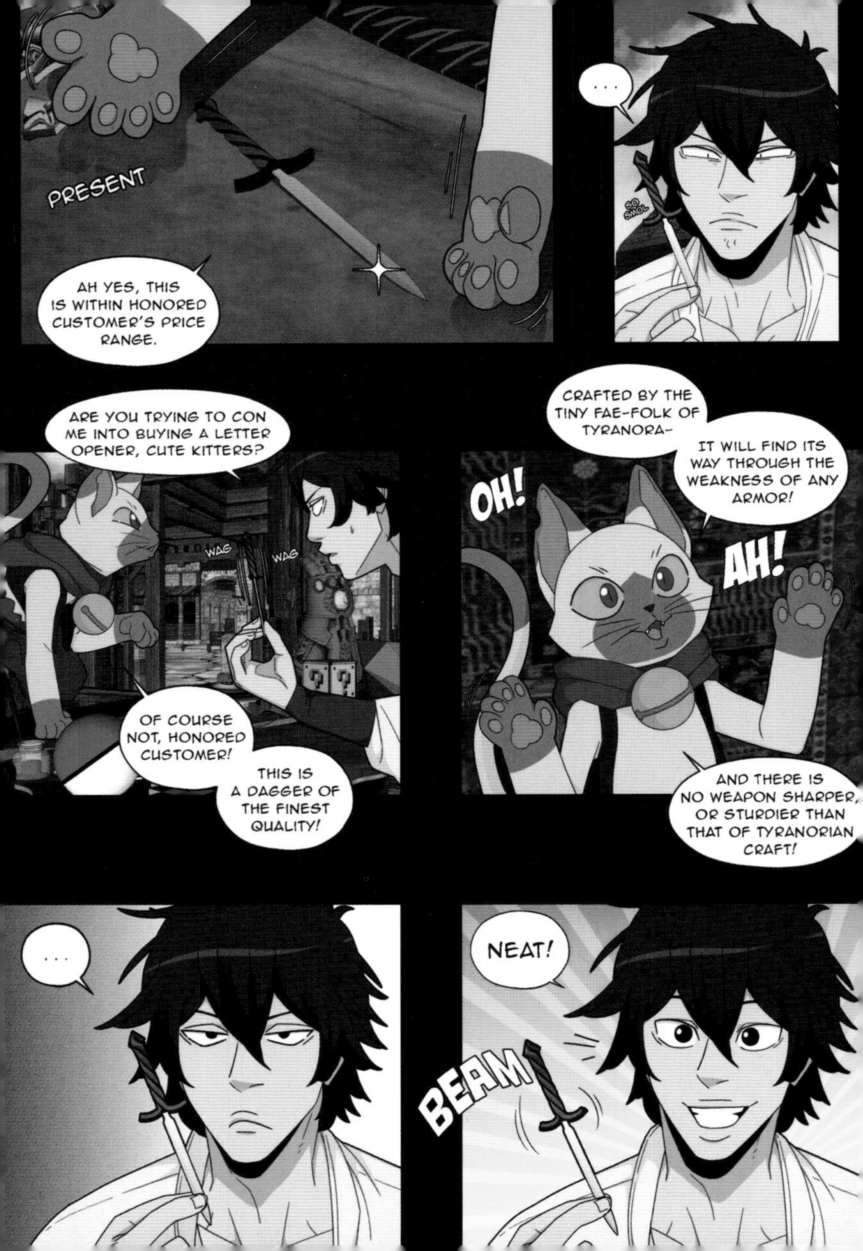

PRESENT
AH YES, THIS IS WITHIN HONORED CUSTOMER'S PRICE RANGE.
. . .
SO SMOL
ARE YOU TRYING TO CON ME INTO BUYING A LETTER OPENER, CUTE KITTERS?
WAG
WAG
OF COURSE NOT, HONORED CUSTOMER!
THIS IS A DAGGER OF THE FINEST QUALITY!
CRAFTED BY THE TINY FAE-FOLK OF TYRANORA-
IT WILL FIND ITS WAY THROUGH THE WEAKNESS OF ANY ARMOR!
OH!
AH!
AND THERE IS NO WEAPON SHARPER, OR STURDIER THAN THAT OF TYRANORIAN CRAFT!
. . .
NEAT!
BEAM

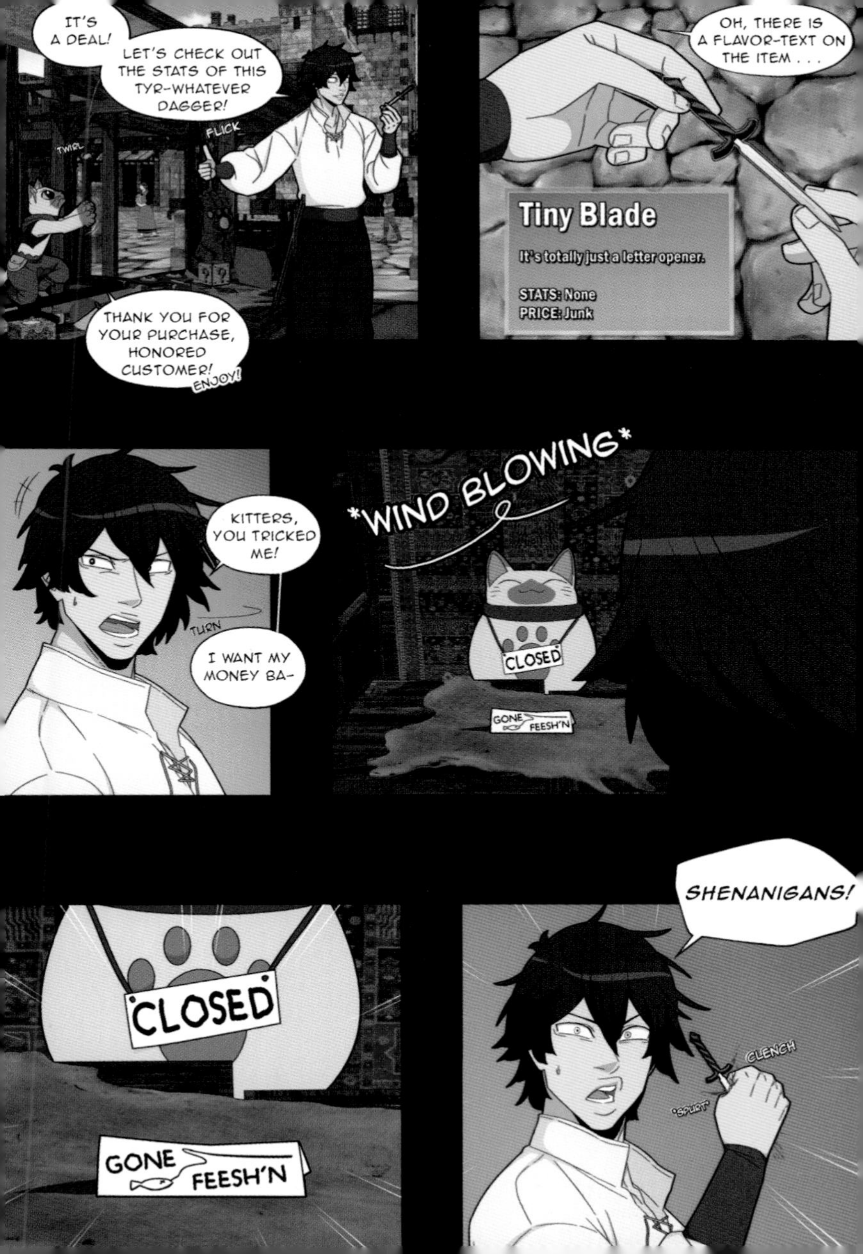
IT'S A DEAL!
LET'S CHECK OUT THE STATS OF THIS TYR-WHATEVER DAGGER!
FLICK
TWIRL
THANK YOU FOR YOUR PURCHASE, HONORED CUSTOMER!
ENJOY!
OH, THERE IS A FLAVOR-TEXT ON THE ITEM . . .
Tiny Blade
It's totally just a letter opener.
STATS: None
PRICE: Junk
KITTERS, YOU TRICKED ME!
TURN
I WANT MY MONEY BA-
WIND BLOWING
CLOSED
GONE FEESH'N
CLOSED
GONE FEESH'N
SHENANIGANS!
CLENCH
SPURT

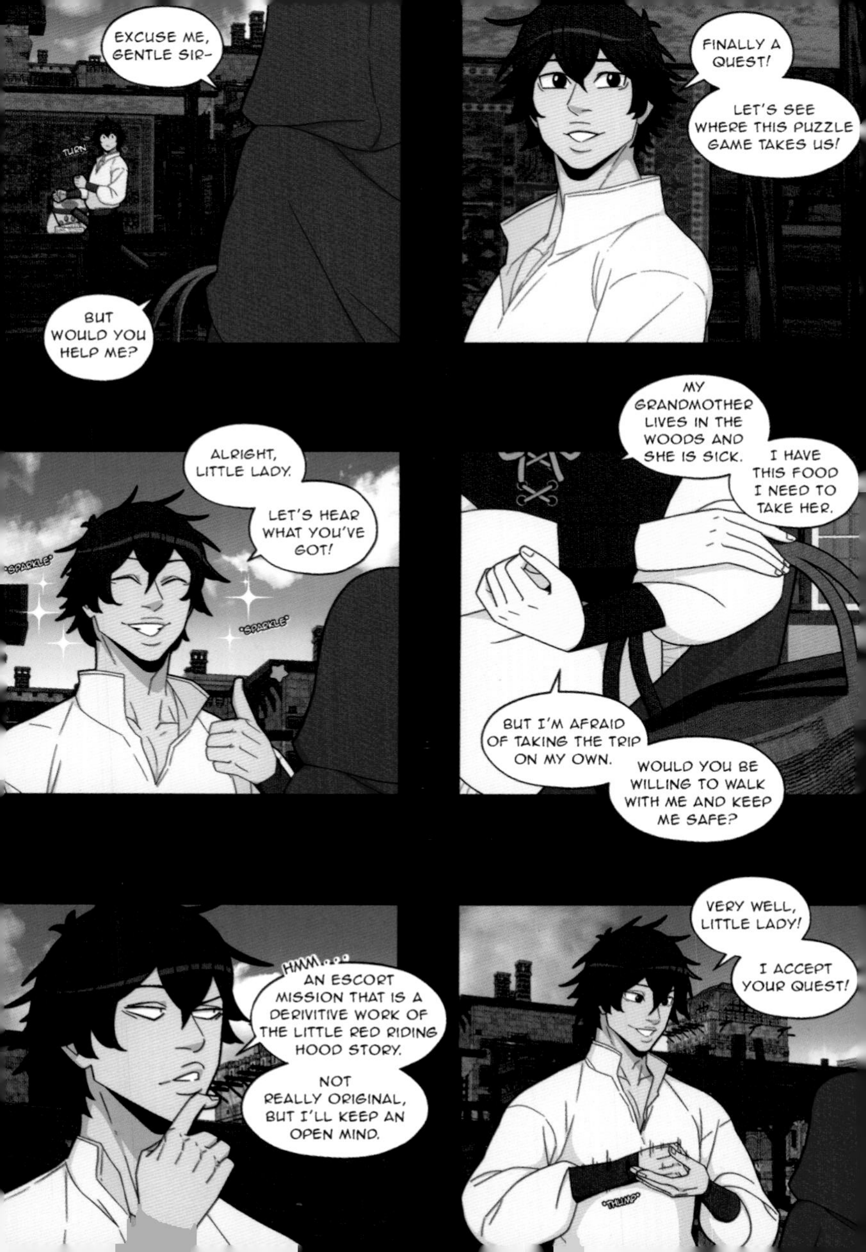
EXCUSE ME, GENTLE SIR-
TURN
BUT WOULD YOU HELP ME?
FINALLY A QUEST!
LET'S SEE WHERE THIS PUZZLE GAME TAKES US!
ALRIGHT, LITTLE LADY.
LET'S HEAR WHAT YOU'VE GOT!
SPARKLE
SPARKLE
MY GRANDMOTHER LIVES IN THE WOODS AND SHE IS SICK.
I HAVE THIS FOOD I NEED TO TAKE HER.
BUT I'M AFRAID OF TAKING THE TRIP ON MY OWN.
WOULD YOU BE WILLING TO WALK WITH ME AND KEEP ME SAFE?
HMM...
AN ESCORT MISSION THAT IS A DERIVITIVE WORK OF THE LITTLE RED RIDING HOOD STORY.
NOT REALLY ORIGINAL, BUT I'LL KEEP AN OPEN MIND.
VERY WELL, LITTLE LADY!
I ACCEPT YOUR QUEST!
THUMP

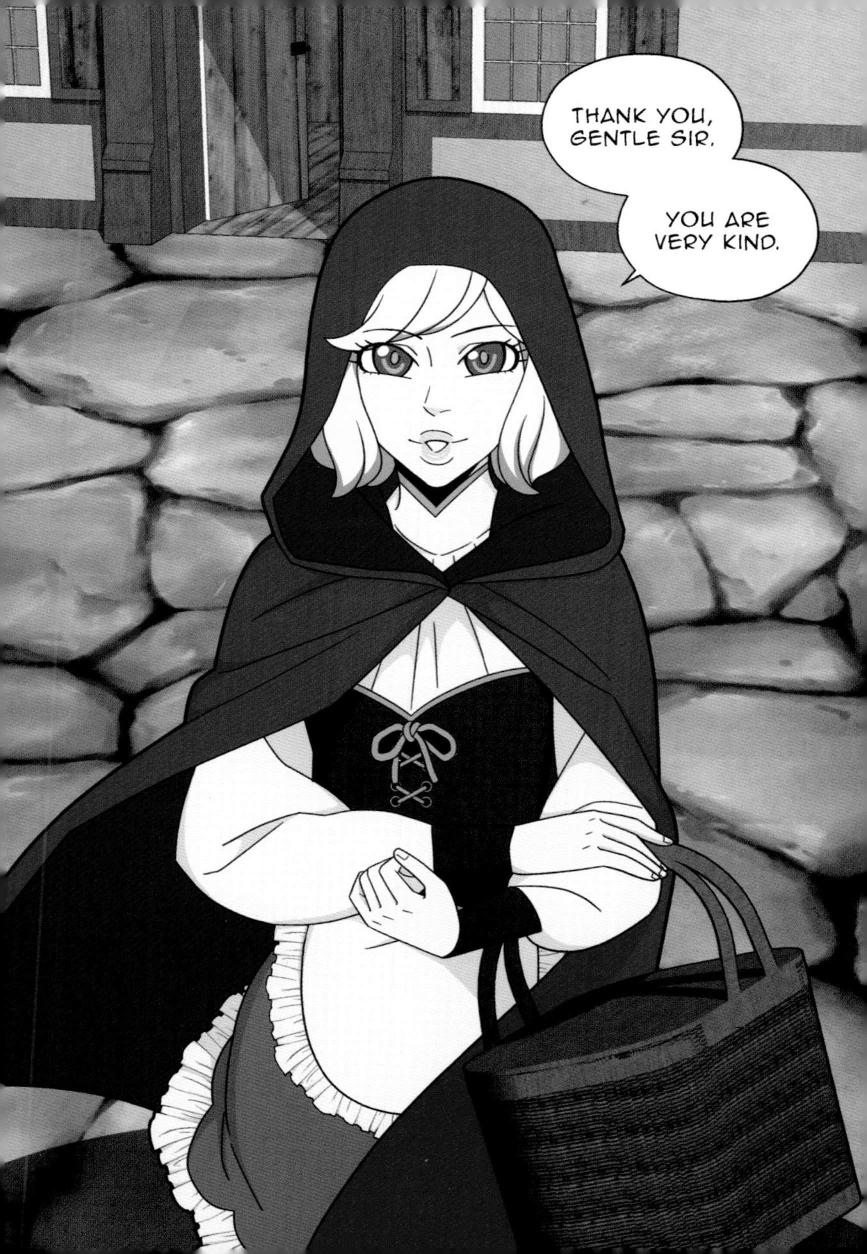
THANK YOU, GENTLE SIR.
YOU ARE VERY KIND.

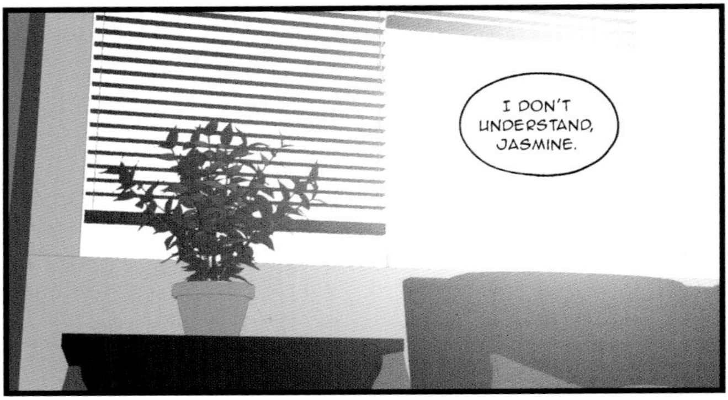
I DON'T UNDERSTAND, JASMINE.

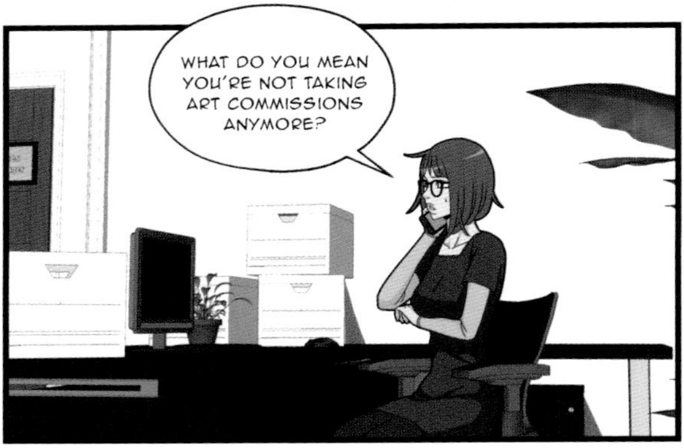
WHAT DO YOU MEAN YOU'RE NOT TAKING ART COMMISSIONS ANYMORE?

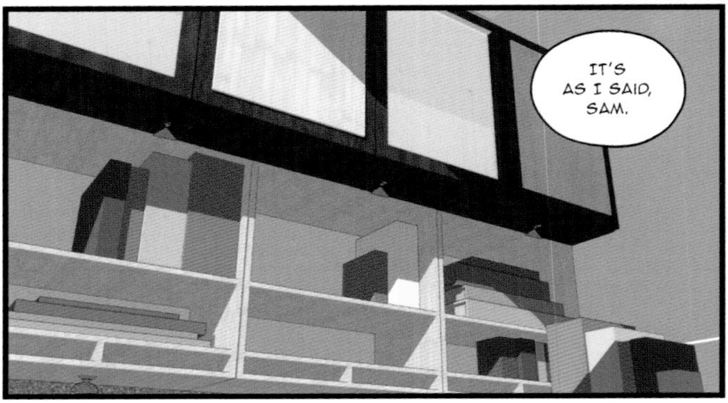
IT'S AS I SAID, SAM.

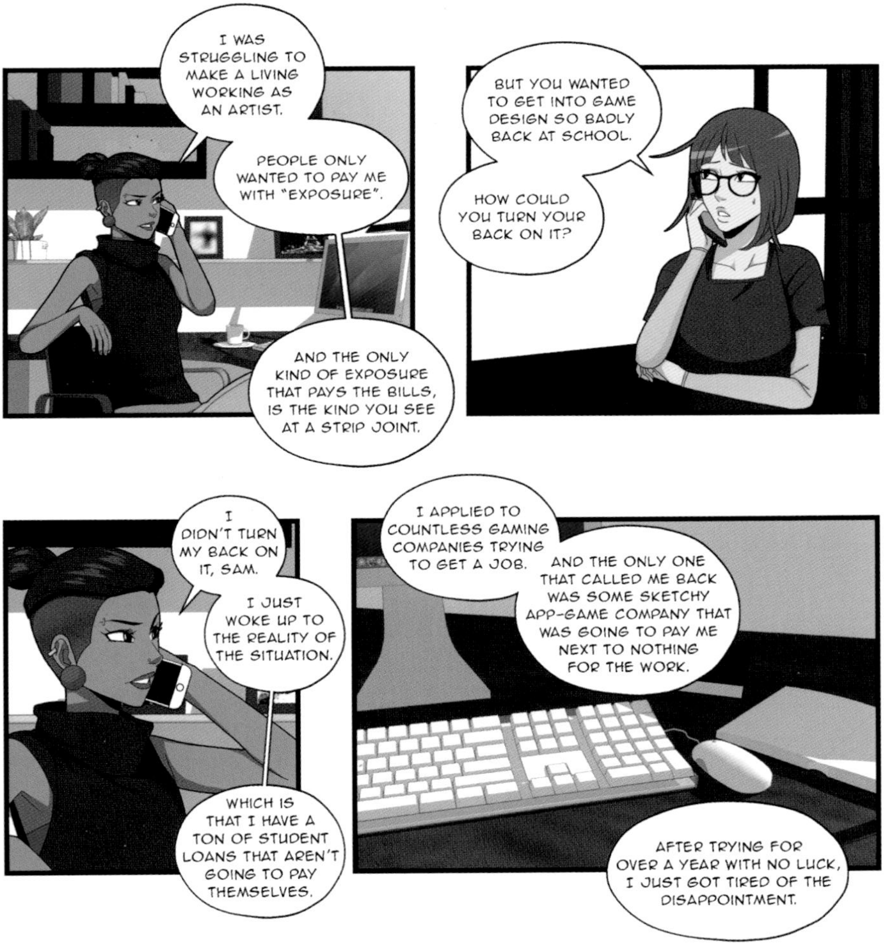
I WAS STRUGGLING TO MAKE A LIVING WORKING AS AN ARTIST.
PEOPLE ONLY WANTED TO PAY ME WITH "EXPOSURE".
AND THE ONLY KIND OF EXPOSURE THAT PAYS THE BILLS, IS THE KIND YOU SEE AT A STRIP JOINT.
BUT YOU WANTED TO GET INTO GAME DESIGN SO BADLY BACK AT SCHOOL.
HOW COULD YOU TURN YOUR BACK ON IT?
I DIDN'T TURN MY BACK ON IT, SAM.
I JUST WOKE UP TO THE REALITY OF THE SITUATION.
WHICH IS THAT I HAVE A TON OF STUDENT LOANS THAT AREN'T GOING TO PAY THEMSELVES.
I APPLIED TO COUNTLESS GAMING COMPANIES TRYING TO GET A JOB.
AND THE ONLY ONE THAT CALLED ME BACK WAS SOME SKETCHY APP-GAME COMPANY THAT WAS GOING TO PAY ME NEXT TO NOTHING FOR THE WORK.
AFTER TRYING FOR OVER A YEAR WITH NO LUCK, I JUST GOT TIRED OF THE DISAPPOINTMENT.

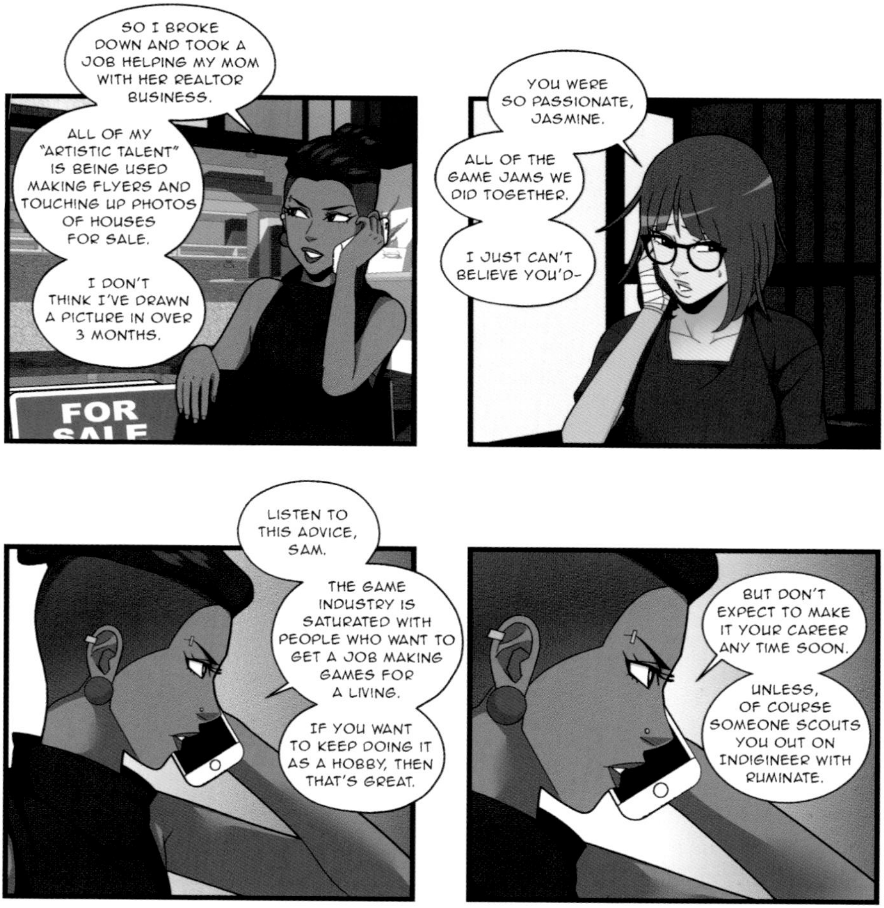
SO I BROKE DOWN AND TOOK A JOB HELPING MY MOM WITH HER REALTOR BUSINESS.
ALL OF MY "ARTISTIC TALENT" IS BEING USED MAKING FLYERS AND TOUCHING UP PHOTOS OF HOUSES FOR SALE.
I DON'T THINK I'VE DRAWN A PICTURE IN OVER 3 MONTHS.
FOR SALE
YOU WERE SO PASSIONATE, JASMINE.
ALL OF THE GAME JAMS WE DID TOGETHER.
I JUST CAN'T BELIEVE YOU'D-
LISTEN TO THIS ADVICE, SAM.
THE GAME INDUSTRY IS SATURATED WITH PEOPLE WHO WANT TO GET A JOB MAKING GAMES FOR A LIVING.
IF YOU WANT TO KEEP DOING IT AS A HOBBY, THEN THAT'S GREAT.
BUT DON'T EXPECT TO MAKE IT YOUR CAREER ANY TIME SOON.
UNLESS, OF COURSE SOMEONE SCOUTS YOU OUT ON INDIGINEER WITH RUMINATE.

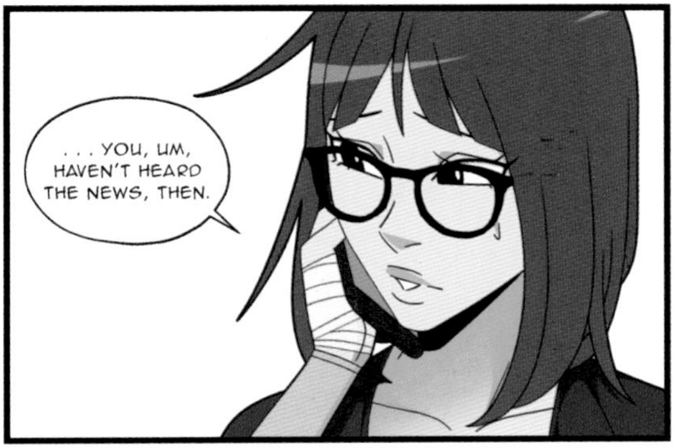
. . . YOU, UM, HAVEN'T HEARD THE NEWS, THEN.

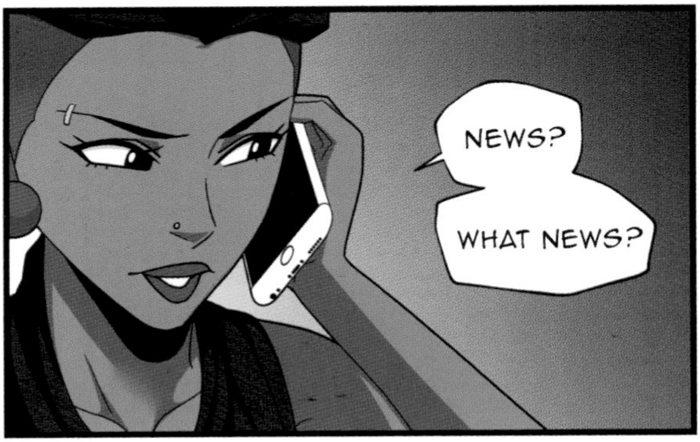
NEWS?
WHAT NEWS?

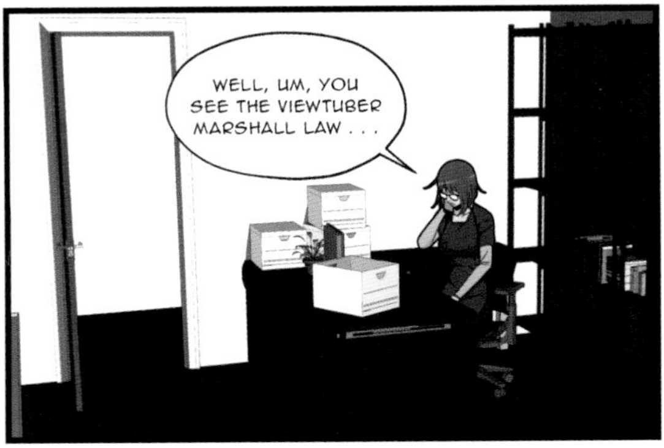
WELL, UM, YOU SEE THE VIEWTUBER MARSHALL LAW . . .

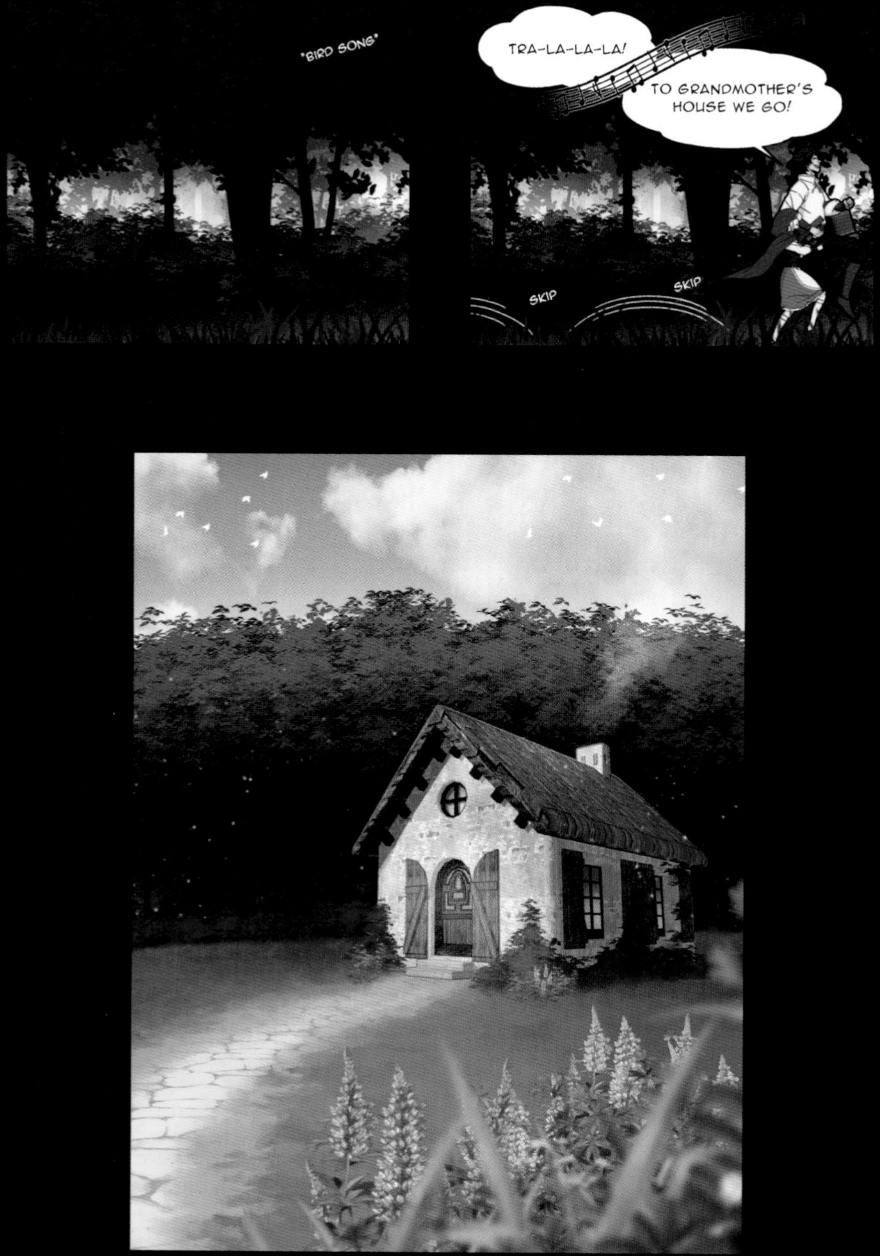
BIRD SONG
TRA-LA-LA-LA!
TO GRANDMOTHER'S HOUSE WE GO!
SKIP
SKIP

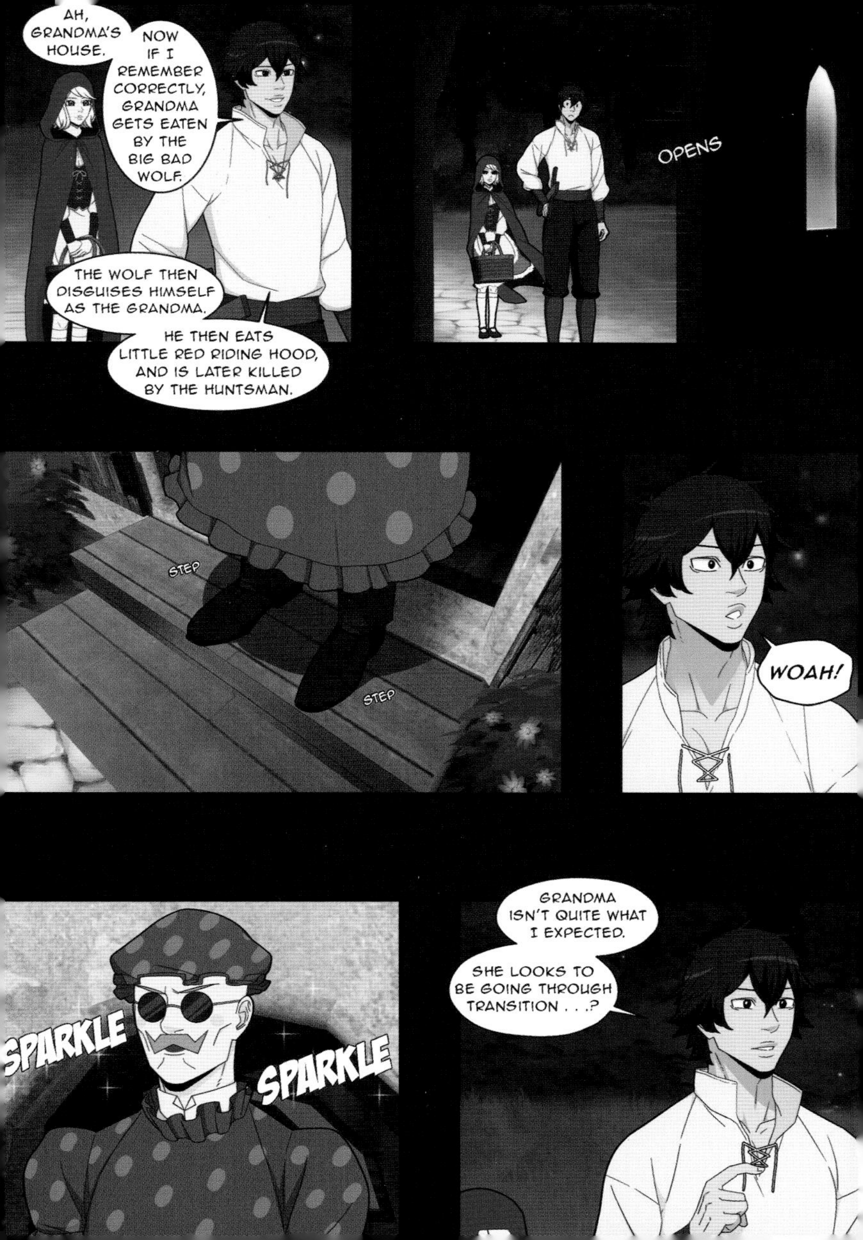
AH, GRANDMA'S HOUSE.
NOW IF I REMEMBER CORRECTLY, GRANDMA GETS EATEN BY THE BIG BAD WOLF.
THE WOLF THEN DISGUISES HIMSELF AS THE GRANDMA.
HE THEN EATS LITTLE RED RIDING HOOD, AND IS LATER KILLED BY THE HUNTSMAN.
OPENS
STEP
STEP
WOAH!
SPARKLE
SPARKLE
GRANDMA ISN'T QUITE WHAT I EXPECTED.
SHE LOOKS TO BE GOING THROUGH TRANSITION . . .?

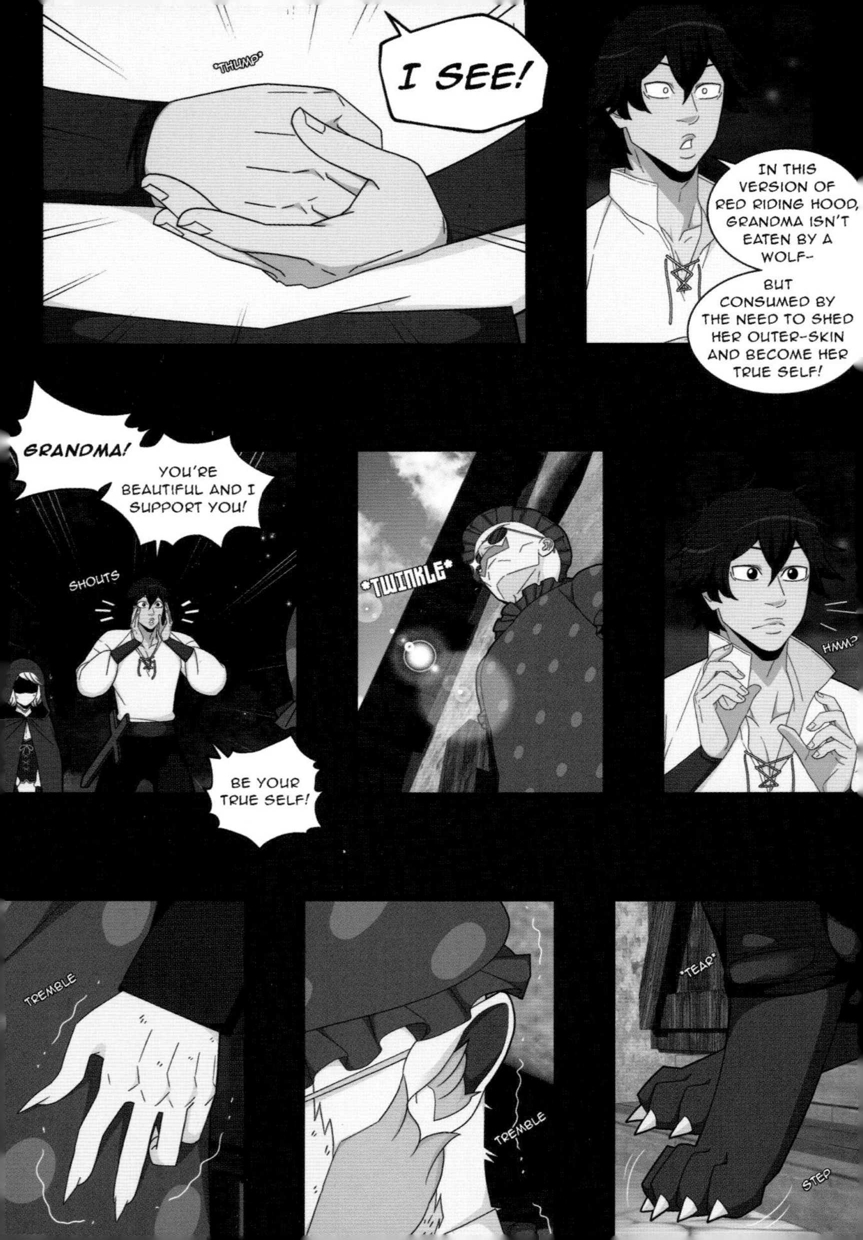
THUMP
I SEE!
IN THIS VERSION OF RED RIDING HOOD, GRANDMA ISN'T EATEN BY A WOLF-
BUT CONSUMED BY THE NEED TO SHED HER OUTER-SKIN AND BECOME HER TRUE SELF!
GRANDMA!
YOU'RE BEAUTIFUL AND I SUPPORT YOU!
SHOUTS
BE YOUR TRUE SELF!
TWINKLE
HMM?
TREMBLE
TREMBLE
TEAR
STEP

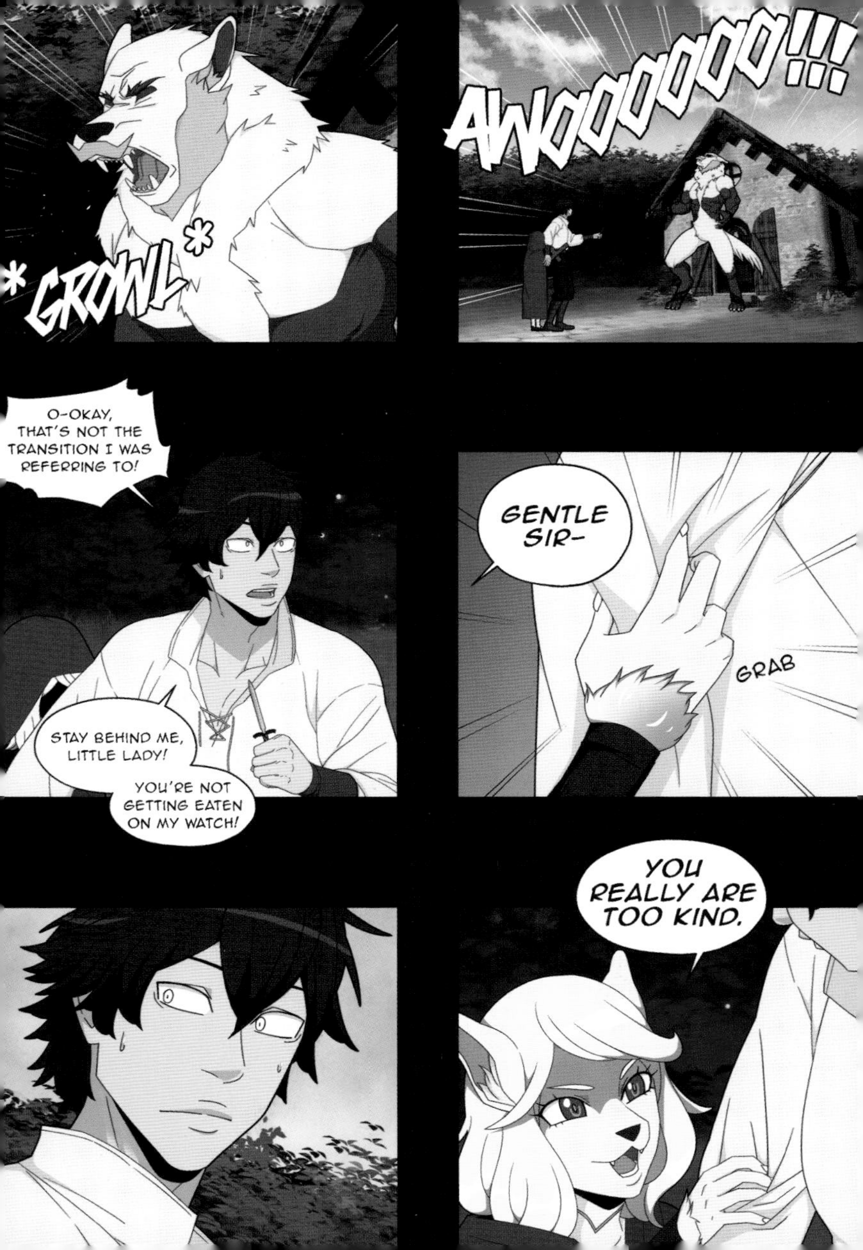
GROWL
AWOOOOOOO!!!
O-OKAY, THAT'S NOT THE TRANSITION I WAS REFERRING TO!
STAY BEHIND ME, LITTLE LADY!
YOU'RE NOT GETTING EATEN ON MY WATCH!
GENTLE SIR-
GRAB
YOU REALLY ARE TOO KIND.

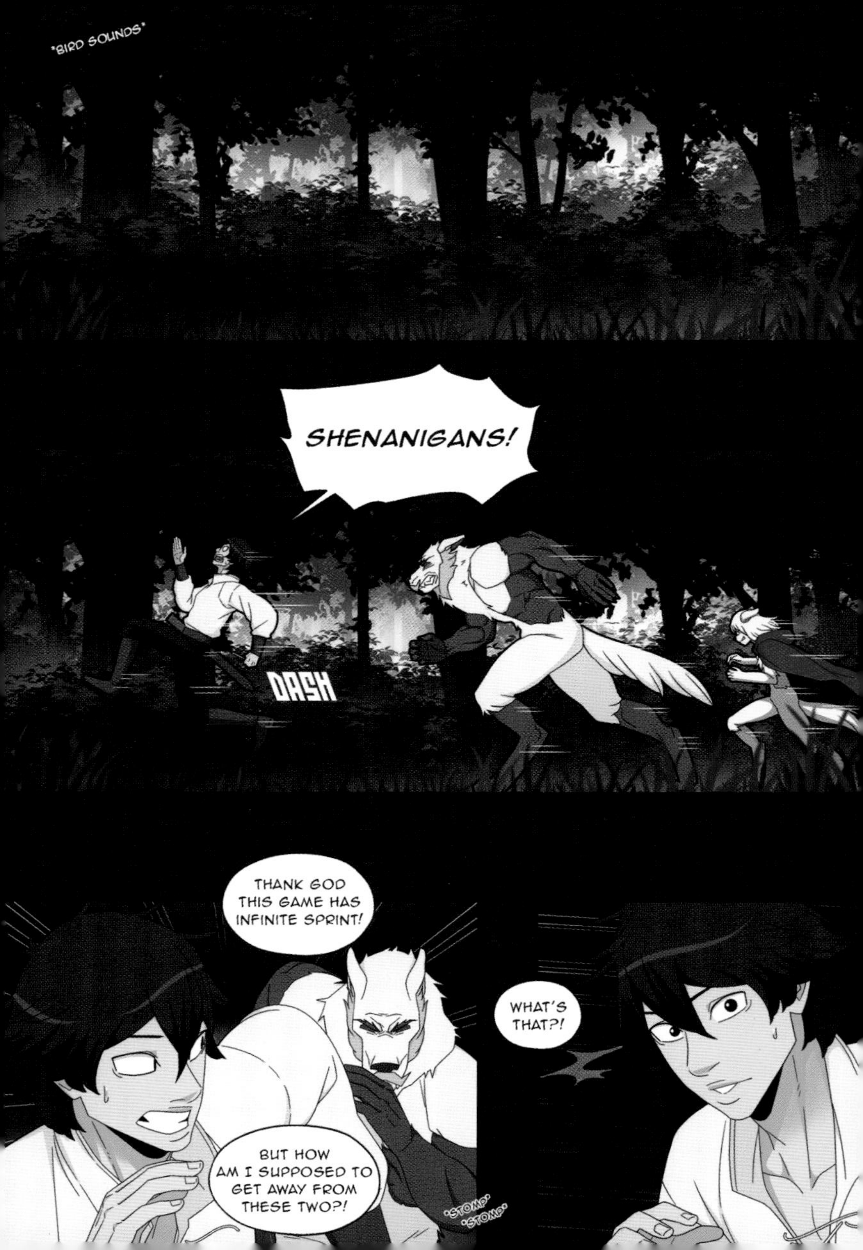
BIRD SOUNDS
SHENANIGANS!
DASH
THANK GOD THIS GAME HAS INFINITE SPRINT!
BUT HOW AM I SUPPOSED TO GET AWAY FROM THESE TWO?!
STOMP *STOMP*
WHAT'S THAT?!

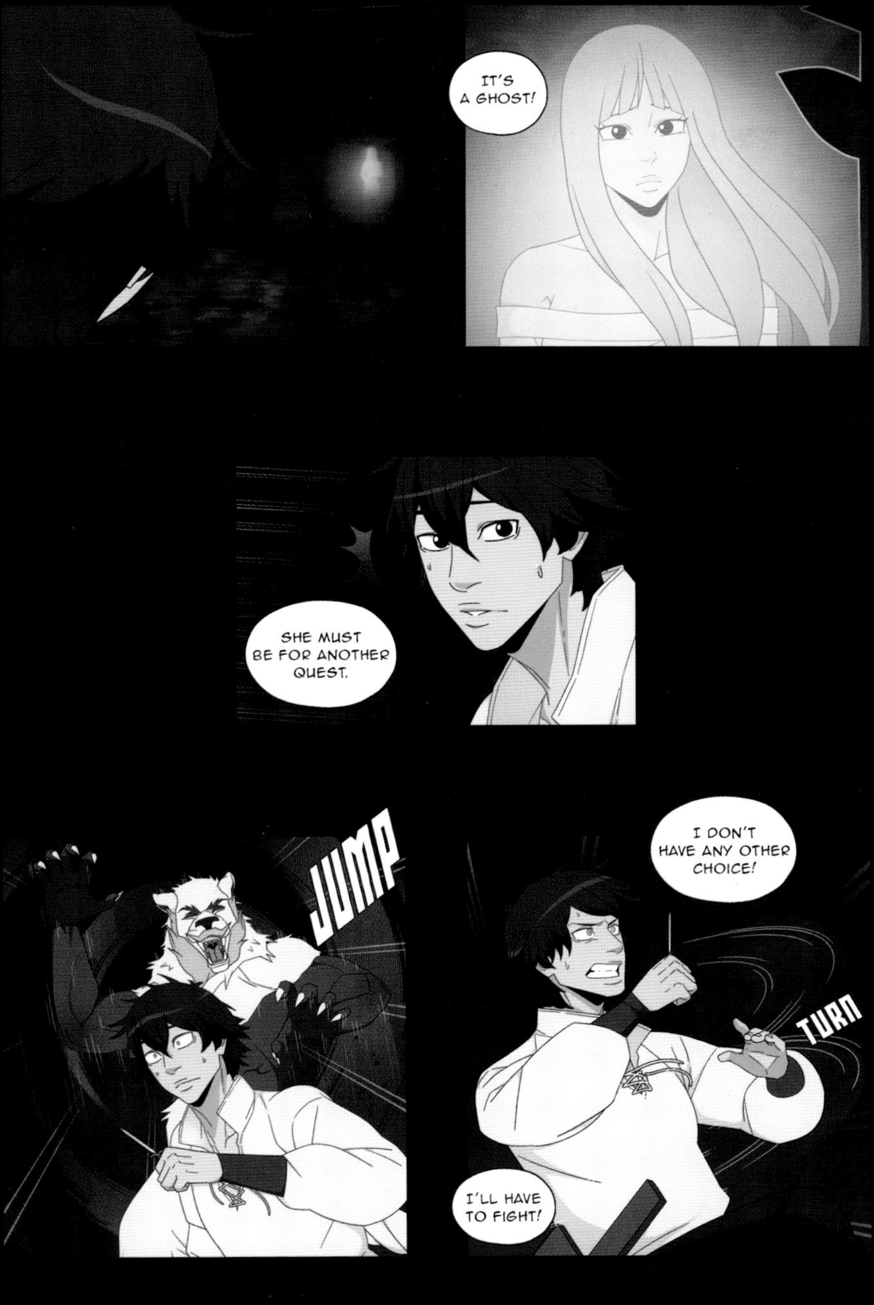
IT'S A GHOST!
SHE MUST BE FOR ANOTHER QUEST.
JUMP
I DON'T HAVE ANY OTHER CHOICE!
TURN
I'LL HAVE TO FIGHT!

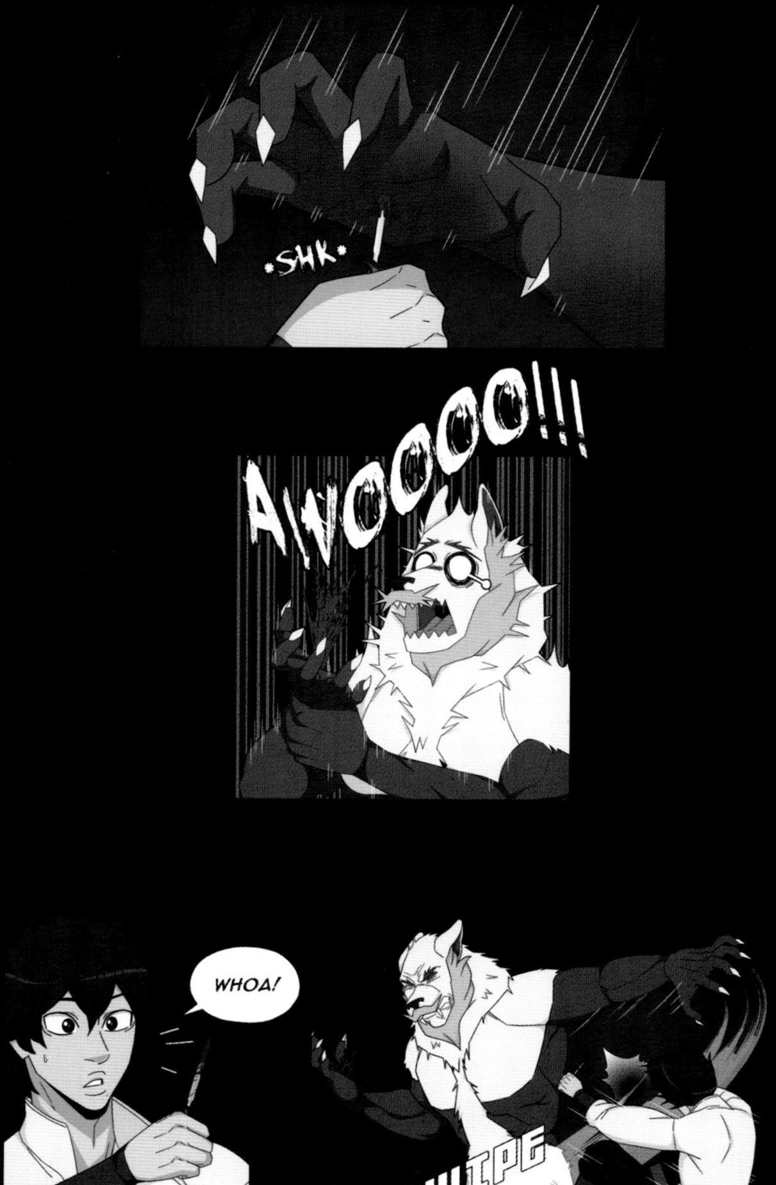
SHK
AWOOOOO!!!
WHOA!
SWIPE

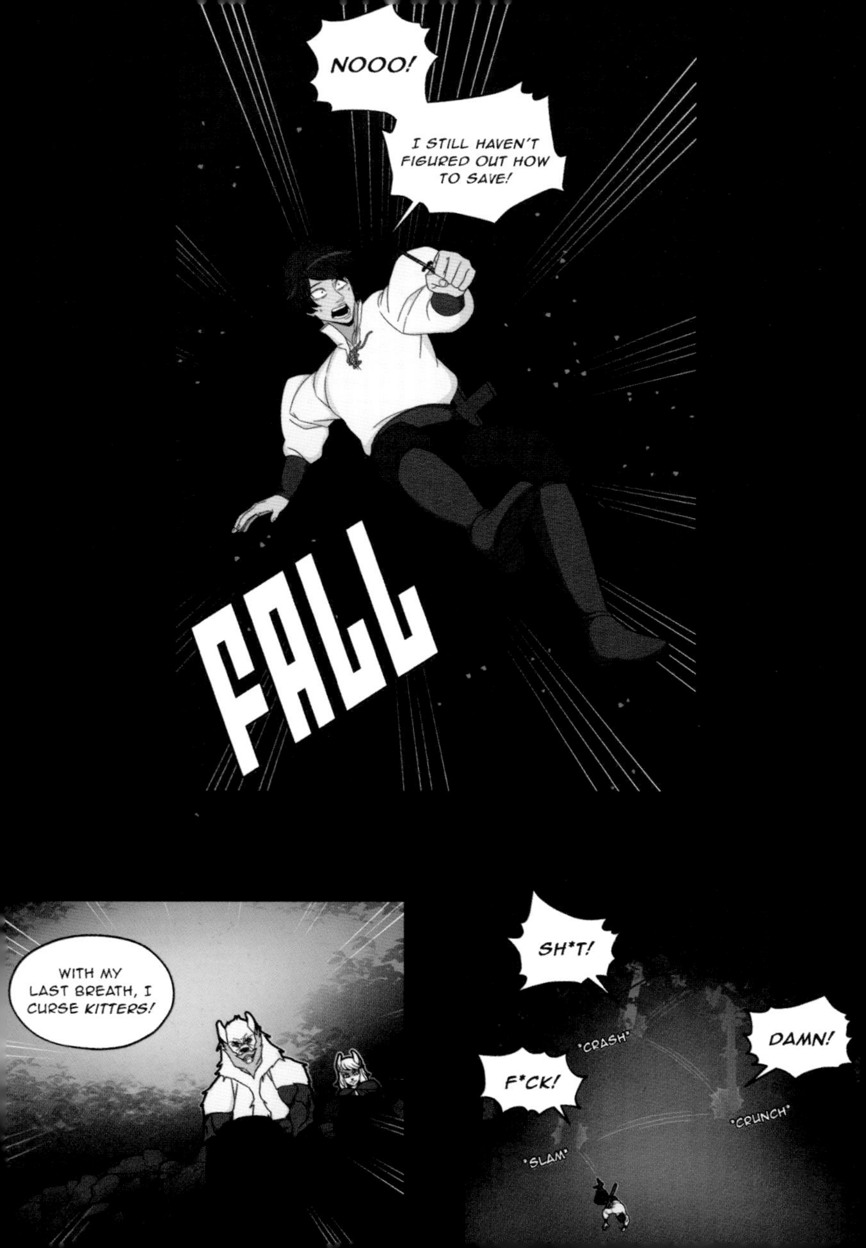
NOOO!
I STILL HAVEN'T FIGURED OUT HOW TO SAVE!
FALL
WITH MY LAST BREATH, I CURSE KITTERS!
SH*T!
CRASH
DAMN!
F*CK!
CRUNCH
SLAM

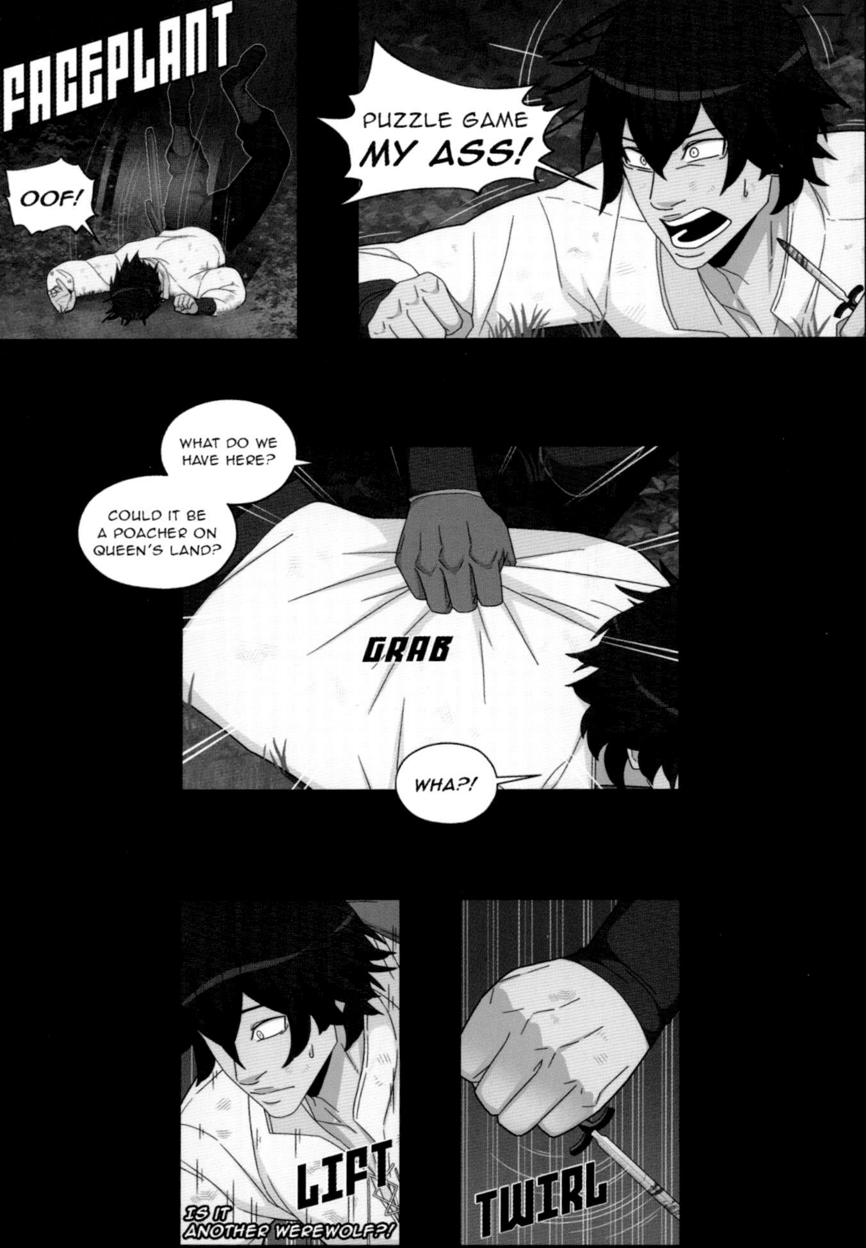
FACEPLANT
OOF!
PUZZLE GAME MY ASS!
WHAT DO WE HAVE HERE?
COULD IT BE A POACHER ON QUEEN'S LAND?
GRAB
WHA?!
LIFT
IS IT ANOTHER WEREWOLF?!
TWIRL

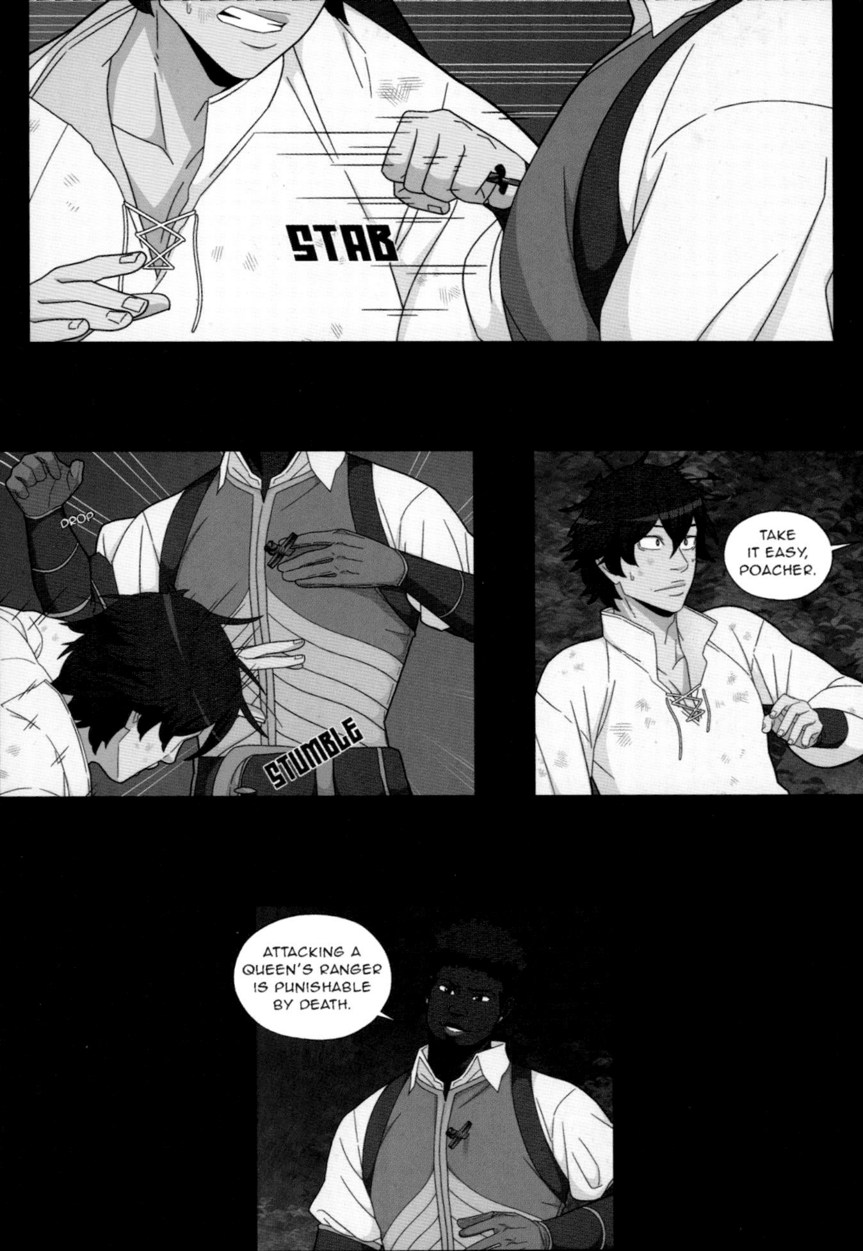
STAB
DROP
STUMBLE
TAKE IT EASY, POACHER.
ATTACKING A QUEEN'S RANGER IS PUNISHABLE BY DEATH.

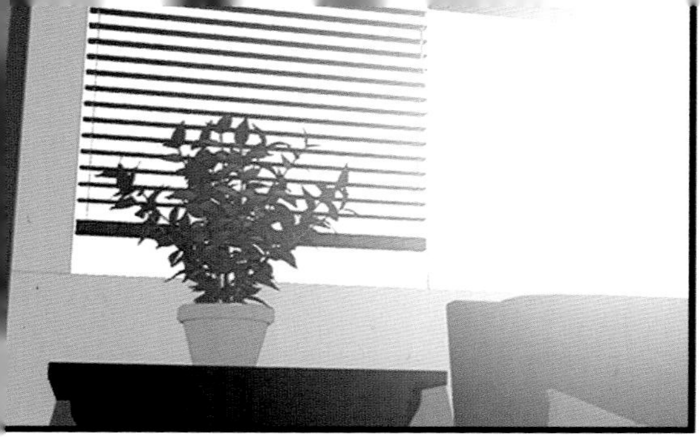

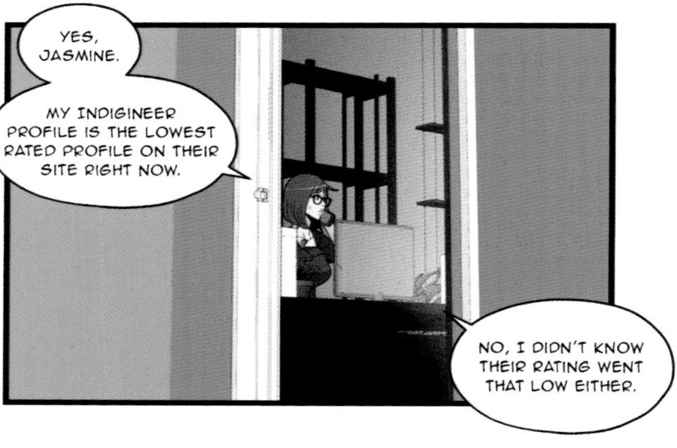
YES, JASMINE.
MY INDIGINEER PROFILE IS THE LOWEST RATED PROFILE ON THEIR SITE RIGHT NOW.
NO, I DIDN'T KNOW THEIR RATING WENT THAT LOW EITHER.

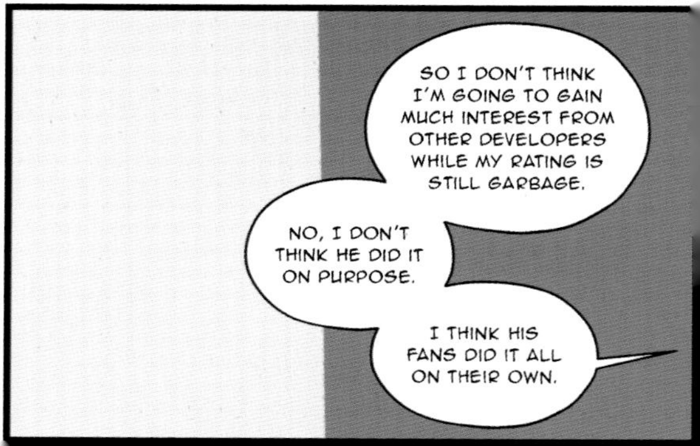
SO I DON'T THINK I'M GOING TO GAIN MUCH INTEREST FROM OTHER DEVELOPERS WHILE MY RATING IS STILL GARBAGE.
NO, I DON'T THINK HE DID IT ON PURPOSE.
I THINK HIS FANS DID IT ALL ON THEIR OWN.

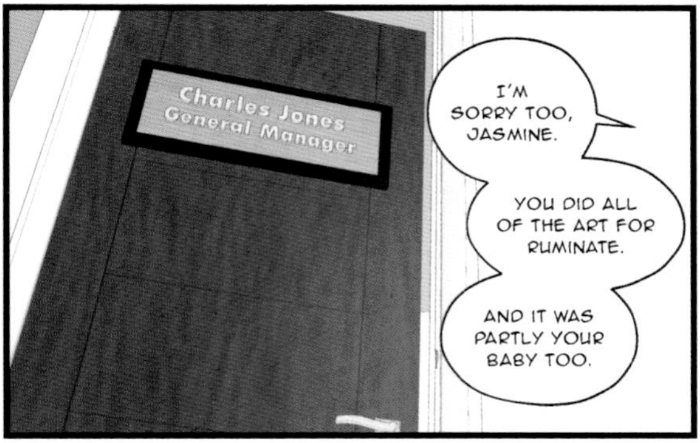
Charles Jones
General Manager
I'M SORRY TOO, JASMINE.
YOU DID ALL OF THE ART FOR RUMINATE.
AND IT WAS PARTLY YOUR BABY TOO.

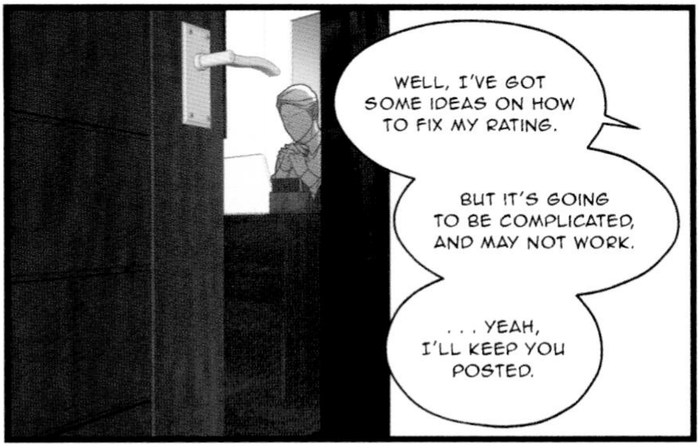
WELL, I'VE GOT SOME IDEAS ON HOW TO FIX MY RATING.
BUT IT'S GOING TO BE COMPLICATED, AND MAY NOT WORK.
. . . YEAH, I'LL KEEP YOU POSTED.

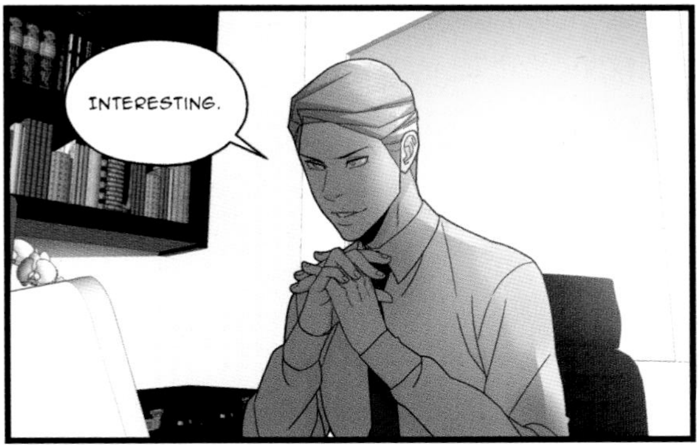
INTERESTING.

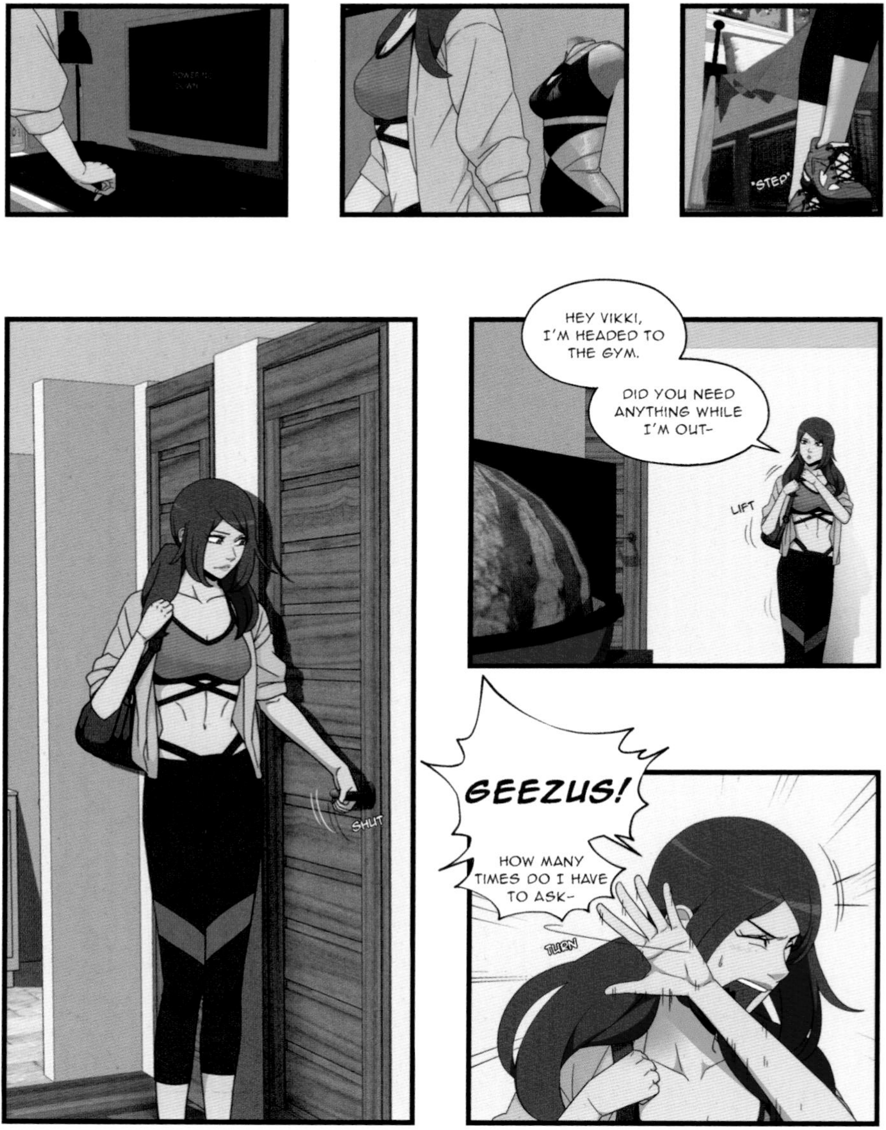
STEP
SHUT
HEY VIKKI, I'M HEADED TO THE GYM.
DID YOU NEED ANYTHING WHILE I'M OUT-
LIFT
GEEZUS!
HOW MANY TIMES DO I HAVE TO ASK-
TURN

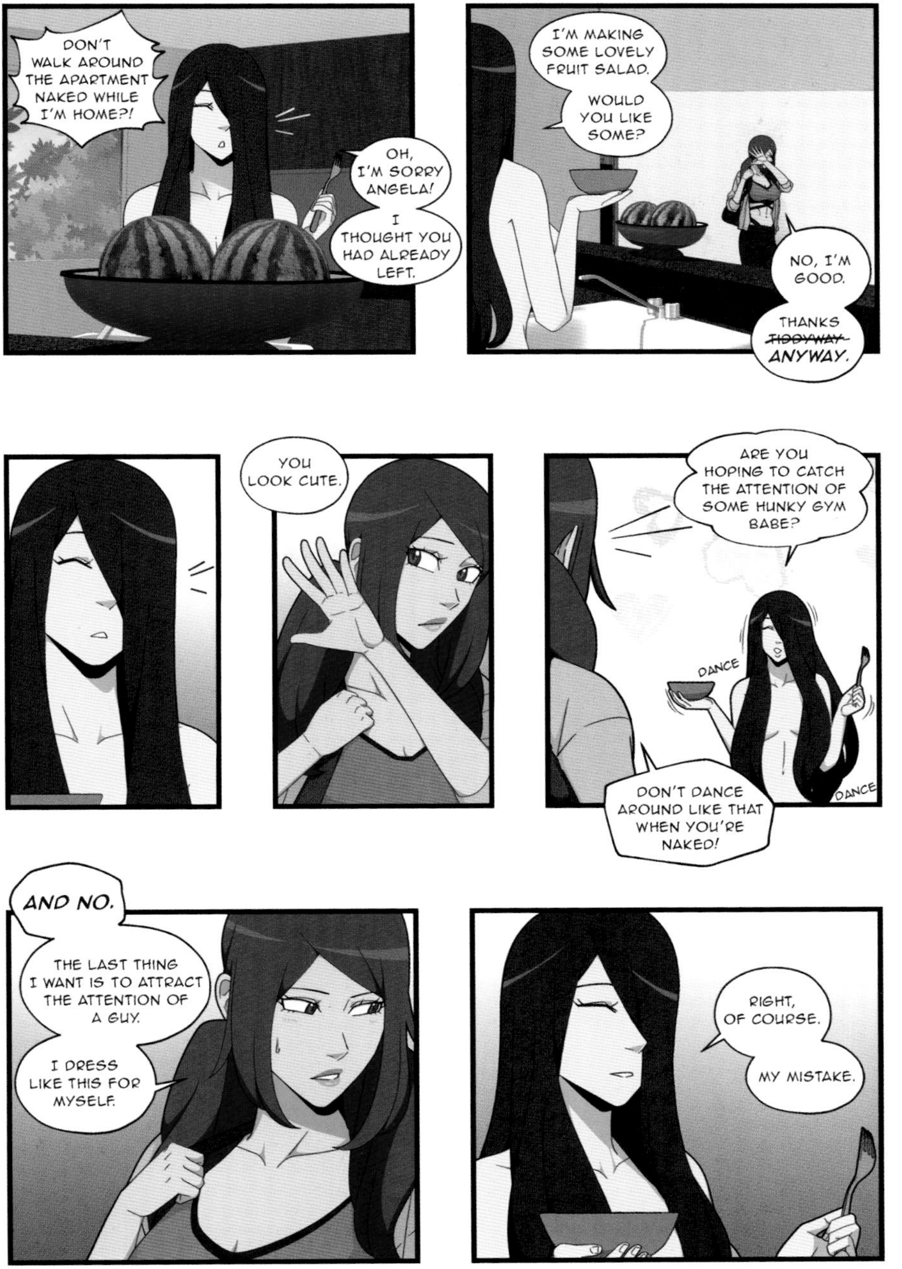
DON'T WALK AROUND THE APARTMENT NAKED WHILE I'M HOME?!
OH, I'M SORRY ANGELA!
I THOUGHT YOU HAD ALREADY LEFT.
I'M MAKING SOME LOVELY FRUIT SALAD.
WOULD YOU LIKE SOME?
NO, I'M GOOD.
THANKS ~~TIDDYWAY~~ *ANYWAY.*
YOU LOOK CUTE.
ARE YOU HOPING TO CATCH THE ATTENTION OF SOME HUNKY GYM BABE?
DANCE
DANCE
DON'T DANCE AROUND LIKE THAT WHEN YOU'RE NAKED!
AND NO.
THE LAST THING I WANT IS TO ATTRACT THE ATTENTION OF A GUY.
I DRESS LIKE THIS FOR MYSELF.
RIGHT, OF COURSE.
MY MISTAKE.

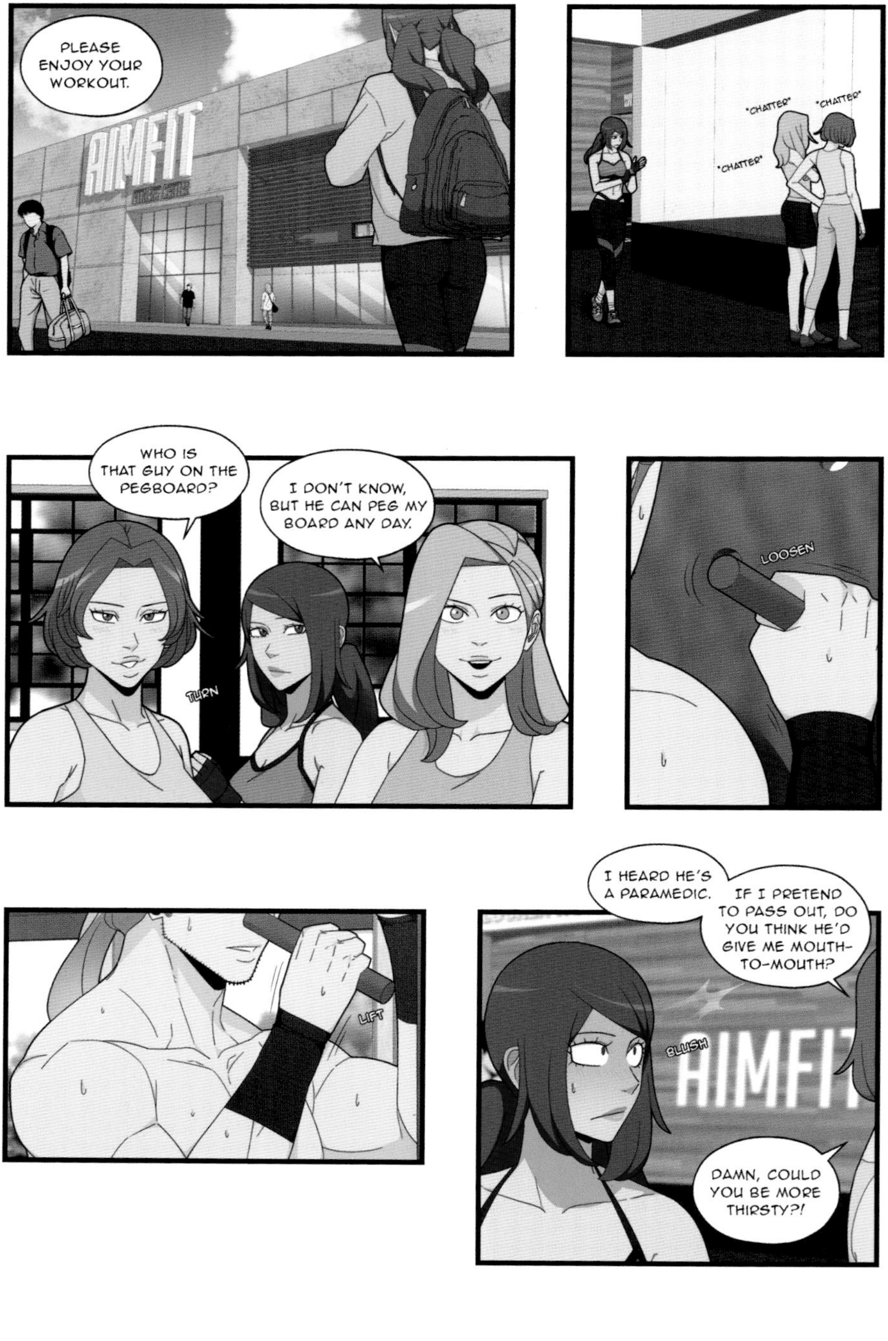
PLEASE ENJOY YOUR WORKOUT.
AIMFIT
CHATTER
CHATTER
CHATTER
WHO IS THAT GUY ON THE PEGBOARD?
I DON'T KNOW, BUT HE CAN PEG MY BOARD ANY DAY.
TURN
LOOSEN
LIFT
I HEARD HE'S A PARAMEDIC.
IF I PRETEND TO PASS OUT, DO YOU THINK HE'D GIVE ME MOUTH-TO-MOUTH?
BLUSH
AIMFIT
DAMN, COULD YOU BE MORE THIRSTY?!

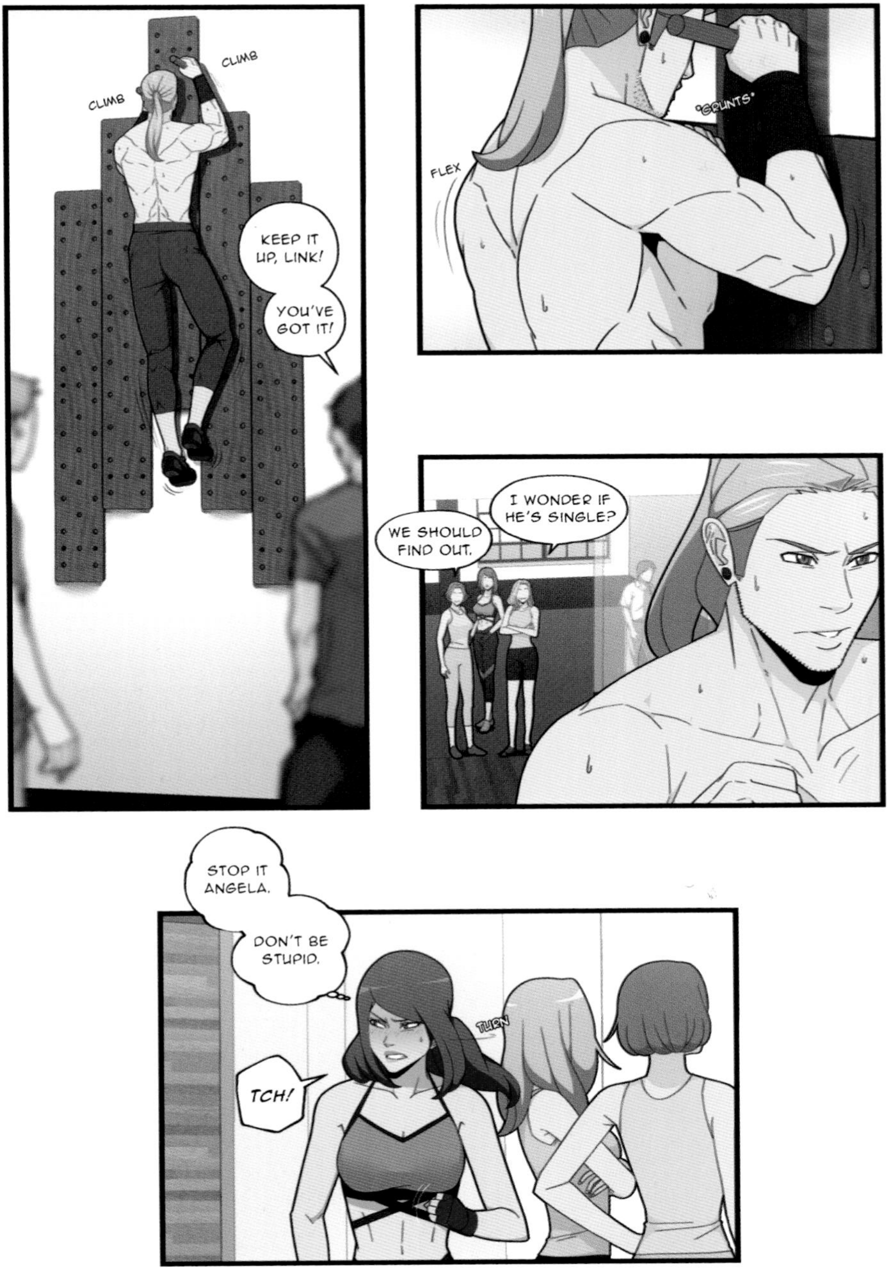
CLIMB
CLIMB
KEEP IT UP, LINK!
YOU'VE GOT IT!
GRUNTS
FLEX
WE SHOULD FIND OUT.
I WONDER IF HE'S SINGLE?
STOP IT ANGELA.
DON'T BE STUPID.
TURN
TCH!

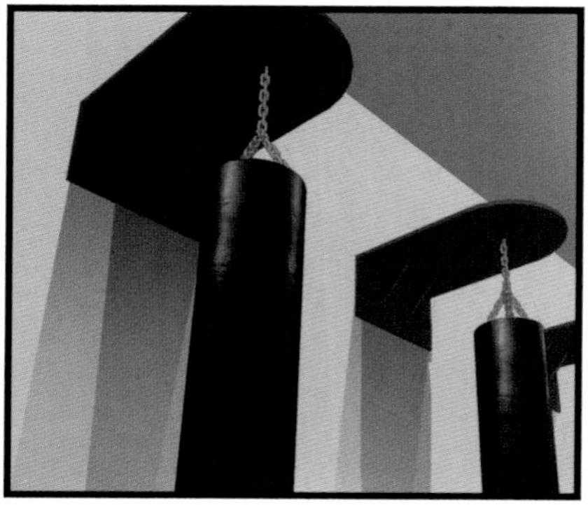

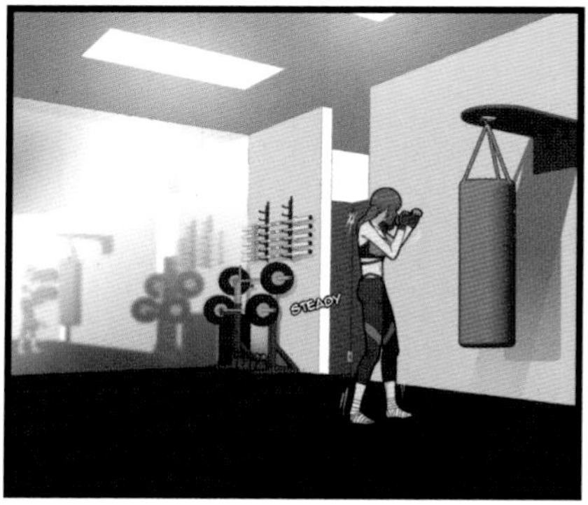
STEADY

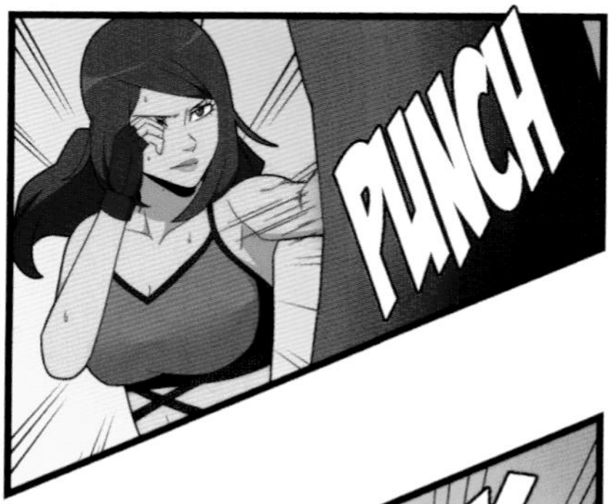
PUNCH

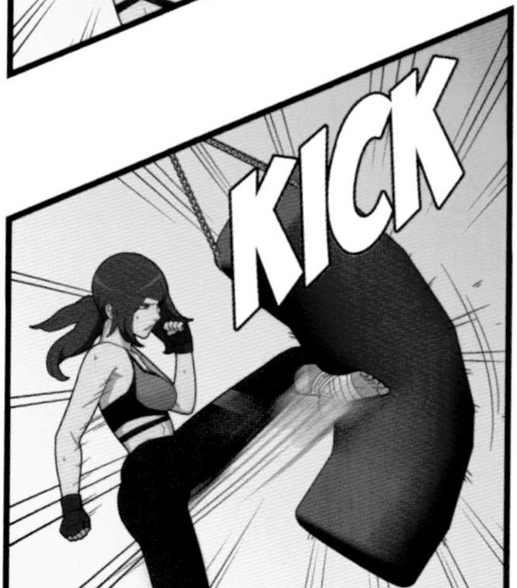
KICK

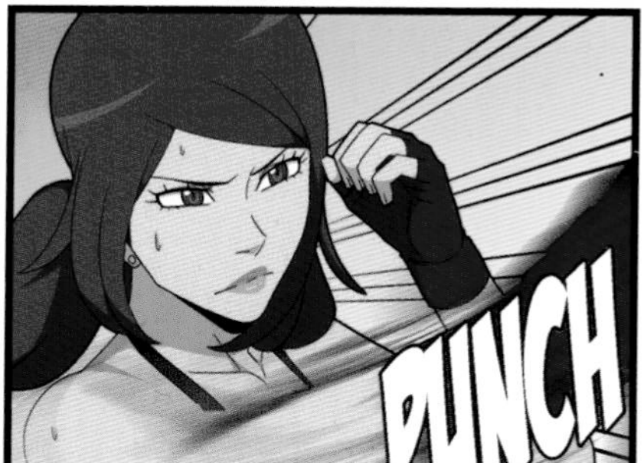
PUNCH

RAGE

FEAR

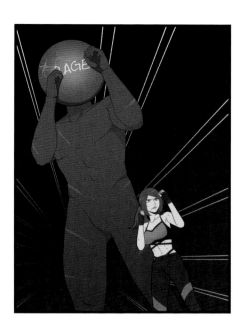

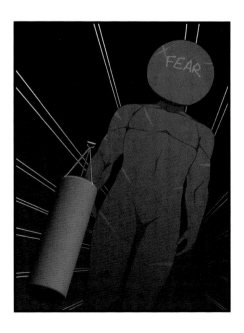

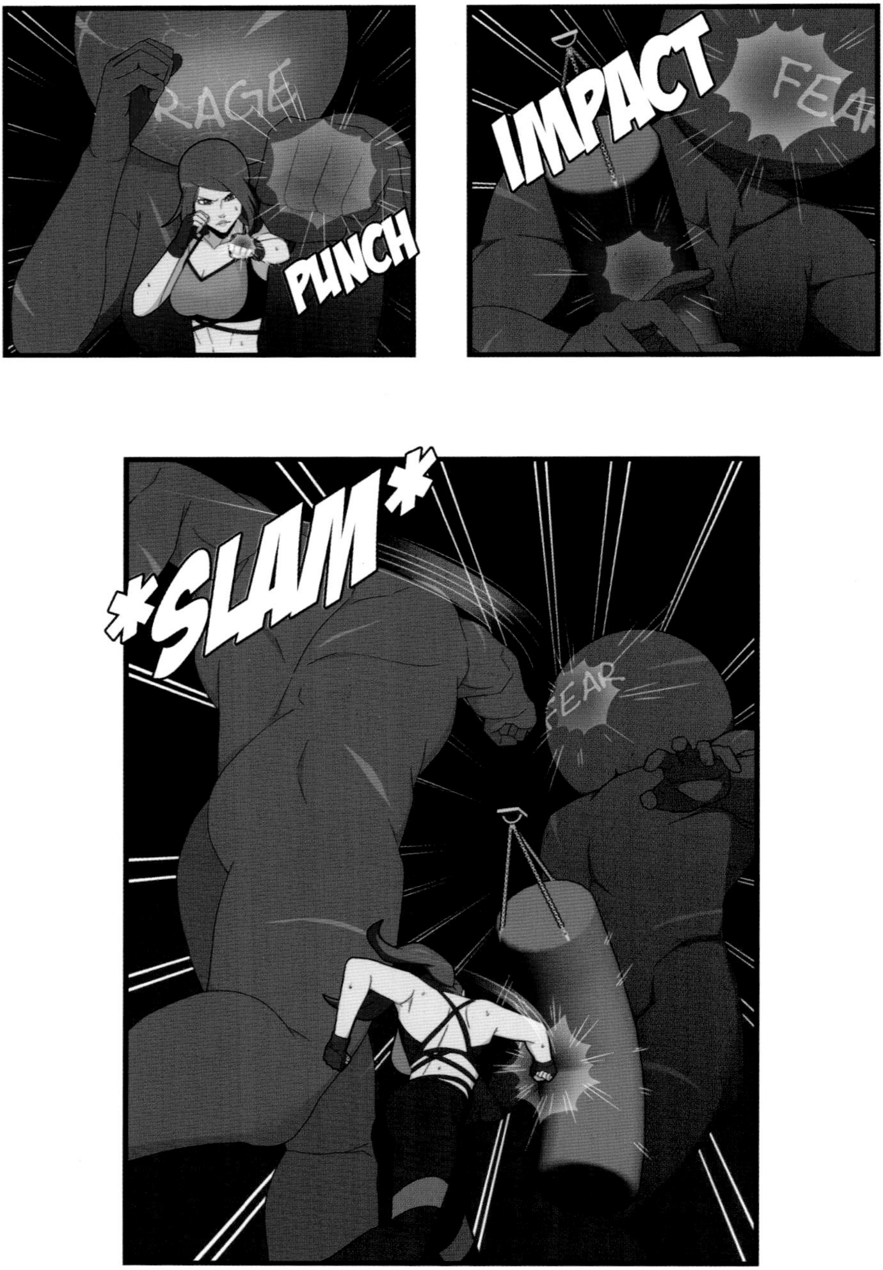
RAGE
PUNCH
IMPACT
FEAR
SLAM
FEAR

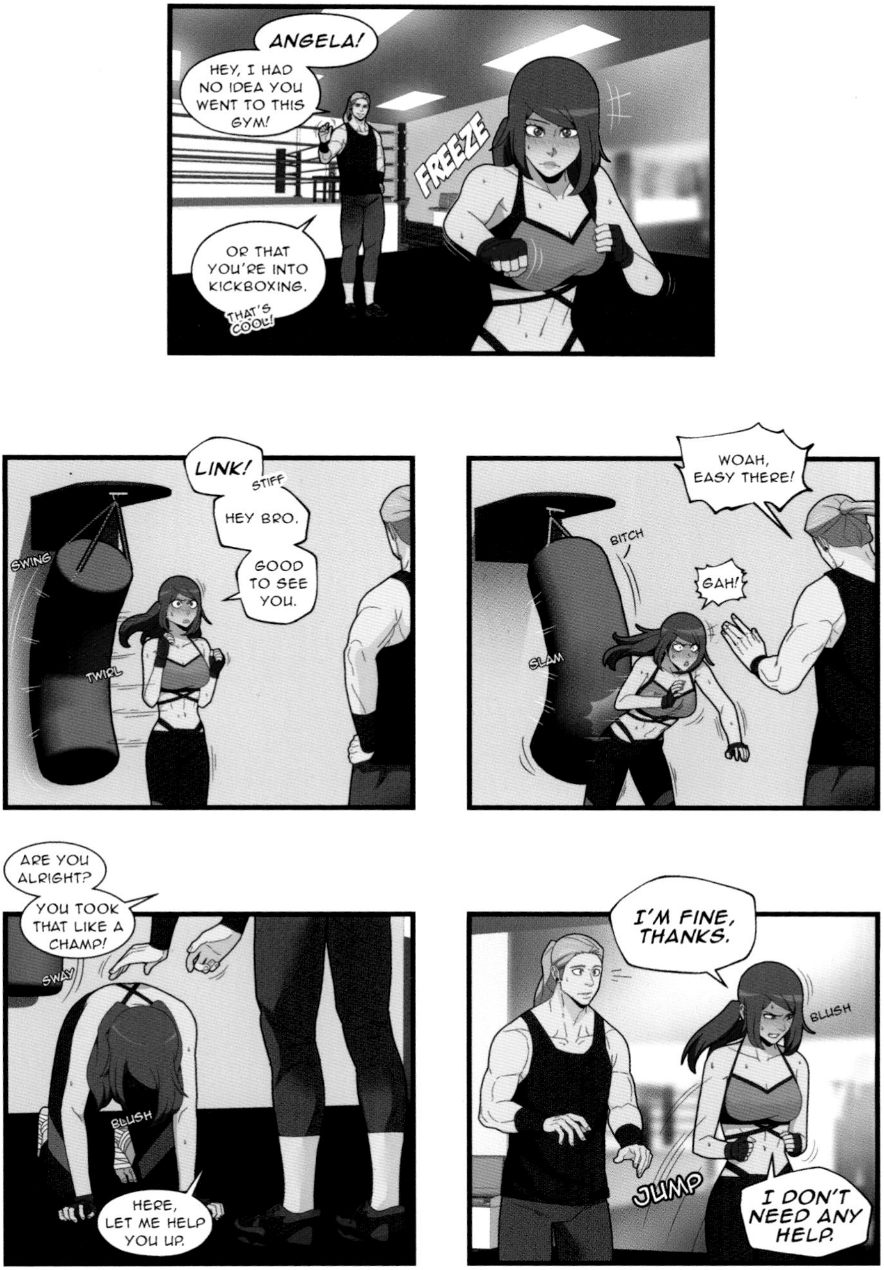
ANGELA!
HEY, I HAD NO IDEA YOU WENT TO THIS GYM!
FREEZE
OR THAT YOU'RE INTO KICKBOXING.
THAT'S COOL!
LINK!
STIFF
HEY BRO.
GOOD TO SEE YOU.
SWING
TWIRL
WOAH, EASY THERE!
BITCH
GAH!
SLAM
ARE YOU ALRIGHT?
YOU TOOK THAT LIKE A CHAMP!
SWAY
BLUSH
HERE, LET ME HELP YOU UP.
I'M FINE, THANKS.
BLUSH
JUMP
I DON'T NEED ANY HELP.

BLUSH

ANGELA HAS BEEN IN A DARK PLACE FOR A WHILE.

IF YOU'RE GOING TO HIT IT THAT HARD . . .

TURN

THEN I'LL SPOT YOU AND MAKE SURE IT DOESN'T SWING BACK AT YOU AGAIN.

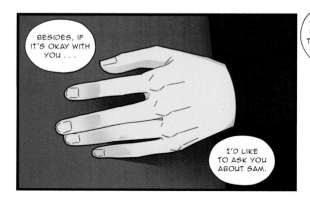

BESIDES, IF IT'S OKAY WITH YOU . . .

I'D LIKE TO ASK YOU ABOUT SAM.

I WAS WONDERING IF SHE EVER TALKS ABOUT ME WITH YOU?

OR TOLD YOU HOW SHE FEELS ABOUT ME?

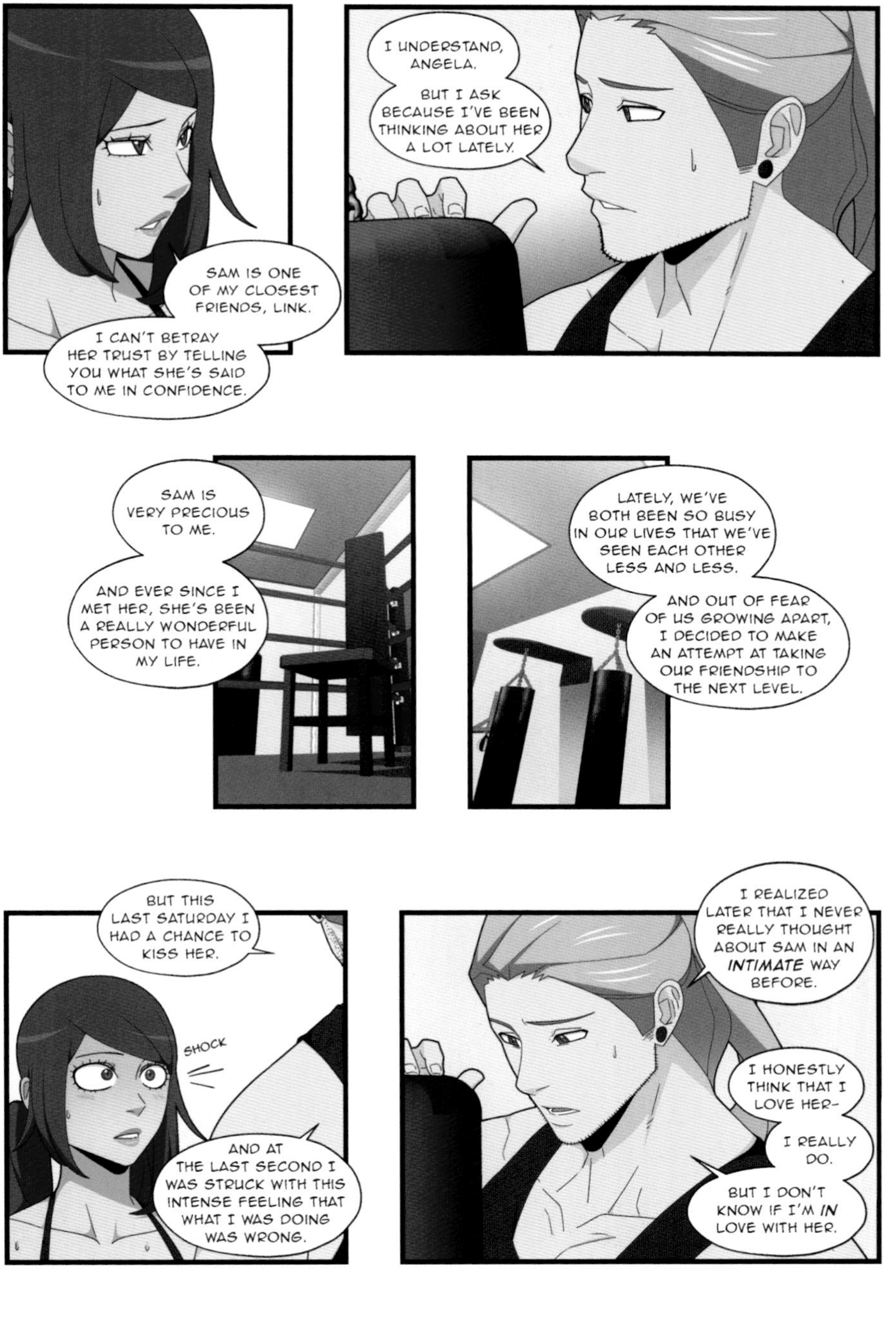
SAM IS ONE OF MY CLOSEST FRIENDS, LINK.
I CAN'T BETRAY HER TRUST BY TELLING YOU WHAT SHE'S SAID TO ME IN CONFIDENCE.
I UNDERSTAND, ANGELA.
BUT I ASK BECAUSE I'VE BEEN THINKING ABOUT HER A LOT LATELY.
SAM IS VERY PRECIOUS TO ME.
AND EVER SINCE I MET HER, SHE'S BEEN A REALLY WONDERFUL PERSON TO HAVE IN MY LIFE.
LATELY, WE'VE BOTH BEEN SO BUSY IN OUR LIVES THAT WE'VE SEEN EACH OTHER LESS AND LESS.
AND OUT OF FEAR OF US GROWING APART, I DECIDED TO MAKE AN ATTEMPT AT TAKING OUR FRIENDSHIP TO THE NEXT LEVEL.
BUT THIS LAST SATURDAY I HAD A CHANCE TO KISS HER.
SHOCK
AND AT THE LAST SECOND I WAS STRUCK WITH THIS INTENSE FEELING THAT WHAT I WAS DOING WAS WRONG.
I REALIZED LATER THAT I NEVER REALLY THOUGHT ABOUT SAM IN AN *INTIMATE* WAY BEFORE.
I HONESTLY THINK THAT I LOVE HER-
I REALLY DO.
BUT I DON'T KNOW IF I'M *IN* LOVE WITH HER.

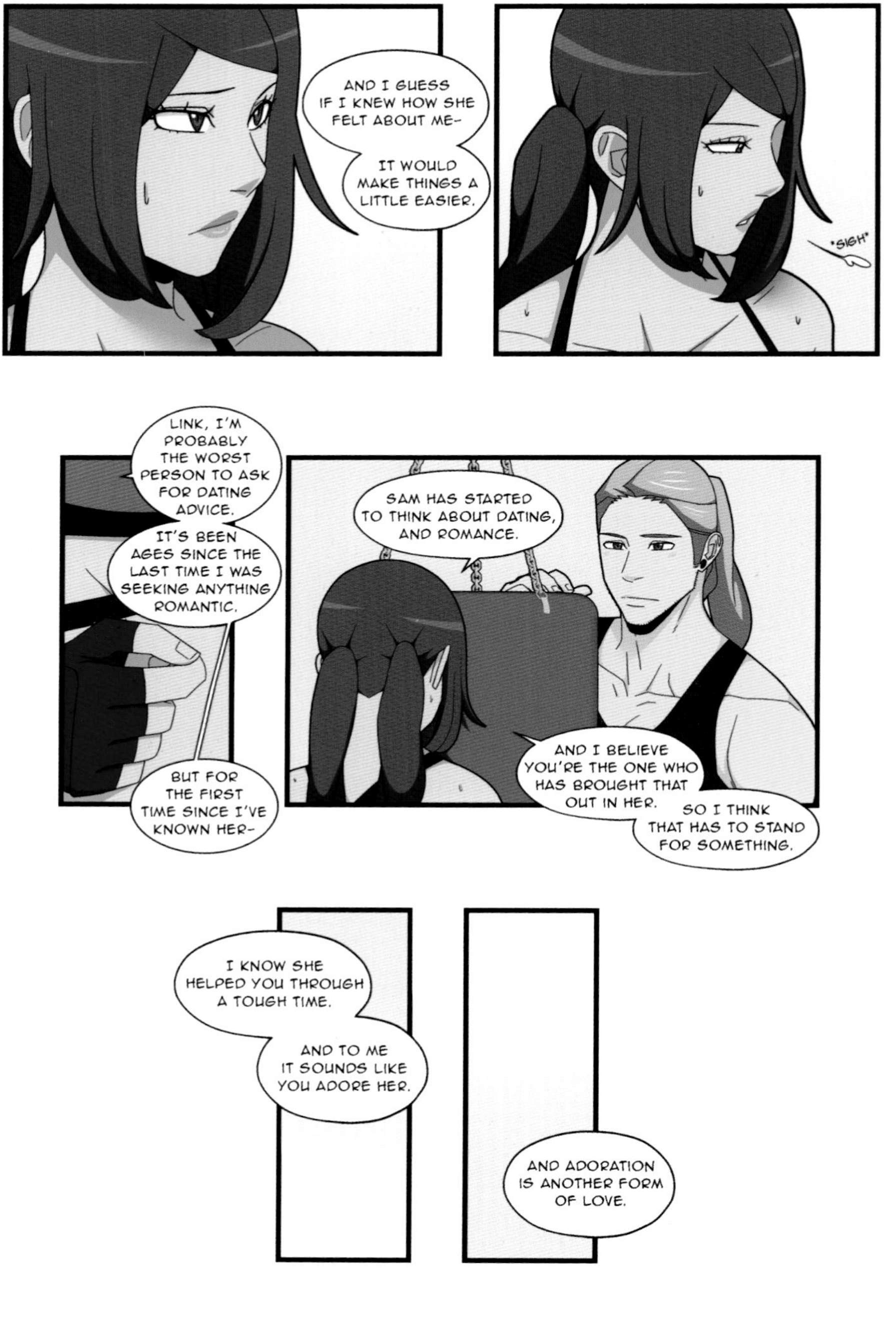
AND I GUESS IF I KNEW HOW SHE FELT ABOUT ME-
IT WOULD MAKE THINGS A LITTLE EASIER.
SIGH
LINK, I'M PROBABLY THE WORST PERSON TO ASK FOR DATING ADVICE.
IT'S BEEN AGES SINCE THE LAST TIME I WAS SEEKING ANYTHING ROMANTIC.
BUT FOR THE FIRST TIME SINCE I'VE KNOWN HER-
SAM HAS STARTED TO THINK ABOUT DATING, AND ROMANCE.
AND I BELIEVE YOU'RE THE ONE WHO HAS BROUGHT THAT OUT IN HER.
SO I THINK THAT HAS TO STAND FOR SOMETHING.
I KNOW SHE HELPED YOU THROUGH A TOUGH TIME.
AND TO ME IT SOUNDS LIKE YOU ADORE HER.
AND ADORATION IS ANOTHER FORM OF LOVE.

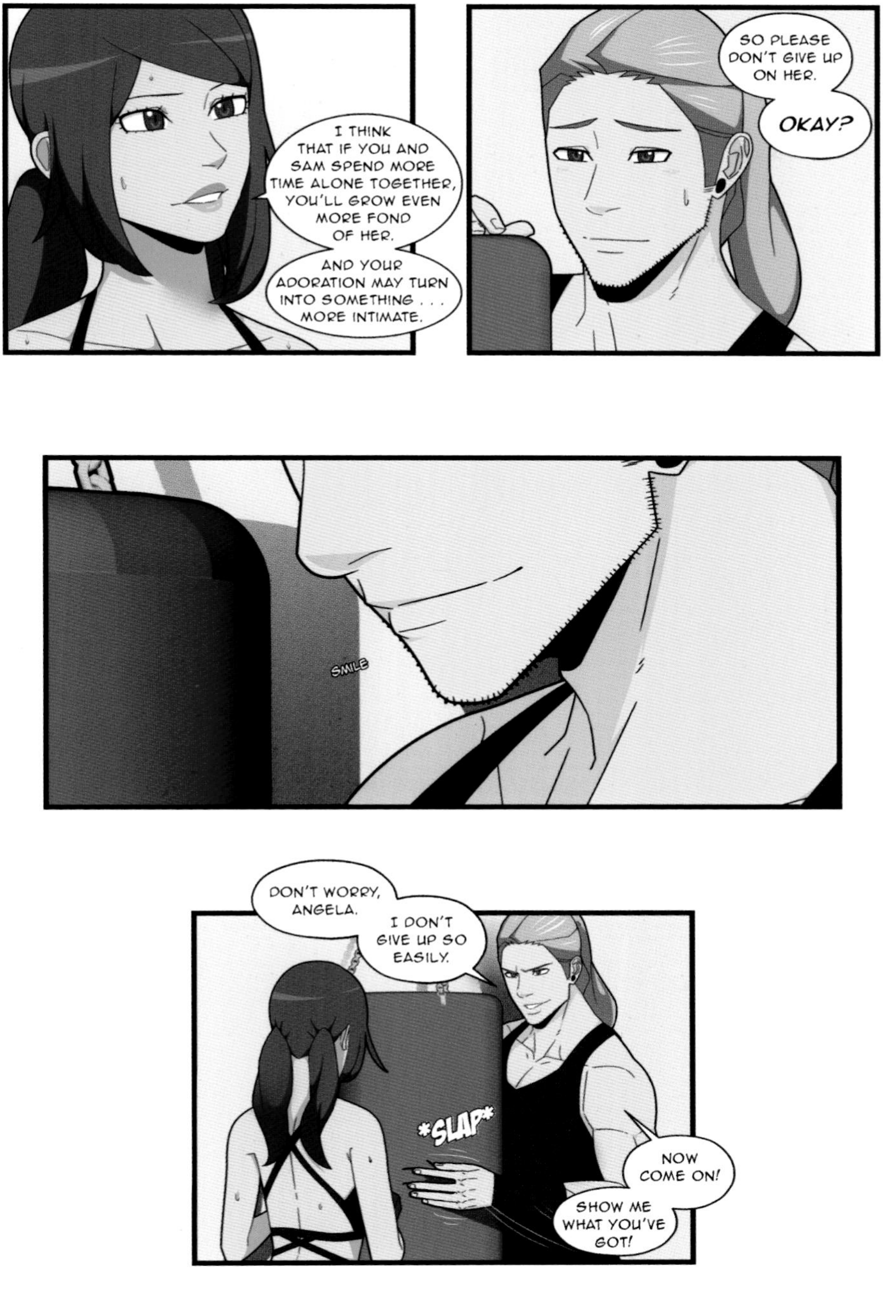
I THINK THAT IF YOU AND SAM SPEND MORE TIME ALONE TOGETHER, YOU'LL GROW EVEN MORE FOND OF HER.
AND YOUR ADORATION MAY TURN INTO SOMETHING . . . MORE INTIMATE.
SO PLEASE DON'T GIVE UP ON HER.
OKAY?
SMILE
DON'T WORRY, ANGELA.
I DON'T GIVE UP SO EASILY.
SLAP
NOW COME ON!
SHOW ME WHAT YOU'VE GOT!

GOOD!

PAP *PAP* *PAP*

KEEP IT UP!

PAP

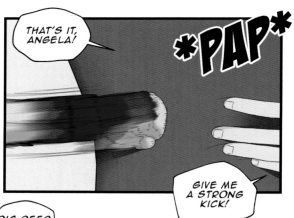

THAT'S IT, ANGELA!

PAP

GIVE ME A STRONG KICK!

HUFF *HUFF* *HUFF*

H-HANG ON . . . A SECOND.

I NEED . . . TO CATCH . . . MY BREATH.

DIG DEEP, ANGELA—

AND FINISH STRONG!

HUFF *HUFF*

PUMP

CHANNEL YOUR INNER WARRIOR!

YOU'VE GOT THIS!

HUFF

HUFF

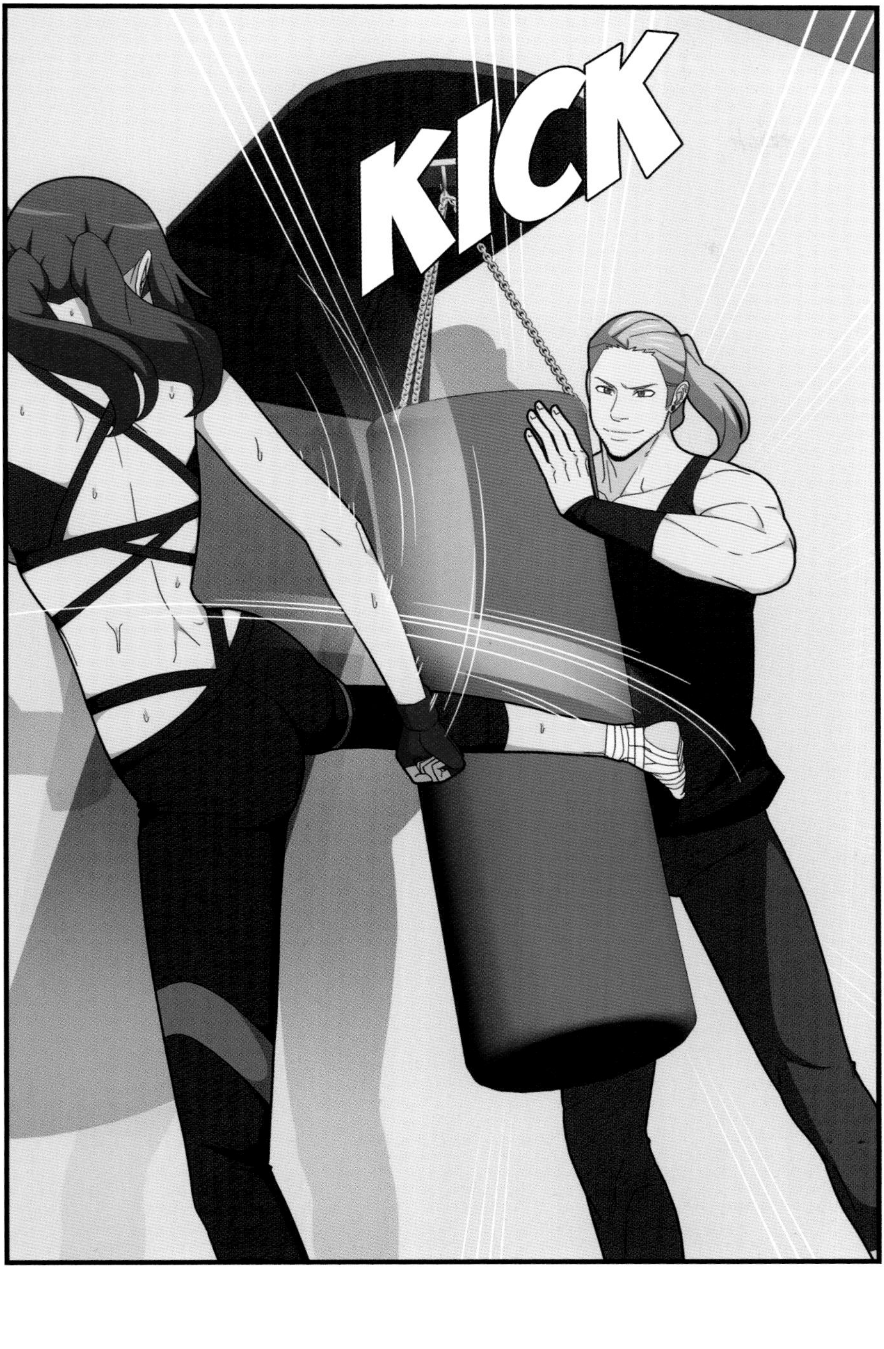
KICK

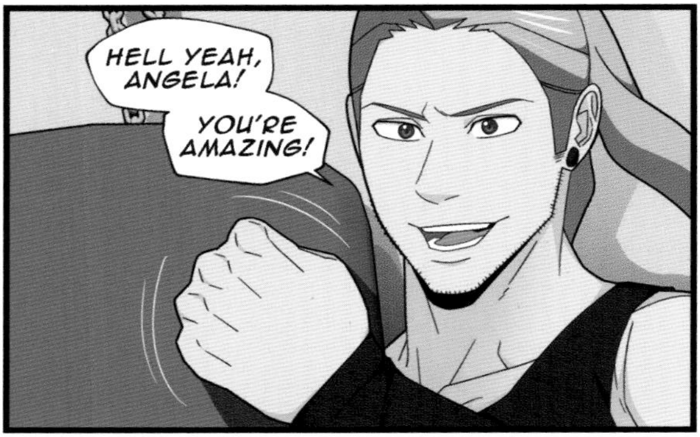
HELL YEAH, ANGELA!
YOU'RE AMAZING!
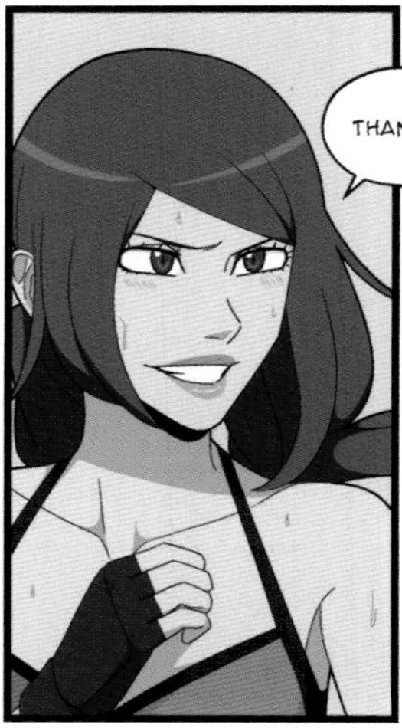
THANKS!
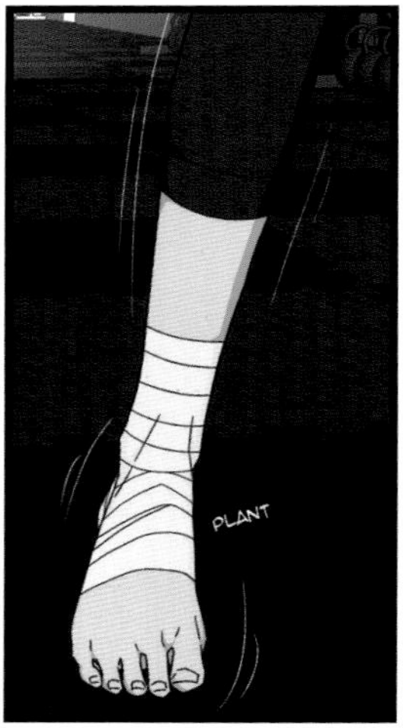
PLANT
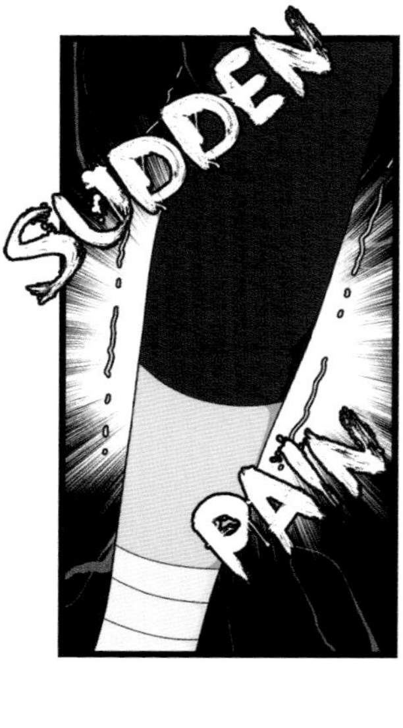
SUDDEN
PAIN

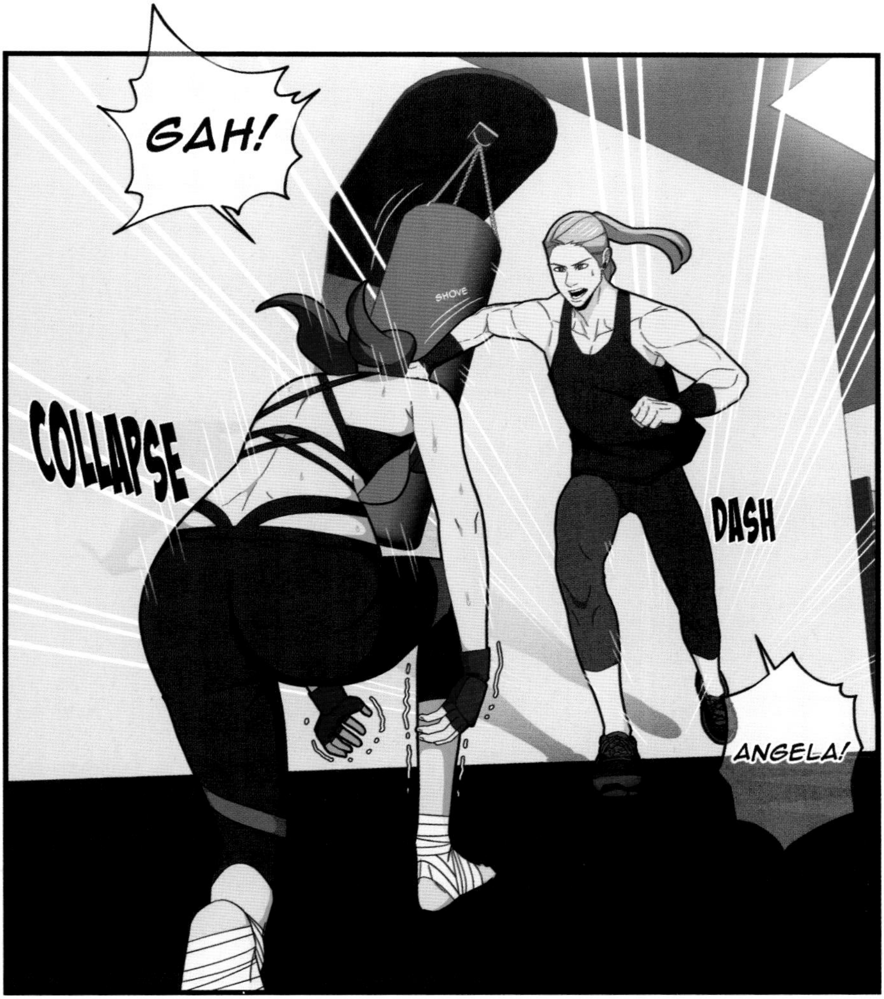
GAH!
SHOVE
COLLAPSE
DASH
ANGELA!

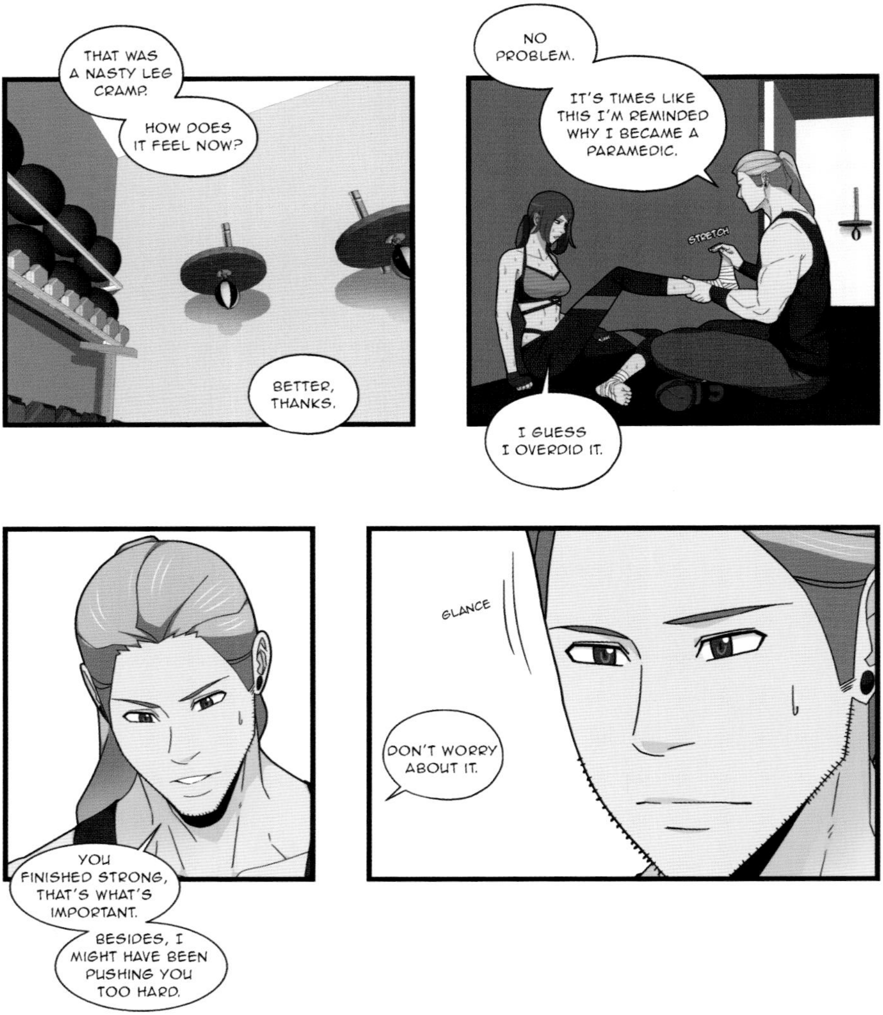
THAT WAS A NASTY LEG CRAMP.
HOW DOES IT FEEL NOW?
BETTER, THANKS.
NO PROBLEM.
IT'S TIMES LIKE THIS I'M REMINDED WHY I BECAME A PARAMEDIC.
STRETCH
I GUESS I OVERDID IT.
YOU FINISHED STRONG, THAT'S WHAT'S IMPORTANT.
BESIDES, I MIGHT HAVE BEEN PUSHING YOU TOO HARD.
GLANCE
DON'T WORRY ABOUT IT.

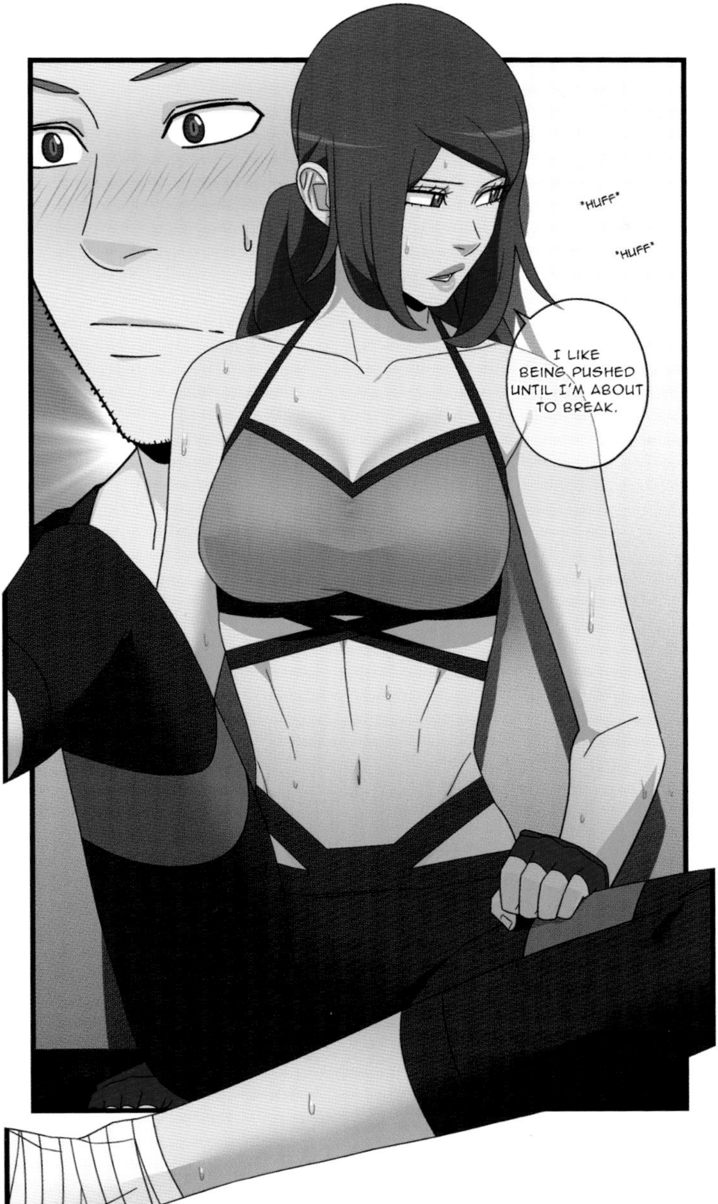
HUFF
HUFF
I LIKE BEING PUSHED UNTIL I'M ABOUT TO BREAK.

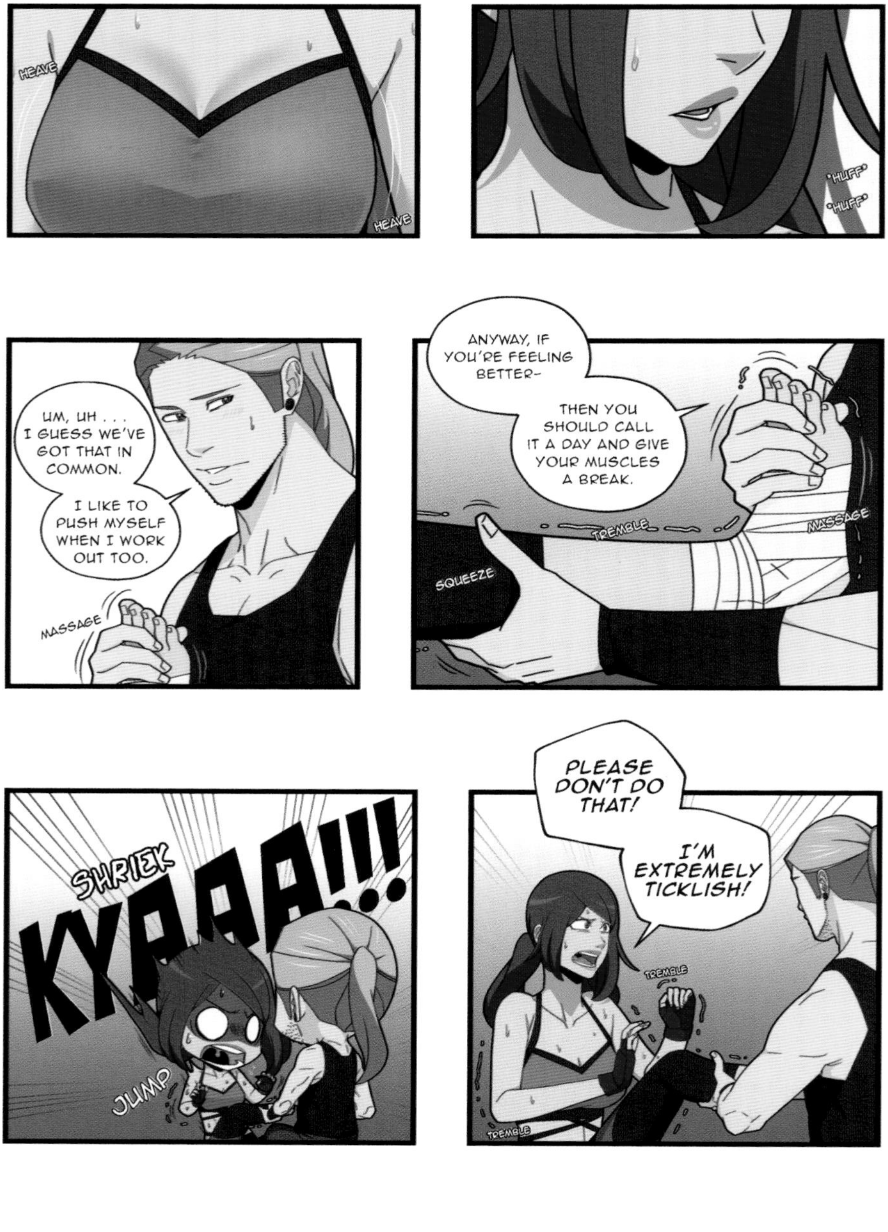
HEAVE
HEAVE
HUFF
HUFF
UM, UH . . . I GUESS WE'VE GOT THAT IN COMMON.
I LIKE TO PUSH MYSELF WHEN I WORK OUT TOO.
MASSAGE
ANYWAY, IF YOU'RE FEELING BETTER-
THEN YOU SHOULD CALL IT A DAY AND GIVE YOUR MUSCLES A BREAK.
TREMBLE
MASSAGE
SQUEEZE
SHRIEK
KYAAAA!!!
JUMP
PLEASE DON'T DO THAT!
I'M EXTREMELY TICKLISH!
TREMBLE
TREMBLE

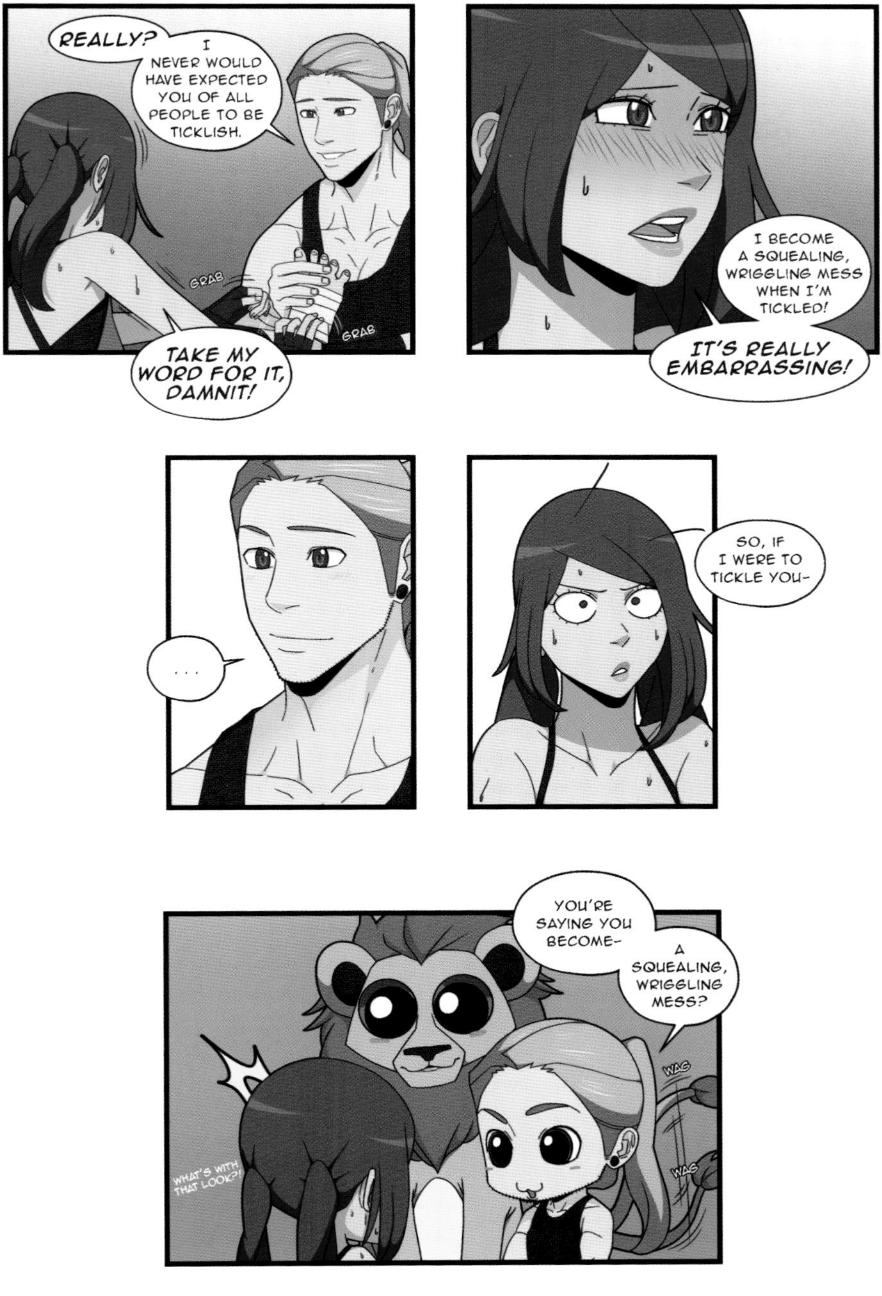
REALLY?
I NEVER WOULD HAVE EXPECTED YOU OF ALL PEOPLE TO BE TICKLISH.
GRAB
GRAB
TAKE MY WORD FOR IT, DAMNIT!
I BECOME A SQUEALING, WRIGGLING MESS WHEN I'M TICKLED!
IT'S REALLY EMBARRASSING!
. . .
SO, IF I WERE TO TICKLE YOU-
YOU'RE SAYING YOU BECOME-
A SQUEALING, WRIGGLING MESS?
WAG
WAG
WHAT'S WITH THAT LOOK?!

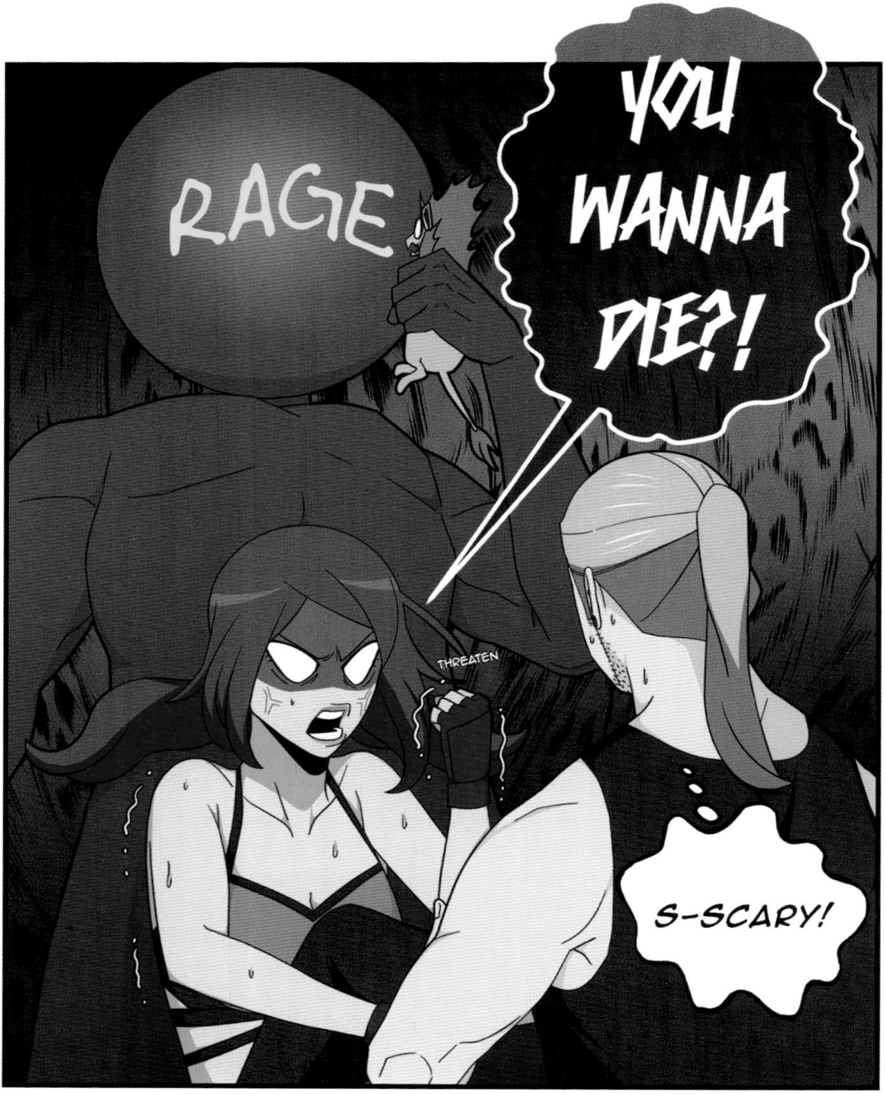
RAGE
YOU WANNA DIE?!
THREATEN
S-SCARY!

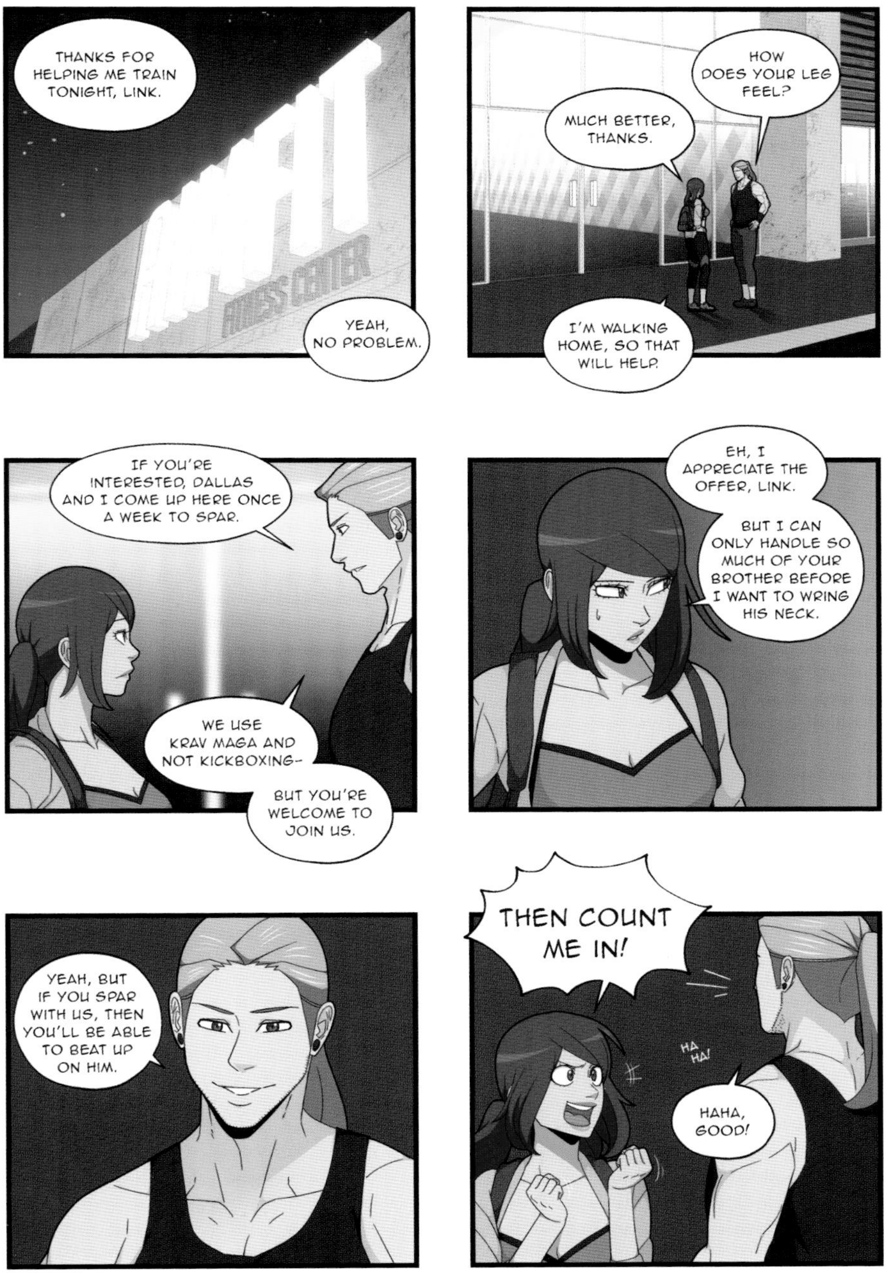
THANKS FOR HELPING ME TRAIN TONIGHT, LINK.
FITNESS CENTER
YEAH, NO PROBLEM.
HOW DOES YOUR LEG FEEL?
MUCH BETTER, THANKS.
I'M WALKING HOME, SO THAT WILL HELP.
IF YOU'RE INTERESTED, DALLAS AND I COME UP HERE ONCE A WEEK TO SPAR.
WE USE KRAV MAGA AND NOT KICKBOXING-
BUT YOU'RE WELCOME TO JOIN US.
EH, I APPRECIATE THE OFFER, LINK.
BUT I CAN ONLY HANDLE SO MUCH OF YOUR BROTHER BEFORE I WANT TO WRING HIS NECK.
YEAH, BUT IF YOU SPAR WITH US, THEN YOU'LL BE ABLE TO BEAT UP ON HIM.
THEN COUNT ME IN!
HA HA!
HAHA, GOOD!

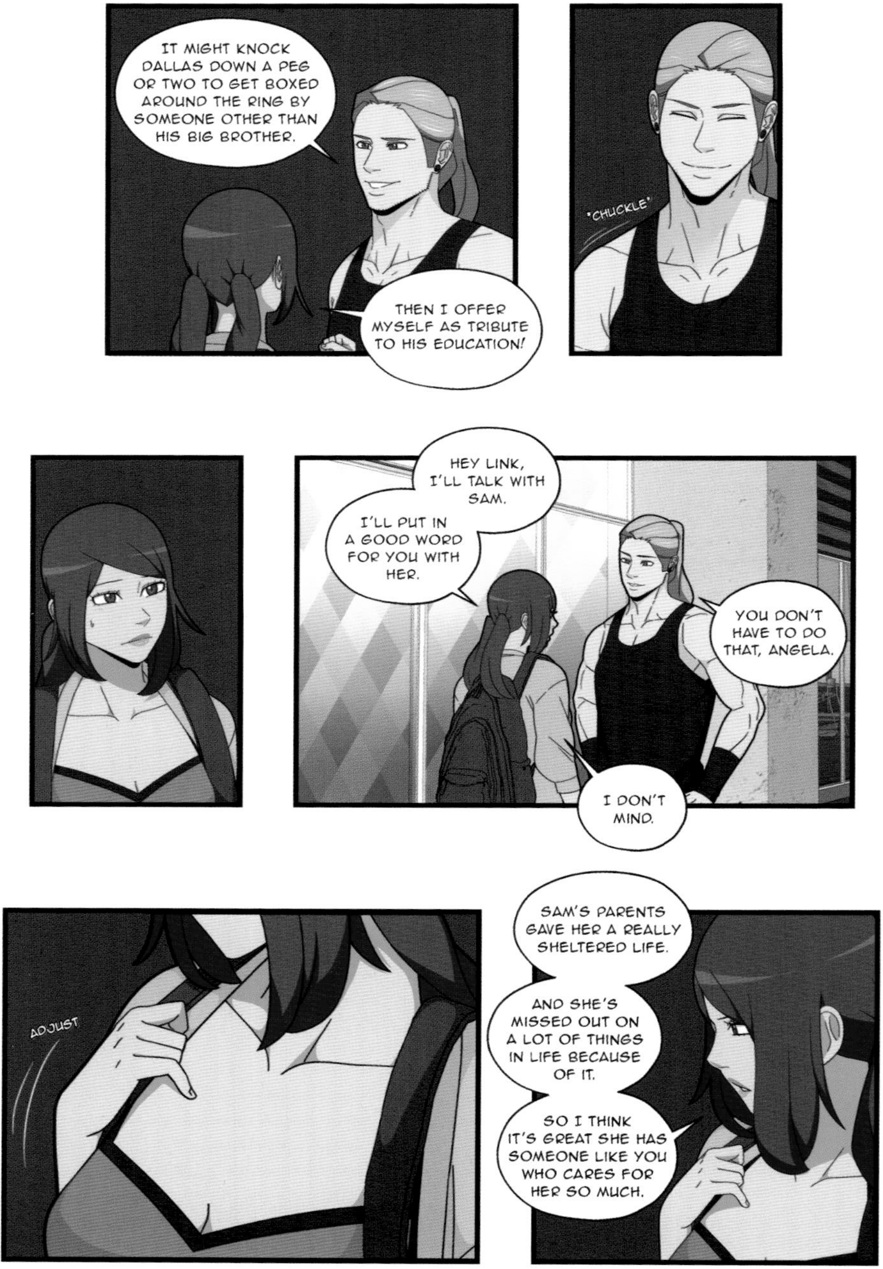
IT MIGHT KNOCK DALLAS DOWN A PEG OR TWO TO GET BOXED AROUND THE RING BY SOMEONE OTHER THAN HIS BIG BROTHER.
THEN I OFFER MYSELF AS TRIBUTE TO HIS EDUCATION!
CHUCKLE
HEY LINK, I'LL TALK WITH SAM.
I'LL PUT IN A GOOD WORD FOR YOU WITH HER.
YOU DON'T HAVE TO DO THAT, ANGELA.
I DON'T MIND.
ADJUST
SAM'S PARENTS GAVE HER A REALLY SHELTERED LIFE.
AND SHE'S MISSED OUT ON A LOT OF THINGS IN LIFE BECAUSE OF IT.
SO I THINK IT'S GREAT SHE HAS SOMEONE LIKE YOU WHO CARES FOR HER SO MUCH.

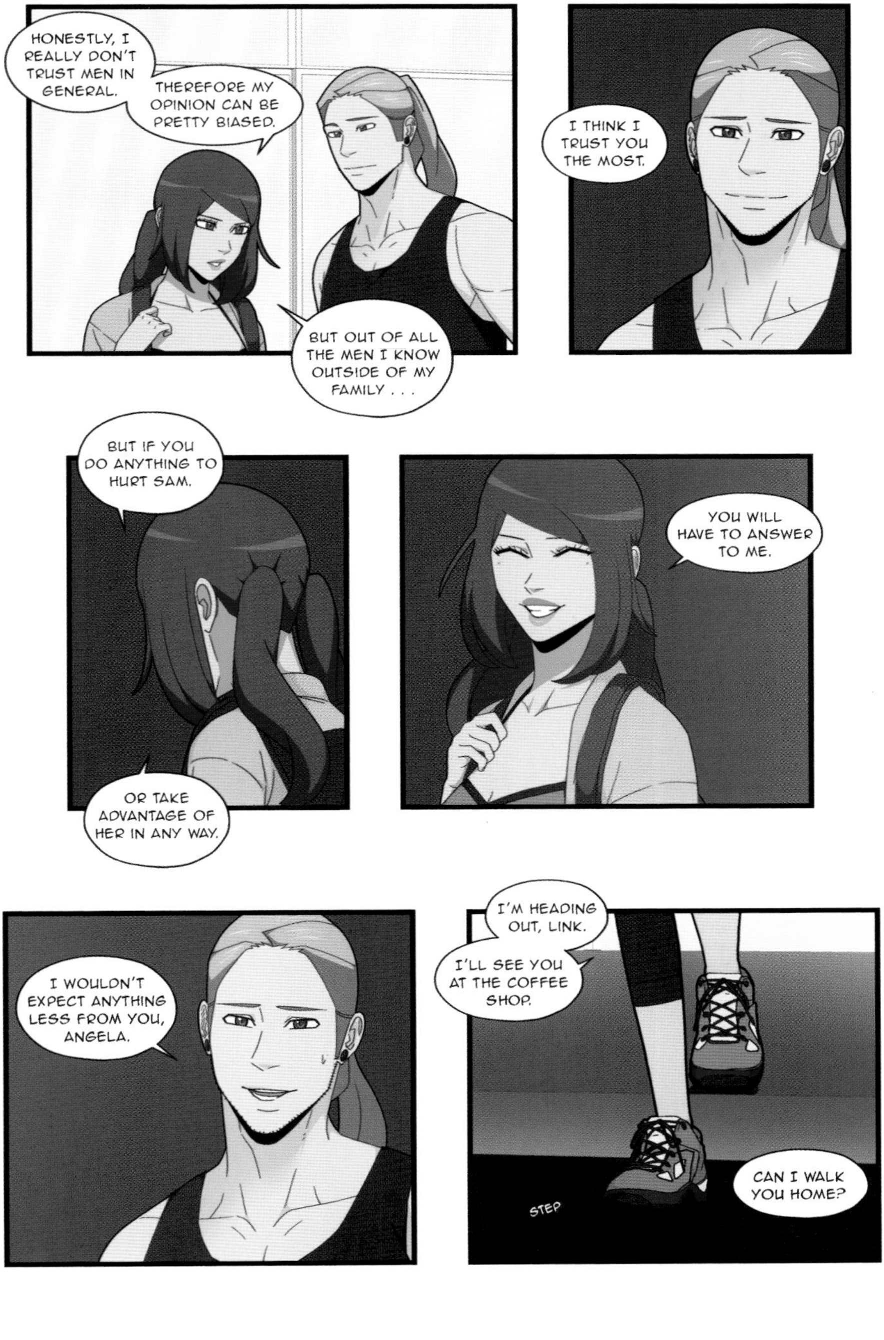
HONESTLY, I REALLY DON'T TRUST MEN IN GENERAL.
THEREFORE MY OPINION CAN BE PRETTY BIASED.
BUT OUT OF ALL THE MEN I KNOW OUTSIDE OF MY FAMILY . . .
I THINK I TRUST YOU THE MOST.
BUT IF YOU DO ANYTHING TO HURT SAM.
OR TAKE ADVANTAGE OF HER IN ANY WAY.
YOU WILL HAVE TO ANSWER TO ME.
I WOULDN'T EXPECT ANYTHING LESS FROM YOU, ANGELA.
I'M HEADING OUT, LINK.
I'LL SEE YOU AT THE COFFEE SHOP.
STEP
CAN I WALK YOU HOME?

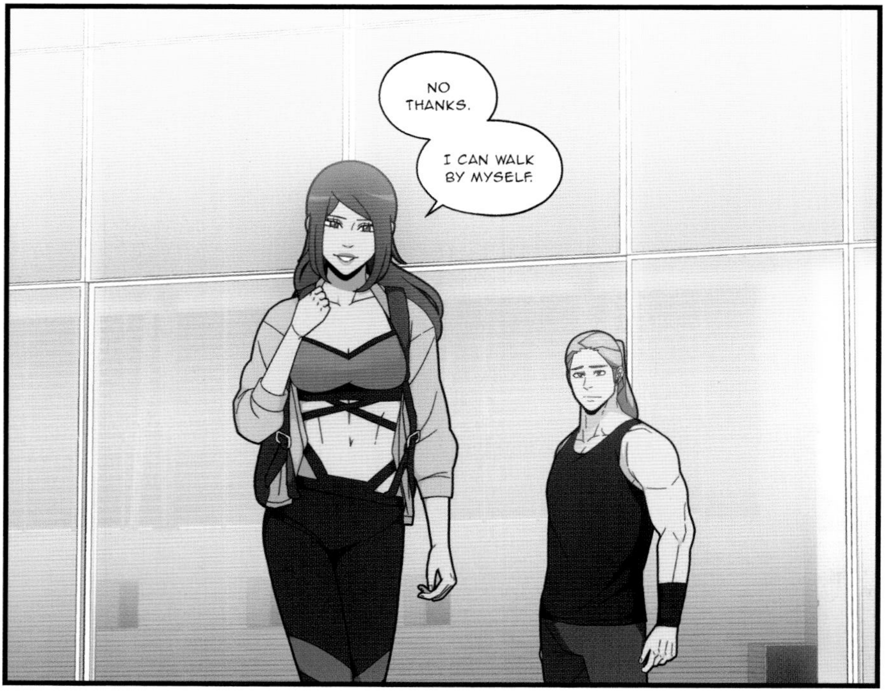
NO THANKS.
I CAN WALK BY MYSELF.

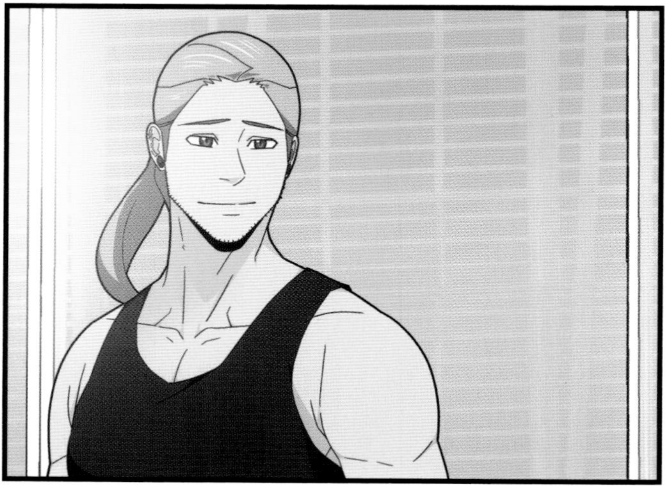

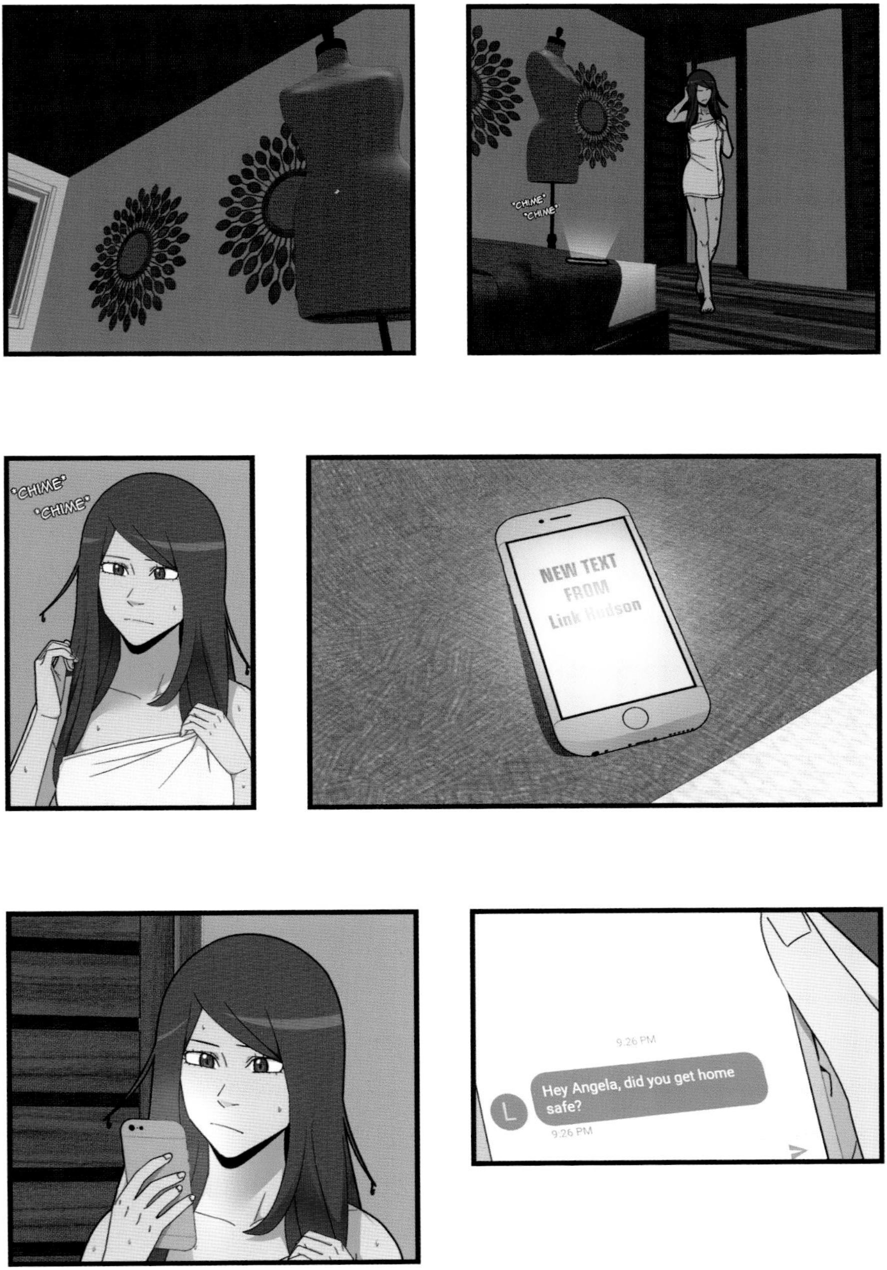
CHIME
CHIME
CHIME
CHIME
NEW TEXT
FROM
Link Hudson
9:26 PM
Hey Angela, did you get home safe?
9:26 PM

CHUCKLE
TOSS
Hey Angela, did you get home safe?
9:26 PM
Nope.
I'm totally dead in a ditch somewhere.
9:28 PM
Secured SMS
SMS
Hey Angela, did you get hom
safe?
9:26 PM
Nope.
I'm totally dead in a ditch somewhere.
Haha, very funny.
9:29 PM
Secured SMS
DROP
ADJUST

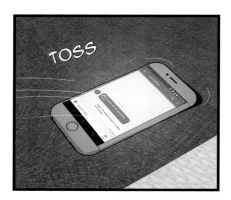

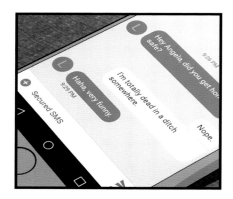

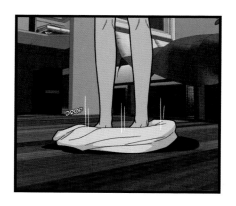

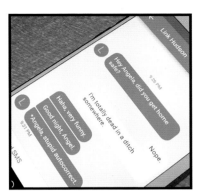

Link Hudson

Hey Angela did you get home safe?
9:26 PM

I'm totally dead in a ditch somewhere.

Nope.

Haha very funny

Good night, Angel.

*Angela stupid autocorrect

9:37 PM

SMS

ANGELA, AND VIKKI
. . .

LET ME INTRODUCE YOU TO LINK.

HIS DAD IS A PATIENT HERE.

HI!

WAVE

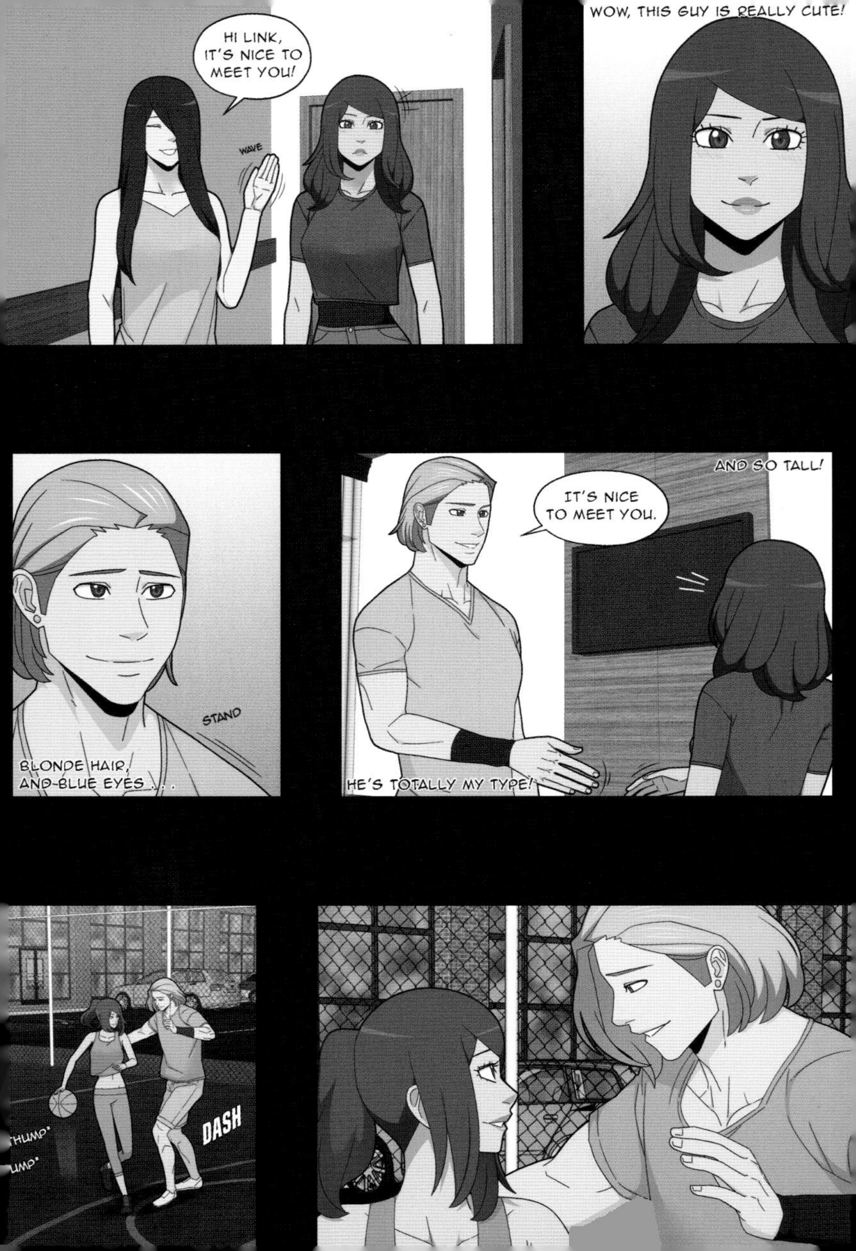
HI LINK, IT'S NICE TO MEET YOU!
WAVE
WOW, THIS GUY IS REALLY CUTE!
STAND
BLONDE HAIR, AND BLUE EYES . . .
AND SO TALL!
IT'S NICE TO MEET YOU.
HE'S TOTALLY MY TYPE!
DASH

HA
HA
HA
HA

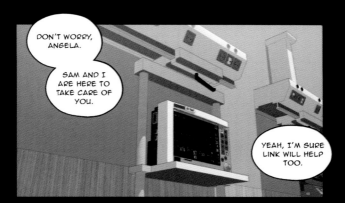

DON'T WORRY, ANGELA.

SAM AND I ARE HERE TO TAKE CARE OF YOU.

YEAH, I'M SURE LINK WILL HELP TOO.

NO, PLEASE DON'T TELL LINK WHAT HAPPENED!

I DON'T WANT HIM TO KNOW!

in a ditch
somewhere.
Haha, very funny.
Good night, Angel.
*Angela, stupid autocorrect.
9:31 PM
Good night.
SMS

SIGH

DELETE
DELETE
SMS

PLACE

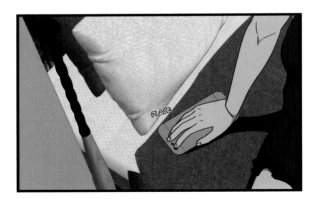

I DON'T WANT
FOR HIM TO KNOW
HOW BROKEN I AM.

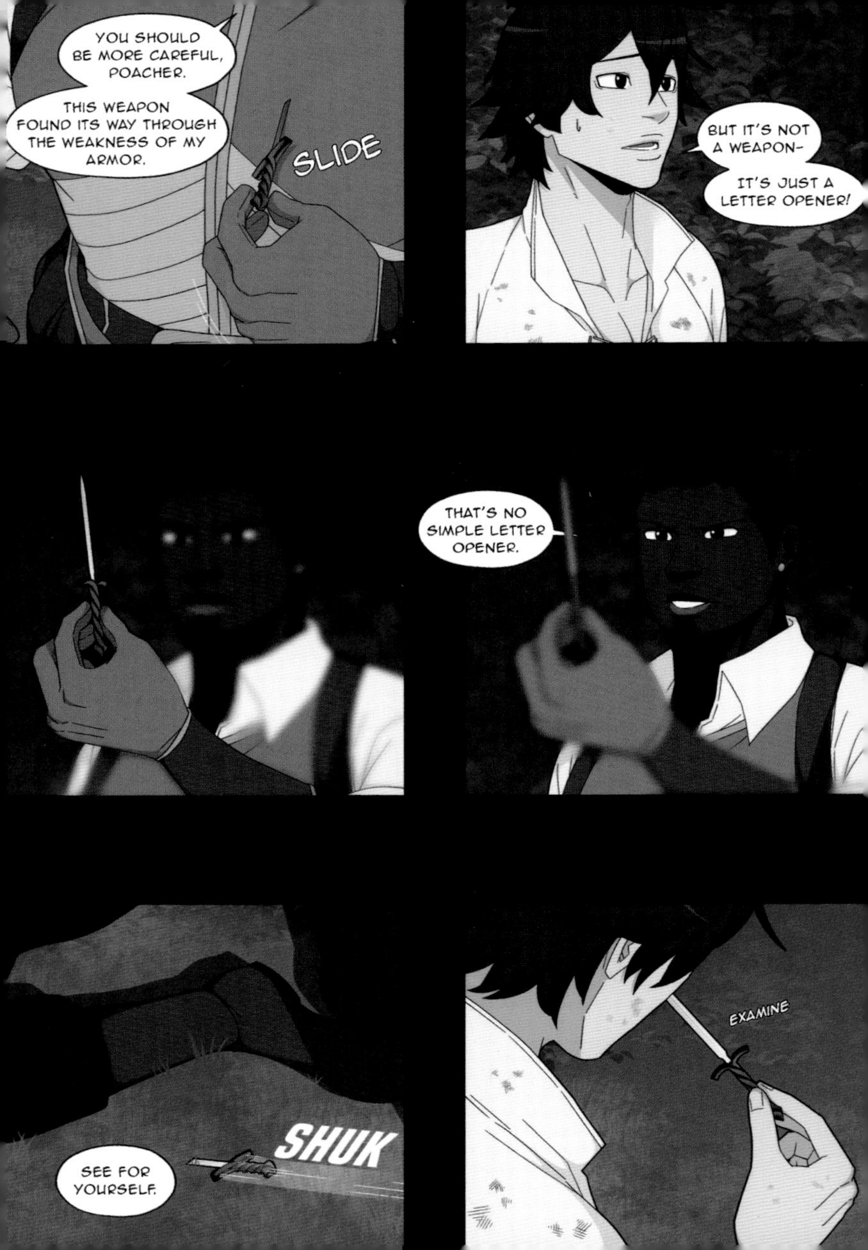
YOU SHOULD BE MORE CAREFUL, POACHER.
THIS WEAPON FOUND ITS WAY THROUGH THE WEAKNESS OF MY ARMOR.
SLIDE
BUT IT'S NOT A WEAPON-
IT'S JUST A LETTER OPENER!
THAT'S NO SIMPLE LETTER OPENER.
SHUK
SEE FOR YOURSELF.
EXAMINE

WAIT A MINUTE, THE TITLE HAS CHANGED!

Tiny Silvered Blade

It's totally just a silvered letter opener.

STATS: Full damage to lycanthropes
PRICE: 200g

IT SAYS IT'S NOW "SILVERED".

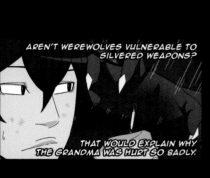

AREN'T WEREWOLVES VULNERABLE TO SILVERED WEAPONS?

THAT WOULD EXPLAIN WHY THE GRANDMA WAS HURT SO BADLY.

ALRIGHT, POACHER.

COME WITH ME QUIETLY, AND DON'T CAUSE ANY PROBLEMS.

I'M NOT A POACHER!

I'M—

I'm a chicken chaser! [HUMOR]

I am dragonborn! [INTIMIDATION]

Your dream come true! [SEDUCE]

I'm completely lost! [TRUTH]

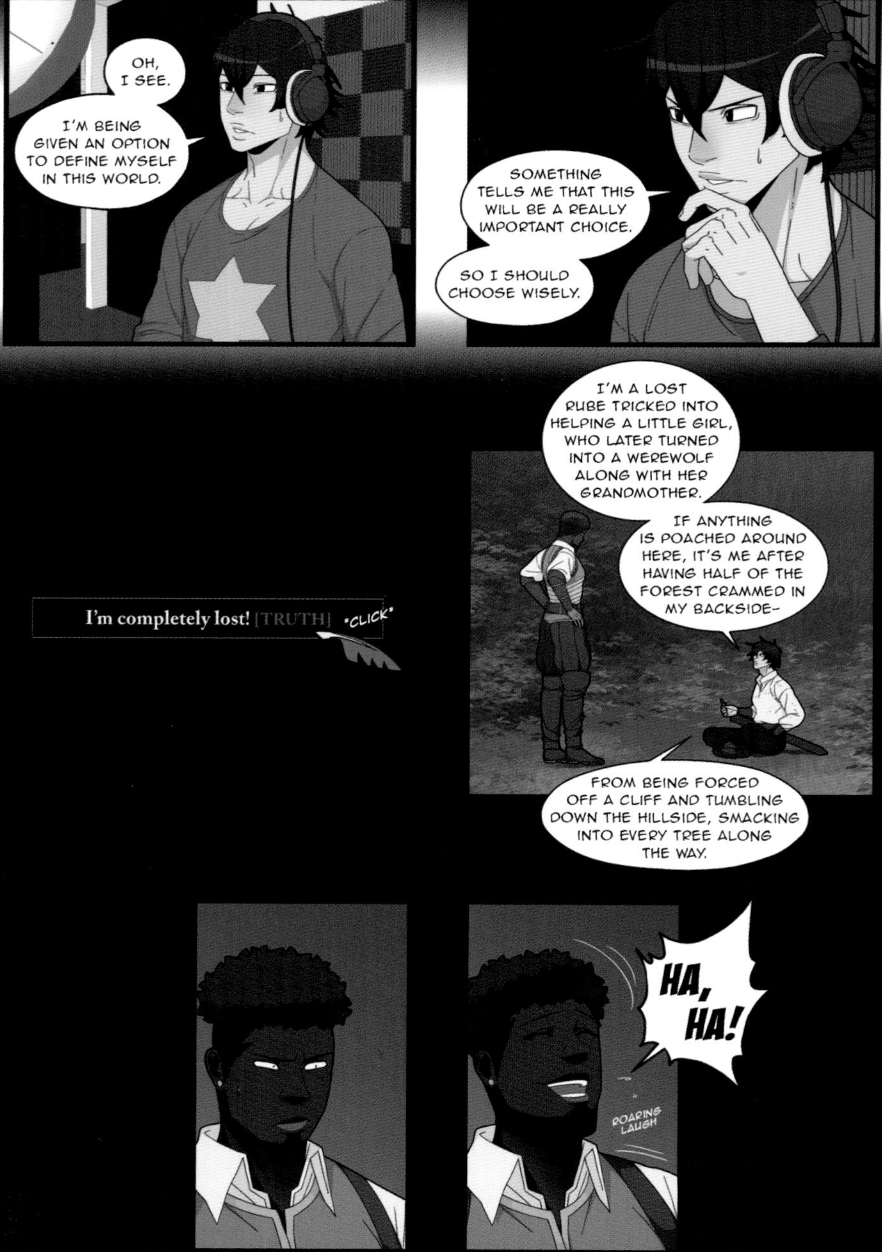
OH, I SEE.
I'M BEING GIVEN AN OPTION TO DEFINE MYSELF IN THIS WORLD.
SOMETHING TELLS ME THAT THIS WILL BE A REALLY IMPORTANT CHOICE.
SO I SHOULD CHOOSE WISELY.
I'm completely lost! [TRUTH]
CLICK
I'M A LOST RUBE TRICKED INTO HELPING A LITTLE GIRL, WHO LATER TURNED INTO A WEREWOLF ALONG WITH HER GRANDMOTHER.
IF ANYTHING IS POACHED AROUND HERE, IT'S ME AFTER HAVING HALF OF THE FOREST CRAMMED IN MY BACKSIDE-
FROM BEING FORCED OFF A CLIFF AND TUMBLING DOWN THE HILLSIDE, SMACKING INTO EVERY TREE ALONG THE WAY.
HA, HA!
ROARING LAUGH

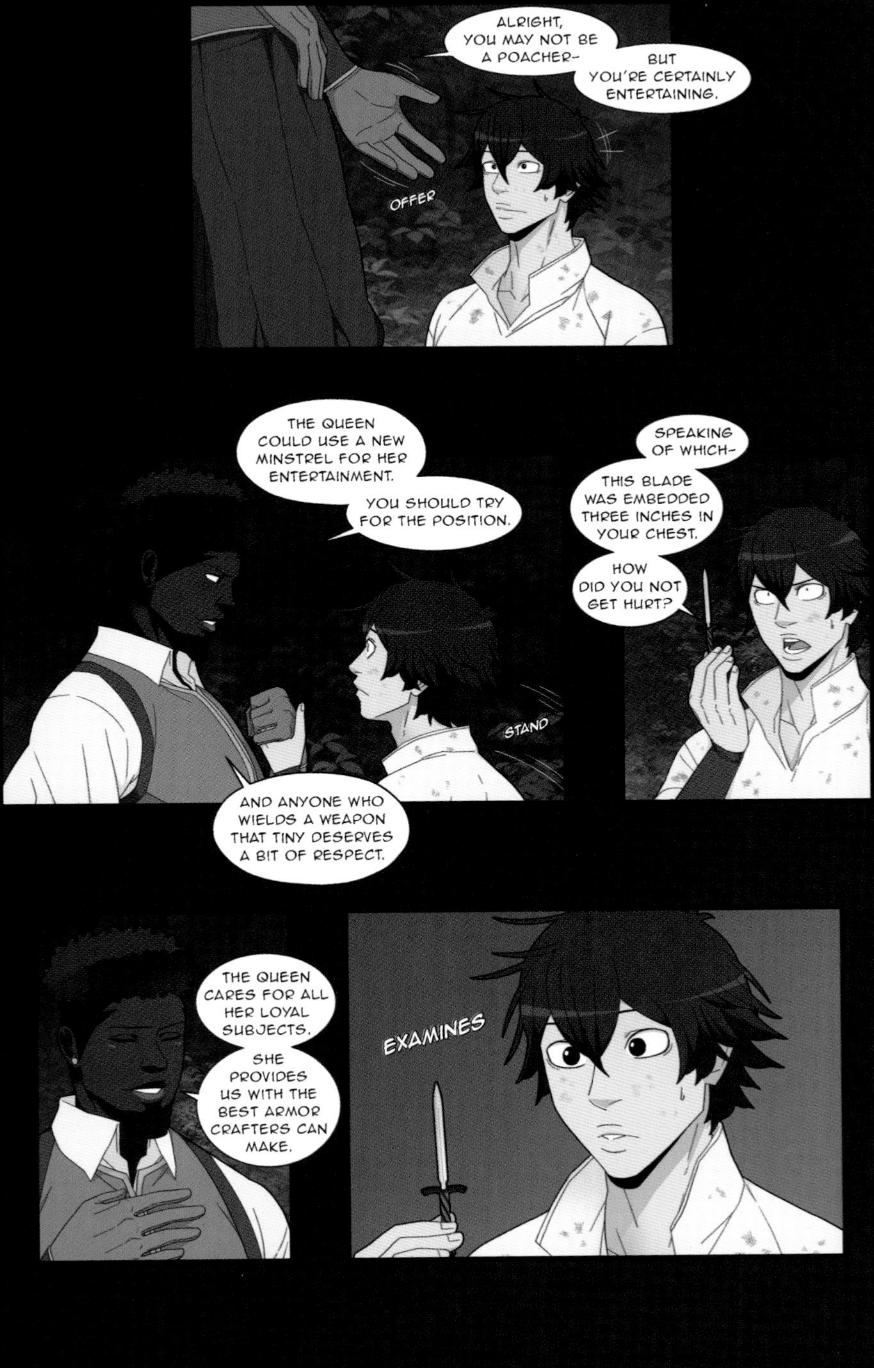
ALRIGHT, YOU MAY NOT BE A POACHER-
BUT YOU'RE CERTAINLY ENTERTAINING.
OFFER
THE QUEEN COULD USE A NEW MINSTREL FOR HER ENTERTAINMENT.
YOU SHOULD TRY FOR THE POSITION.
STAND
AND ANYONE WHO WIELDS A WEAPON THAT TINY DESERVES A BIT OF RESPECT.
SPEAKING OF WHICH-
THIS BLADE WAS EMBEDDED THREE INCHES IN YOUR CHEST.
HOW DID YOU NOT GET HURT?
THE QUEEN CARES FOR ALL HER LOYAL SUBJECTS.
SHE PROVIDES US WITH THE BEST ARMOR CRAFTERS CAN MAKE.
EXAMINES

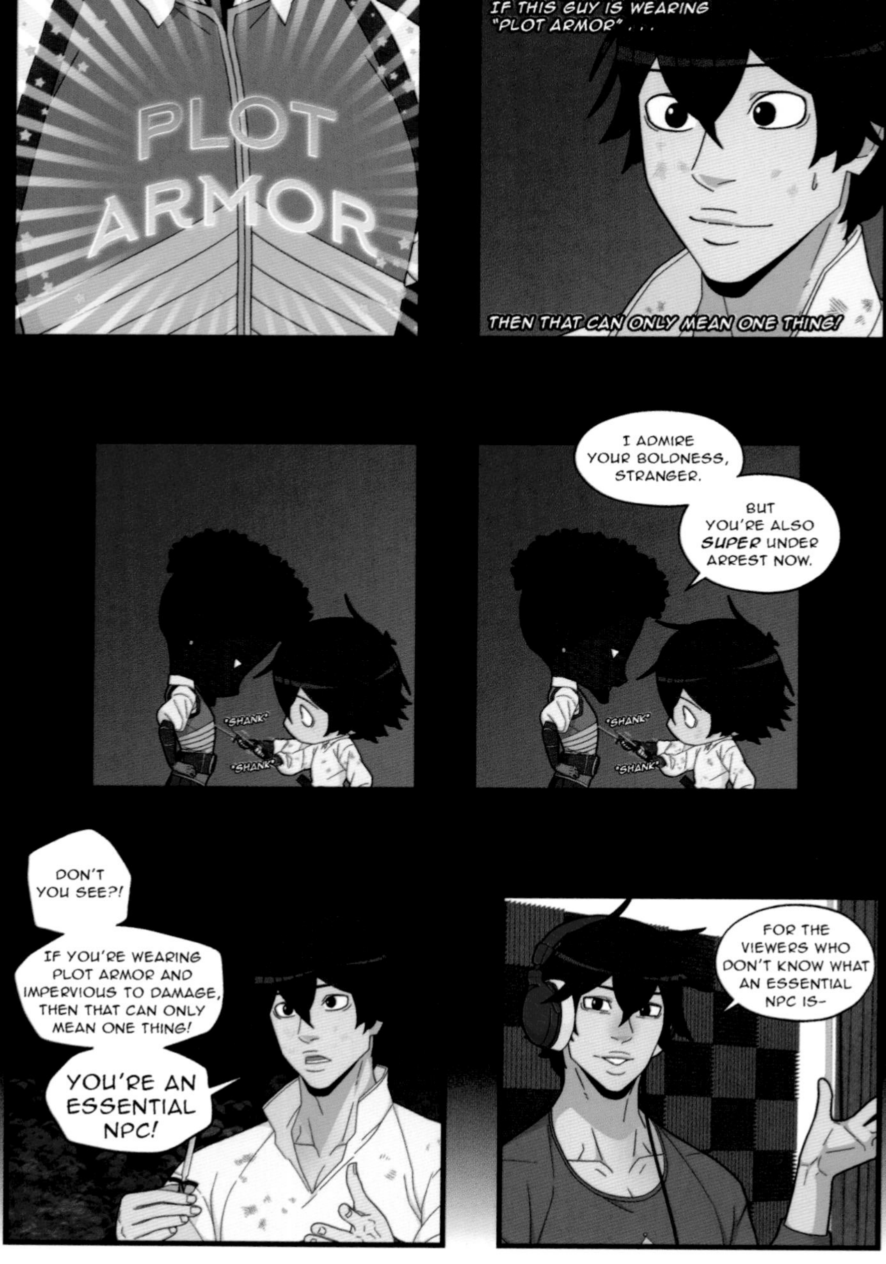
PLOT ARMOR
IF THIS GUY IS WEARING "PLOT ARMOR" . . .
THEN THAT CAN ONLY MEAN ONE THING!
SHANK
SHANK
I ADMIRE YOUR BOLDNESS, STRANGER.
BUT YOU'RE ALSO **SUPER** UNDER ARREST NOW.
SHANK
SHANK
DON'T YOU SEE?!
IF YOU'RE WEARING PLOT ARMOR AND IMPERVIOUS TO DAMAGE, THEN THAT CAN ONLY MEAN ONE THING!
YOU'RE AN ESSENTIAL NPC!
FOR THE VIEWERS WHO DON'T KNOW WHAT AN ESSENTIAL NPC IS–

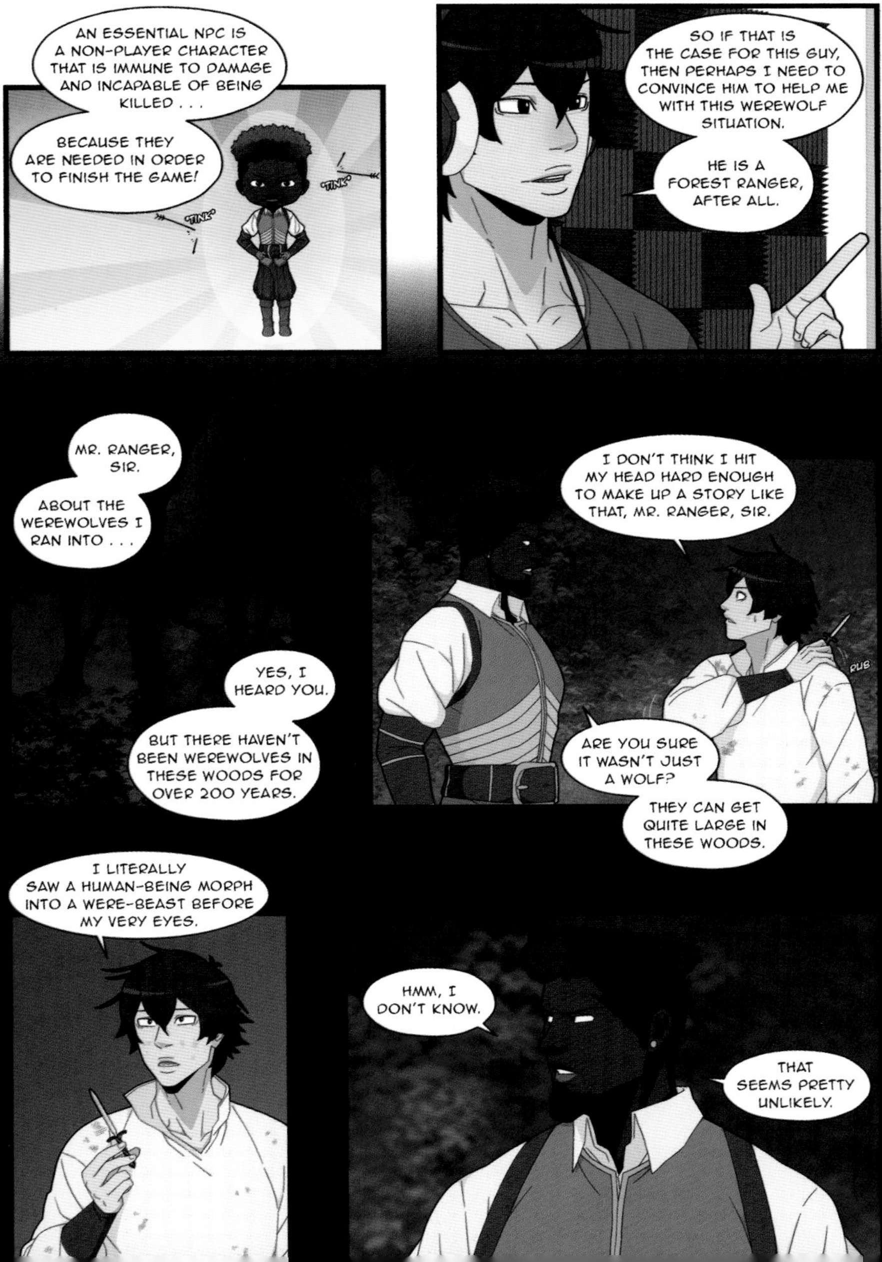
AN ESSENTIAL NPC IS A NON-PLAYER CHARACTER THAT IS IMMUNE TO DAMAGE AND INCAPABLE OF BEING KILLED . . .
BECAUSE THEY ARE NEEDED IN ORDER TO FINISH THE GAME!
TINK
TINK
SO IF THAT IS THE CASE FOR THIS GUY, THEN PERHAPS I NEED TO CONVINCE HIM TO HELP ME WITH THIS WEREWOLF SITUATION.
HE IS A FOREST RANGER, AFTER ALL.
MR. RANGER, SIR.
ABOUT THE WEREWOLVES I RAN INTO . . .
YES, I HEARD YOU.
BUT THERE HAVEN'T BEEN WEREWOLVES IN THESE WOODS FOR OVER 200 YEARS.
I DON'T THINK I HIT MY HEAD HARD ENOUGH TO MAKE UP A STORY LIKE THAT, MR. RANGER, SIR.
RUB
ARE YOU SURE IT WASN'T JUST A WOLF?
THEY CAN GET QUITE LARGE IN THESE WOODS.
I LITERALLY SAW A HUMAN-BEING MORPH INTO A WERE-BEAST BEFORE MY VERY EYES.
HMM, I DON'T KNOW.
THAT SEEMS PRETTY UNLIKELY.

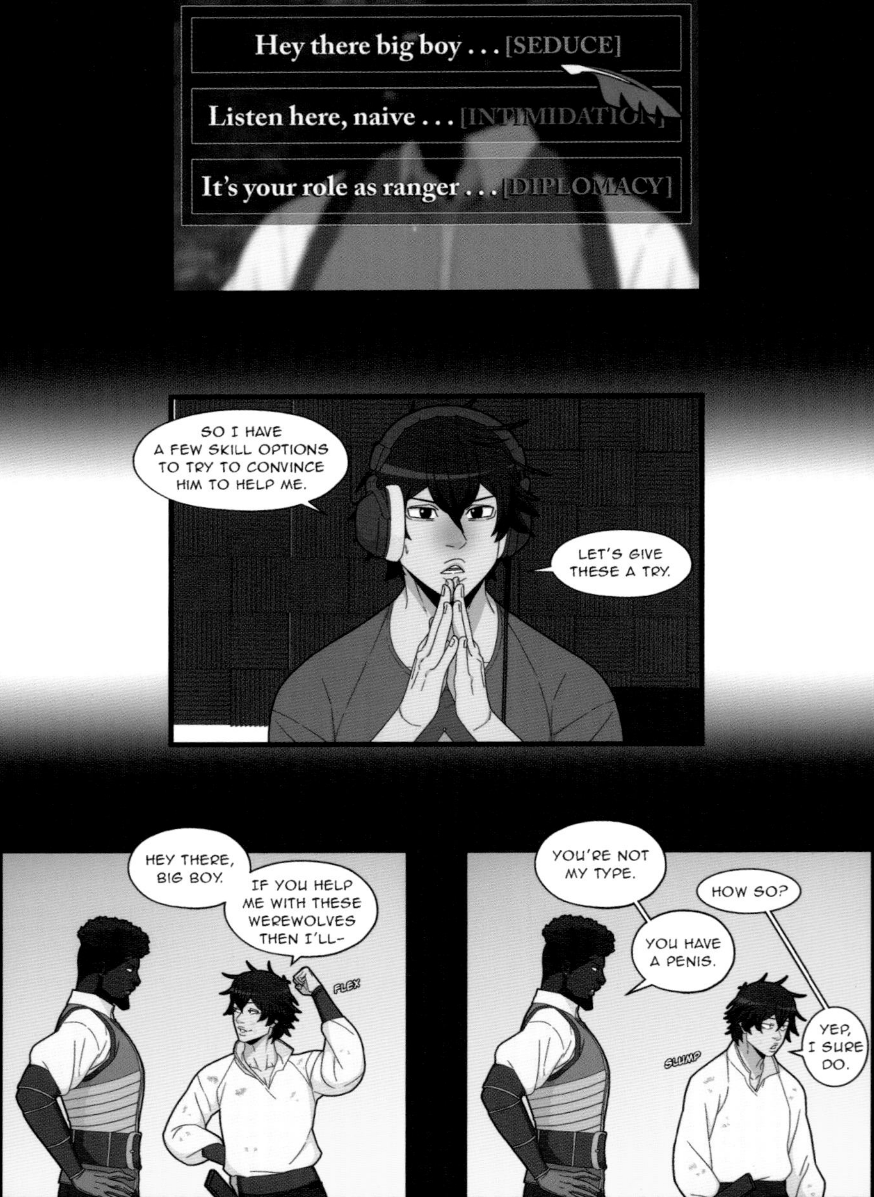
Hey there big boy . . . [SEDUCE]
Listen here, naive . . . [INTIMIDATION]
It's your role as ranger . . . [DIPLOMACY]
SO I HAVE A FEW SKILL OPTIONS TO TRY TO CONVINCE HIM TO HELP ME.
LET'S GIVE THESE A TRY.
HEY THERE, BIG BOY.
IF YOU HELP ME WITH THESE WEREWOLVES THEN I'LL-
FLEX
YOU'RE NOT MY TYPE.
HOW SO?
YOU HAVE A PENIS.
SLUMP
YEP, I SURE DO.

The ranger was not seduced.

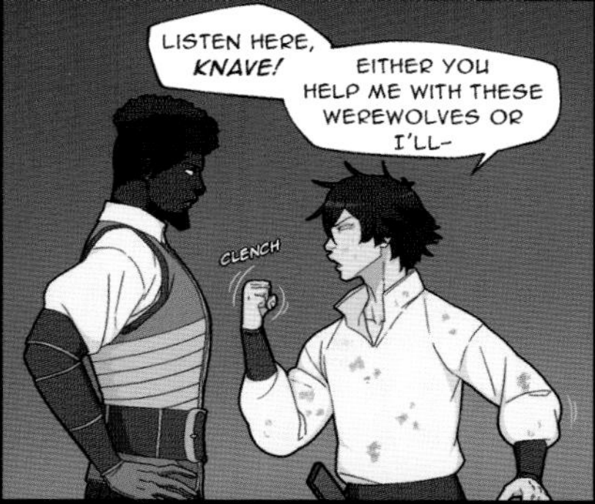
LISTEN HERE, KNAVE!
EITHER YOU HELP ME WITH THESE WEREWOLVES OR I'LL-
CLENCH

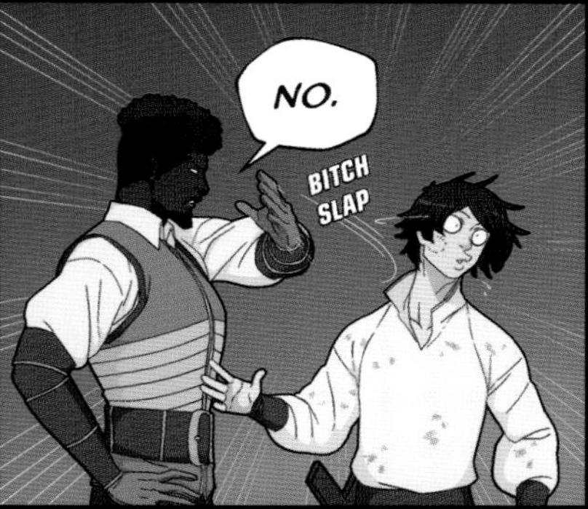
NO.
BITCH SLAP

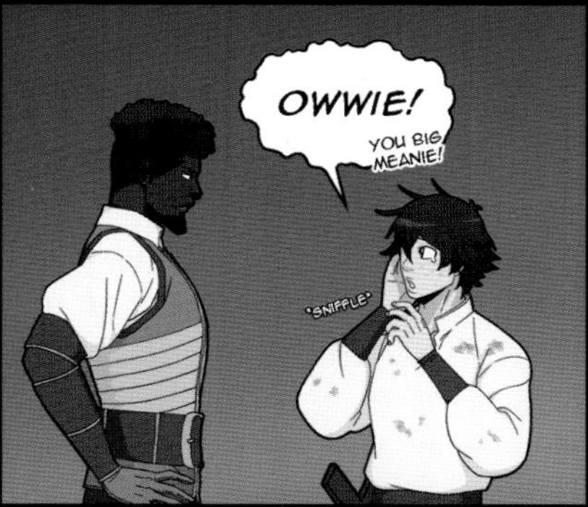
OWWIE!
YOU BIG MEANIE!
SNIFFLE

The ranger was not intimidated.

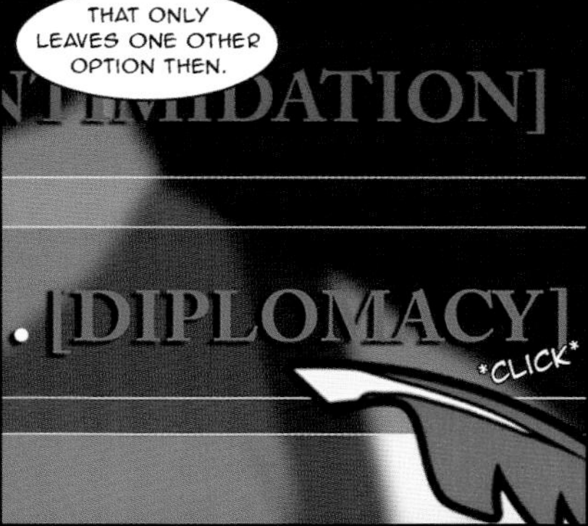
THAT ONLY LEAVES ONE OTHER OPTION THEN.
[DIPLOMACY]
CLICK

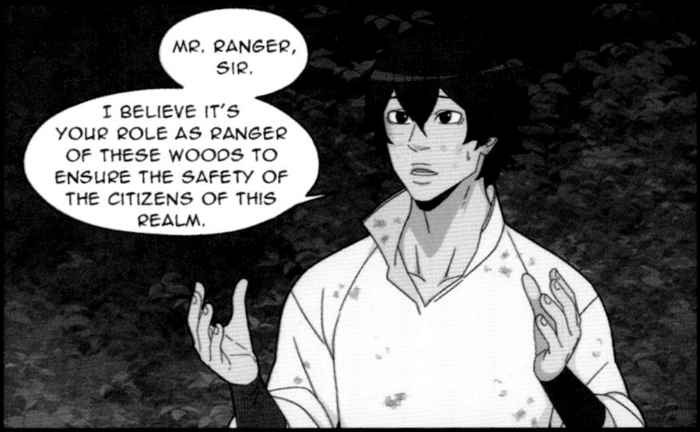
MR. RANGER, SIR.
I BELIEVE IT'S YOUR ROLE AS RANGER OF THESE WOODS TO ENSURE THE SAFETY OF THE CITIZENS OF THIS REALM.

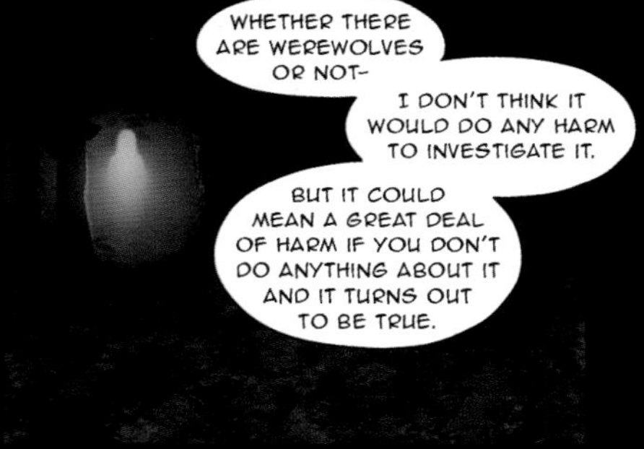
WHETHER THERE ARE WEREWOLVES OR NOT-
I DON'T THINK IT WOULD DO ANY HARM TO INVESTIGATE IT.
BUT IT COULD MEAN A GREAT DEAL OF HARM IF YOU DON'T DO ANYTHING ABOUT IT AND IT TURNS OUT TO BE TRUE.

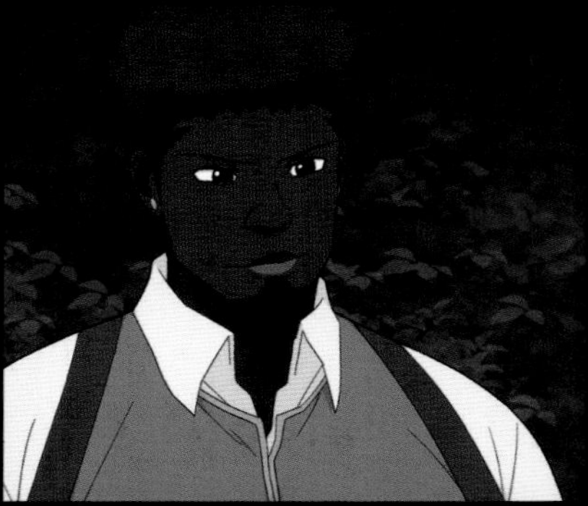

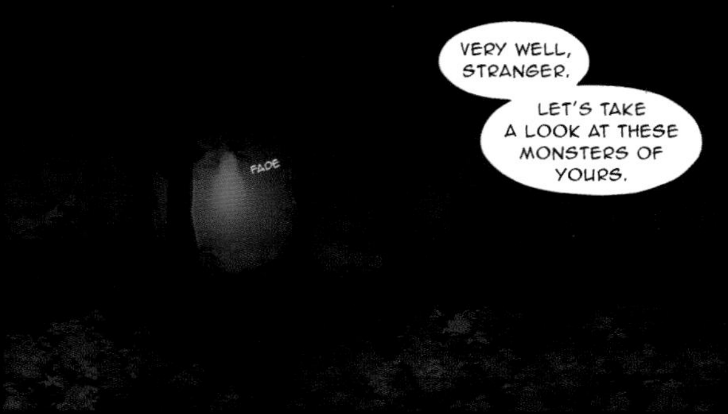
VERY WELL, STRANGER.
LET'S TAKE A LOOK AT THESE MONSTERS OF YOURS.
FADE

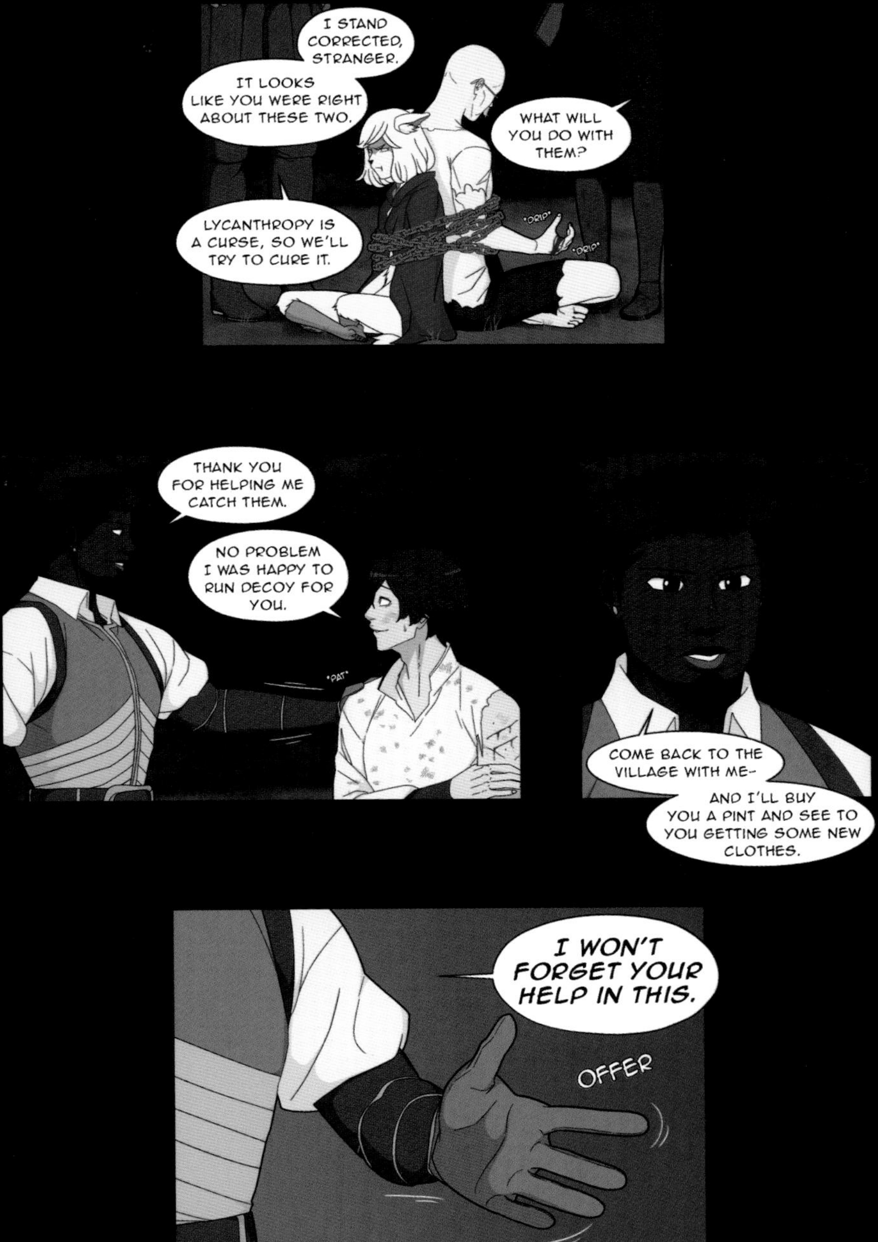
I STAND CORRECTED, STRANGER.
IT LOOKS LIKE YOU WERE RIGHT ABOUT THESE TWO.
WHAT WILL YOU DO WITH THEM?
LYCANTHROPY IS A CURSE, SO WE'LL TRY TO CURE IT.
DRIP
DRIP
THANK YOU FOR HELPING ME CATCH THEM.
NO PROBLEM I WAS HAPPY TO RUN DECOY FOR YOU.
PAT
COME BACK TO THE VILLAGE WITH ME-
AND I'LL BUY YOU A PINT AND SEE TO YOU GETTING SOME NEW CLOTHES.
I WON'T FORGET YOUR HELP IN THIS.
OFFER

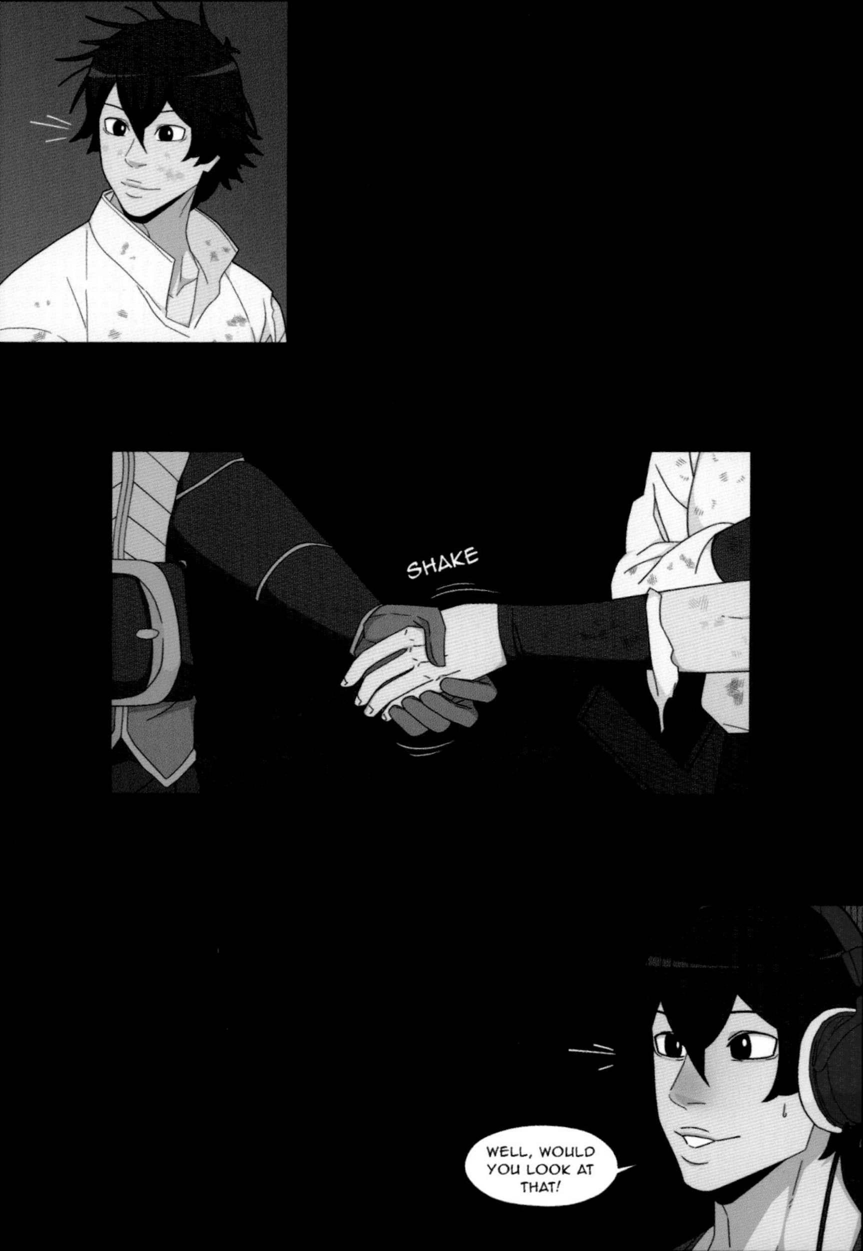
SHAKE
WELL, WOULD YOU LOOK AT THAT!

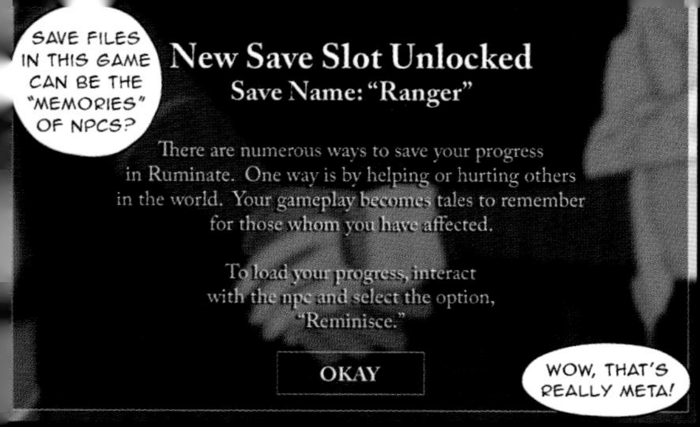
SAVE FILES IN THIS GAME CAN BE THE "MEMORIES" OF NPCS?
New Save Slot Unlocked
Save Name: "Ranger"
There are numerous ways to save your progress in Ruminate. One way is by helping or hurting others in the world. Your gameplay becomes tales to remember for those whom you have affected.
To load your progress, interact with the npc and select the option, "Reminisce."
OKAY
WOW, THAT'S REALLY META!

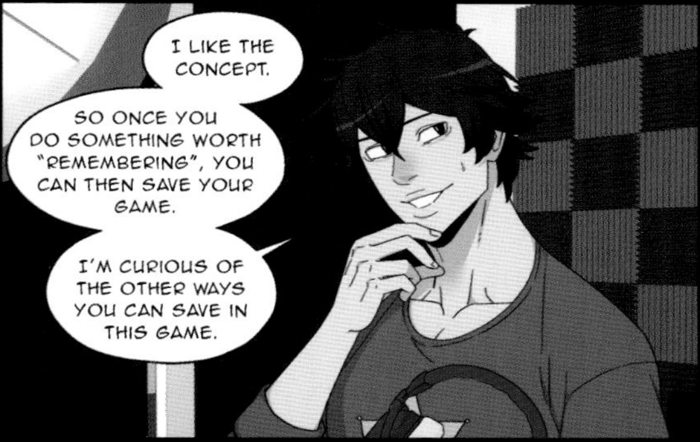
I LIKE THE CONCEPT.
SO ONCE YOU DO SOMETHING WORTH "REMEMBERING", YOU CAN THEN SAVE YOUR GAME.
I'M CURIOUS OF THE OTHER WAYS YOU CAN SAVE IN THIS GAME.

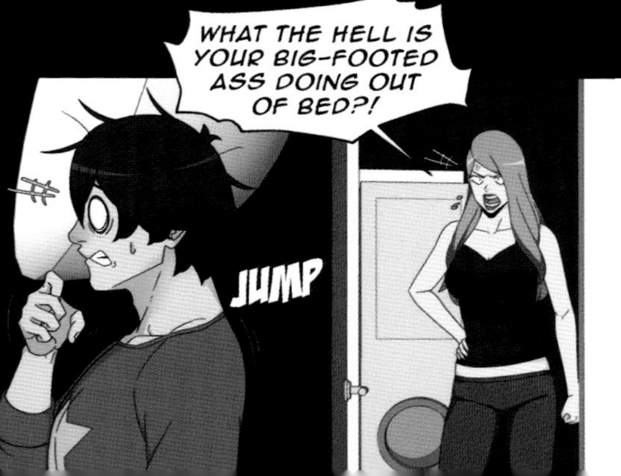
WHAT THE HELL IS YOUR BIG-FOOTED ASS DOING OUT OF BED?!
JUMP

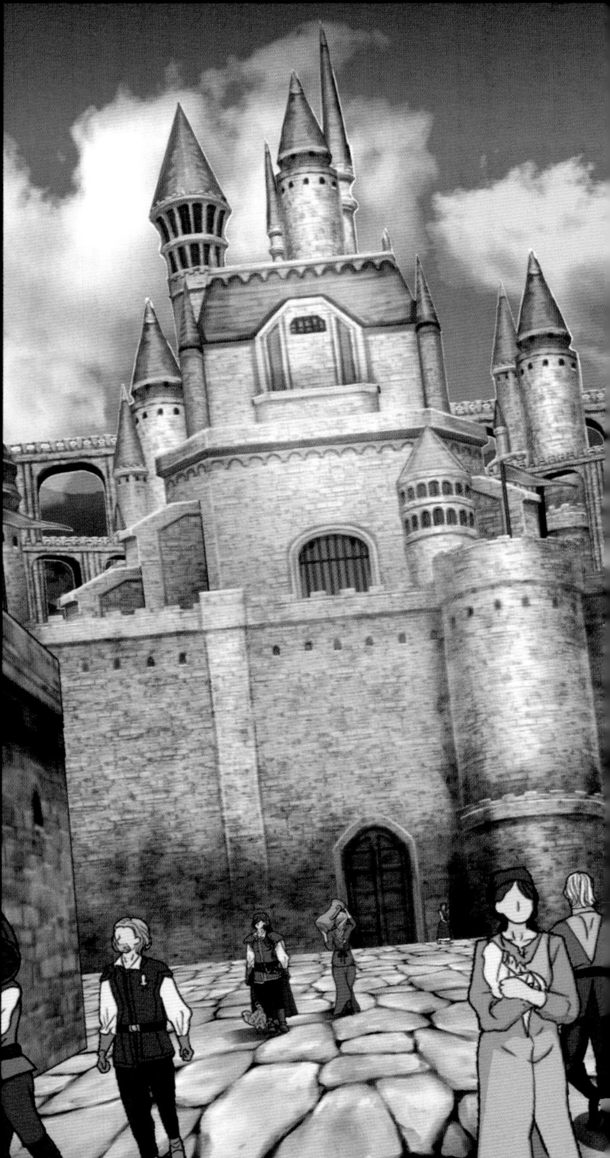

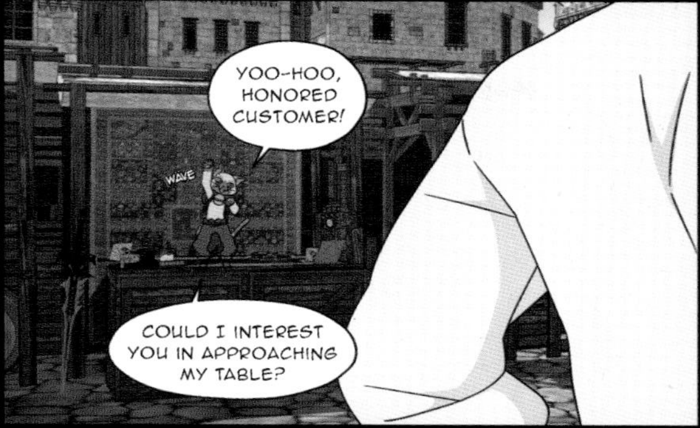
YOO-HOO, HONORED CUSTOMER!
WAVE
COULD I INTEREST YOU IN APPROACHING MY TABLE?
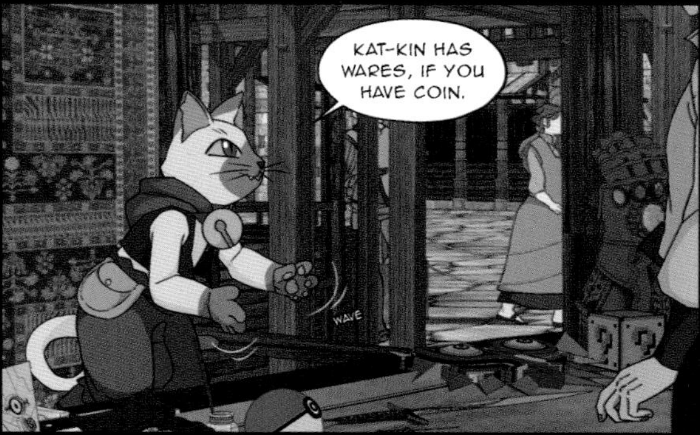
KAT-KIN HAS WARES, IF YOU HAVE COIN.
WAVE
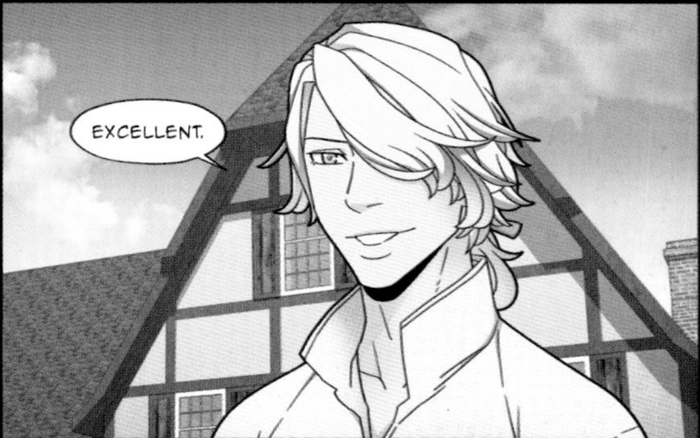
EXCELLENT.

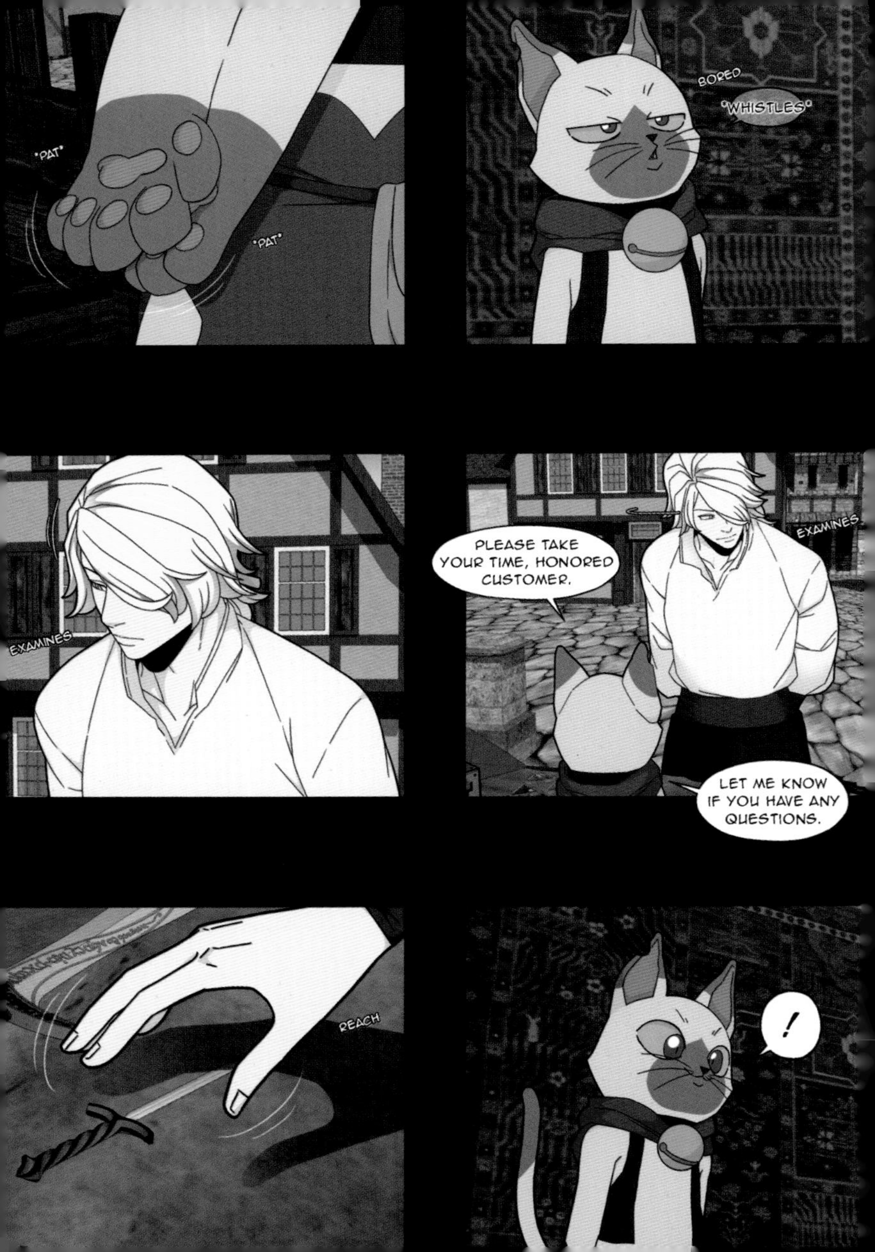
PAT
PAT
BORED
WHISTLES
EXAMINES
PLEASE TAKE YOUR TIME, HONORED CUSTOMER.
EXAMINES
LET ME KNOW IF YOU HAVE ANY QUESTIONS.
REACH
!

GASP

MOVE
PAST

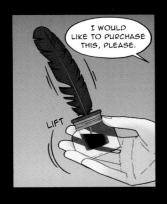

I WOULD
LIKE TO PURCHASE
THIS, PLEASE.

LIFT

MY APOLOGIES,
HONORED CUSTOMER!

BUT THAT
QUILL AND INK ISN'T
FOR SALE!

I ONLY USE
IT FOR WRITING
RECEIPTS.

I'LL GIVE YOU
A GOLD PIECE
FOR IT.

DEAL!

THUMB
UP

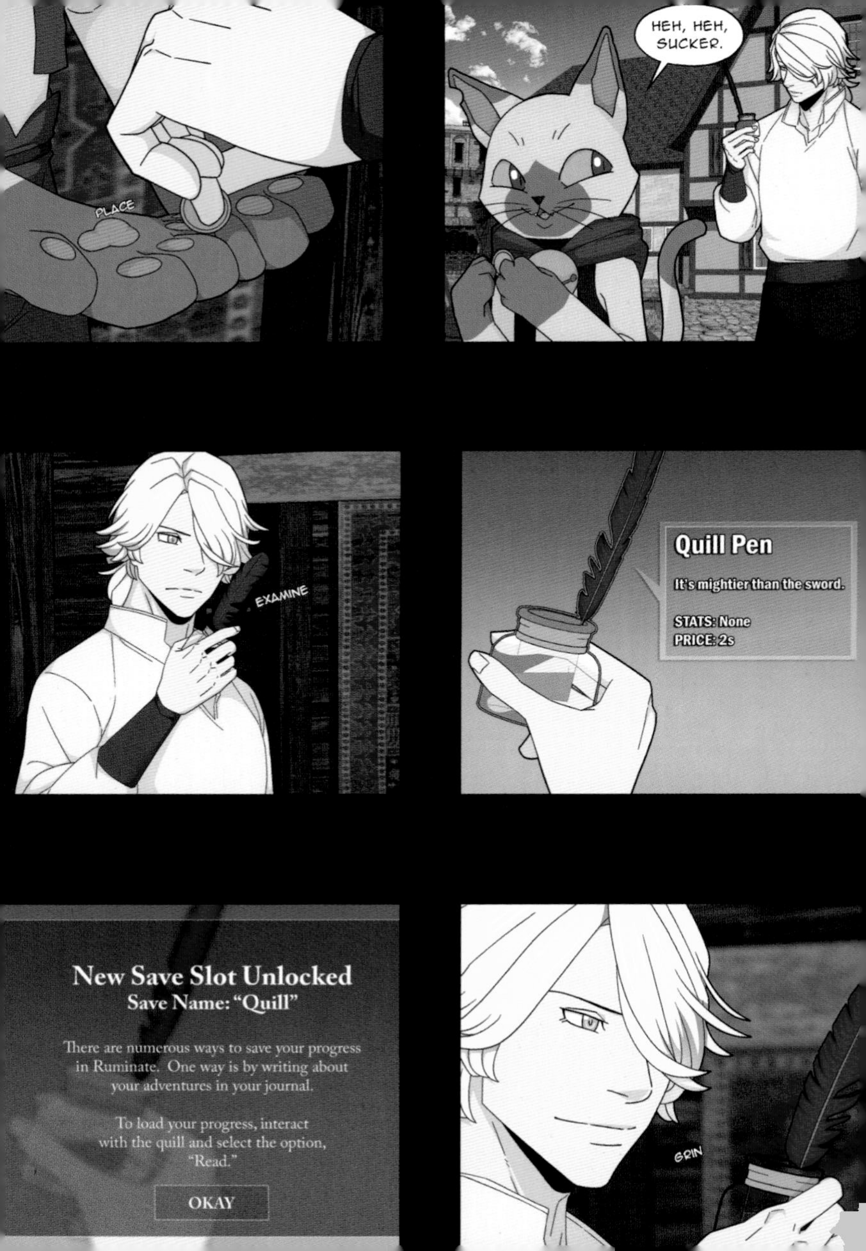
PLACE
HEH, HEH, SUCKER.
EXAMINE
Quill Pen
It's mightier than the sword.
STATS: None
PRICE: 2s
New Save Slot Unlocked
Save Name: "Quill"
There are numerous ways to save your progress in Ruminate. One way is by writing about your adventures in your journal.
To load your progress, interact with the quill and select the option, "Read."
OKAY
GRIN

EXCUSE ME, GENTLE SIR—

BUT WOULD YOU HELP ME?

MY GRANDMOTHER LIVES IN THE WOODS AND SHE IS SICK.

I HAVE THIS FOOD I NEED TO TAKE HER.

BUT I'M AFRAID OF TAKING THE TRIP ON MY OWN.

WOULD YOU BE WILLING TO WALK WITH ME AND KEEP ME SAFE?

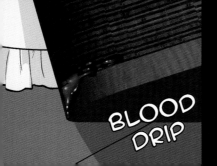

BLOOD DRIP

CHUCKLE

PLACE

*DOMINATE
MUSIC*

BZZT
BZZT

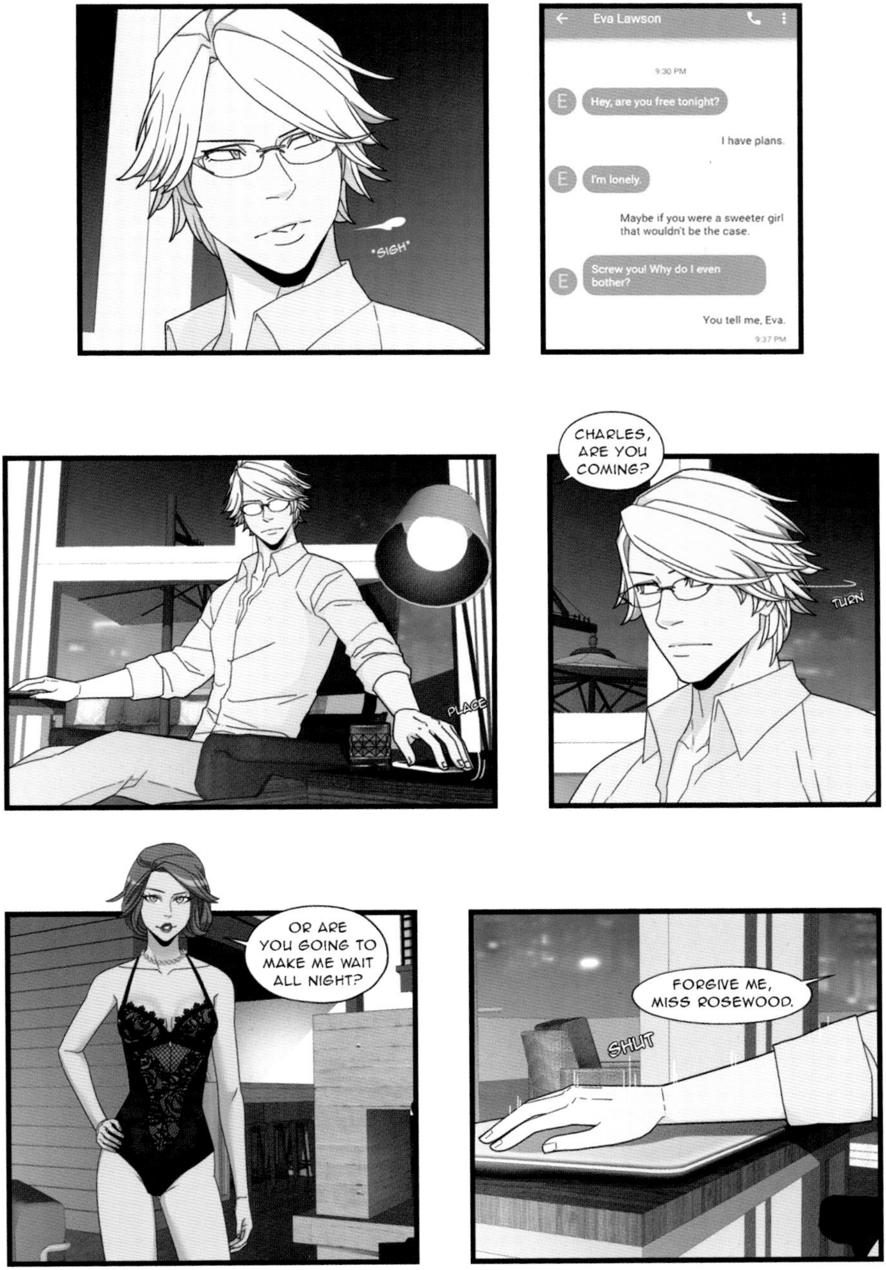
SIGH
Eva Lawson
9:30 PM
Hey, are you free tonight?
I have plans.
I'm lonely.
Maybe if you were a sweeter girl that wouldn't be the case.
Screw you! Why do I even bother?
You tell me, Eva.
9:37 PM
PLACE
CHARLES, ARE YOU COMING?
TURN
OR ARE YOU GOING TO MAKE ME WAIT ALL NIGHT?
FORGIVE ME, MISS ROSEWOOD.
SHUT

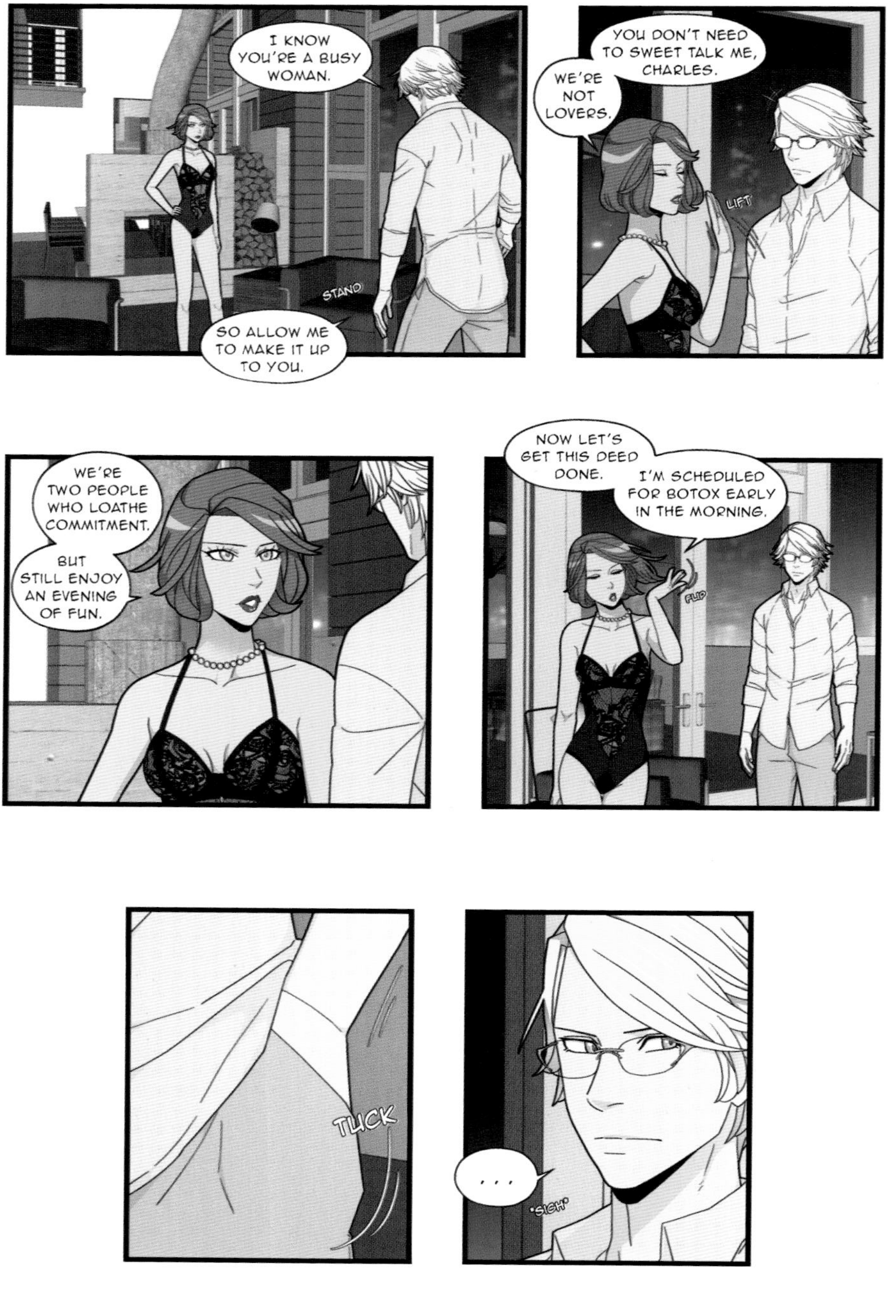
I KNOW YOU'RE A BUSY WOMAN.
STAND
SO ALLOW ME TO MAKE IT UP TO YOU.
YOU DON'T NEED TO SWEET TALK ME, CHARLES.
WE'RE NOT LOVERS.
LIFT
WE'RE TWO PEOPLE WHO LOATHE COMMITMENT.
BUT STILL ENJOY AN EVENING OF FUN.
NOW LET'S GET THIS DEED DONE.
I'M SCHEDULED FOR BOTOX EARLY IN THE MORNING.
FLIP
TUCK
. . .
SIGH

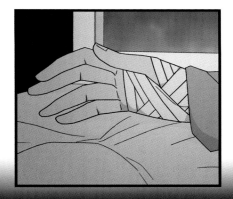

TREMBLE

. . .
ON S-SATURDAY,
DID YOU WANT TO
. . .
K-KISS ME?

TREMBLE

HONESTLY,
. . .
I THOUGHT
I DID.

BUT IN
THE MOMENT,
IT JUST FELT
. . . WRONG.

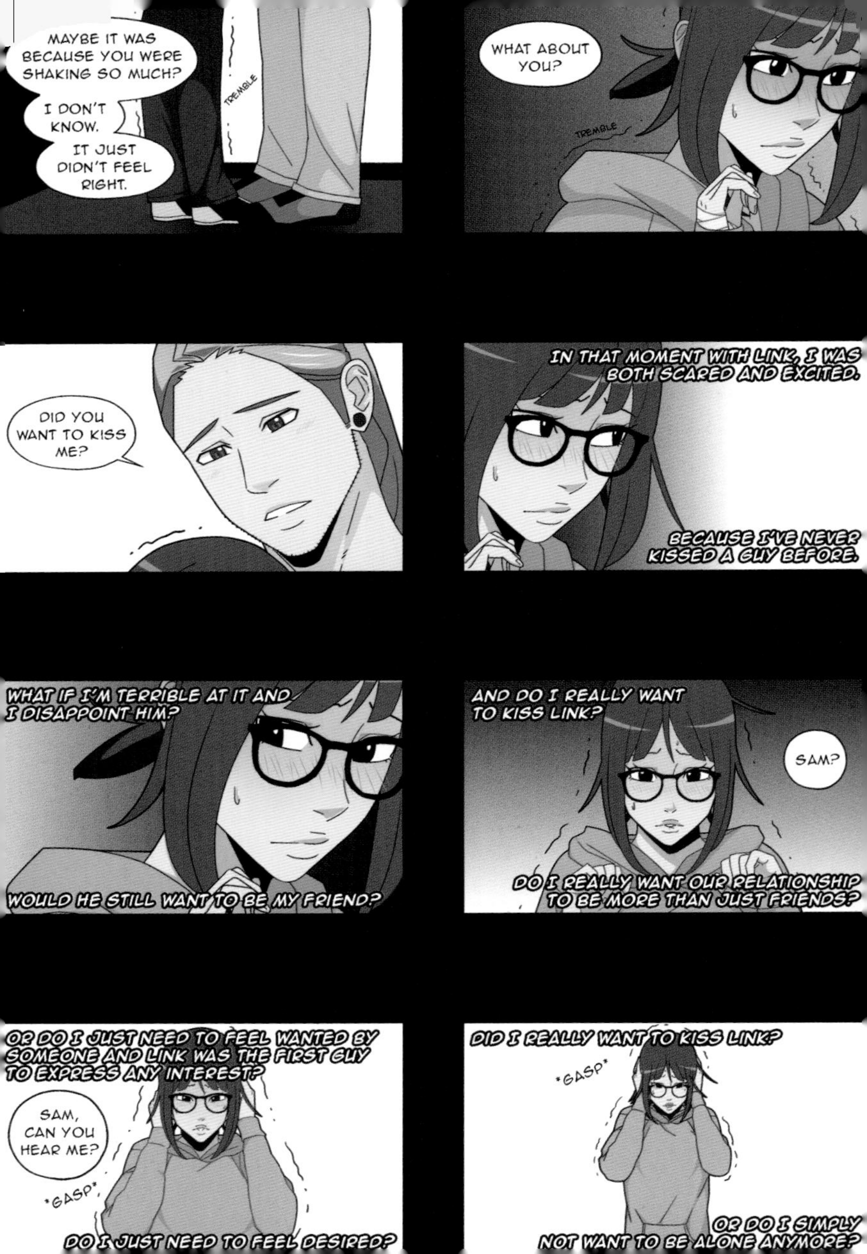
MAYBE IT WAS BECAUSE YOU WERE SHAKING SO MUCH?
I DON'T KNOW.
IT JUST DIDN'T FEEL RIGHT.
TREMBLE
WHAT ABOUT YOU?
TREMBLE
DID YOU WANT TO KISS ME?
IN THAT MOMENT WITH LINK, I WAS BOTH SCARED AND EXCITED.
BECAUSE I'VE NEVER KISSED A GUY BEFORE.
WHAT IF I'M TERRIBLE AT IT AND I DISAPPOINT HIM?
WOULD HE STILL WANT TO BE MY FRIEND?
AND DO I REALLY WANT TO KISS LINK?
SAM?
DO I REALLY WANT OUR RELATIONSHIP TO BE MORE THAN JUST FRIENDS?
OR DO I JUST NEED TO FEEL WANTED BY SOMEONE AND LINK WAS THE FIRST GUY TO EXPRESS ANY INTEREST?
SAM, CAN YOU HEAR ME?
GASP
DO I JUST NEED TO FEEL DESIRED?
DID I REALLY WANT TO KISS LINK?
GASP
OR DO I SIMPLY NOT WANT TO BE ALONE ANYMORE?

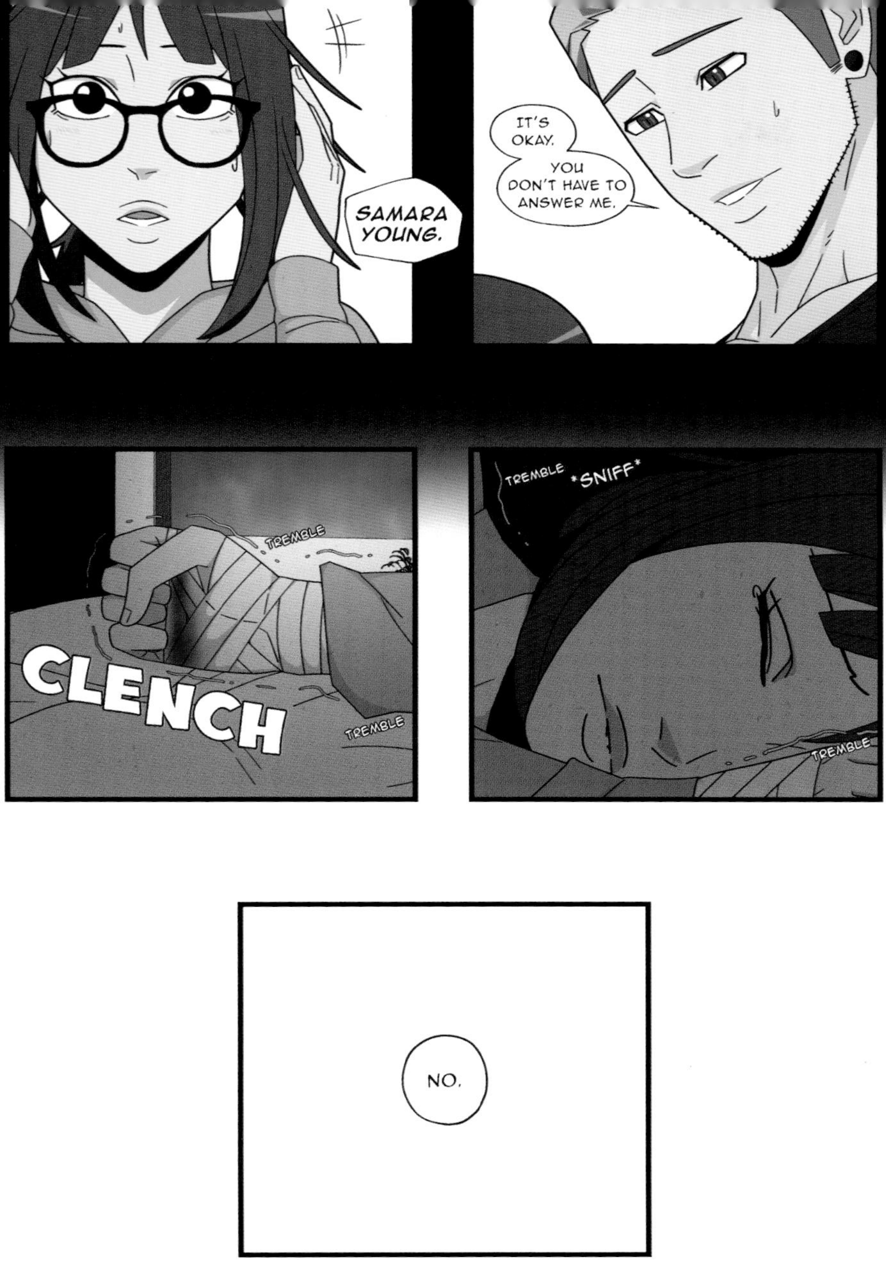
SAMARA YOUNG.
IT'S OKAY.
YOU DON'T HAVE TO ANSWER ME.
TREMBLE
CLENCH
TREMBLE
TREMBLE
SNIFF
TREMBLE
NO.

FEVERISH

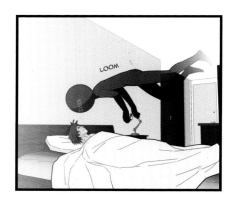

LOOM

PANT

PANT

IT LOOKS LIKE I'VE LOST WEIGHT.

TUG

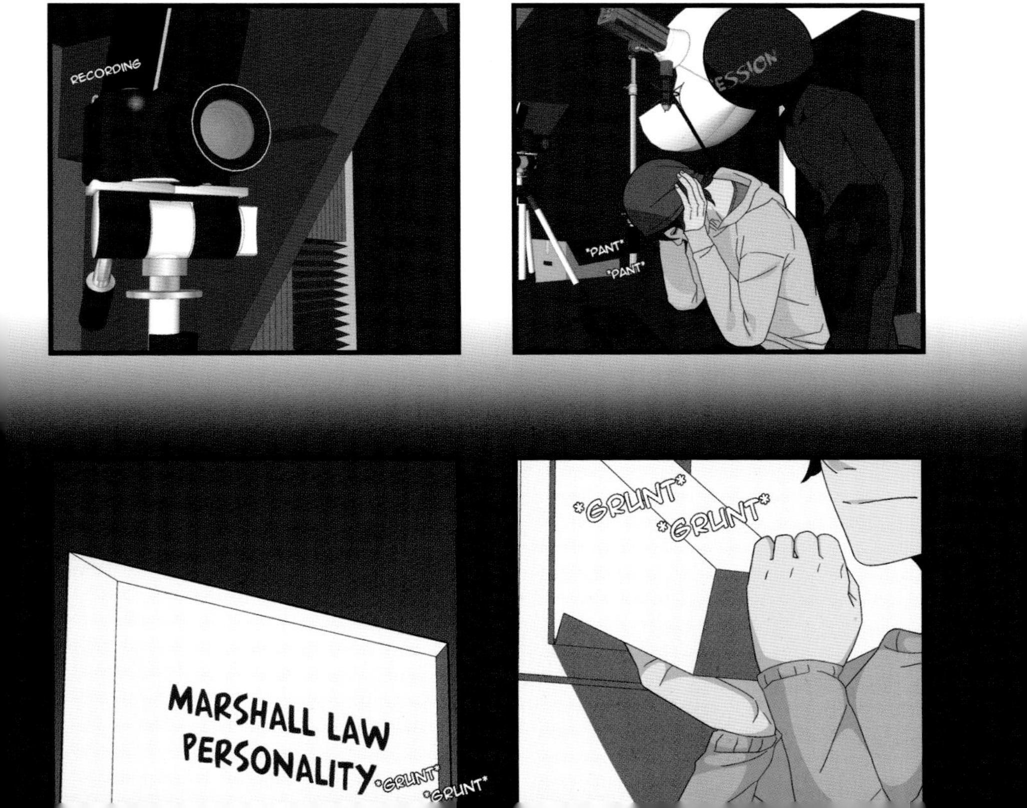
RECORDING
ESSION
PANT
PANT
MARSHALL LAW
PERSONALITY
GRUNT
GRUNT
GRUNT
GRUNT

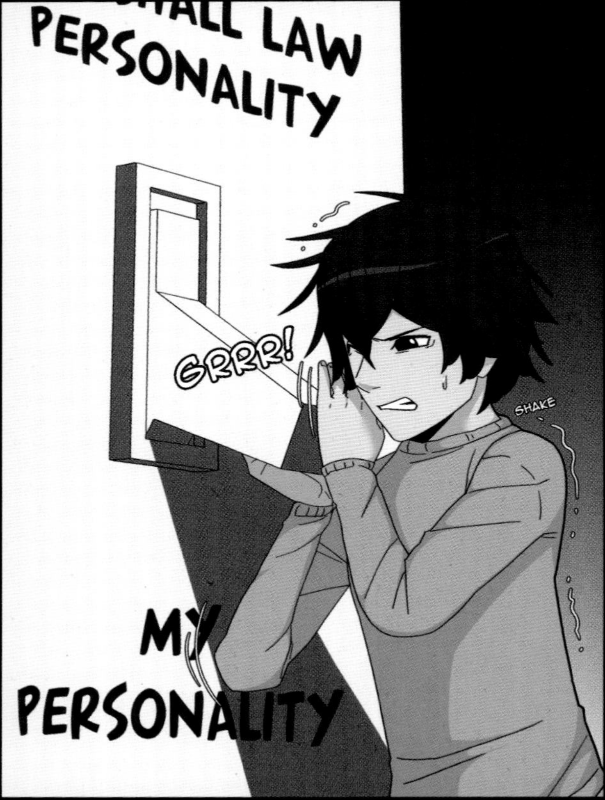
LAW
PERSONALITY
GRRR!
SHAKE
MY
PERSONALITY

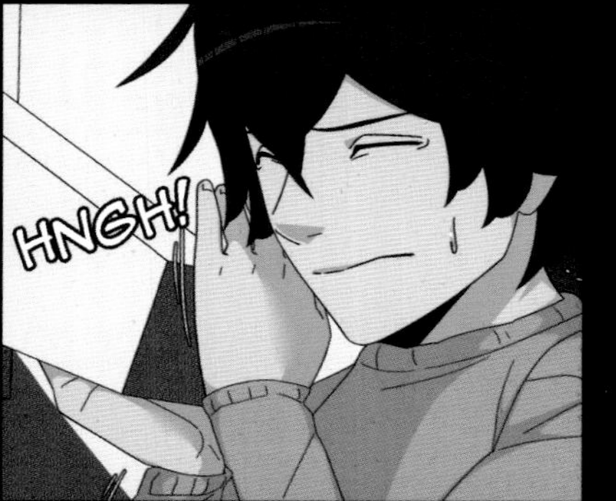
HNGH!

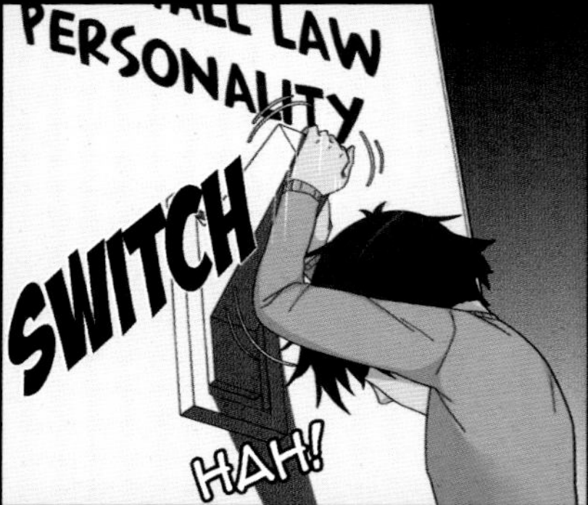
LAW
PERSONALITY
SWITCH
HAH!

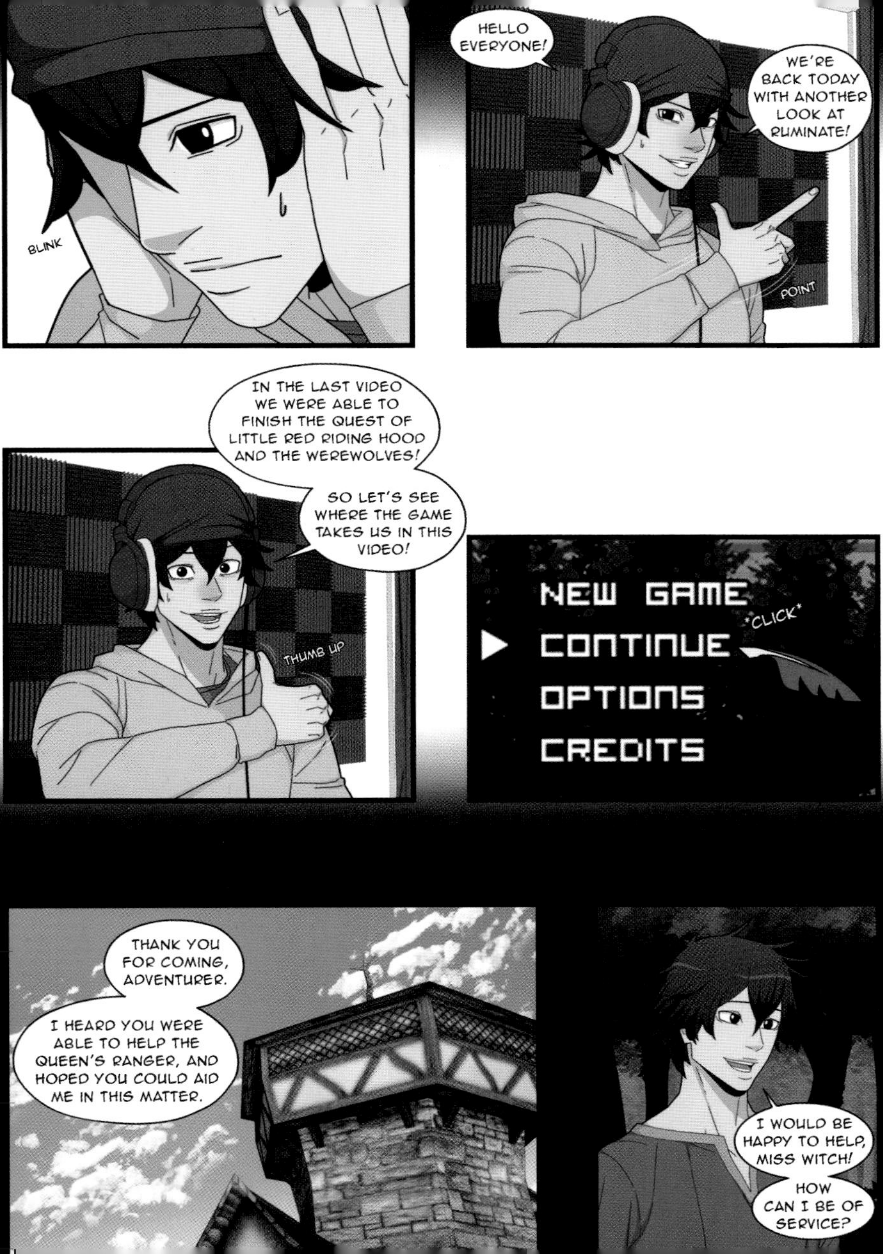
BLINK
HELLO EVERYONE!
WE'RE BACK TODAY WITH ANOTHER LOOK AT RUMINATE!
POINT
IN THE LAST VIDEO WE WERE ABLE TO FINISH THE QUEST OF LITTLE RED RIDING HOOD AND THE WEREWOLVES!
SO LET'S SEE WHERE THE GAME TAKES US IN THIS VIDEO!
THUMB UP
NEW GAME
CONTINUE
CLICK
OPTIONS
CREDITS
THANK YOU FOR COMING, ADVENTURER.
I HEARD YOU WERE ABLE TO HELP THE QUEEN'S RANGER, AND HOPED YOU COULD AID ME IN THIS MATTER.
I WOULD BE HAPPY TO HELP, MISS WITCH!
HOW CAN I BE OF SERVICE?

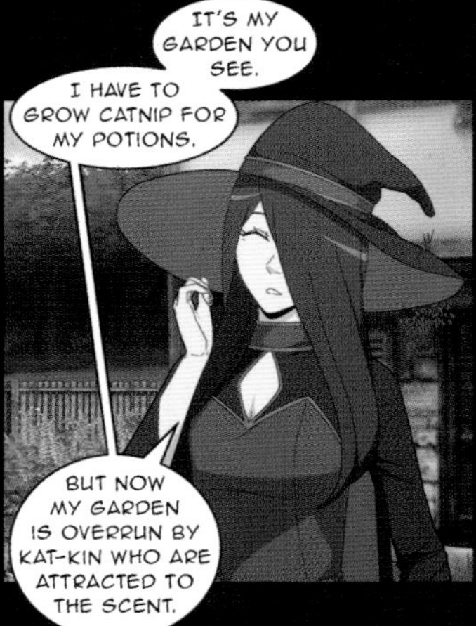
IT'S MY GARDEN YOU SEE.
I HAVE TO GROW CATNIP FOR MY POTIONS.
BUT NOW MY GARDEN IS OVERRUN BY KAT-KIN WHO ARE ATTRACTED TO THE SCENT.

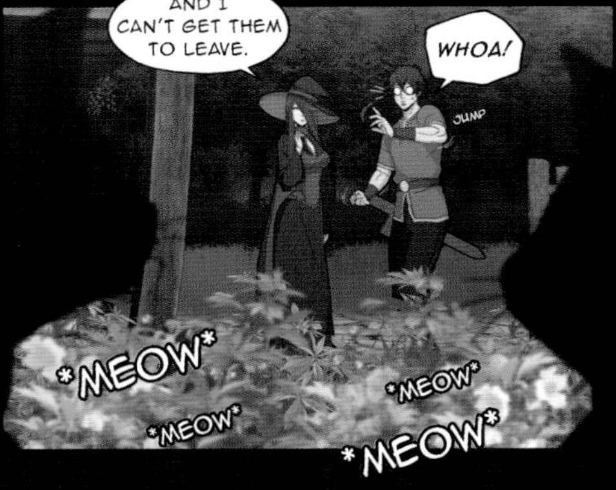
AND I CAN'T GET THEM TO LEAVE.
WHOA!
JUMP
MEOW
MEOW
MEOW
MEOW

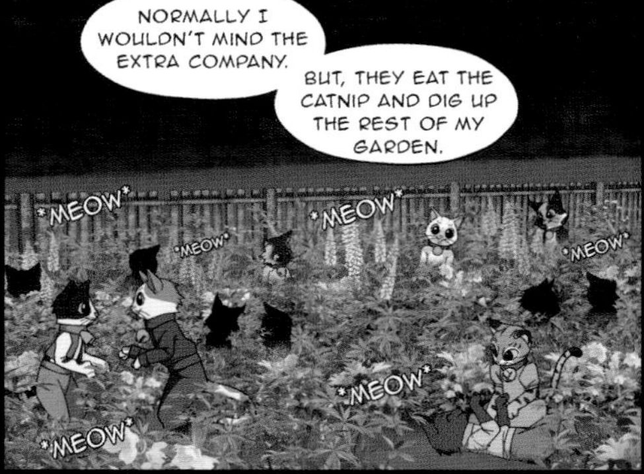
NORMALLY I WOULDN'T MIND THE EXTRA COMPANY.
BUT, THEY EAT THE CATNIP AND DIG UP THE REST OF MY GARDEN.
MEOW
MEOW
MEOW
MEOW
MEOW
MEOW

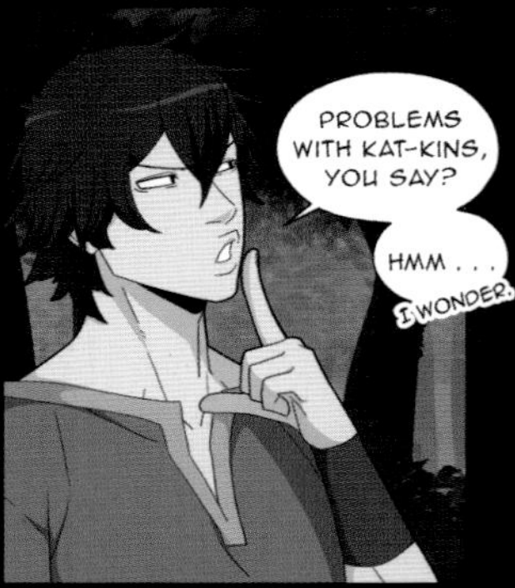
PROBLEMS WITH KAT-KINS, YOU SAY?
HMM . . .
I WONDER.

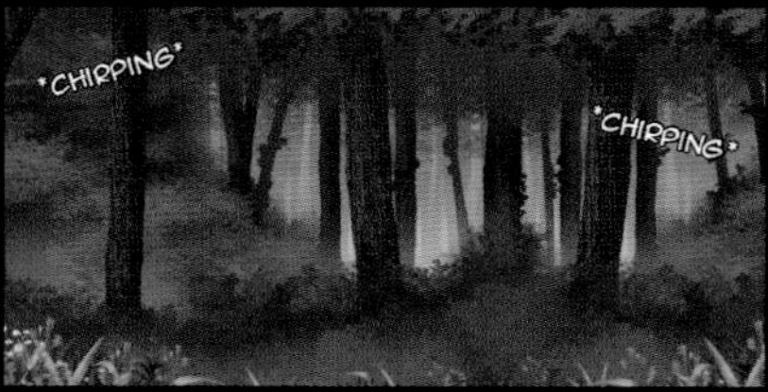
CHIRPING
CHIRPING

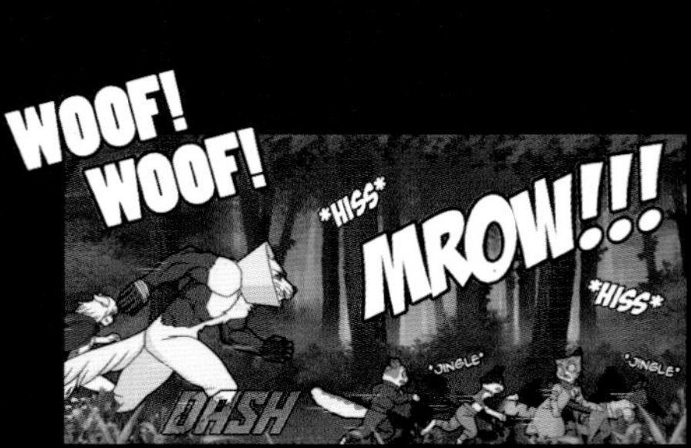
WOOF!
WOOF!
HISS
MROW!!!
HISS
JINGLE
JINGLE
DASH

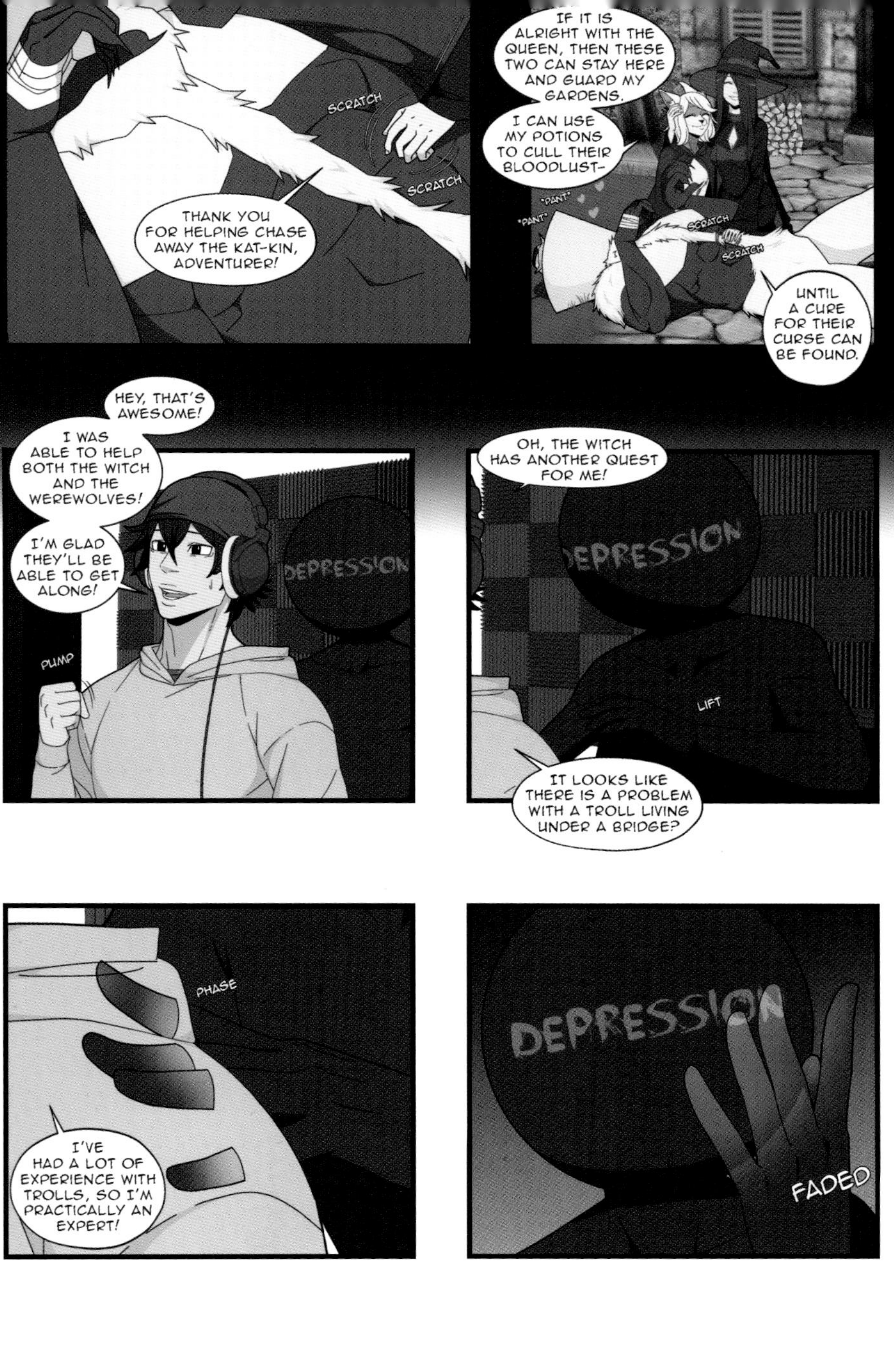
SCRATCH
SCRATCH
THANK YOU FOR HELPING CHASE AWAY THE KAT-KIN, ADVENTURER!
IF IT IS ALRIGHT WITH THE QUEEN, THEN THESE TWO CAN STAY HERE AND GUARD MY GARDENS.
I CAN USE MY POTIONS TO CULL THEIR BLOODLUST-
PANT
PANT
SCRATCH
SCRATCH
UNTIL A CURE FOR THEIR CURSE CAN BE FOUND.
HEY, THAT'S AWESOME!
I WAS ABLE TO HELP BOTH THE WITCH AND THE WEREWOLVES!
I'M GLAD THEY'LL BE ABLE TO GET ALONG!
DEPRESSION
PUMP
OH, THE WITCH HAS ANOTHER QUEST FOR ME!
DEPRESSION
LIFT
IT LOOKS LIKE THERE IS A PROBLEM WITH A TROLL LIVING UNDER A BRIDGE?
PHASE
I'VE HAD A LOT OF EXPERIENCE WITH TROLLS, SO I'M PRACTICALLY AN EXPERT!
DEPRESSION
FADED

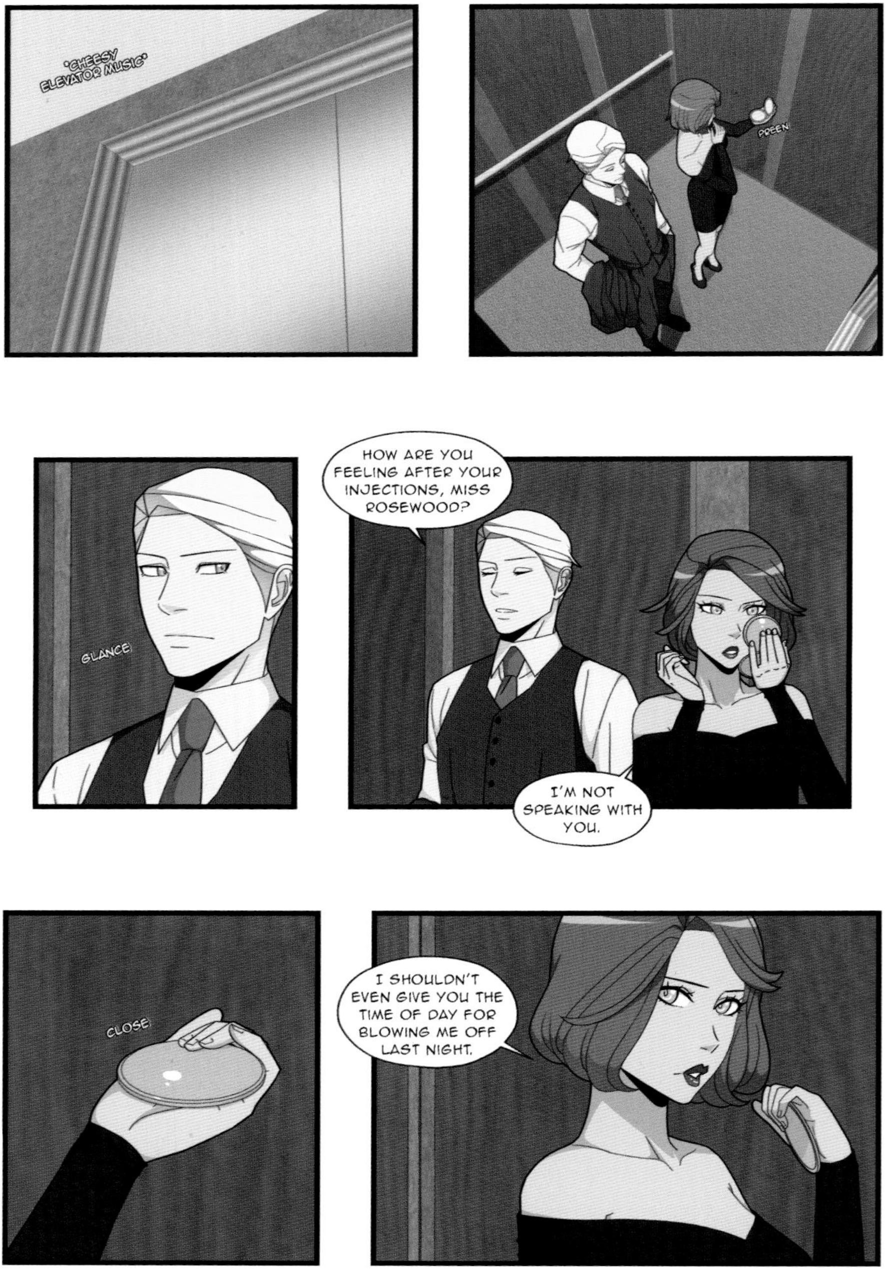
CHEESY ELEVATOR MUSIC
PREEN
GLANCE
HOW ARE YOU FEELING AFTER YOUR INJECTIONS, MISS ROSEWOOD?
I'M NOT SPEAKING WITH YOU.
CLOSE
I SHOULDN'T EVEN GIVE YOU THE TIME OF DAY FOR BLOWING ME OFF LAST NIGHT.

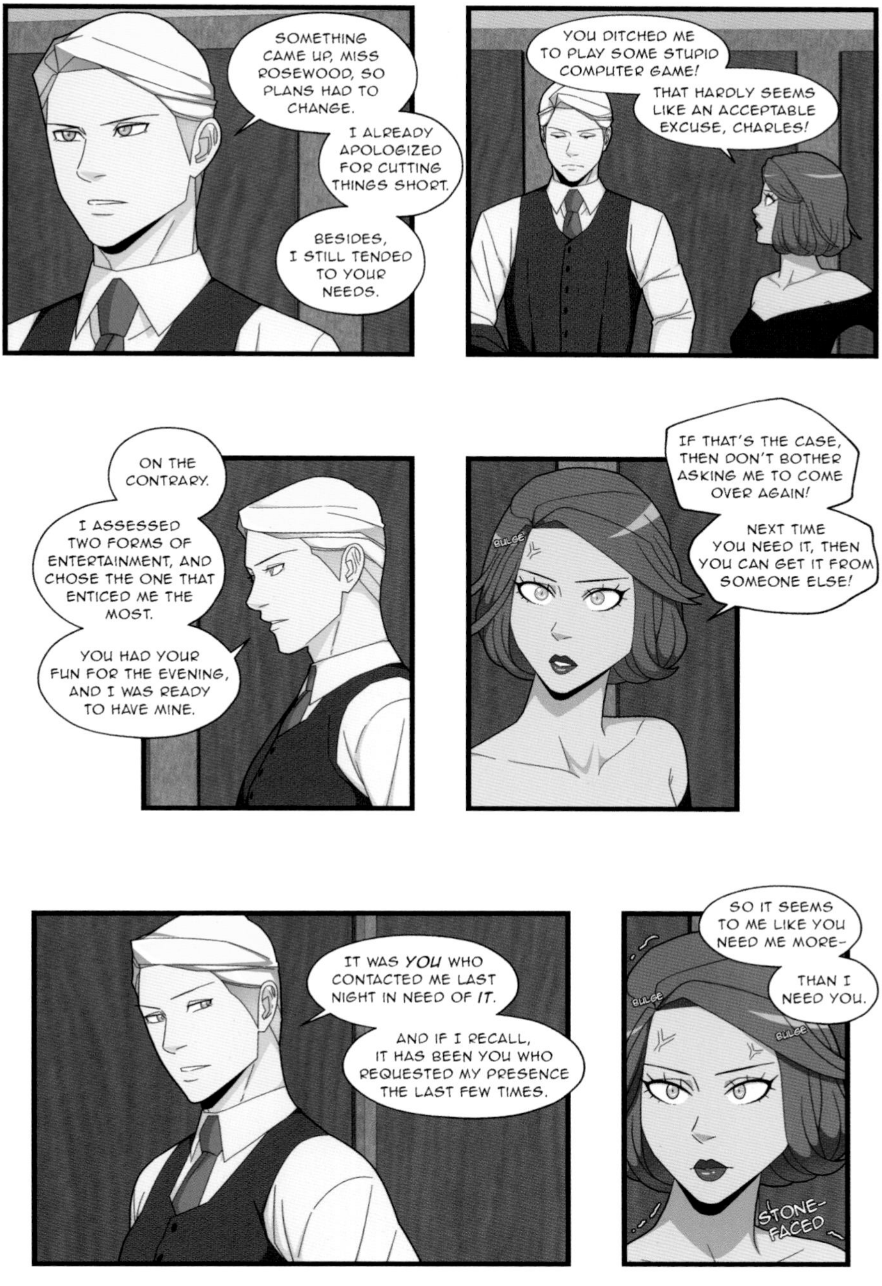
SOMETHING CAME UP, MISS ROSEWOOD, SO PLANS HAD TO CHANGE.
I ALREADY APOLOGIZED FOR CUTTING THINGS SHORT.
BESIDES, I STILL TENDED TO YOUR NEEDS.
YOU DITCHED ME TO PLAY SOME STUPID COMPUTER GAME!
THAT HARDLY SEEMS LIKE AN ACCEPTABLE EXCUSE, CHARLES!
ON THE CONTRARY.
I ASSESSED TWO FORMS OF ENTERTAINMENT, AND CHOSE THE ONE THAT ENTICED ME THE MOST.
YOU HAD YOUR FUN FOR THE EVENING, AND I WAS READY TO HAVE MINE.
BULGE
IF THAT'S THE CASE, THEN DON'T BOTHER ASKING ME TO COME OVER AGAIN!
NEXT TIME YOU NEED IT, THEN YOU CAN GET IT FROM SOMEONE ELSE!
IT WAS *YOU* WHO CONTACTED ME LAST NIGHT IN NEED OF *IT*.
AND IF I RECALL, IT HAS BEEN YOU WHO REQUESTED MY PRESENCE THE LAST FEW TIMES.
SO IT SEEMS TO ME LIKE YOU NEED ME MORE-
THAN I NEED YOU.
BULGE
BULGE
STONE-FACED

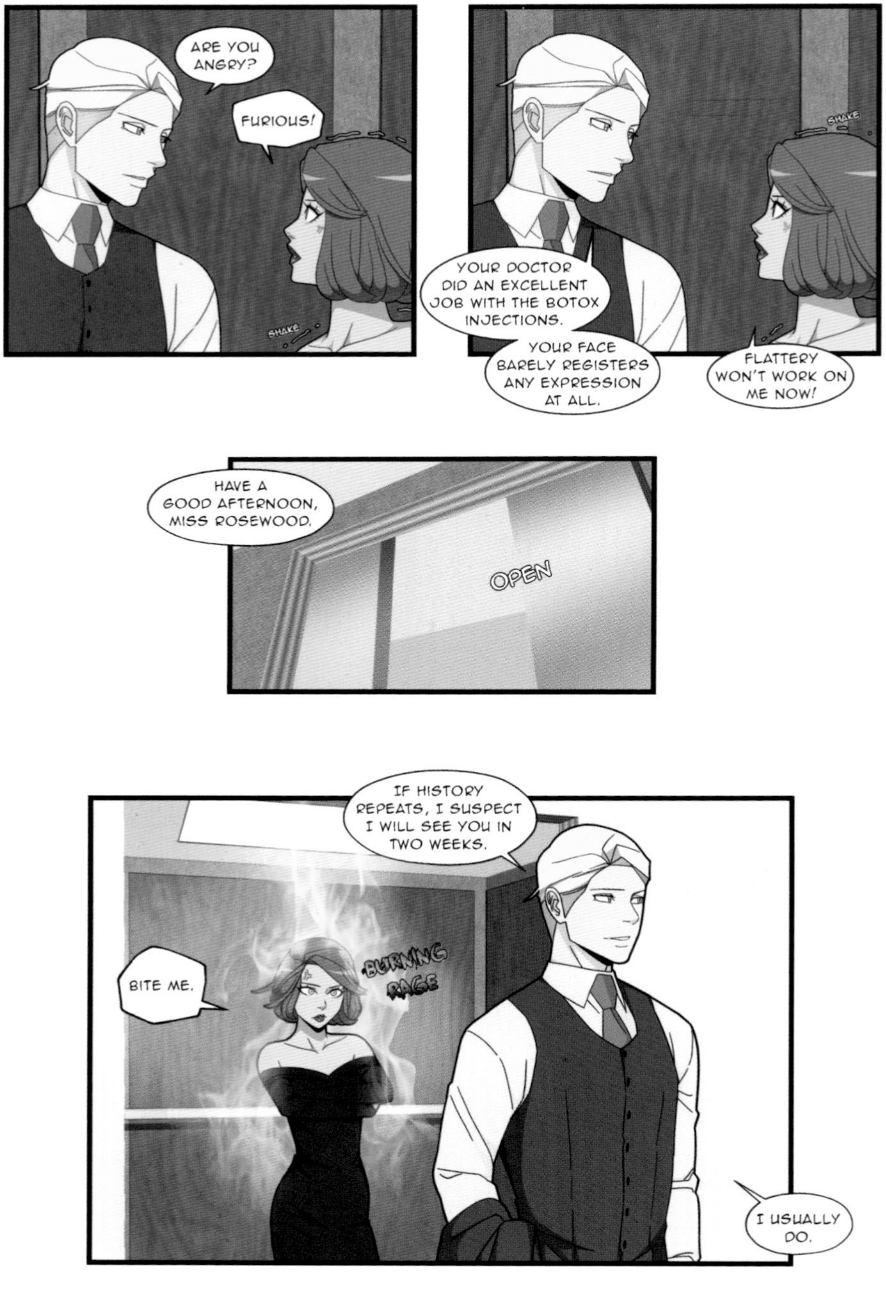
ARE YOU ANGRY?
FURIOUS!
SHAKE
SHAKE
YOUR DOCTOR DID AN EXCELLENT JOB WITH THE BOTOX INJECTIONS.
YOUR FACE BARELY REGISTERS ANY EXPRESSION AT ALL.
FLATTERY WON'T WORK ON ME NOW!
HAVE A GOOD AFTERNOON, MISS ROSEWOOD.
OPEN
IF HISTORY REPEATS, I SUSPECT I WILL SEE YOU IN TWO WEEKS.
BITE ME.
BURNING RAGE
I USUALLY DO.

CHIME

ew you! Why do
ther?

You tell me, Eva.

9:37 PM

Are you free tonight?

9:05 AM

I REALLY DO ATTRACT A LOT OF
DISAGREEABLE PEOPLE, DON'T I?

TUCK

SEEMS AS THOUGH
MY LUCK STILL HASN'T
CHANGED.

ADJUST

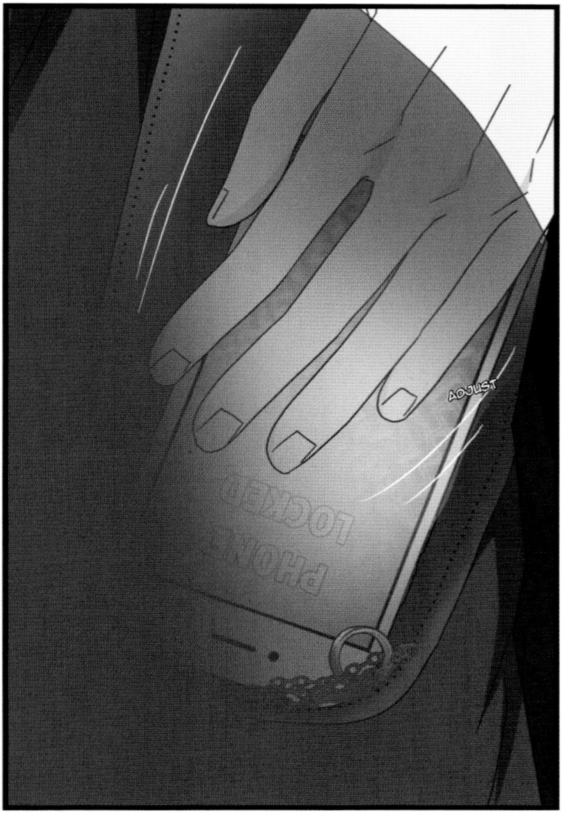
ADJUST

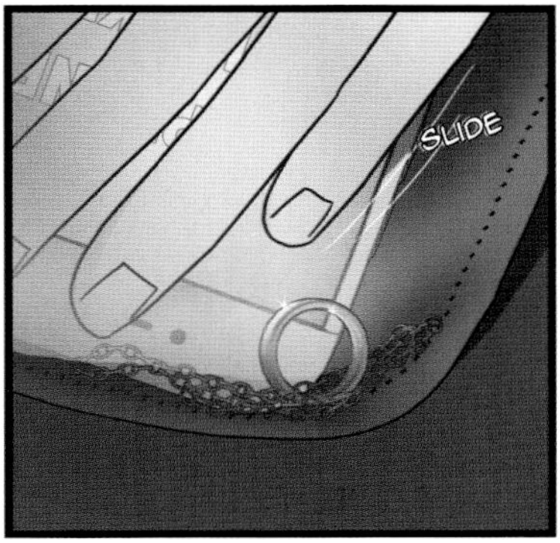
SLIDE

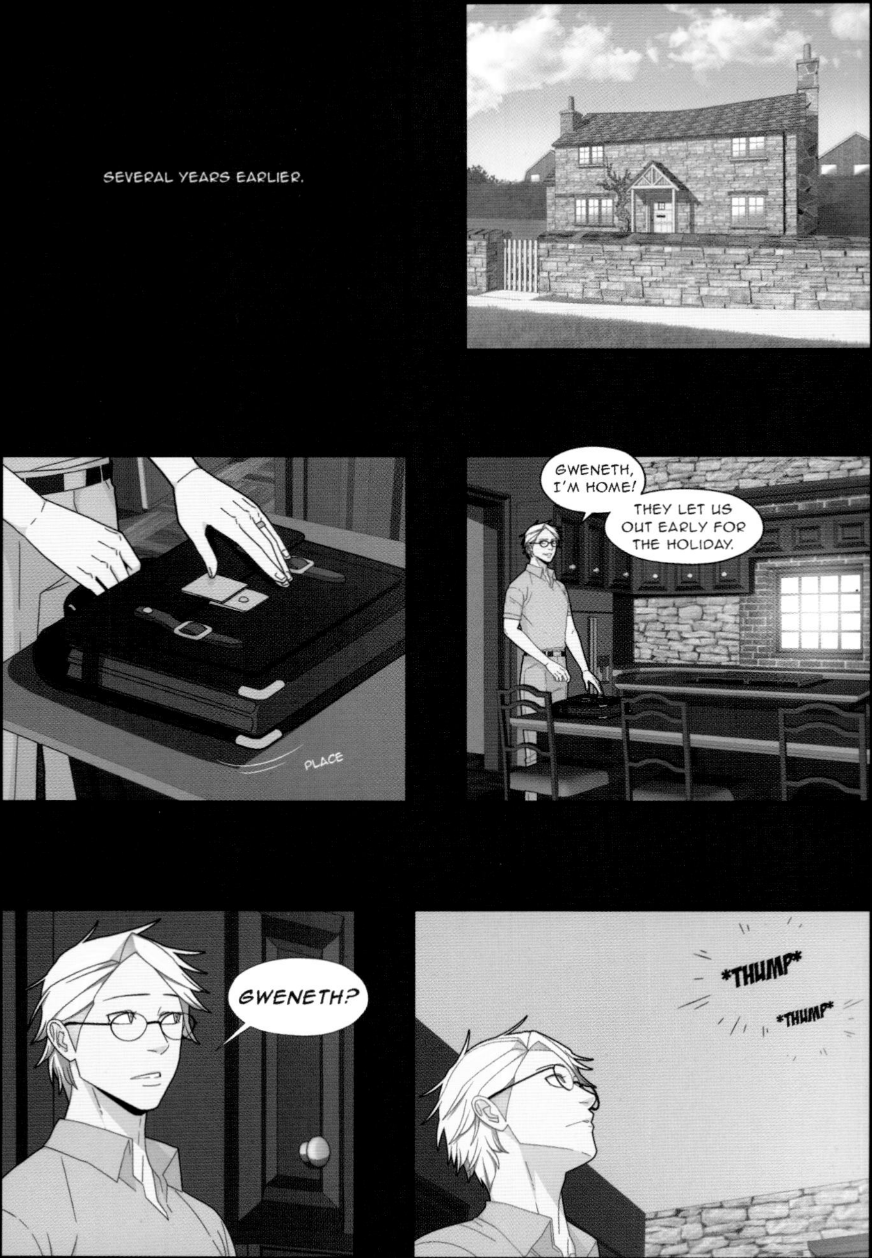
SEVERAL YEARS EARLIER.
PLACE
GWENETH, I'M HOME!
THEY LET US OUT EARLY FOR THE HOLIDAY.
GWENETH?
THUMP
THUMP

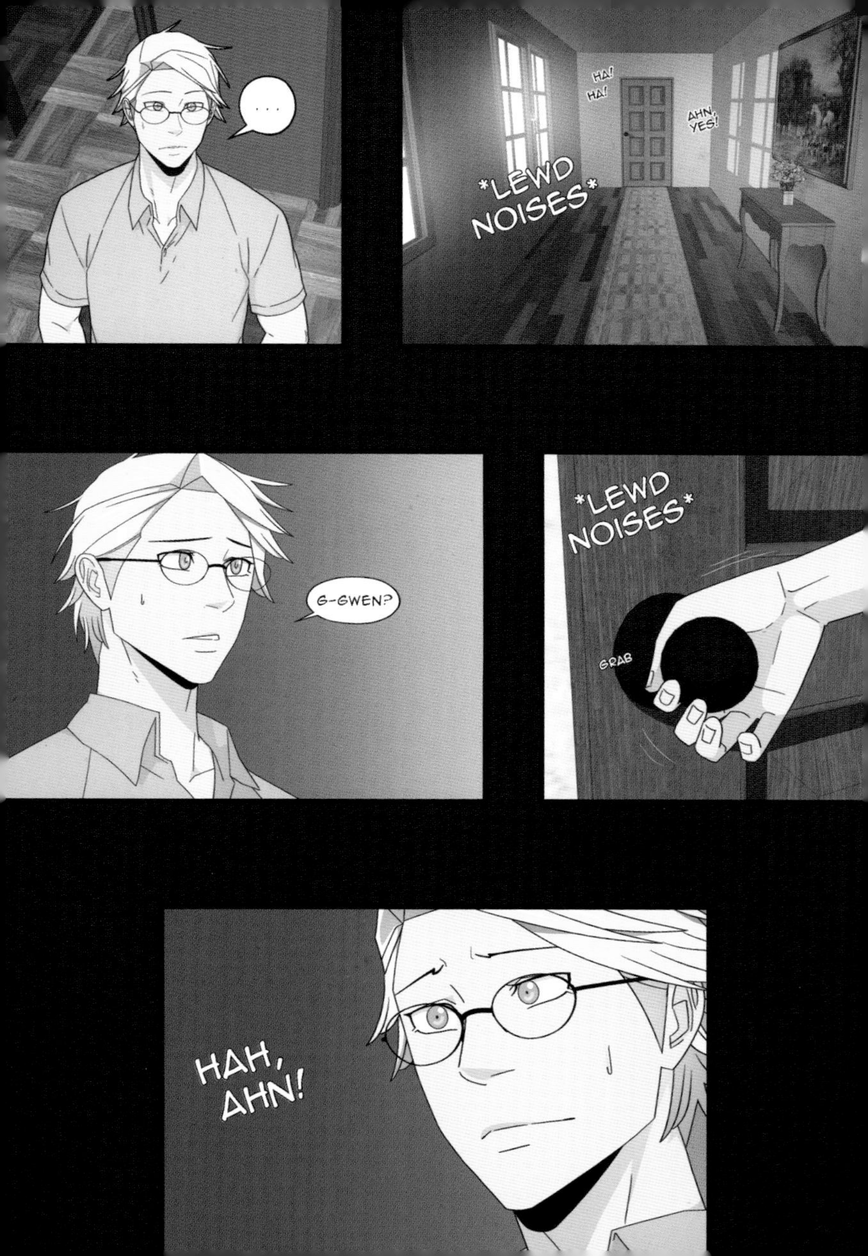
. . .
HA!
HA!
LEWD NOISES
AHN, YES!
G-GWEN?
LEWD NOISES
GRAB
HAH, AHN!

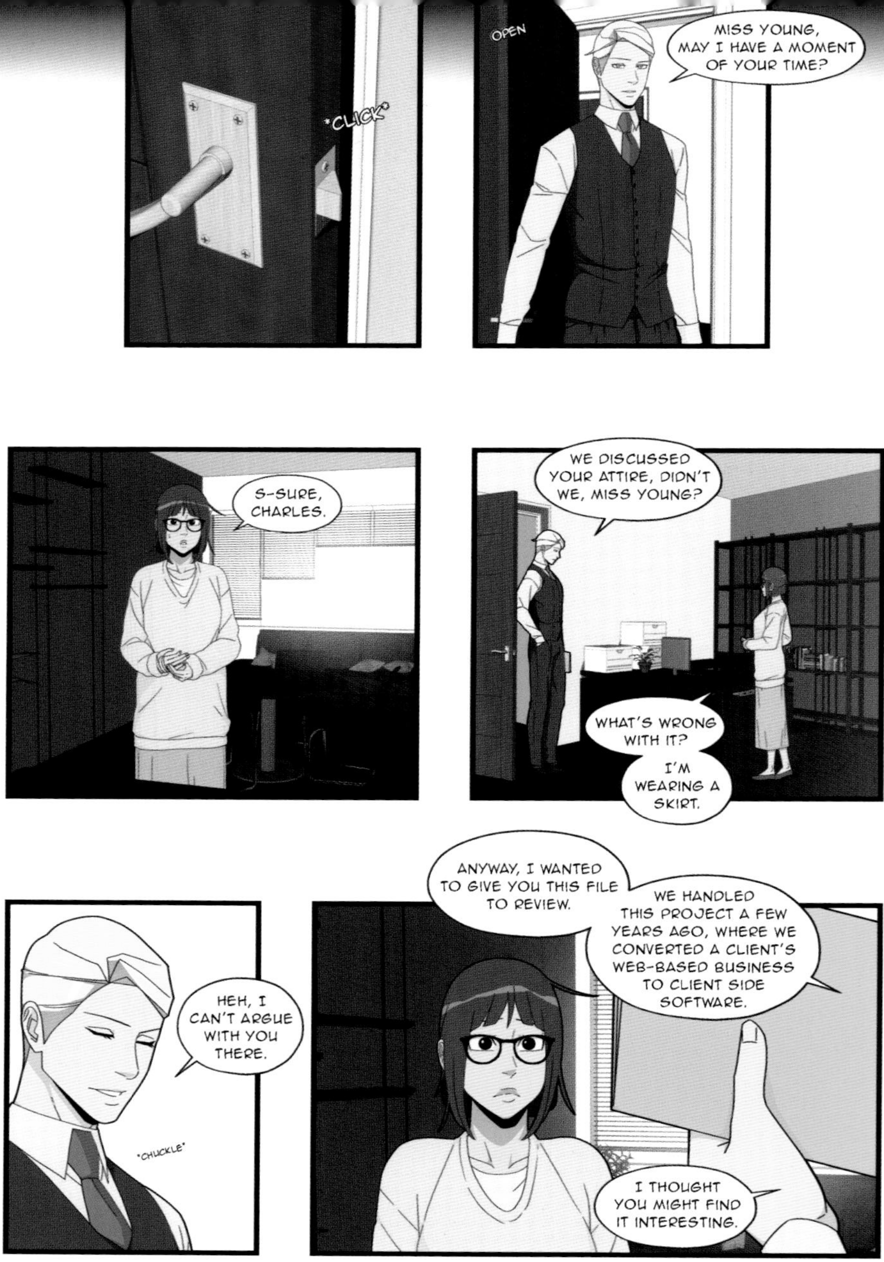
CLICK
OPEN
MISS YOUNG, MAY I HAVE A MOMENT OF YOUR TIME?
S-SURE, CHARLES.
WE DISCUSSED YOUR ATTIRE, DIDN'T WE, MISS YOUNG?
WHAT'S WRONG WITH IT?
I'M WEARING A SKIRT.
HEH, I CAN'T ARGUE WITH YOU THERE.
CHUCKLE
ANYWAY, I WANTED TO GIVE YOU THIS FILE TO REVIEW.
WE HANDLED THIS PROJECT A FEW YEARS AGO, WHERE WE CONVERTED A CLIENT'S WEB-BASED BUSINESS TO CLIENT SIDE SOFTWARE.
I THOUGHT YOU MIGHT FIND IT INTERESTING.

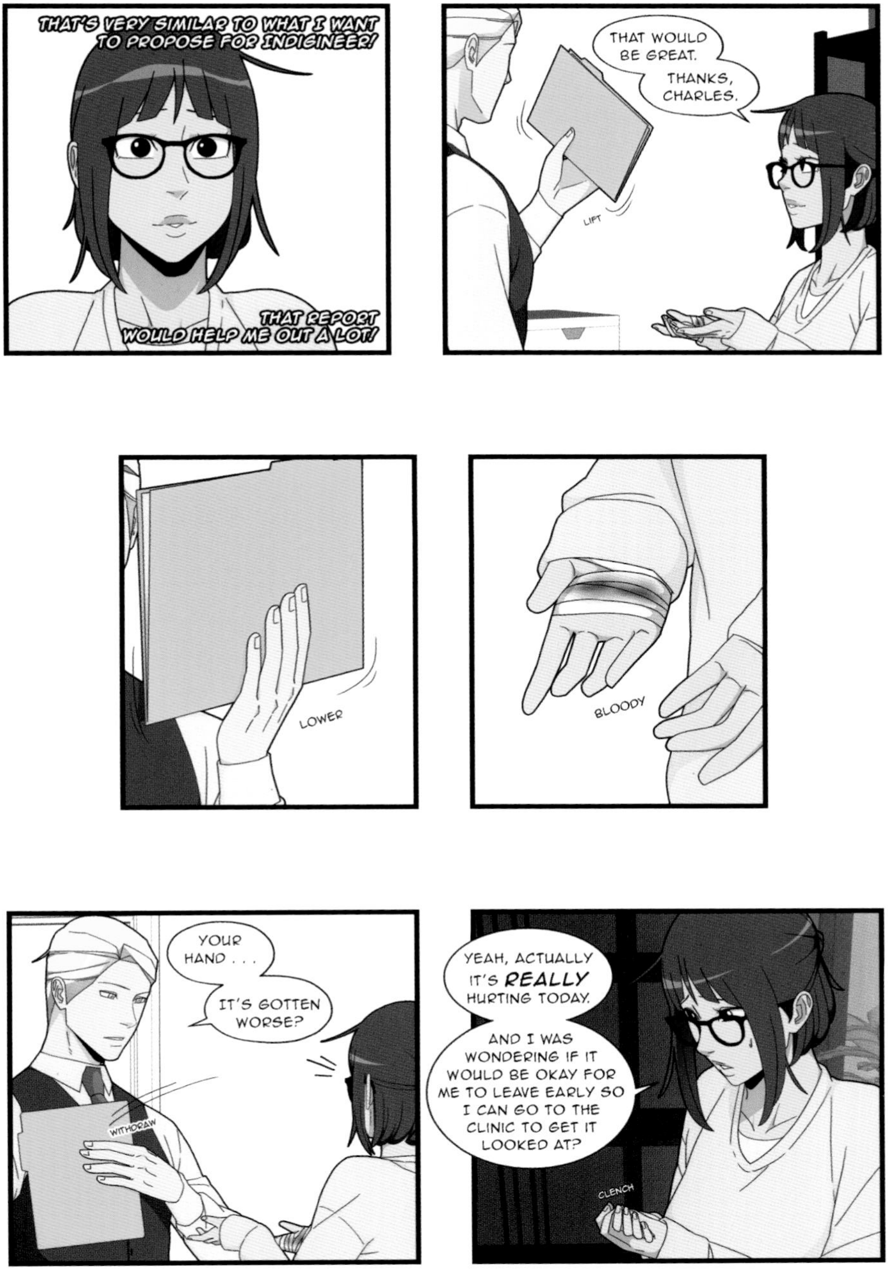
THAT'S VERY SIMILAR TO WHAT I WANT TO PROPOSE FOR INDIGINEER!
THAT REPORT WOULD HELP ME OUT A LOT!
THAT WOULD BE GREAT.
THANKS, CHARLES.
LIFT
LOWER
BLOODY
YOUR HAND . . .
IT'S GOTTEN WORSE?
WITHDRAW
YEAH, ACTUALLY IT'S REALLY HURTING TODAY.
AND I WAS WONDERING IF IT WOULD BE OKAY FOR ME TO LEAVE EARLY SO I CAN GO TO THE CLINIC TO GET IT LOOKED AT?
CLENCH

IF I LEAVE NOW, I SHOULD BE ABLE TO CATCH THE BUS.

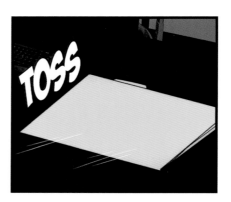

GET YOUR THINGS TOGETHER, MISS YOUNG.

I WILL TAKE YOU THERE MYSELF.

CHARLES, YOU DON'T HAVE TO DO THAT!

I DON'T MIND TAKING THE BUS!

IT'S NO TROUBLE.

BESIDES, I DON'T LIKE THE IDEA OF YOU RIDING THE BUS ANYWAY.

GET READY TO LEAVE AND I'LL INFORM LUCY WE'LL BE UNAVAILABLE.

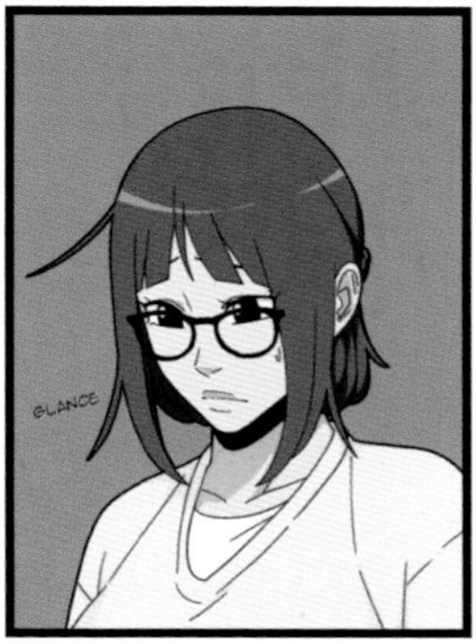
GLANCE

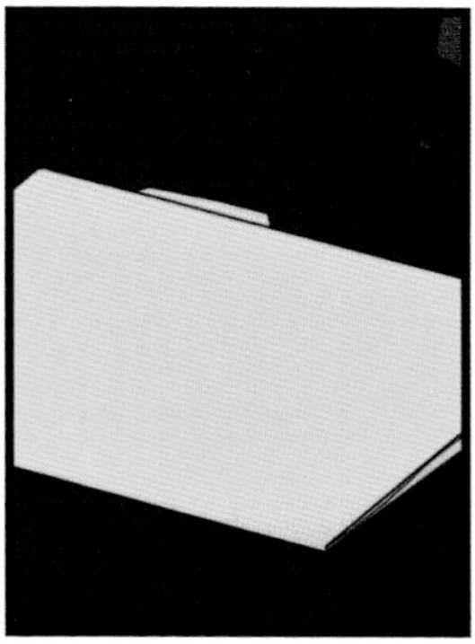

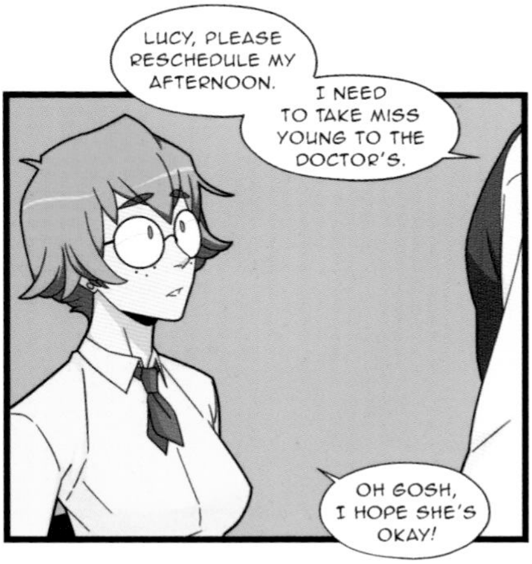
LUCY, PLEASE RESCHEDULE MY AFTERNOON.
I NEED TO TAKE MISS YOUNG TO THE DOCTOR'S.
OH GOSH, I HOPE SHE'S OKAY!

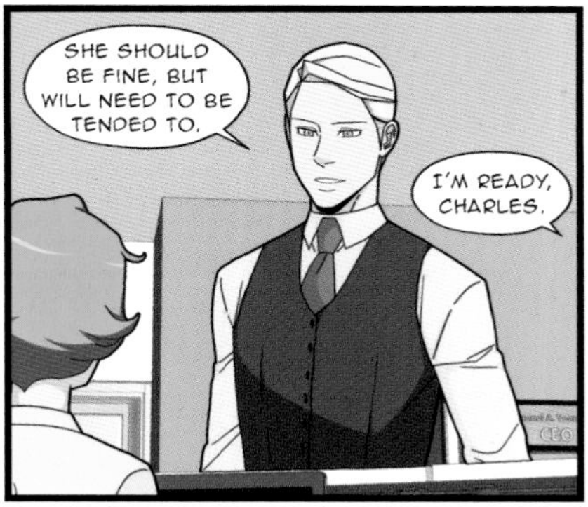
SHE SHOULD BE FINE, BUT WILL NEED TO BE TENDED TO.
I'M READY, CHARLES.

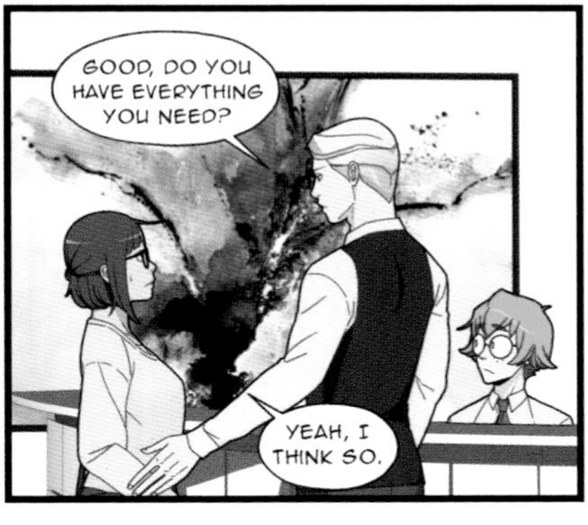
GOOD, DO YOU HAVE EVERYTHING YOU NEED?
YEAH, I THINK SO.

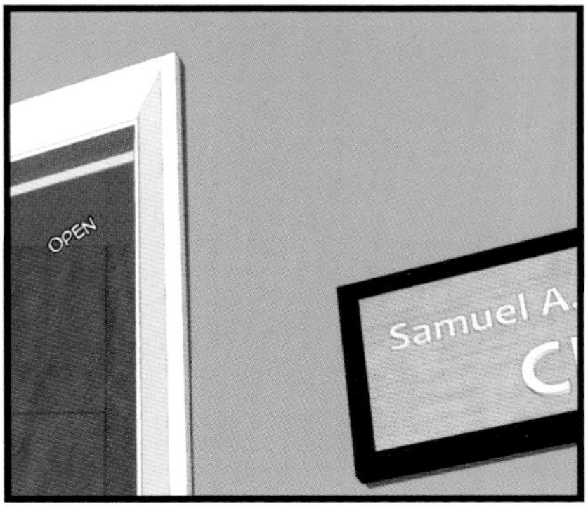
OPEN
Samuel A.

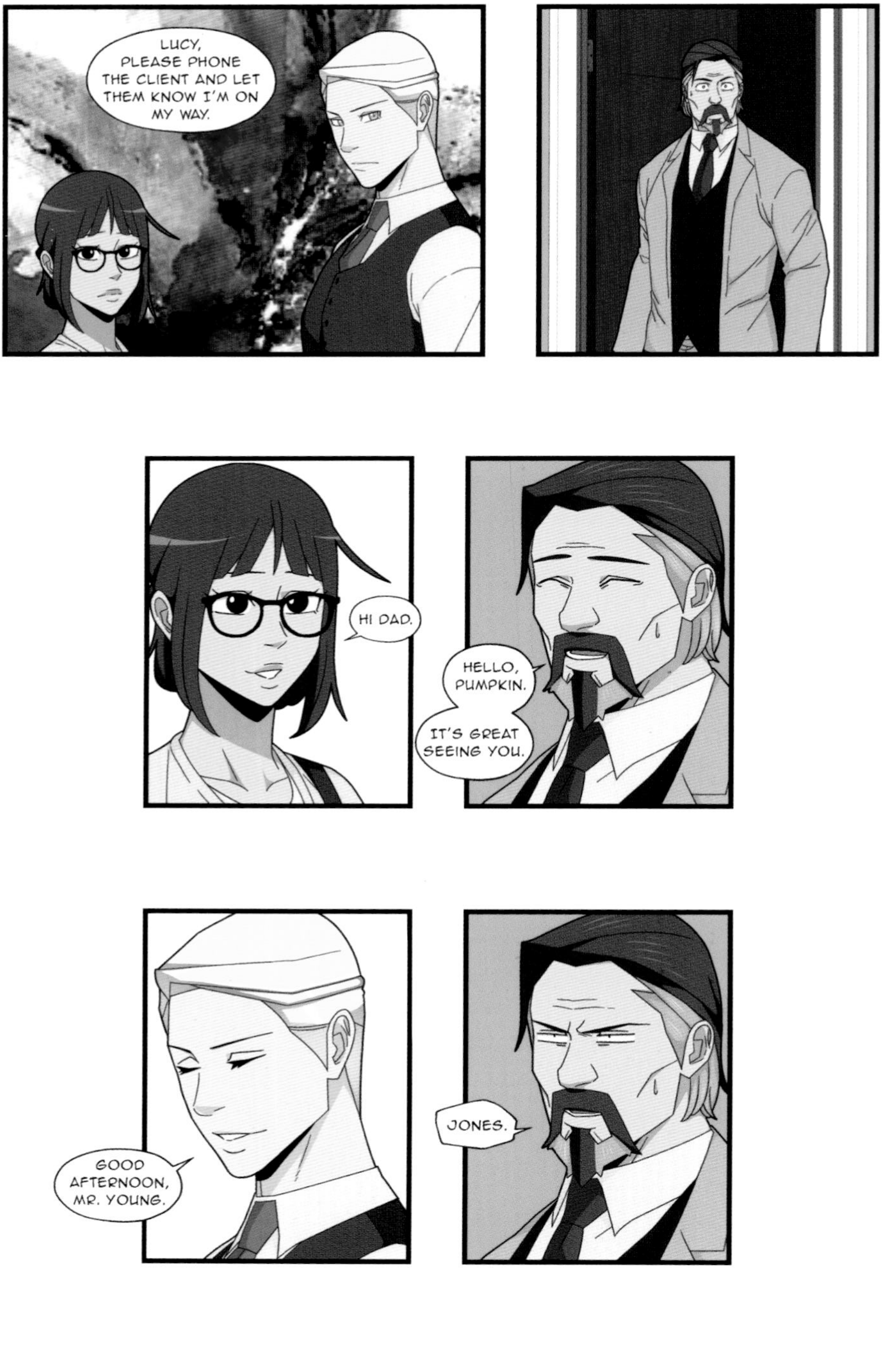
LUCY, PLEASE PHONE THE CLIENT AND LET THEM KNOW I'M ON MY WAY.
HI DAD.
HELLO, PUMPKIN.
IT'S GREAT SEEING YOU.
GOOD AFTERNOON, MR. YOUNG.
JONES.

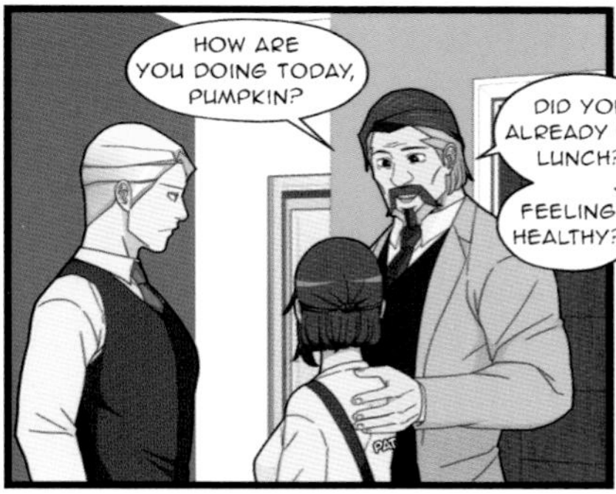
HOW ARE YOU DOING TODAY, PUMPKIN?
DID YOU ALREADY EAT LUNCH?
FEELING HEALTHY?
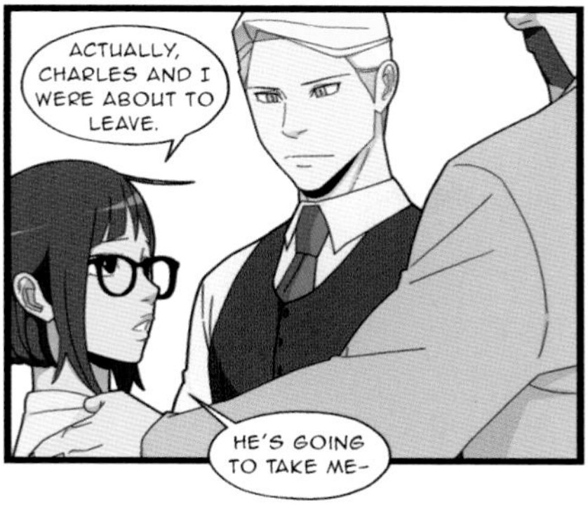
ACTUALLY, CHARLES AND I WERE ABOUT TO LEAVE.
HE'S GOING TO TAKE ME-
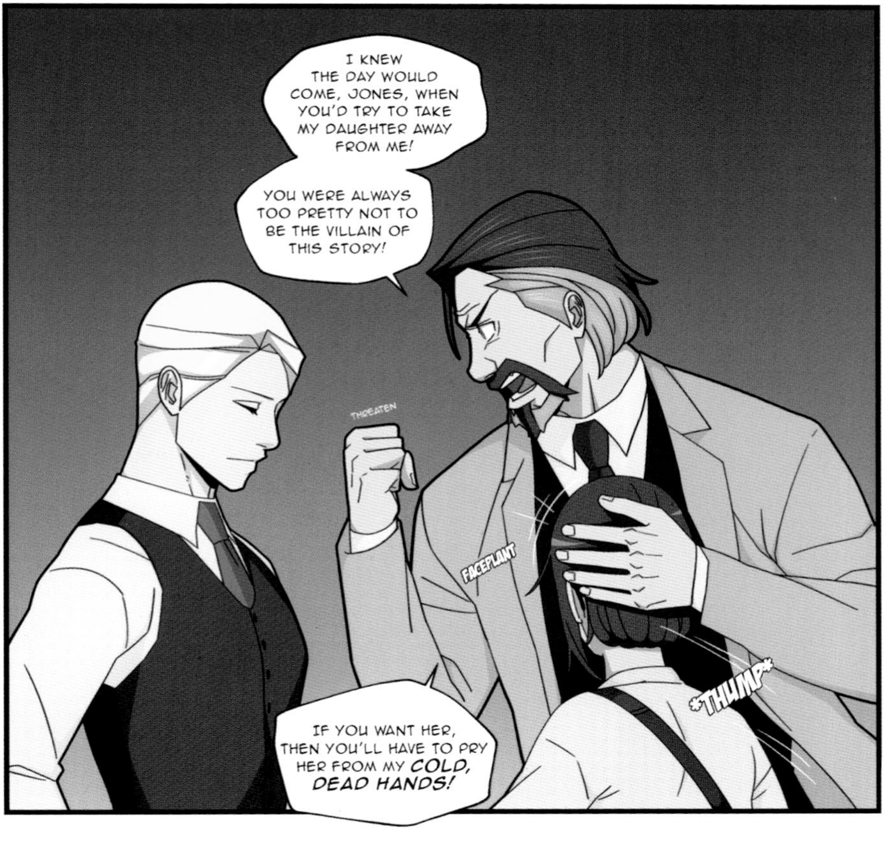
I KNEW THE DAY WOULD COME, JONES, WHEN YOU'D TRY TO TAKE MY DAUGHTER AWAY FROM ME!
YOU WERE ALWAYS TOO PRETTY NOT TO BE THE VILLAIN OF THIS STORY!
THREATEN
FACEPLANT
THUMP
IF YOU WANT HER, THEN YOU'LL HAVE TO PRY HER FROM MY *COLD, DEAD HANDS!*

PUSH

DAD, THAT'S NOT WHAT'S HAPPENING!

DON'T BE RIDICULOUS!

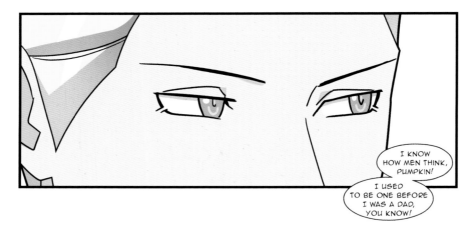

I KNOW HOW MEN THINK, PUMPKIN!

I USED TO BE ONE BEFORE I WAS A DAD, YOU KNOW!

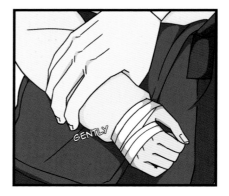

GENTLY

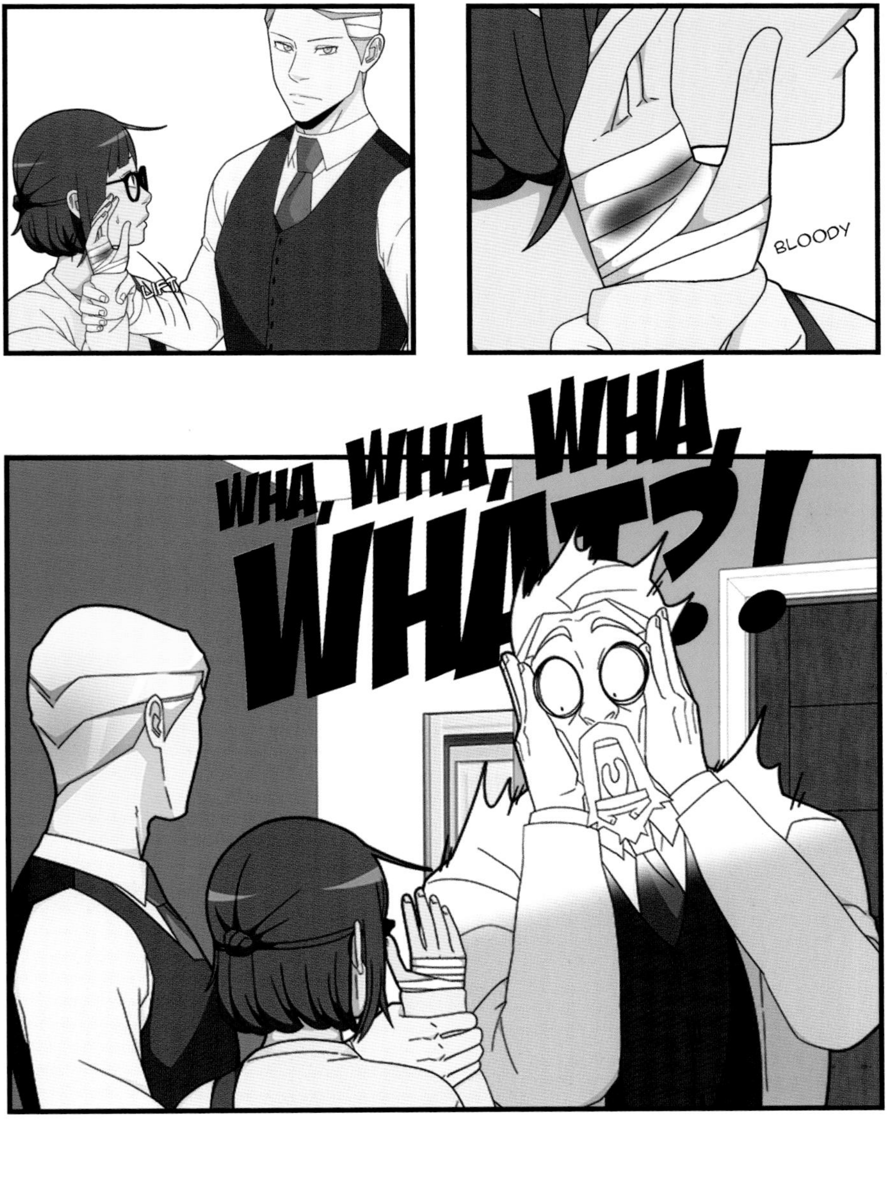
LIFT
BLOODY
WHA, WHA, WHA, WHAT?!

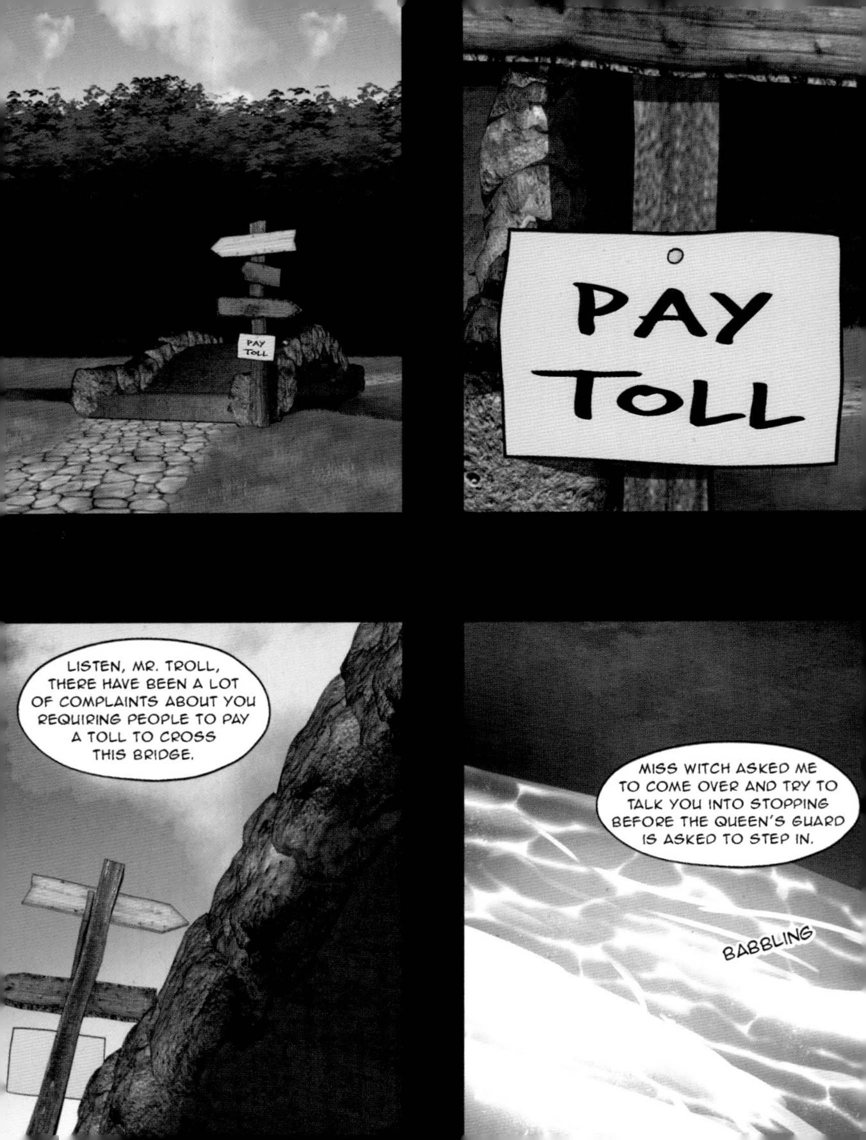
PAY TOLL
PAY TOLL
LISTEN, MR. TROLL, THERE HAVE BEEN A LOT OF COMPLAINTS ABOUT YOU REQUIRING PEOPLE TO PAY A TOLL TO CROSS THIS BRIDGE.
MISS WITCH ASKED ME TO COME OVER AND TRY TO TALK YOU INTO STOPPING BEFORE THE QUEEN'S GUARD IS ASKED TO STEP IN.
BABBLING

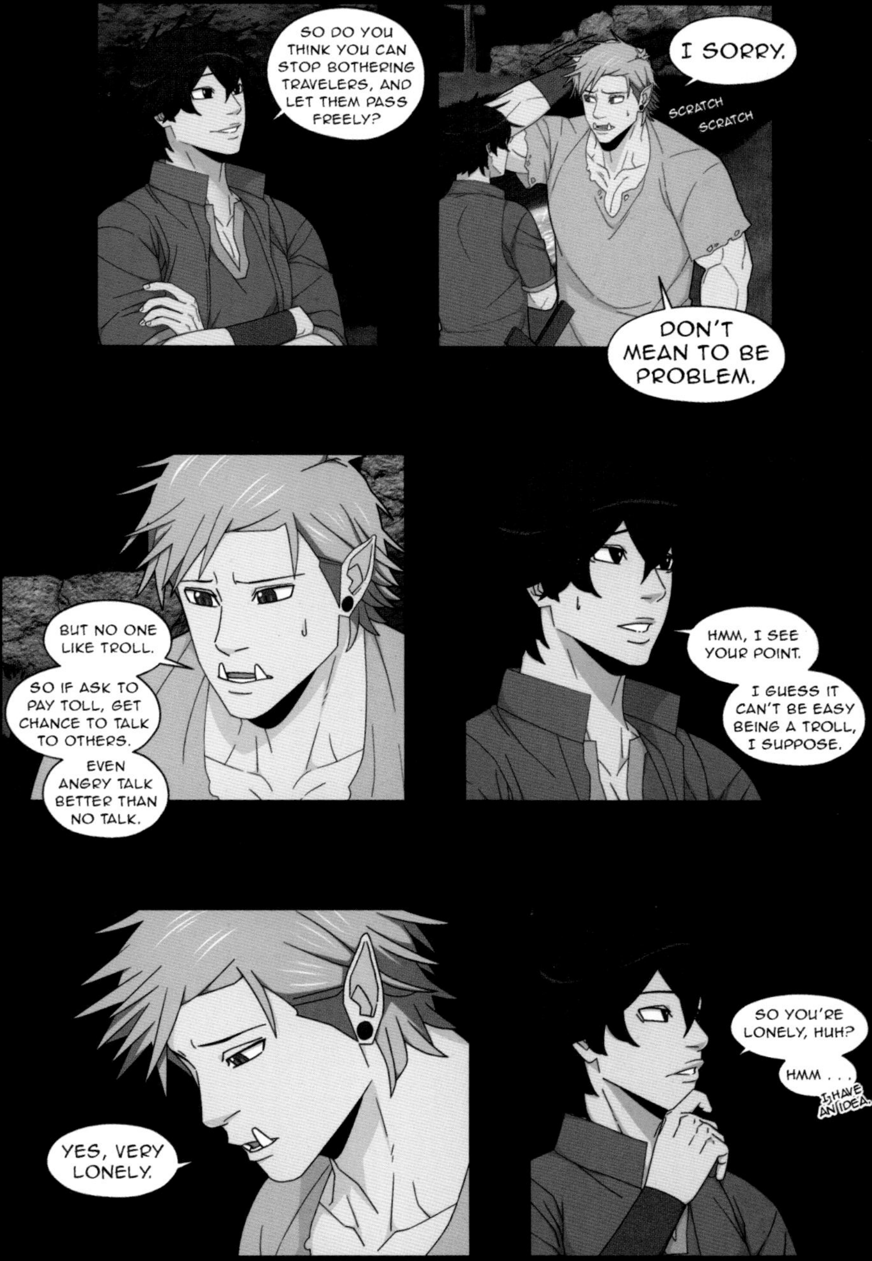
SO DO YOU THINK YOU CAN STOP BOTHERING TRAVELERS, AND LET THEM PASS FREELY?
I SORRY.
SCRATCH
SCRATCH
DON'T MEAN TO BE PROBLEM.
BUT NO ONE LIKE TROLL.
SO IF ASK TO PAY TOLL, GET CHANCE TO TALK TO OTHERS.
EVEN ANGRY TALK BETTER THAN NO TALK.
HMM, I SEE YOUR POINT.
I GUESS IT CAN'T BE EASY BEING A TROLL, I SUPPOSE.
YES, VERY LONELY.
SO YOU'RE LONELY, HUH?
HMM . . .
I HAVE AN IDEA.

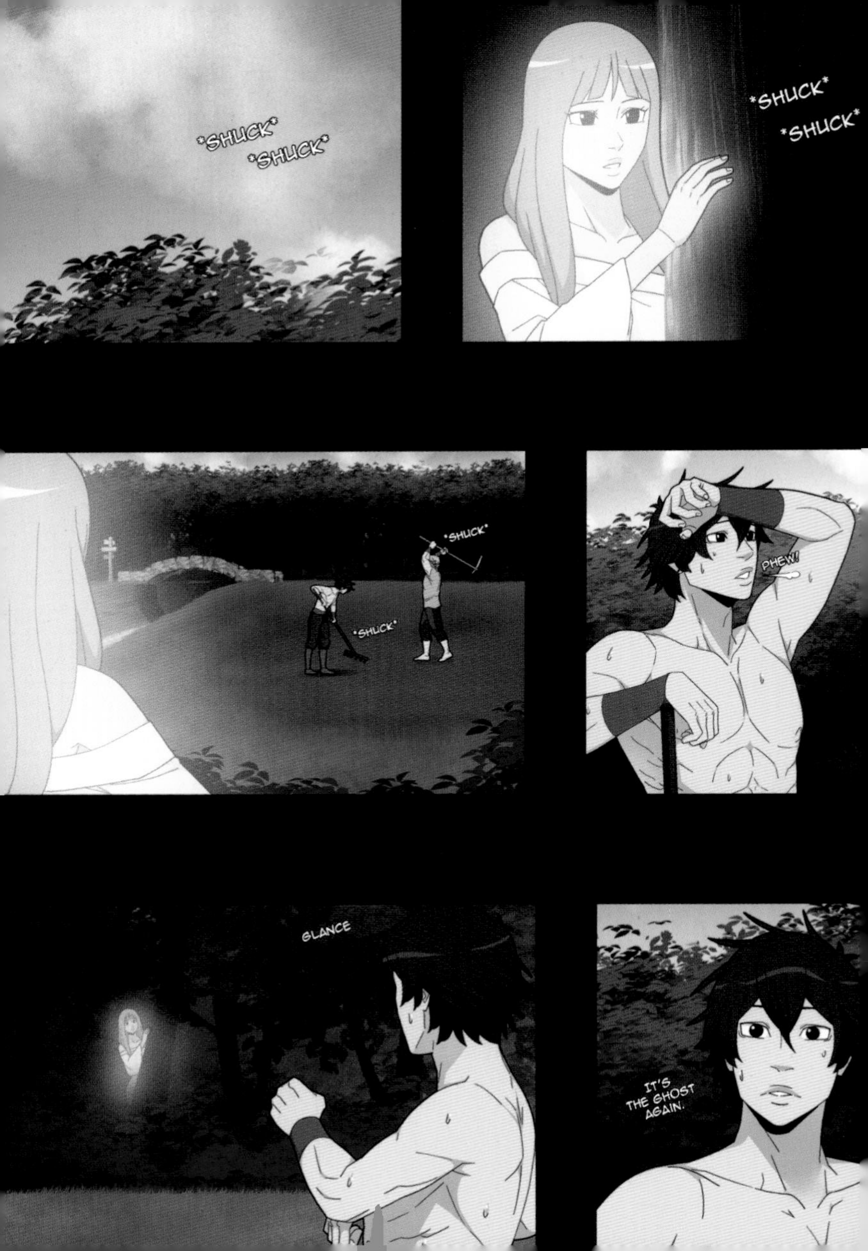
SHUCK
SHUCK
SHUCK
SHUCK
SHUCK
SHUCK
PHEW!
GLANCE
IT'S THE GHOST AGAIN.

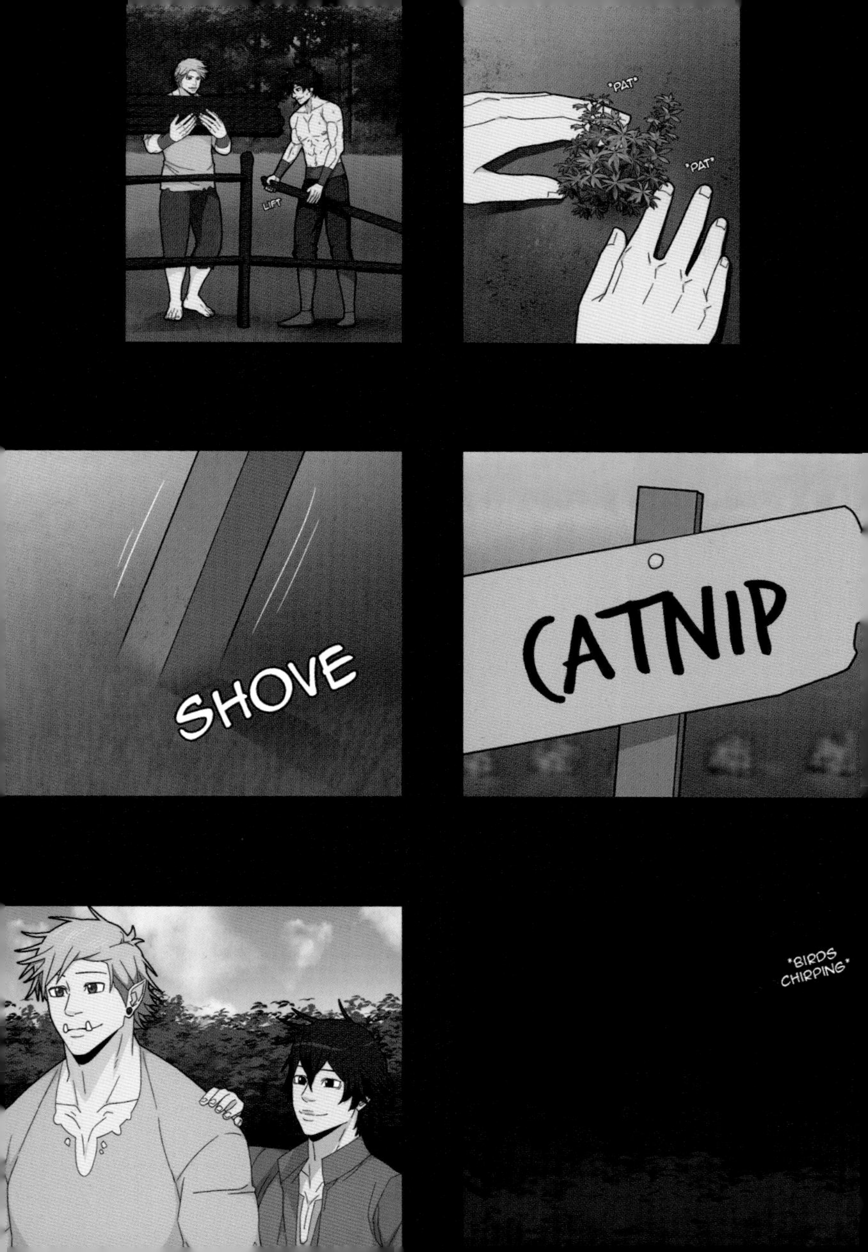
LIFT
PAT
PAT
SHOVE
CATNIP
BIRDS CHIRPING

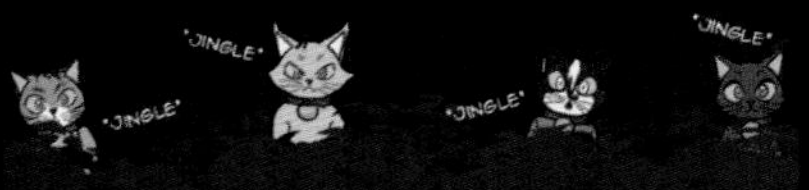
JINGLE
JINGLE
JINGLE
JINGLE

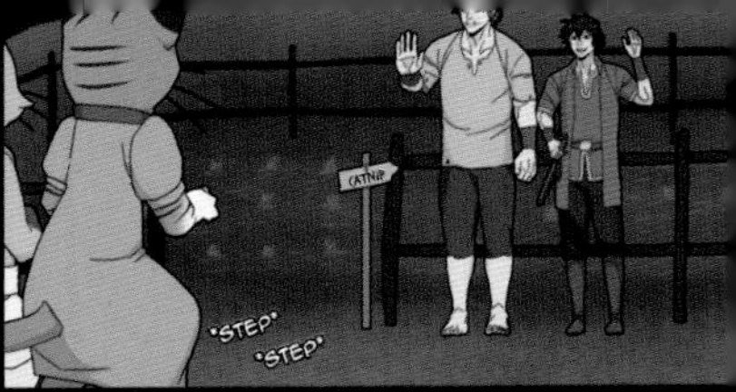
STEP
STEP

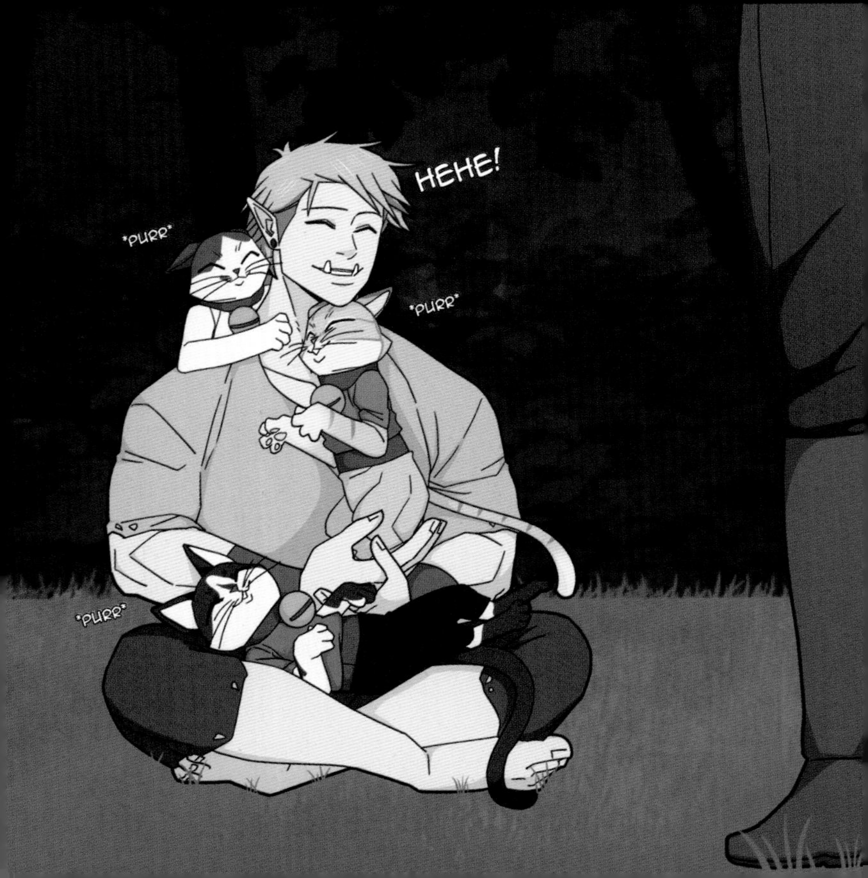
HEHE!
PURR
PURR
PURR

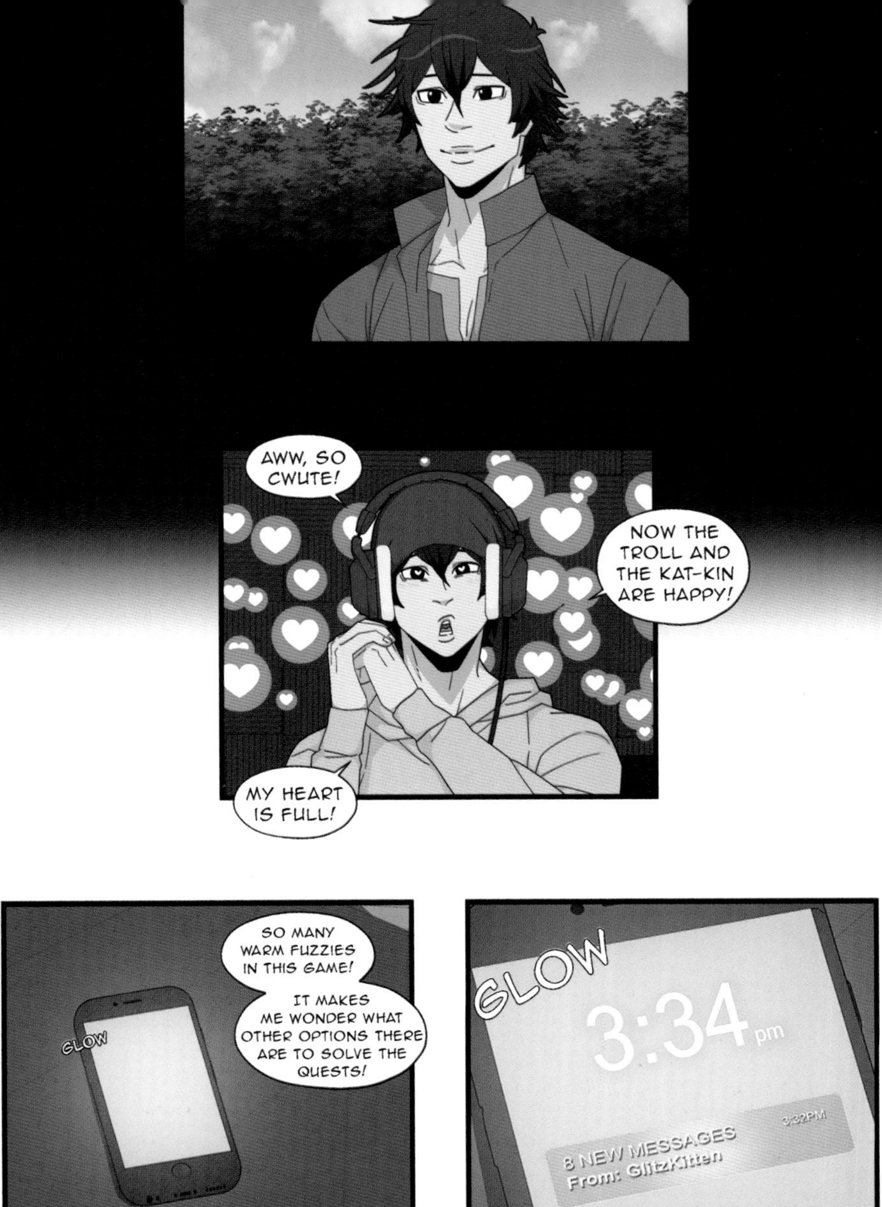
AWW, SO CWUTE!
NOW THE TROLL AND THE KAT-KIN ARE HAPPY!
MY HEART IS FULL!
GLOW
SO MANY WARM FUZZIES IN THIS GAME!
IT MAKES ME WONDER WHAT OTHER OPTIONS THERE ARE TO SOLVE THE QUESTS!
GLOW
3:34 pm
8 NEW MESSAGES
From: GlitzKitten
3:32PM

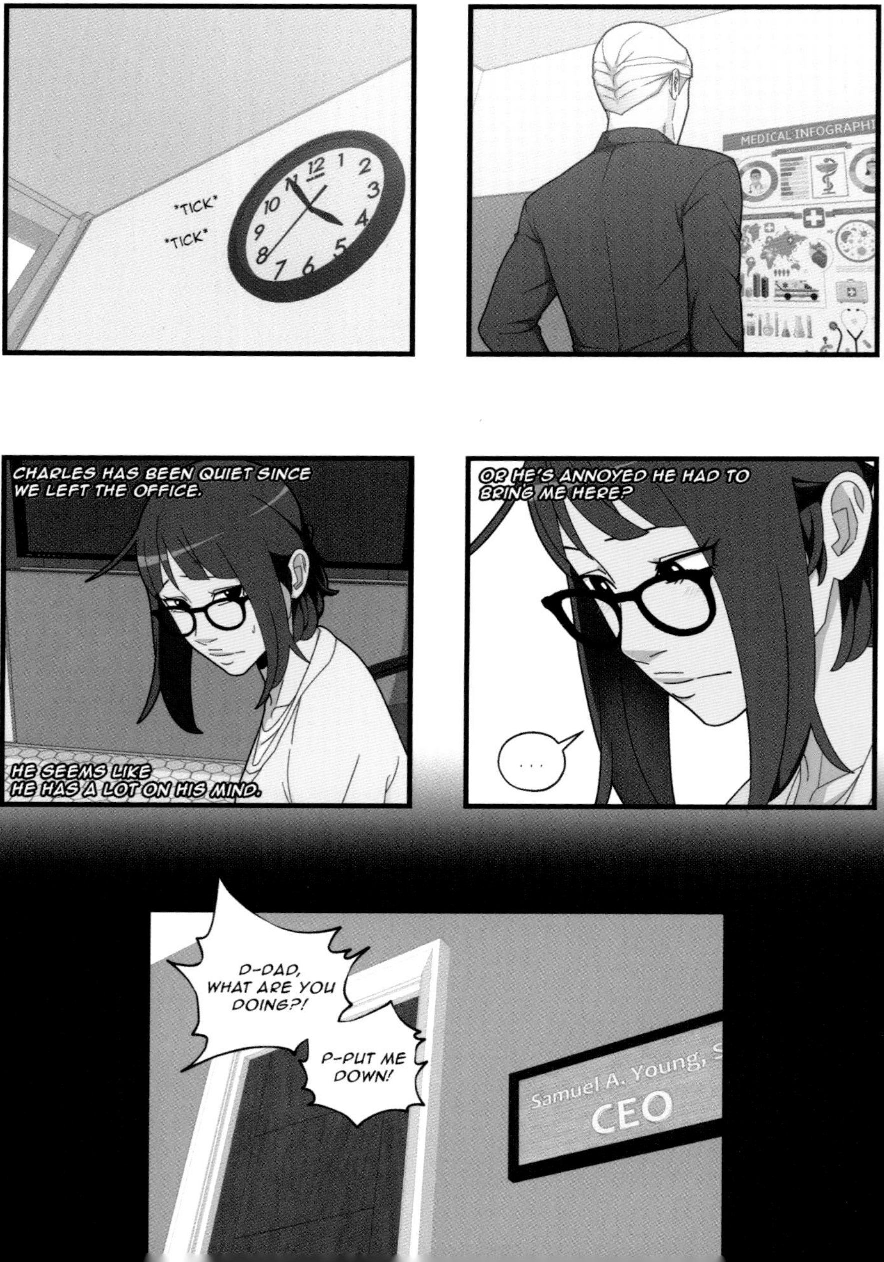
TICK
TICK
CHARLES HAS BEEN QUIET SINCE WE LEFT THE OFFICE.
HE SEEMS LIKE HE HAS A LOT ON HIS MIND.
OR HE'S ANNOYED HE HAD TO BRING ME HERE?
. . .
D-DAD, WHAT ARE YOU DOING?!
P-PUT ME DOWN!
Samuel A. Young,
CEO

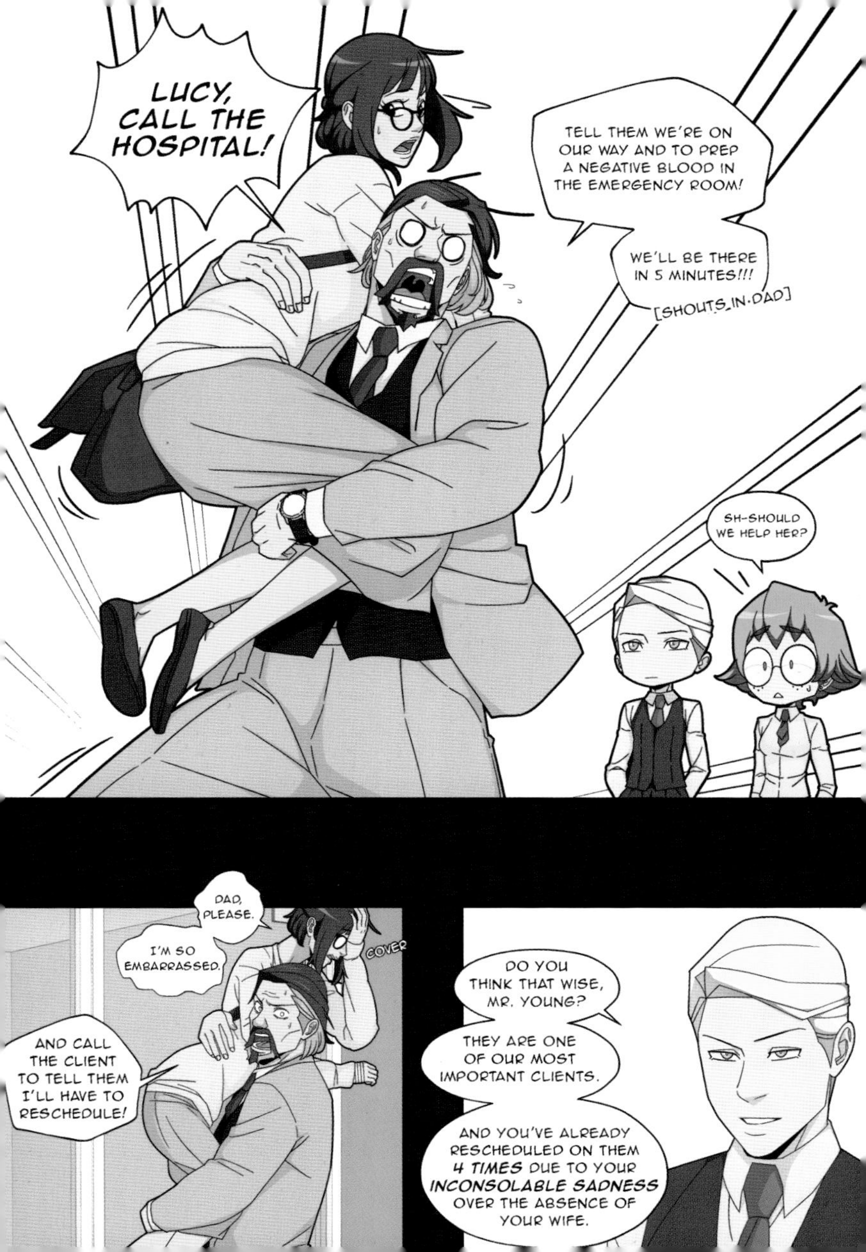
LUCY, CALL THE HOSPITAL!
TELL THEM WE'RE ON OUR WAY AND TO PREP A NEGATIVE BLOOD IN THE EMERGENCY ROOM!
WE'LL BE THERE IN 5 MINUTES!!!
[SHOUTS IN DAD]
SH-SHOULD WE HELP HER?
DAD, PLEASE.
I'M SO EMBARRASSED.
COVER
AND CALL THE CLIENT TO TELL THEM I'LL HAVE TO RESCHEDULE!
DO YOU THINK THAT WISE, MR. YOUNG?
THEY ARE ONE OF OUR MOST IMPORTANT CLIENTS.
AND YOU'VE ALREADY RESCHEDULED ON THEM 4 TIMES DUE TO YOUR INCONSOLABLE SADNESS OVER THE ABSENCE OF YOUR WIFE.

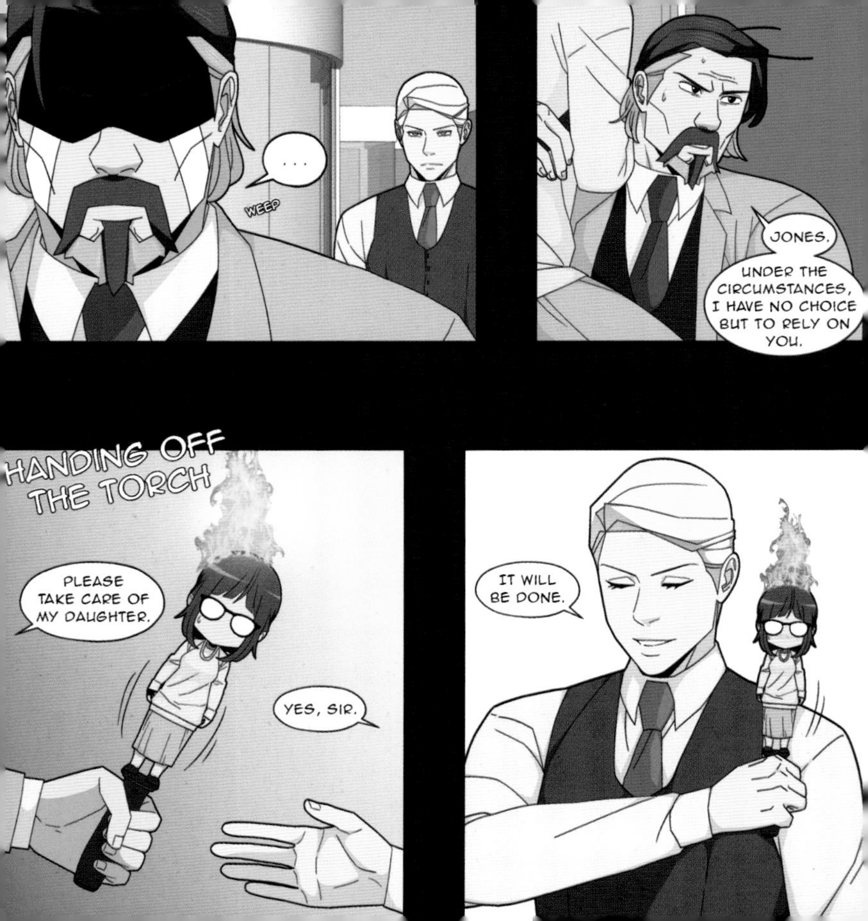

...
WEEP
JONES.
UNDER THE CIRCUMSTANCES, I HAVE NO CHOICE BUT TO RELY ON YOU.
HANDING OFF THE TORCH
PLEASE TAKE CARE OF MY DAUGHTER.
YES, SIR.
IT WILL BE DONE.

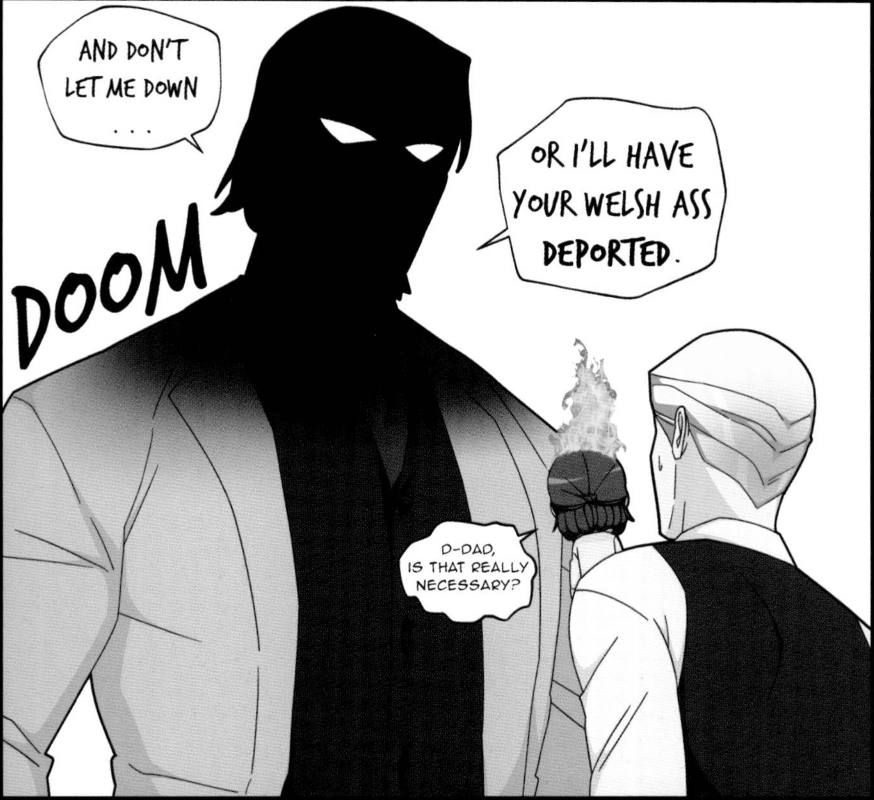
AND DON'T LET ME DOWN . . .
OR I'LL HAVE YOUR WELSH ASS DEPORTED.
DOOM
D-DAD, IS THAT REALLY NECESSARY?

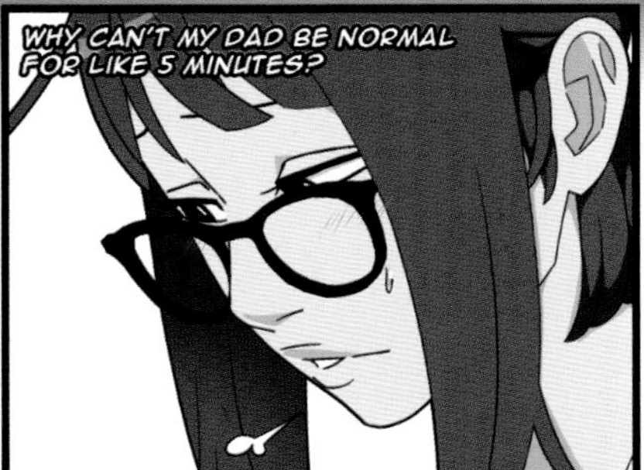
WHY CAN'T MY DAD BE NORMAL FOR LIKE 5 MINUTES?
CHARLES MIGHT BE UPSET WITH WHAT HE SAID!

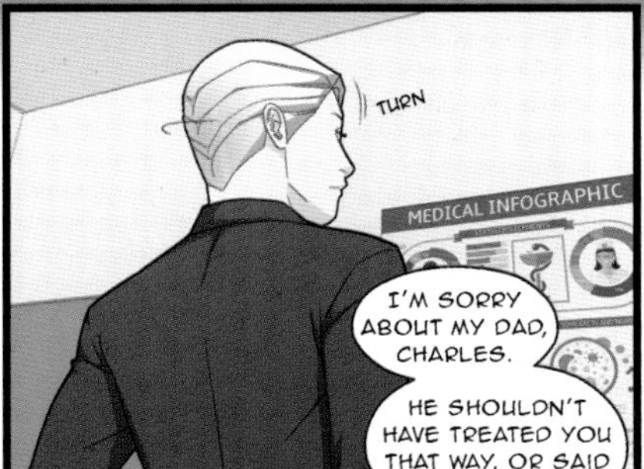
TURN
MEDICAL INFOGRAPHIC
I'M SORRY ABOUT MY DAD, CHARLES.
HE SHOULDN'T HAVE TREATED YOU THAT WAY, OR SAID THOSE THINGS.

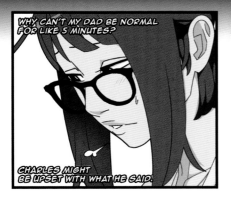

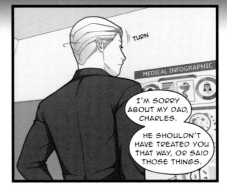

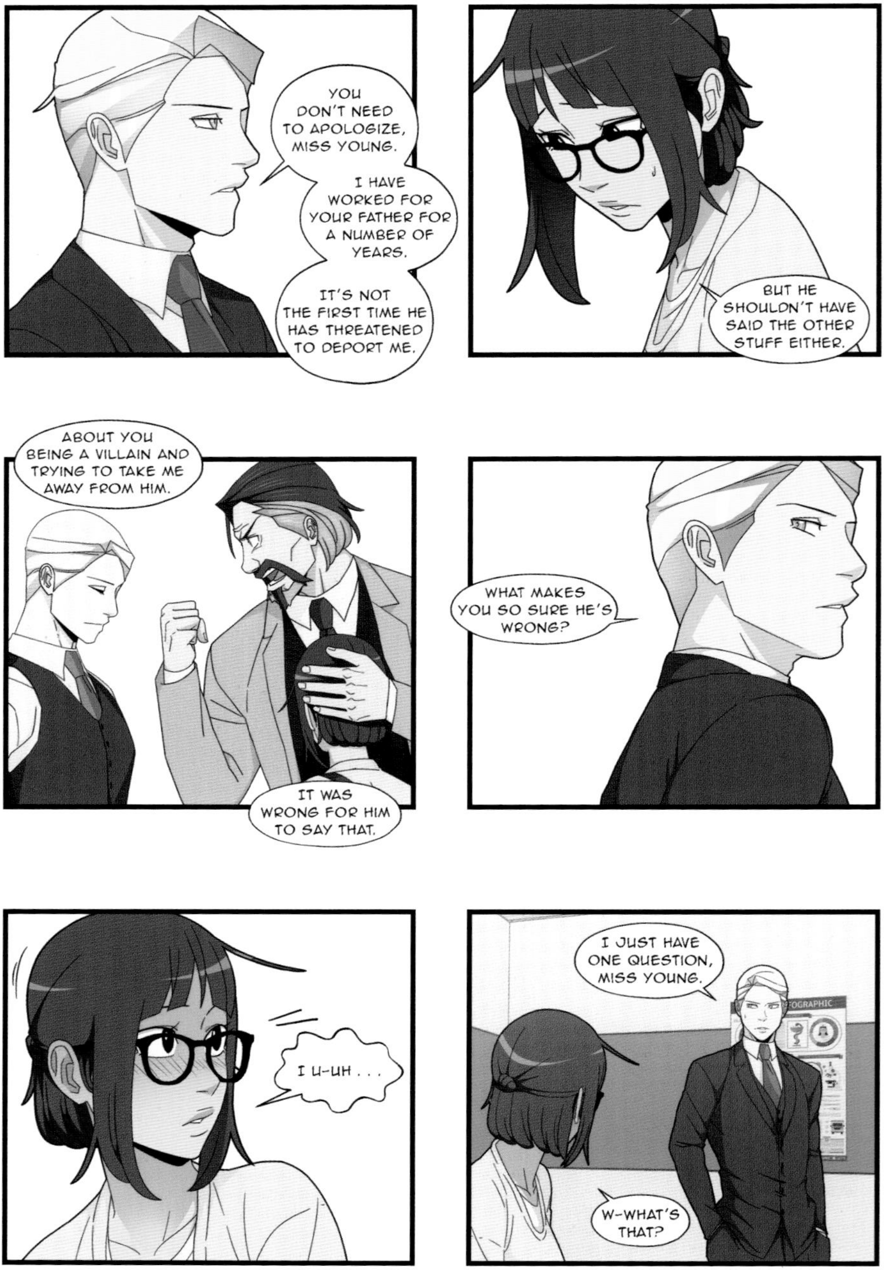
YOU DON'T NEED TO APOLOGIZE, MISS YOUNG.
I HAVE WORKED FOR YOUR FATHER FOR A NUMBER OF YEARS.
IT'S NOT THE FIRST TIME HE HAS THREATENED TO DEPORT ME.
BUT HE SHOULDN'T HAVE SAID THE OTHER STUFF EITHER.
ABOUT YOU BEING A VILLAIN AND TRYING TO TAKE ME AWAY FROM HIM.
IT WAS WRONG FOR HIM TO SAY THAT.
WHAT MAKES YOU SO SURE HE'S WRONG?
I U-UH . . .
I JUST HAVE ONE QUESTION, MISS YOUNG.
W-WHAT'S THAT?

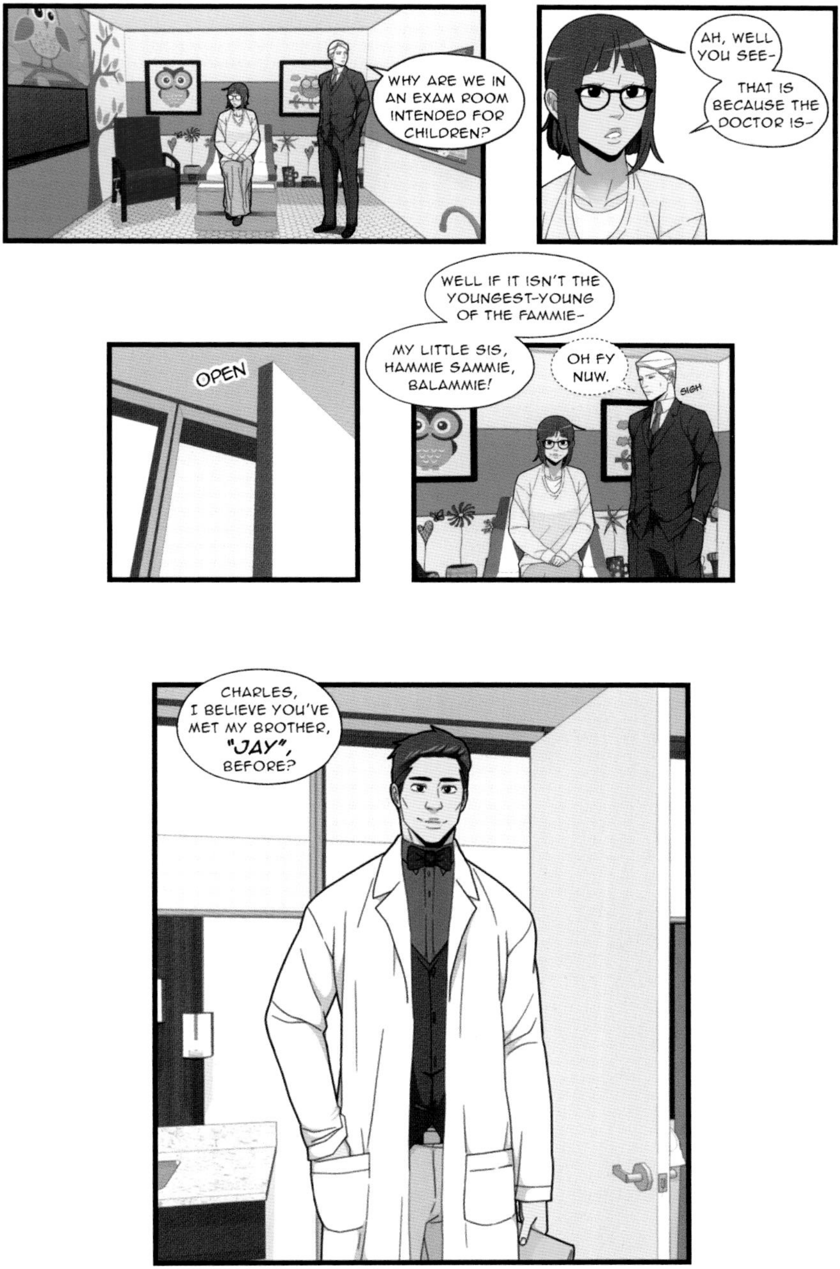
WHY ARE WE IN AN EXAM ROOM INTENDED FOR CHILDREN?
AH, WELL YOU SEE-
THAT IS BECAUSE THE DOCTOR IS-
OPEN
WELL IF IT ISN'T THE YOUNGEST-YOUNG OF THE FAMMIE-
MY LITTLE SIS, HAMMIE SAMMIE, BALAMMIE!
OH FY NUW.
SIGH
CHARLES, I BELIEVE YOU'VE MET MY BROTHER, "JAY", BEFORE?

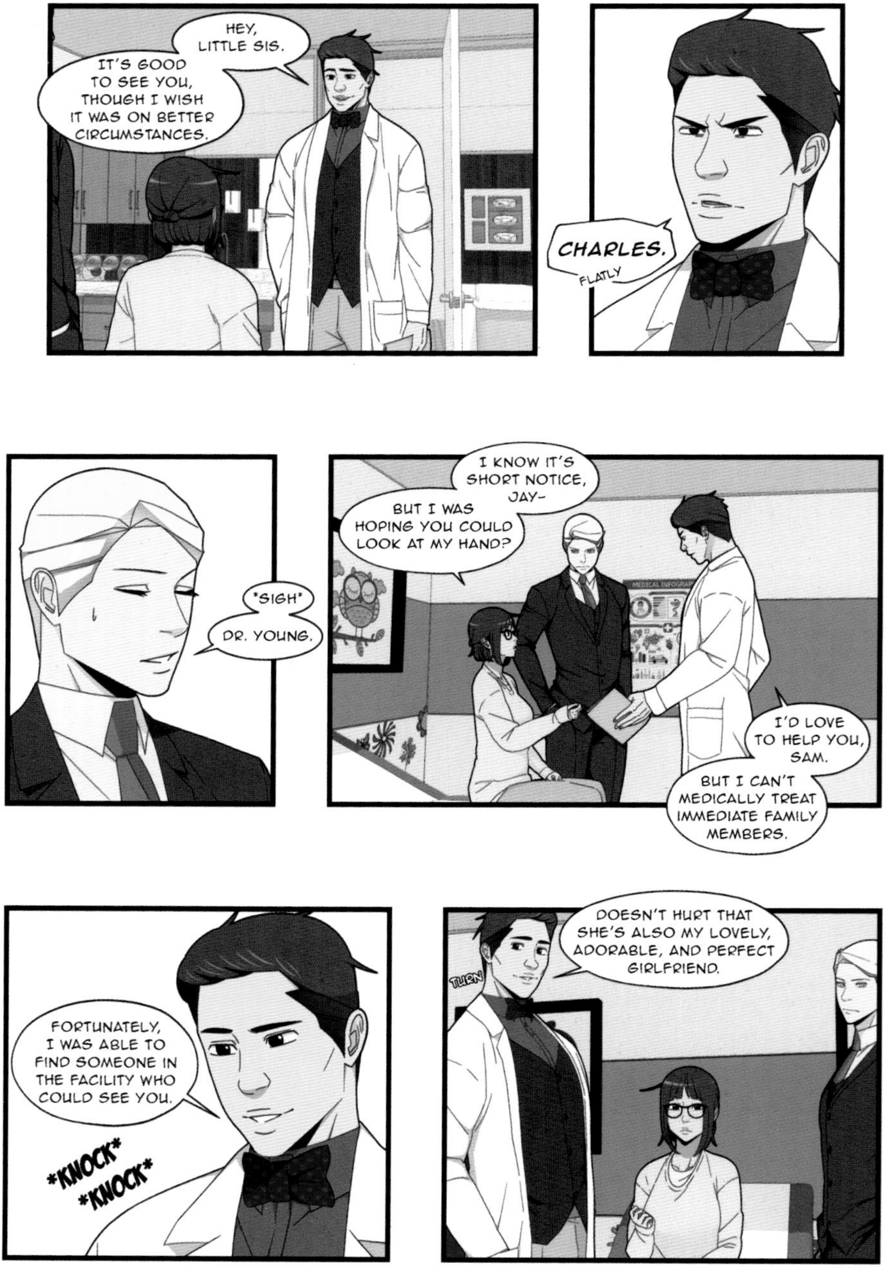
HEY, LITTLE SIS.
IT'S GOOD TO SEE YOU, THOUGH I WISH IT WAS ON BETTER CIRCUMSTANCES.
CHARLES.
FLATLY
SIGH
DR. YOUNG.
I KNOW IT'S SHORT NOTICE, JAY-
BUT I WAS HOPING YOU COULD LOOK AT MY HAND?
I'D LOVE TO HELP YOU, SAM.
BUT I CAN'T MEDICALLY TREAT IMMEDIATE FAMILY MEMBERS.
FORTUNATELY, I WAS ABLE TO FIND SOMEONE IN THE FACILITY WHO COULD SEE YOU.
KNOCK *KNOCK*
TURN
DOESN'T HURT THAT SHE'S ALSO MY LOVELY, ADORABLE, AND PERFECT GIRLFRIEND.

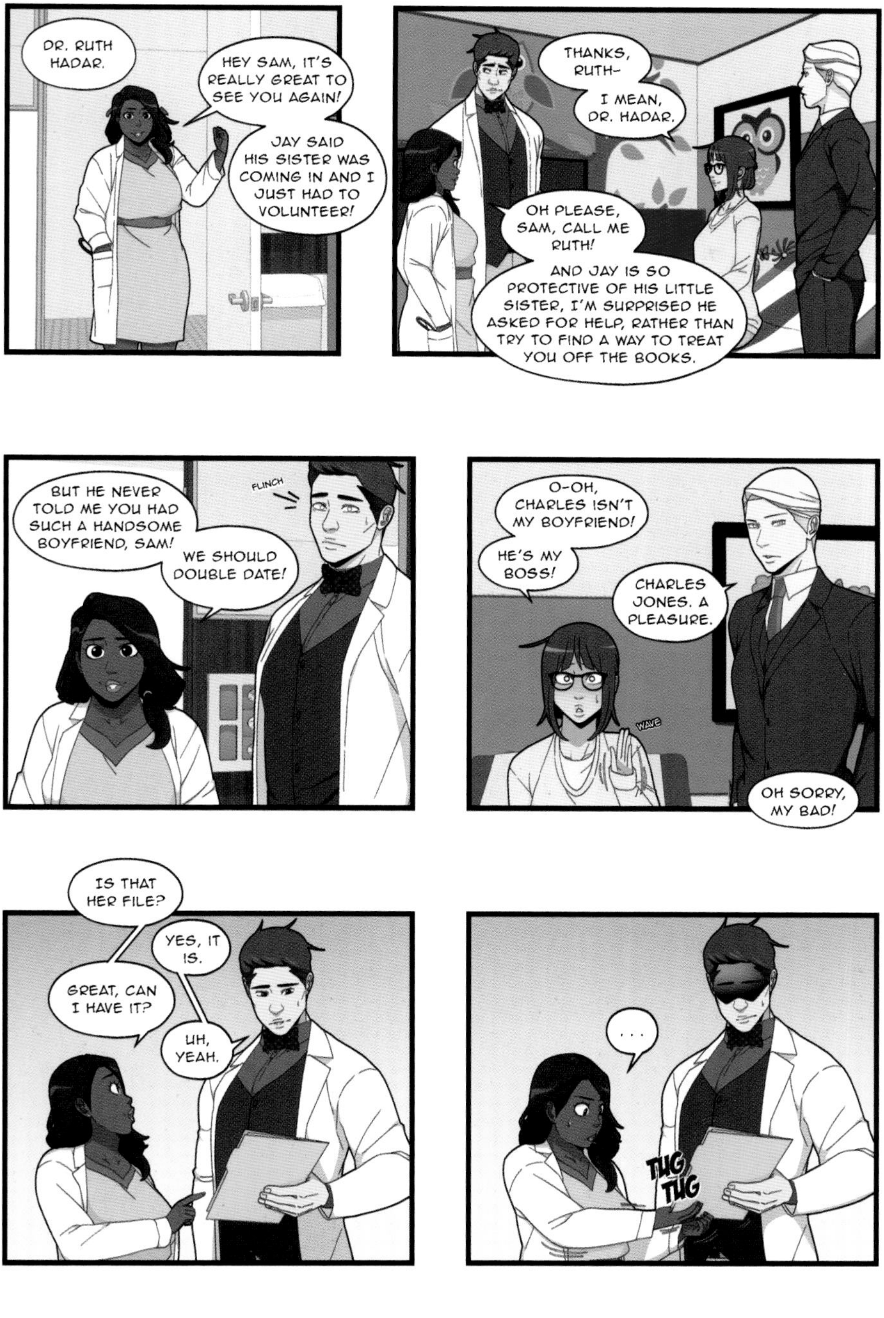
DR. RUTH HADAR.
HEY SAM, IT'S REALLY GREAT TO SEE YOU AGAIN!
JAY SAID HIS SISTER WAS COMING IN AND I JUST HAD TO VOLUNTEER!
THANKS, RUTH-
I MEAN, DR. HADAR.
OH PLEASE, SAM, CALL ME RUTH!
AND JAY IS SO PROTECTIVE OF HIS LITTLE SISTER, I'M SURPRISED HE ASKED FOR HELP, RATHER THAN TRY TO FIND A WAY TO TREAT YOU OFF THE BOOKS.
BUT HE NEVER TOLD ME YOU HAD SUCH A HANDSOME BOYFRIEND, SAM!
FLINCH
WE SHOULD DOUBLE DATE!
O-OH, CHARLES ISN'T MY BOYFRIEND!
HE'S MY BOSS!
CHARLES JONES. A PLEASURE.
WAVE
OH SORRY, MY BAD!
IS THAT HER FILE?
YES, IT IS.
GREAT, CAN I HAVE IT?
UH, YEAH.
. . .
TUG
TUG

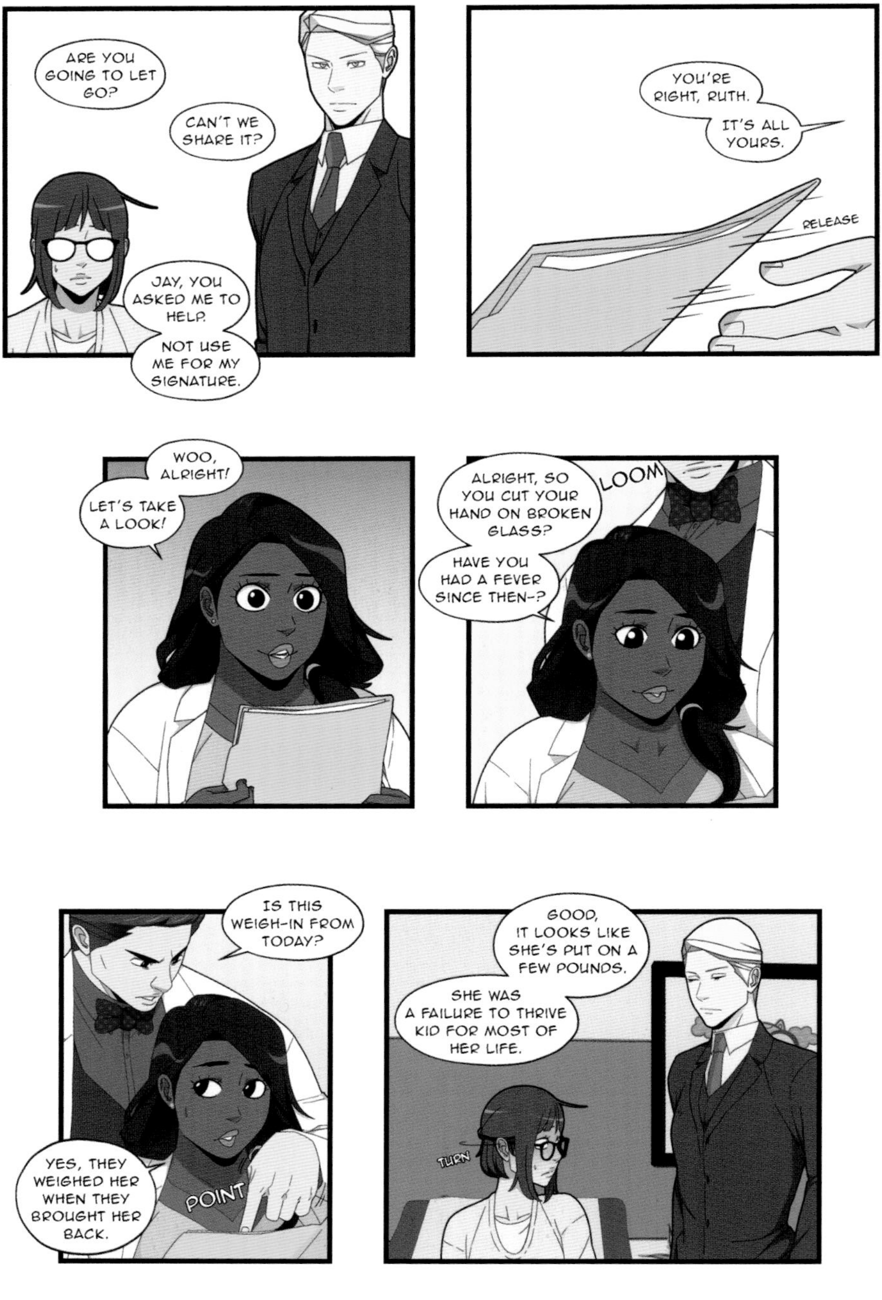
ARE YOU GOING TO LET GO?
CAN'T WE SHARE IT?
JAY, YOU ASKED ME TO HELP.
NOT USE ME FOR MY SIGNATURE.
YOU'RE RIGHT, RUTH.
IT'S ALL YOURS.
RELEASE
WOO, ALRIGHT!
LET'S TAKE A LOOK!
ALRIGHT, SO YOU CUT YOUR HAND ON BROKEN GLASS?
LOOM
HAVE YOU HAD A FEVER SINCE THEN-?
IS THIS WEIGH-IN FROM TODAY?
YES, THEY WEIGHED HER WHEN THEY BROUGHT HER BACK.
POINT
GOOD, IT LOOKS LIKE SHE'S PUT ON A FEW POUNDS.
SHE WAS A FAILURE TO THRIVE KID FOR MOST OF HER LIFE.
TURN

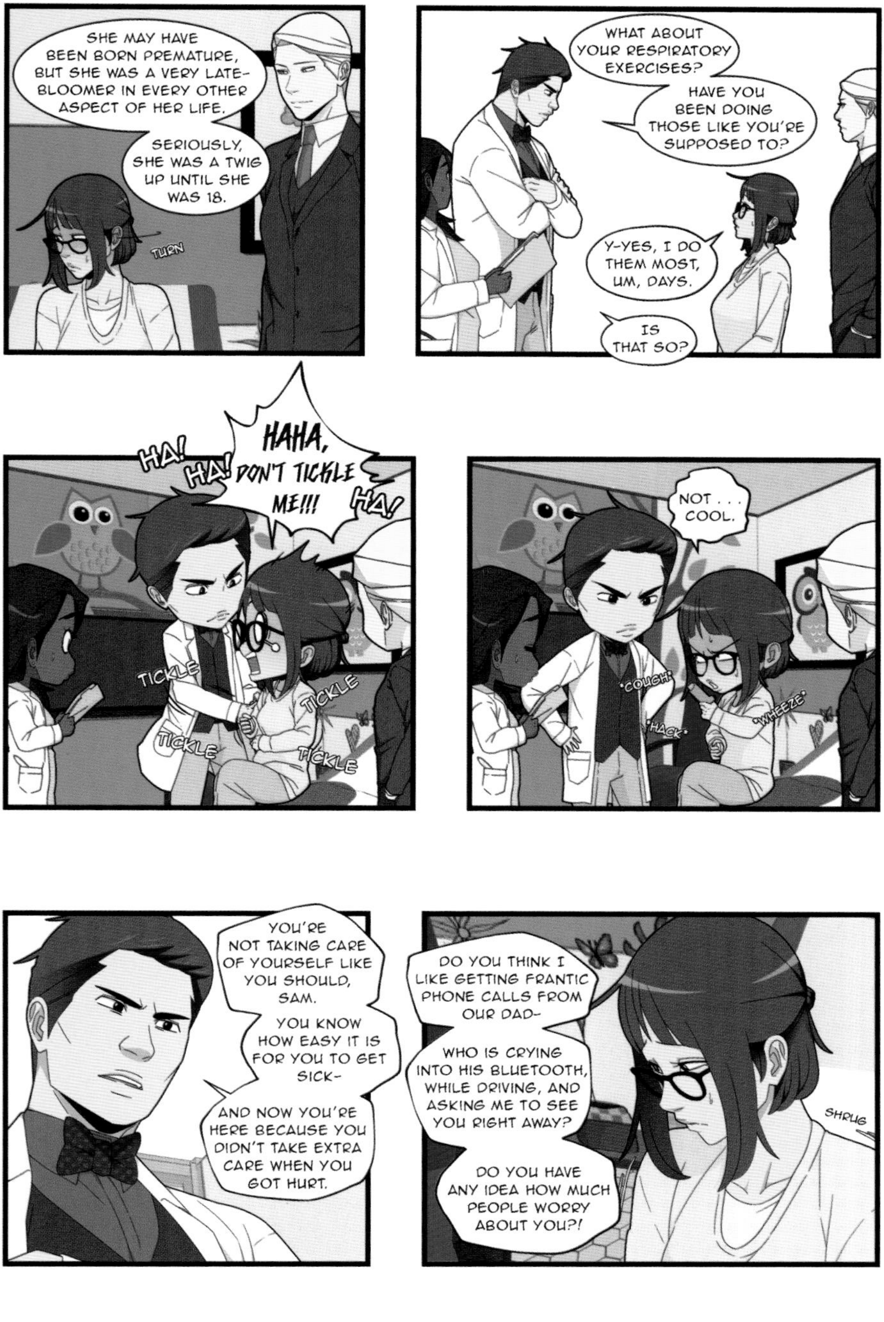
SHE MAY HAVE BEEN BORN PREMATURE, BUT SHE WAS A VERY LATE-BLOOMER IN EVERY OTHER ASPECT OF HER LIFE.
SERIOUSLY, SHE WAS A TWIG UP UNTIL SHE WAS 18.
TURN
WHAT ABOUT YOUR RESPIRATORY EXERCISES?
HAVE YOU BEEN DOING THOSE LIKE YOU'RE SUPPOSED TO?
Y-YES, I DO THEM MOST, UM, DAYS.
IS THAT SO?
HA! HA!
HAHA, DON'T TICKLE ME!!!
HA!
TICKLE
TICKLE
TICKLE
TICKLE
NOT . . . COOL.
COUGH
HACK
WHEEZE
YOU'RE NOT TAKING CARE OF YOURSELF LIKE YOU SHOULD, SAM.
YOU KNOW HOW EASY IT IS FOR YOU TO GET SICK-
AND NOW YOU'RE HERE BECAUSE YOU DIDN'T TAKE EXTRA CARE WHEN YOU GOT HURT.
DO YOU THINK I LIKE GETTING FRANTIC PHONE CALLS FROM OUR DAD-
WHO IS CRYING INTO HIS BLUETOOTH, WHILE DRIVING, AND ASKING ME TO SEE YOU RIGHT AWAY?
DO YOU HAVE ANY IDEA HOW MUCH PEOPLE WORRY ABOUT YOU?!
SHRUG

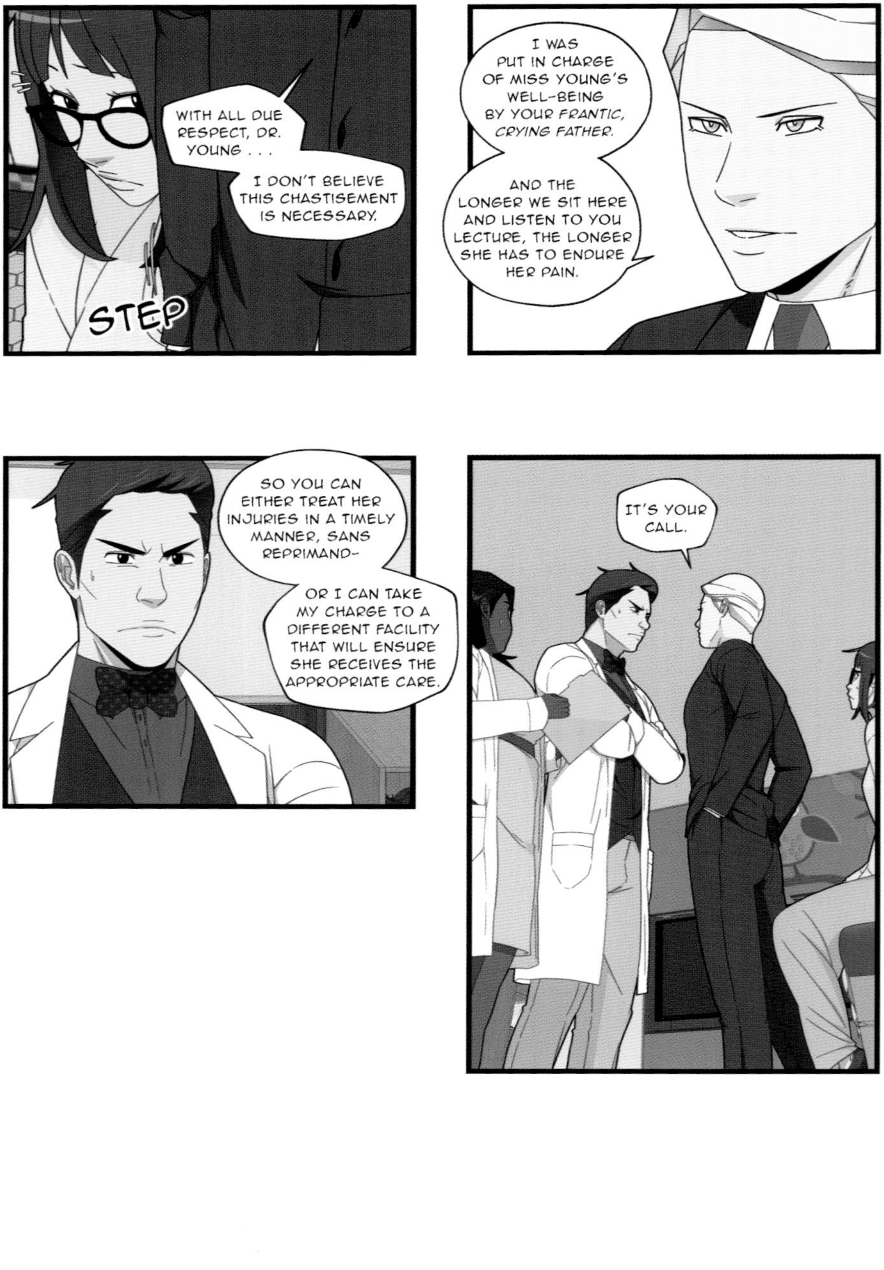
WITH ALL DUE RESPECT, DR. YOUNG . . .
I DON'T BELIEVE THIS CHASTISEMENT IS NECESSARY.
STEP
I WAS PUT IN CHARGE OF MISS YOUNG'S WELL-BEING BY YOUR FRANTIC, CRYING FATHER.
AND THE LONGER WE SIT HERE AND LISTEN TO YOU LECTURE, THE LONGER SHE HAS TO ENDURE HER PAIN.
SO YOU CAN EITHER TREAT HER INJURIES IN A TIMELY MANNER, SANS REPRIMAND-
OR I CAN TAKE MY CHARGE TO A DIFFERENT FACILITY THAT WILL ENSURE SHE RECEIVES THE APPROPRIATE CARE.
IT'S YOUR CALL.

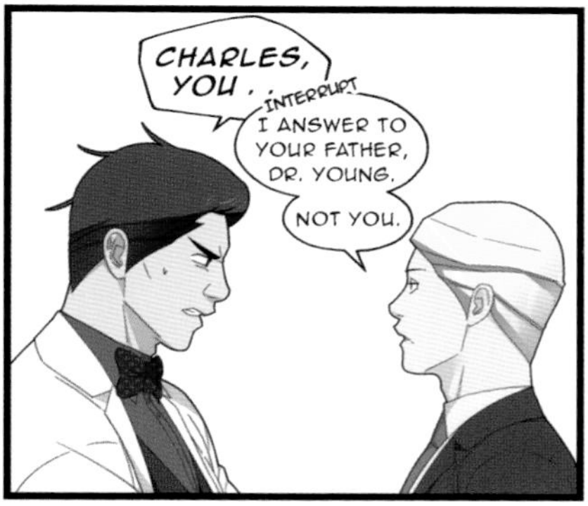
CHARLES, YOU . . .
INTERRUPT
I ANSWER TO YOUR FATHER, DR. YOUNG.
NOT YOU.
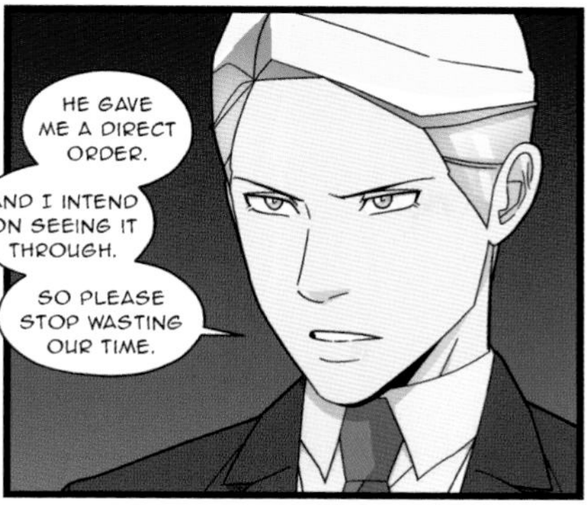
HE GAVE ME A DIRECT ORDER.
AND I INTEND ON SEEING IT THROUGH.
SO PLEASE STOP WASTING OUR TIME.
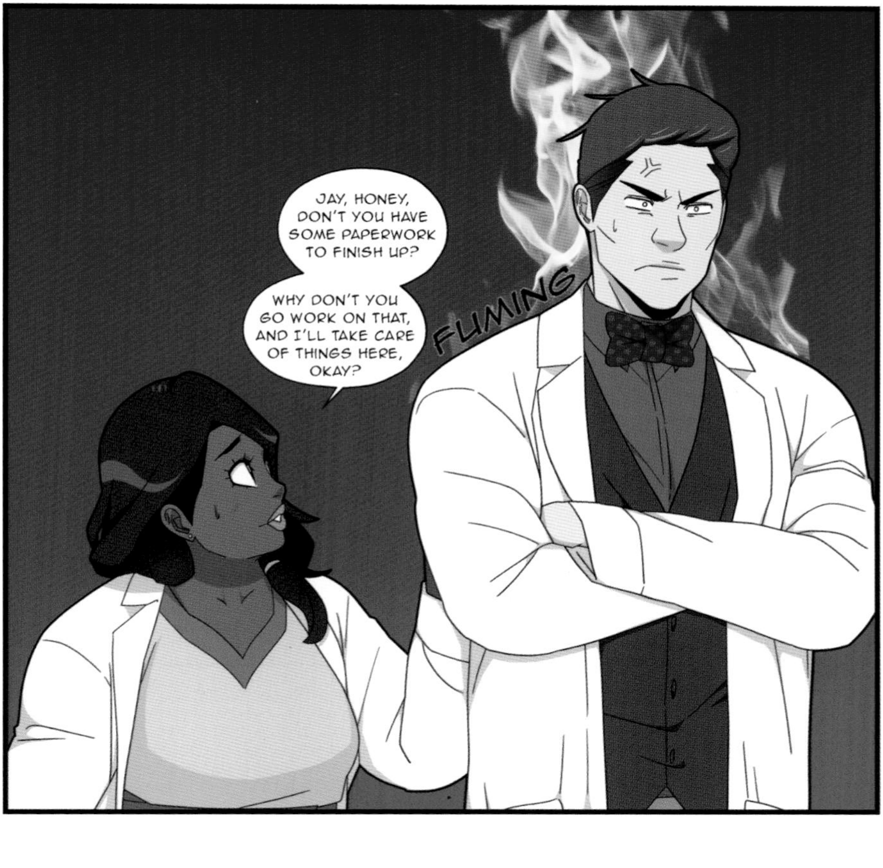
JAY, HONEY, DON'T YOU HAVE SOME PAPERWORK TO FINISH UP?
WHY DON'T YOU GO WORK ON THAT, AND I'LL TAKE CARE OF THINGS HERE, OKAY?
FUMING

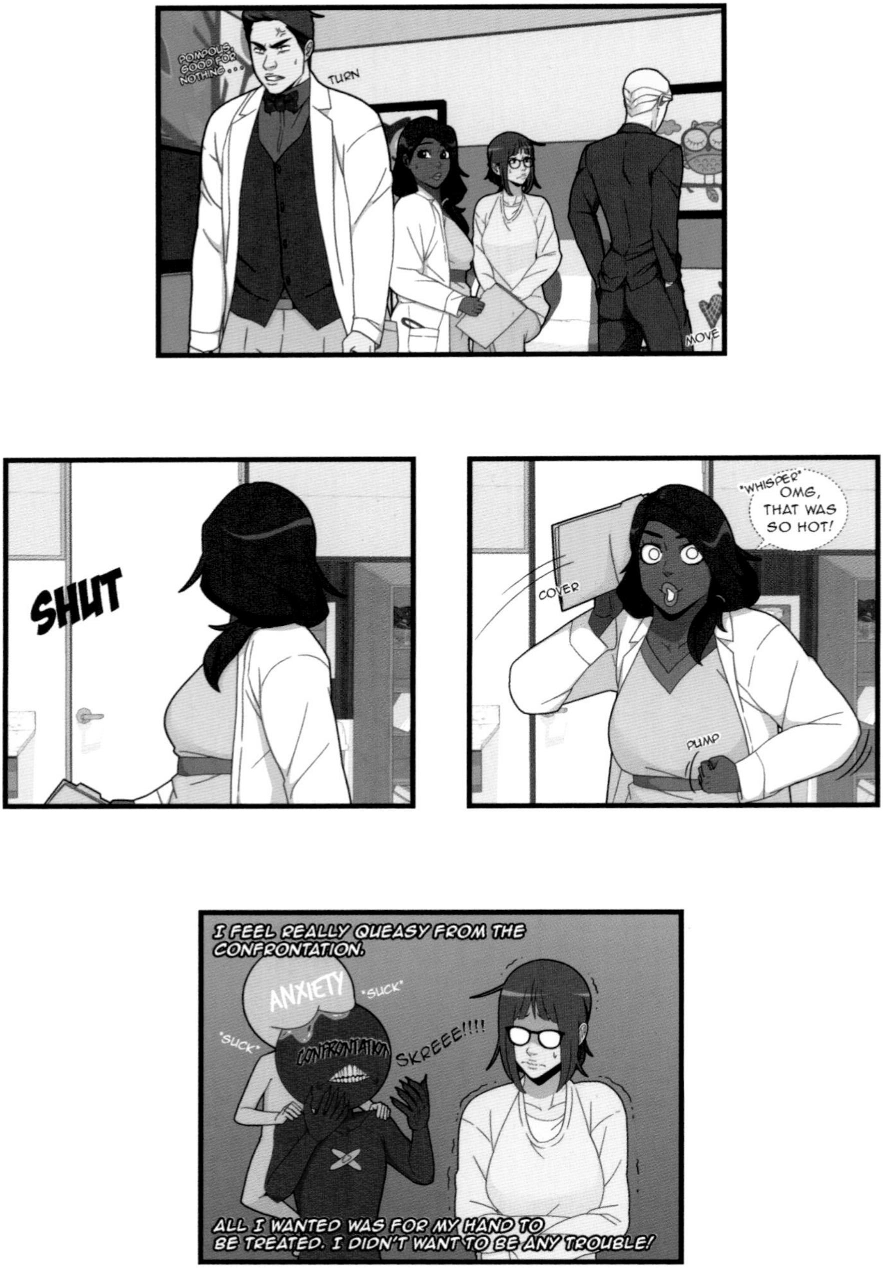
POMPOUS, GOOD FOR NOTHING . . .
TURN
MOVE
SHUT
WHISPER OMG, THAT WAS SO HOT!
COVER
PUMP
I FEEL REALLY QUEASY FROM THE CONFRONTATION.
ANXIETY
SUCK
SUCK
CONFRONTATION
SKREEE!!!!
ALL I WANTED WAS FOR MY HAND TO BE TREATED. I DIDN'T WANT TO BE ANY TROUBLE!

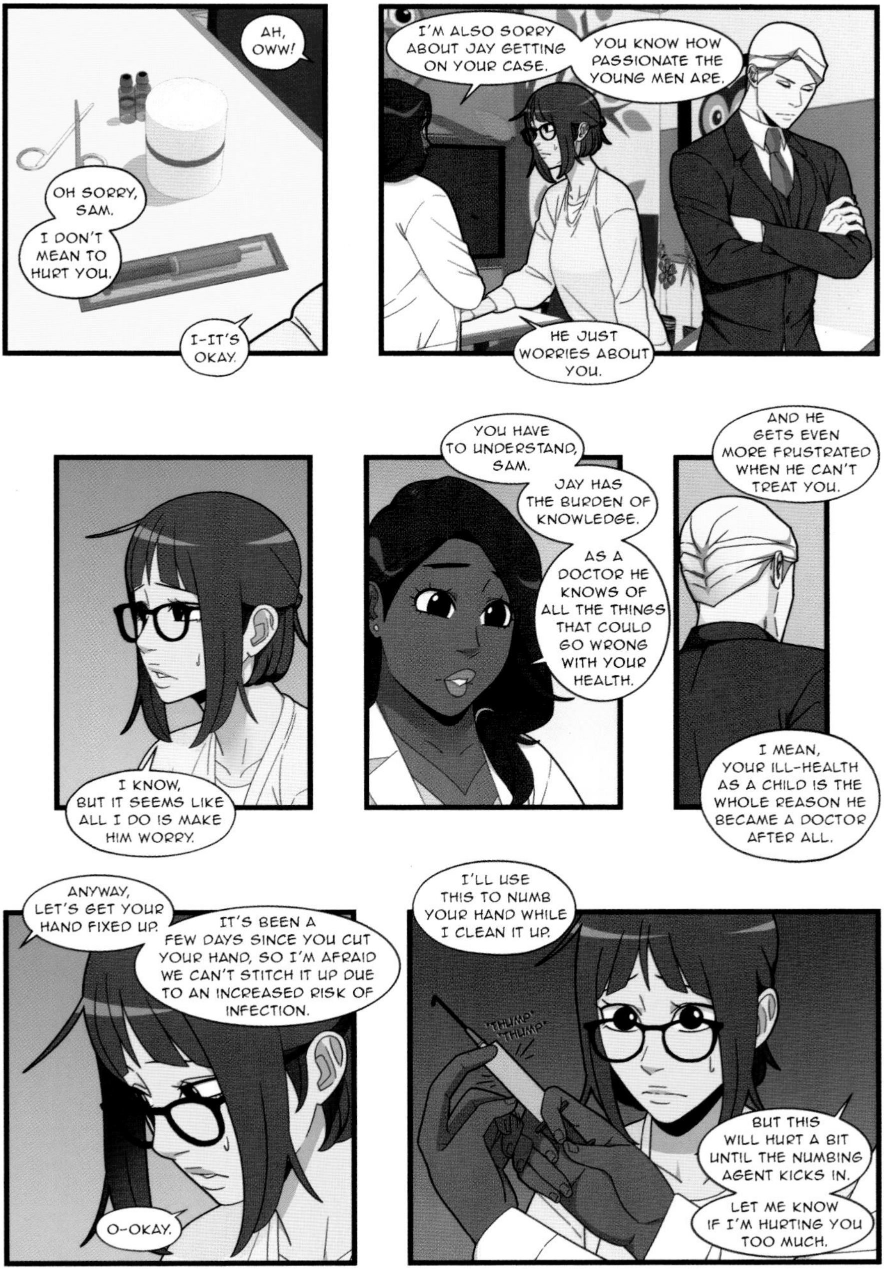
AH, OWW!
OH SORRY, SAM.
I DON'T MEAN TO HURT YOU.
I-IT'S OKAY.
I'M ALSO SORRY ABOUT JAY GETTING ON YOUR CASE.
YOU KNOW HOW PASSIONATE THE YOUNG MEN ARE.
HE JUST WORRIES ABOUT YOU.
I KNOW, BUT IT SEEMS LIKE ALL I DO IS MAKE HIM WORRY.
YOU HAVE TO UNDERSTAND, SAM.
JAY HAS THE BURDEN OF KNOWLEDGE.
AS A DOCTOR HE KNOWS OF ALL THE THINGS THAT COULD GO WRONG WITH YOUR HEALTH.
AND HE GETS EVEN MORE FRUSTRATED WHEN HE CAN'T TREAT YOU.
I MEAN, YOUR ILL-HEALTH AS A CHILD IS THE WHOLE REASON HE BECAME A DOCTOR AFTER ALL.
ANYWAY, LET'S GET YOUR HAND FIXED UP.
IT'S BEEN A FEW DAYS SINCE YOU CUT YOUR HAND, SO I'M AFRAID WE CAN'T STITCH IT UP DUE TO AN INCREASED RISK OF INFECTION.
O-OKAY.
I'LL USE THIS TO NUMB YOUR HAND WHILE I CLEAN IT UP.
THUMP *THUMP*
BUT THIS WILL HURT A BIT UNTIL THE NUMBING AGENT KICKS IN.
LET ME KNOW IF I'M HURTING YOU TOO MUCH.

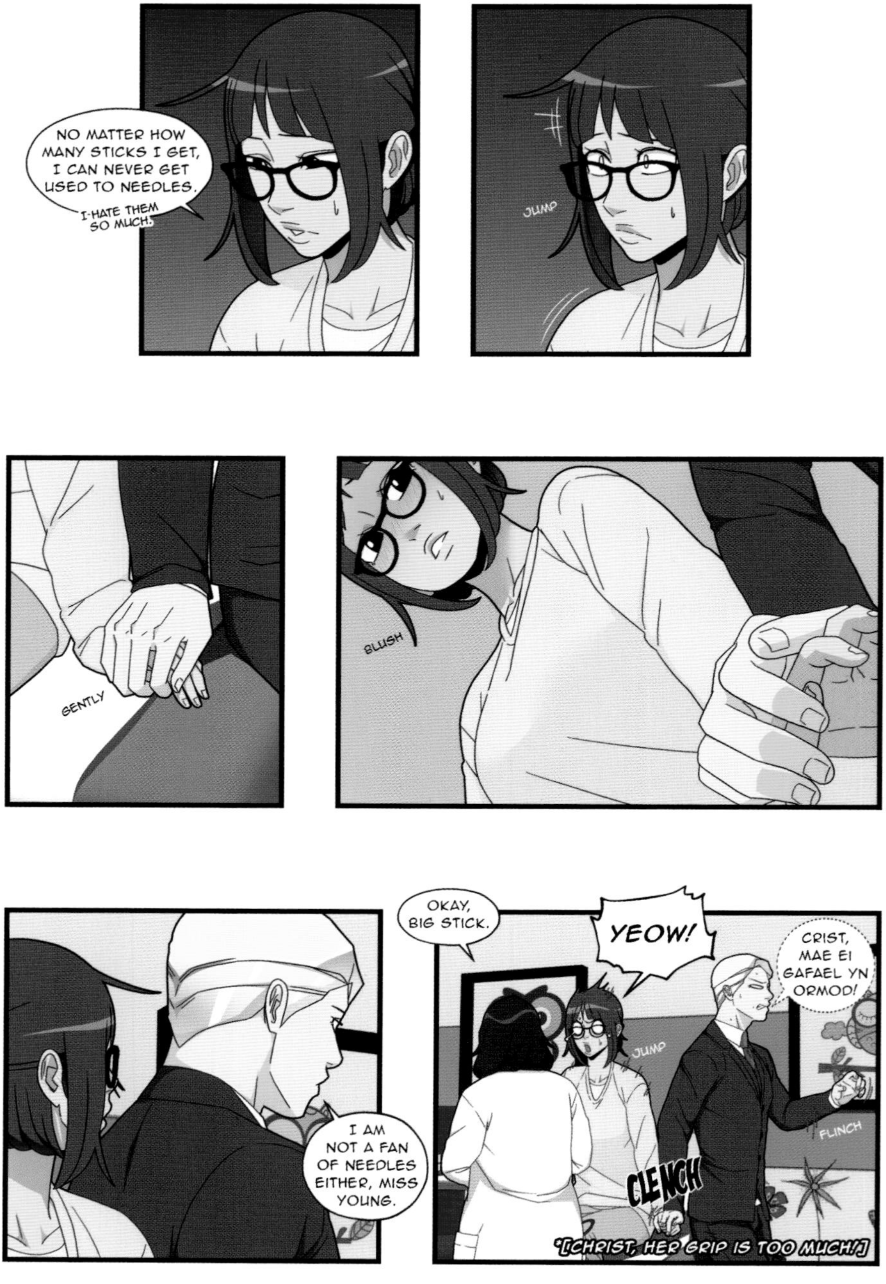
NO MATTER HOW MANY STICKS I GET, I CAN NEVER GET USED TO NEEDLES.
I-HATE THEM SO MUCH.
JUMP
GENTLY
BLUSH
I AM NOT A FAN OF NEEDLES EITHER, MISS YOUNG.
OKAY, BIG STICK.
YEOW!
CRIST, MAE EI GAFAEL YN ORMOD!
JUMP
FLINCH
CLENCH
*[CHRIST, HER GRIP IS TOO MUCH!]

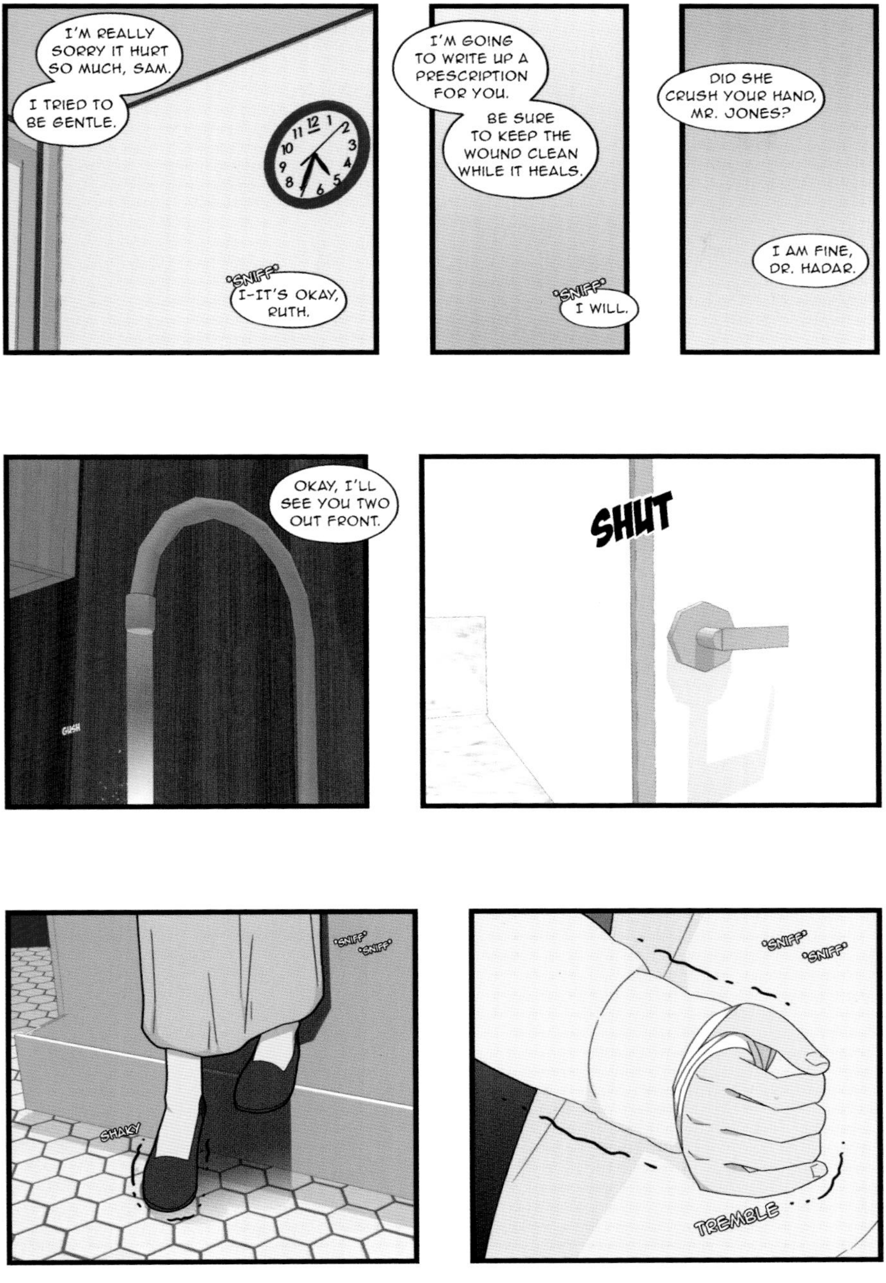
I'M REALLY SORRY IT HURT SO MUCH, SAM.
I TRIED TO BE GENTLE.
SNIFF
I-IT'S OKAY, RUTH.
I'M GOING TO WRITE UP A PRESCRIPTION FOR YOU.
BE SURE TO KEEP THE WOUND CLEAN WHILE IT HEALS.
SNIFF
I WILL.
DID SHE CRUSH YOUR HAND, MR. JONES?
I AM FINE, DR. HADAR.
OKAY, I'LL SEE YOU TWO OUT FRONT.
GUSH
SHUT
SNIFF
SNIFF
SHAKY
SNIFF
SNIFF
TREMBLE

GENTLY, MISS YOUNG.
SNIFF
TAKE YOUR TIME.
SNIFF
DRIP
ARE YOU CRYING, MISS YOUNG?
N-NO, MY EYES ARE WATERING BECAUSE IT HURT SO BAD.
RUB RUB
OF COURSE.
MY MISTAKE.

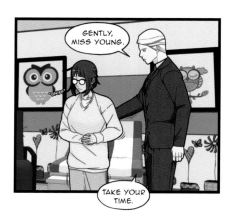

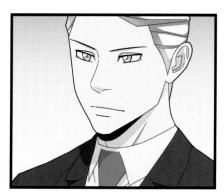

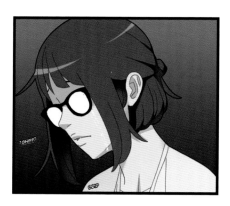

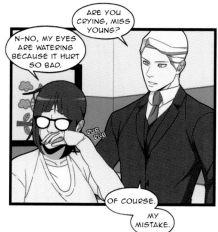

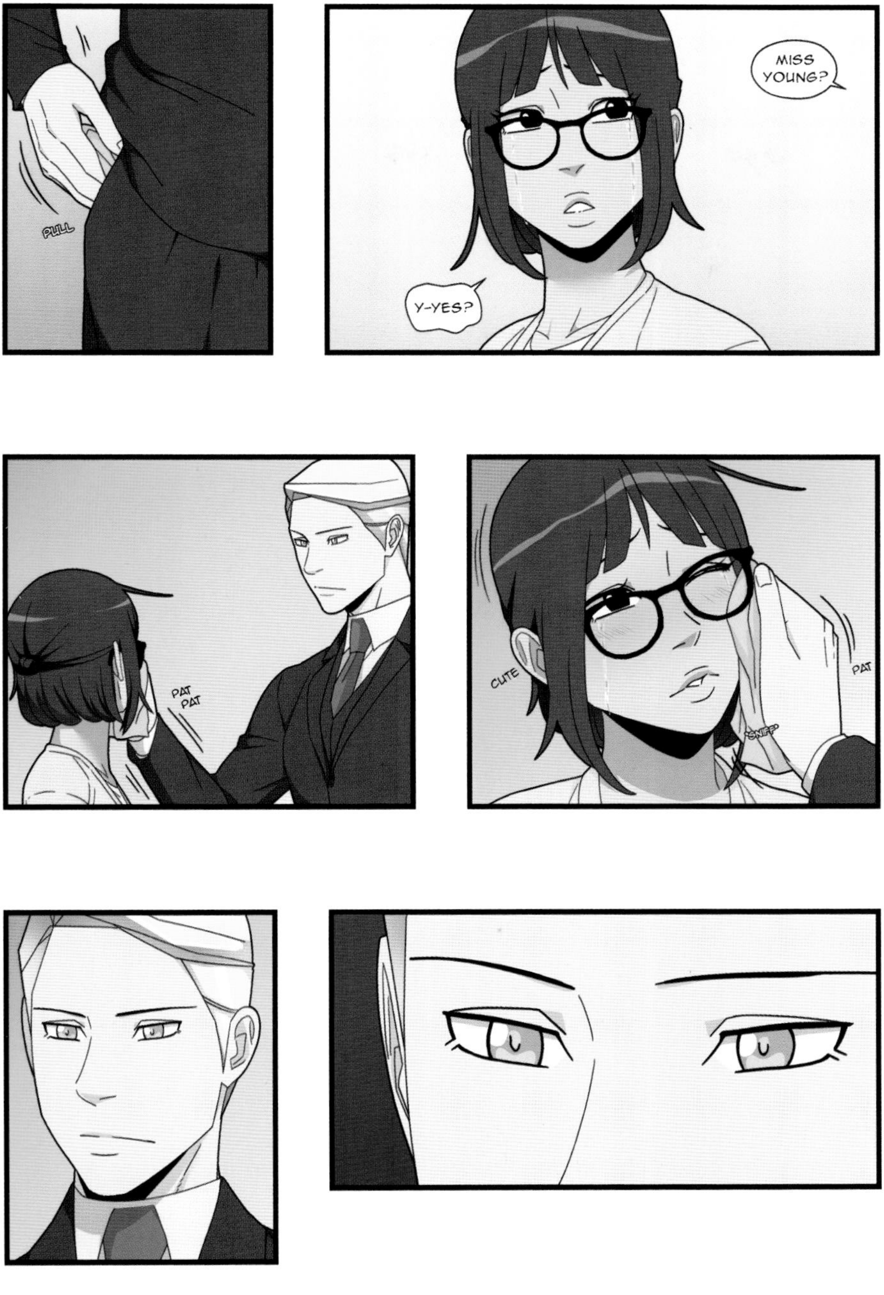
PULL
MISS YOUNG?
Y-YES?
PAT PAT
CUTE
SNIFF
PAT

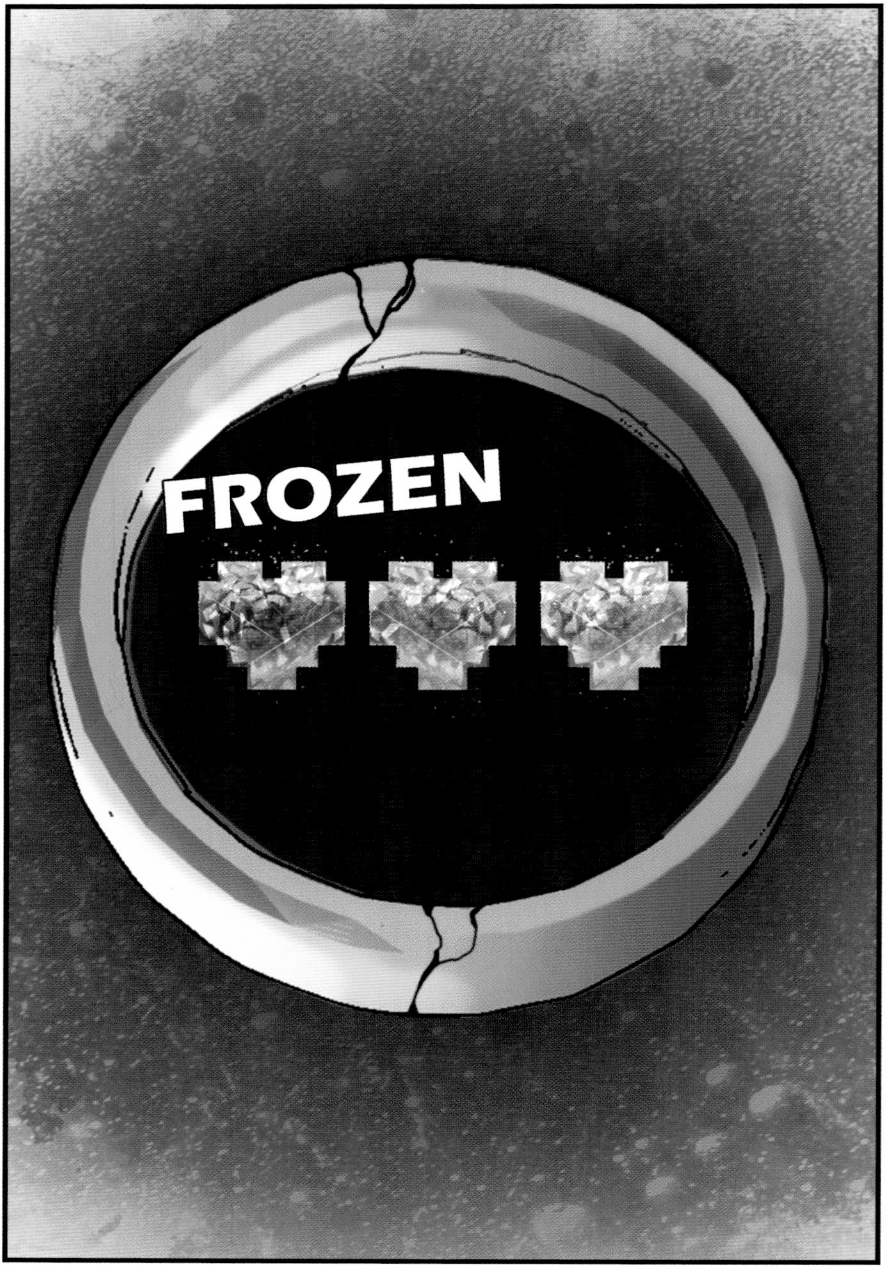
FROZEN

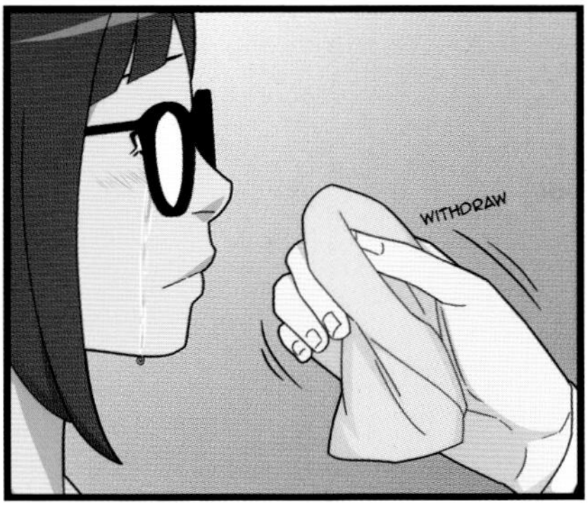
WITHDRAW

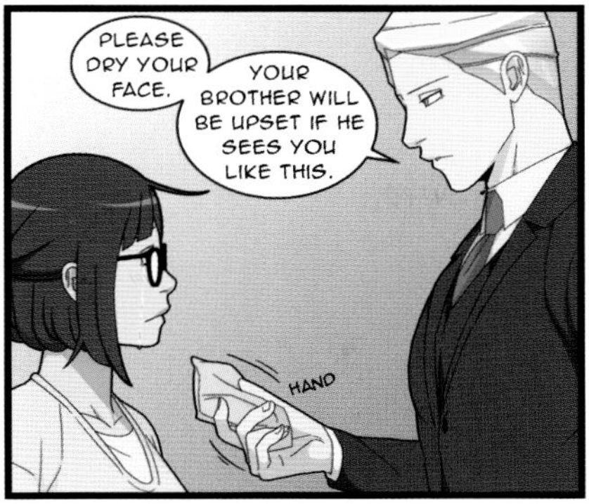
PLEASE DRY YOUR FACE.
YOUR BROTHER WILL BE UPSET IF HE SEES YOU LIKE THIS.
HAND

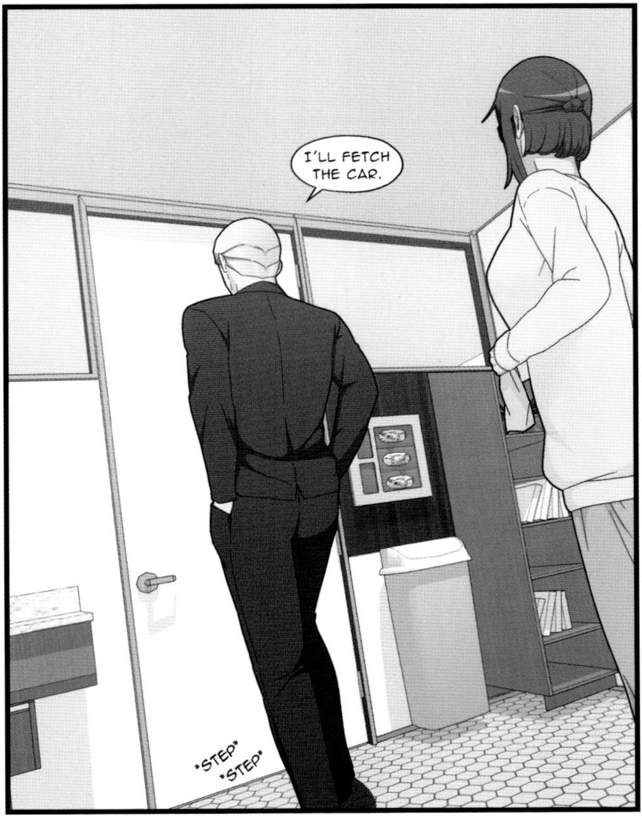
I'LL FETCH THE CAR.
STEP
STEP

SO WE MEET AGAIN, KITTERS.

INDEED, HONORED CUSTOMER.

FOOL ME ONCE, SHAME ON YOU.

BUT YOU SHAN'T BE SO LUCKY A SECOND TIME!

I DON'T KNOW WHAT YOU ARE TALKING ABOUT, HONORED CUSTOMER.

YOU SEEMED HAPPY WITH YOUR LAST PURCHASE.

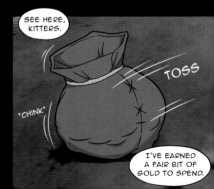

SEE HERE, KITTERS.

CHINK

TOSS

I'VE EARNED A FAIR BIT OF GOLD TO SPEND.

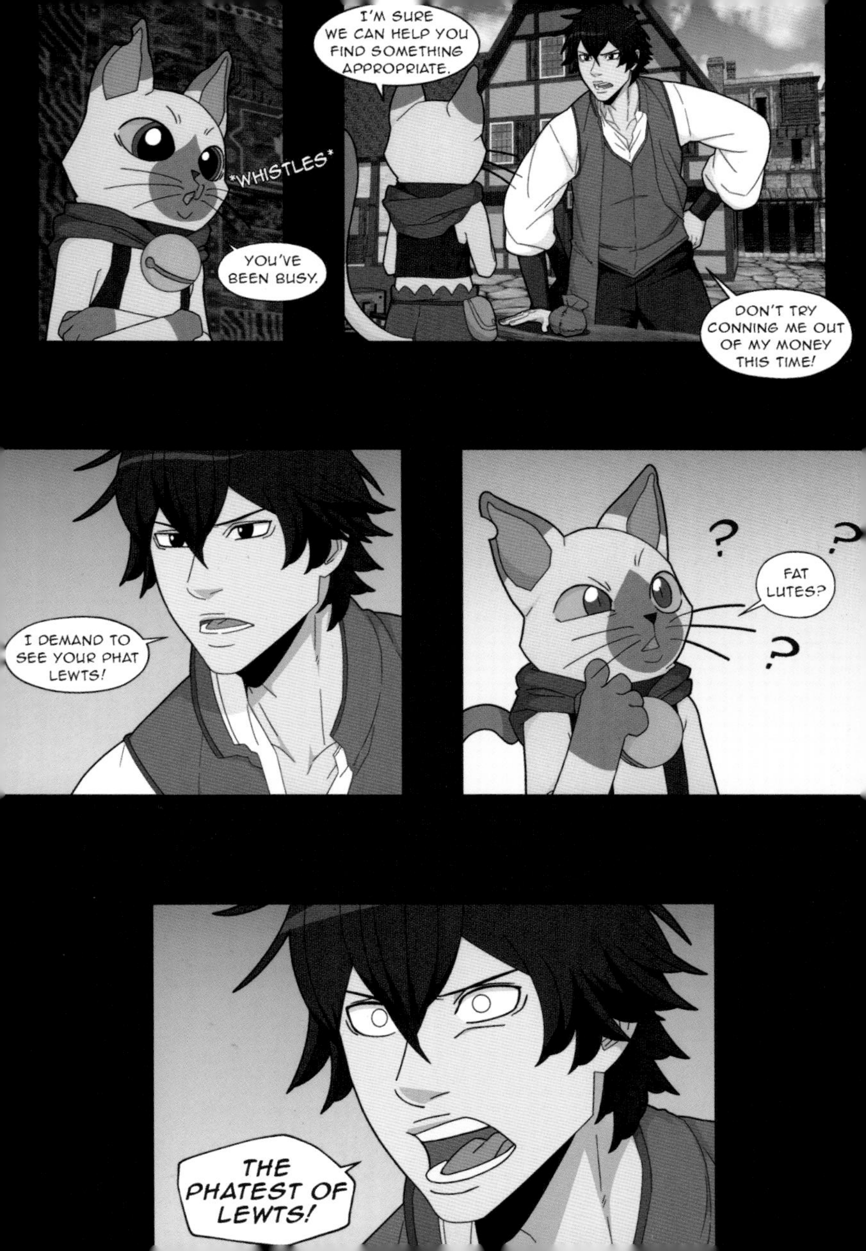
WHISTLES
YOU'VE BEEN BUSY.
I'M SURE WE CAN HELP YOU FIND SOMETHING APPROPRIATE.
DON'T TRY CONNING ME OUT OF MY MONEY THIS TIME!
I DEMAND TO SEE YOUR PHAT LEWTS!
? ? ?
FAT LUTES?
THE PHATEST OF LEWTS!

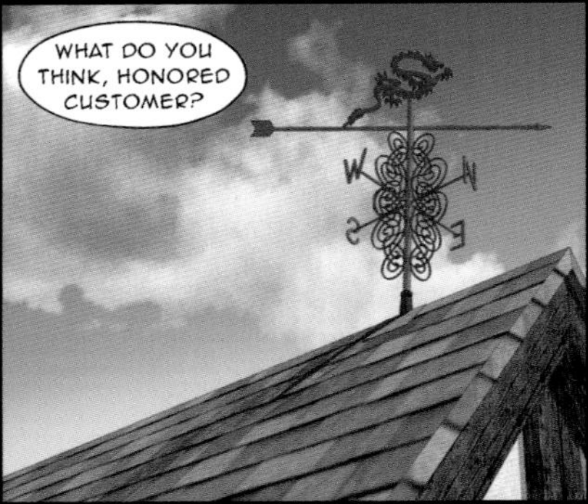
WHAT DO YOU THINK, HONORED CUSTOMER?
W
N
S
E
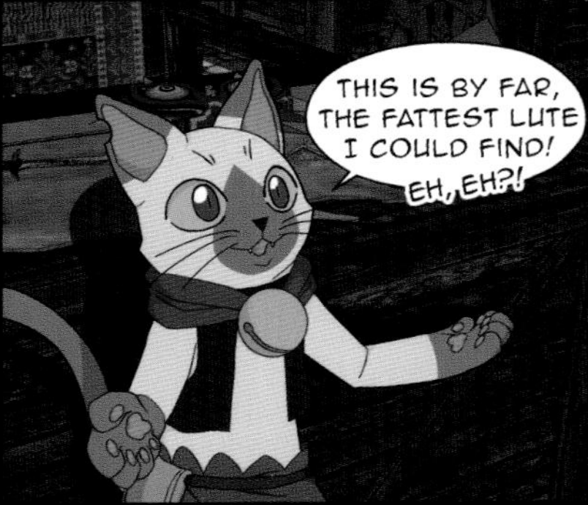
THIS IS BY FAR, THE FATTEST LUTE I COULD FIND!
EH, EH?!
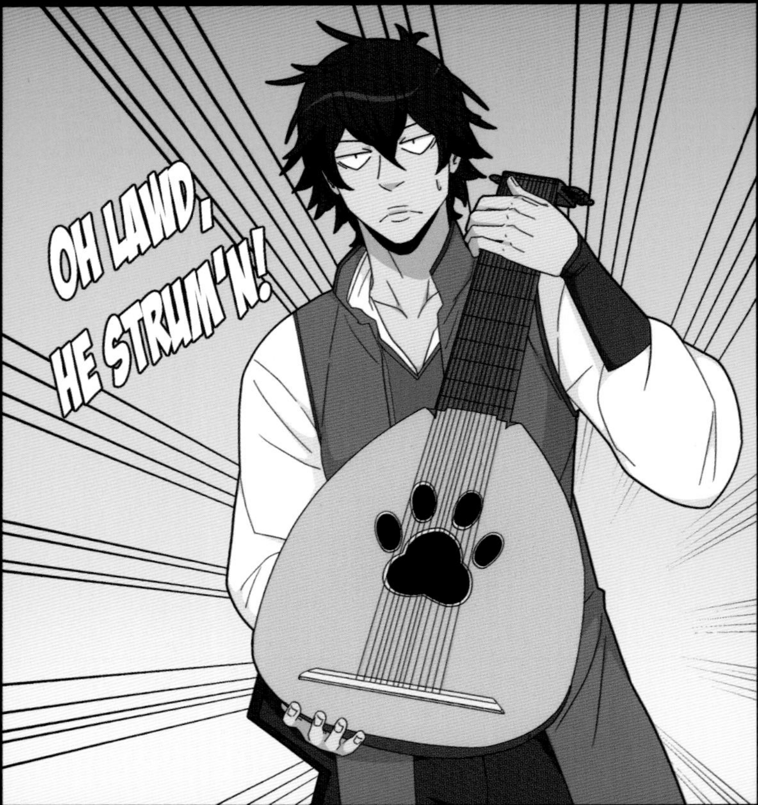
OH LAWD, HE STRUM'N!

...

I LOVE IT!

I HAVE TO GIVE IT TO THIS GAME—

ONE OF THE MOST IMPORTANT ASPECTS TO AN RPG IS PERSONALITY, AND THIS GAME HAS PLENTY OF IT!

I'M REALLY STARTING TO FALL IN LOVE WITH THE CHARACTERS IN THIS GAME — EVEN THE VENDORS!

I ALSO DON'T FEEL LIKE I'M ON ANY RAILS.

THIS GAME REWARDS EXPLORATION.

AND THAT'S PRETTY RARE IN GAMES LIKE THESE.

AND I THINK YOU ALL CAN AGREE WITH ME THAT GAMES LIKE THESE SHOULD BE AN ESCAPE.

A DISTRACTION FROM OUR DAILY TRIALS.

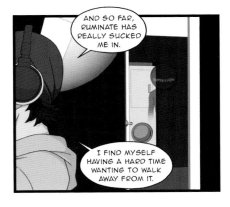

AND SO FAR, RUMINATE HAS REALLY SUCKED ME IN.

I FIND MYSELF HAVING A HARD TIME WANTING TO WALK AWAY FROM IT.

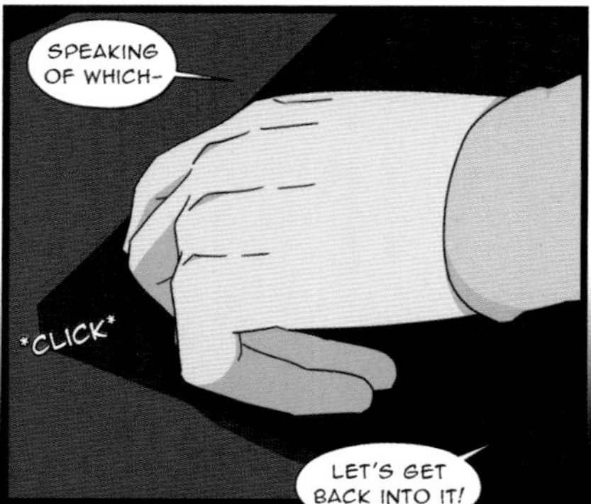
SPEAKING OF WHICH-
CLICK
LET'S GET BACK INTO IT!

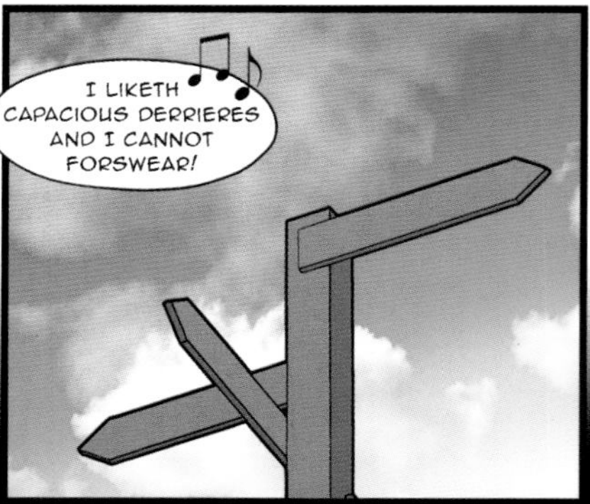
I LIKETH CAPACIOUS DERRIERES AND I CANNOT FORSWEAR!

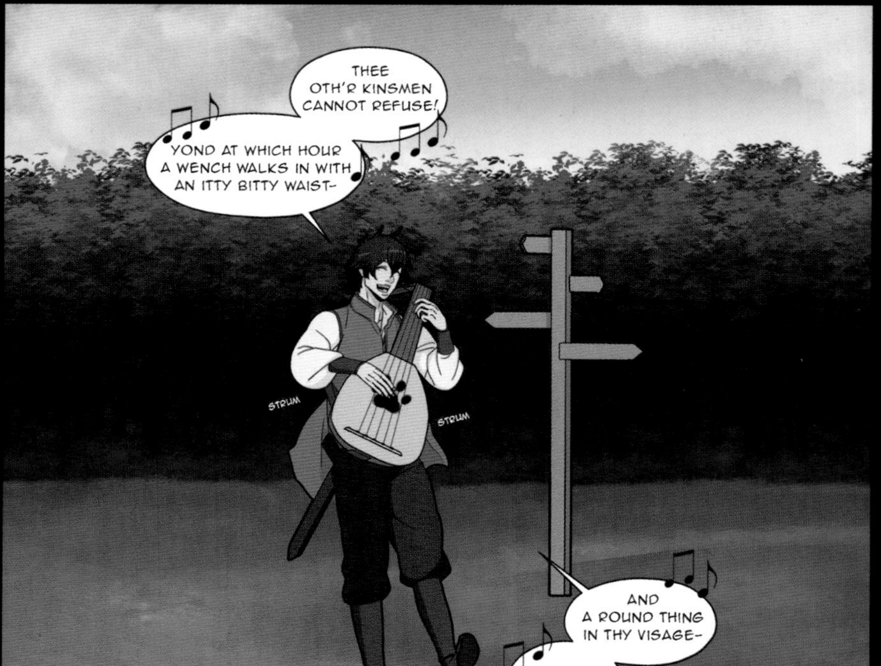
THEE OTH'R KINSMEN CANNOT REFUSE!
YOND AT WHICH HOUR A WENCH WALKS IN WITH AN ITTY BITTY WAIST-
STRUM
STRUM
AND A ROUND THING IN THY VISAGE-
THEE BECOMETH FIRM!

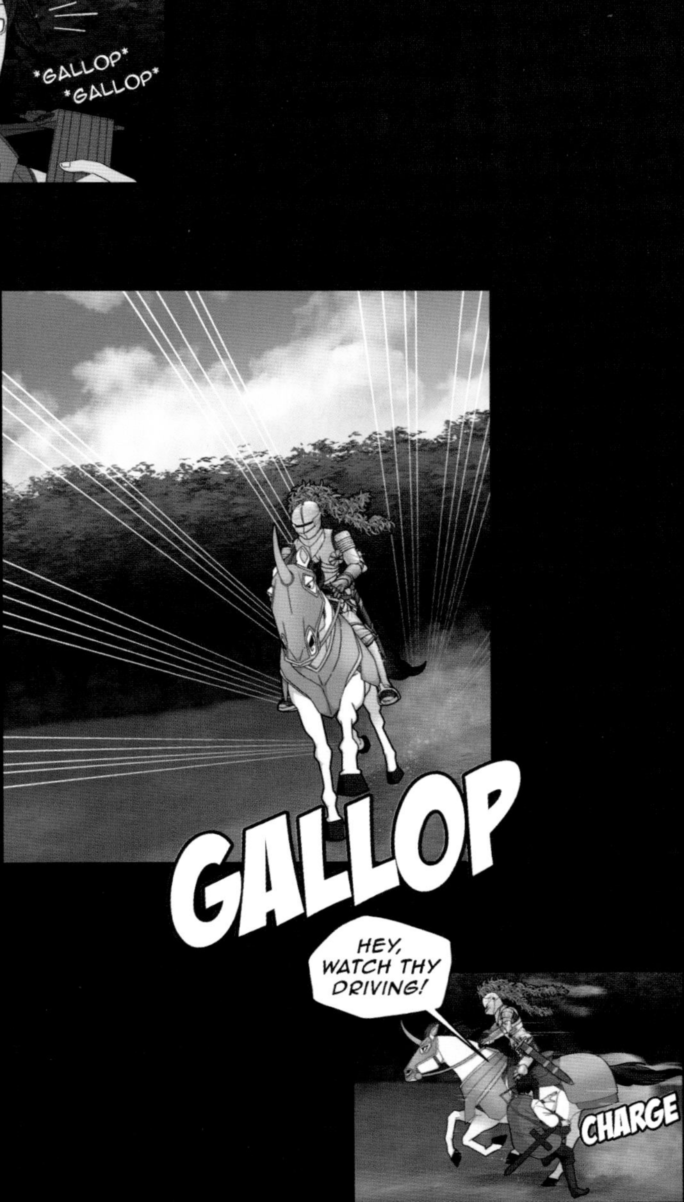
GALLOP
GALLOP
GALLOP
HEY, WATCH THY DRIVING!
CHARGE

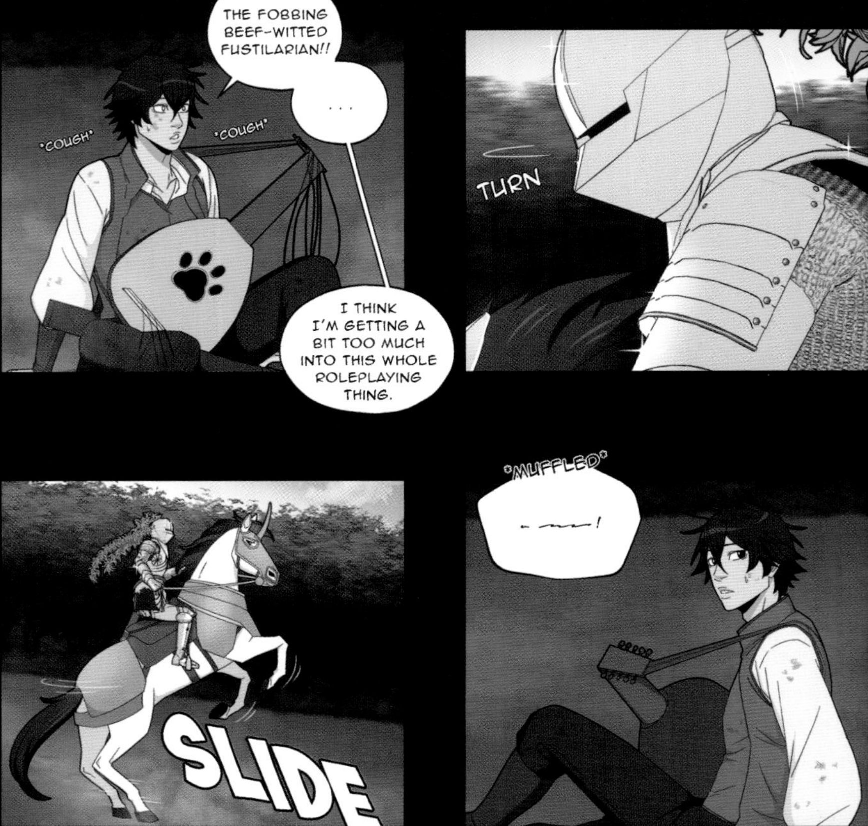
THE FOBBING BEEF-WITTED FUSTILARIAN!!
COUGH
COUGH
. . .
I THINK I'M GETTING A BIT TOO MUCH INTO THIS WHOLE ROLEPLAYING THING.
TURN
SLIDE
MUFFLED

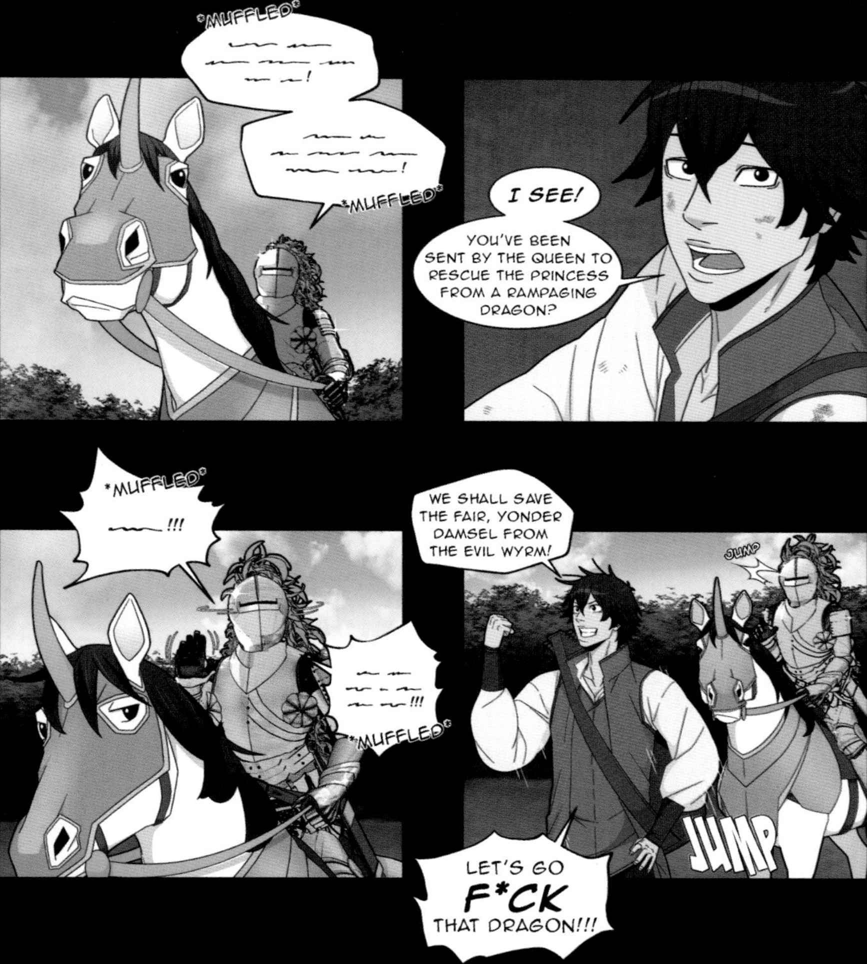
MUFFLED
MUFFLED
I SEE!
YOU'VE BEEN SENT BY THE QUEEN TO RESCUE THE PRINCESS FROM A RAMPAGING DRAGON?
MUFFLED
MUFFLED
WE SHALL SAVE THE FAIR, YONDER DAMSEL FROM THE EVIL WYRM!
JUMP
JUMP
LET'S GO F*CK THAT DRAGON!!!

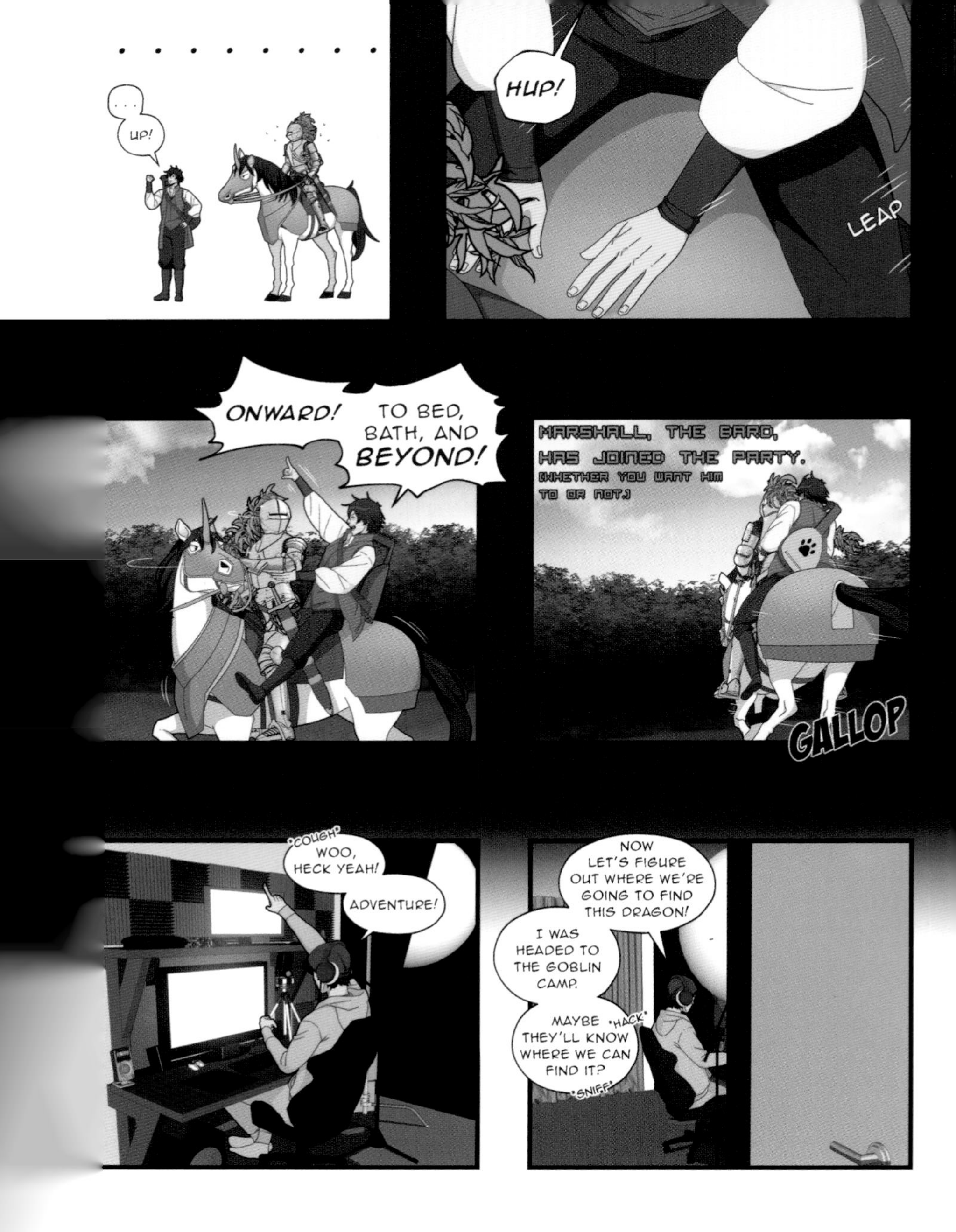
. . . .
. . .
UP!
HUP!
LEAP
ONWARD!
TO BED, BATH, AND BEYOND!
MARSHALL, THE BARD, HAS JOINED THE PARTY.
(WHETHER YOU WANT HIM TO OR NOT.)
GALLOP
COUGH
WOO, HECK YEAH!
ADVENTURE!
NOW LET'S FIGURE OUT WHERE WE'RE GOING TO FIND THIS DRAGON!
I WAS HEADED TO THE GOBLIN CAMP.
MAYBE THEY'LL KNOW WHERE WE CAN FIND IT?
HACK
SNIFF

OR MAYBE THE MINOTAUR KNOWS?
HE'S OUR FRIEND NOW, SO HE MIGHT HELP US.
CLICK

OPEN

EMPTY

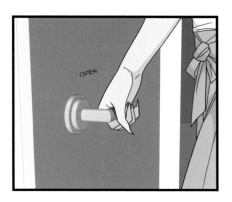

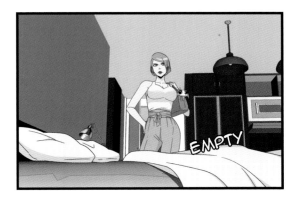

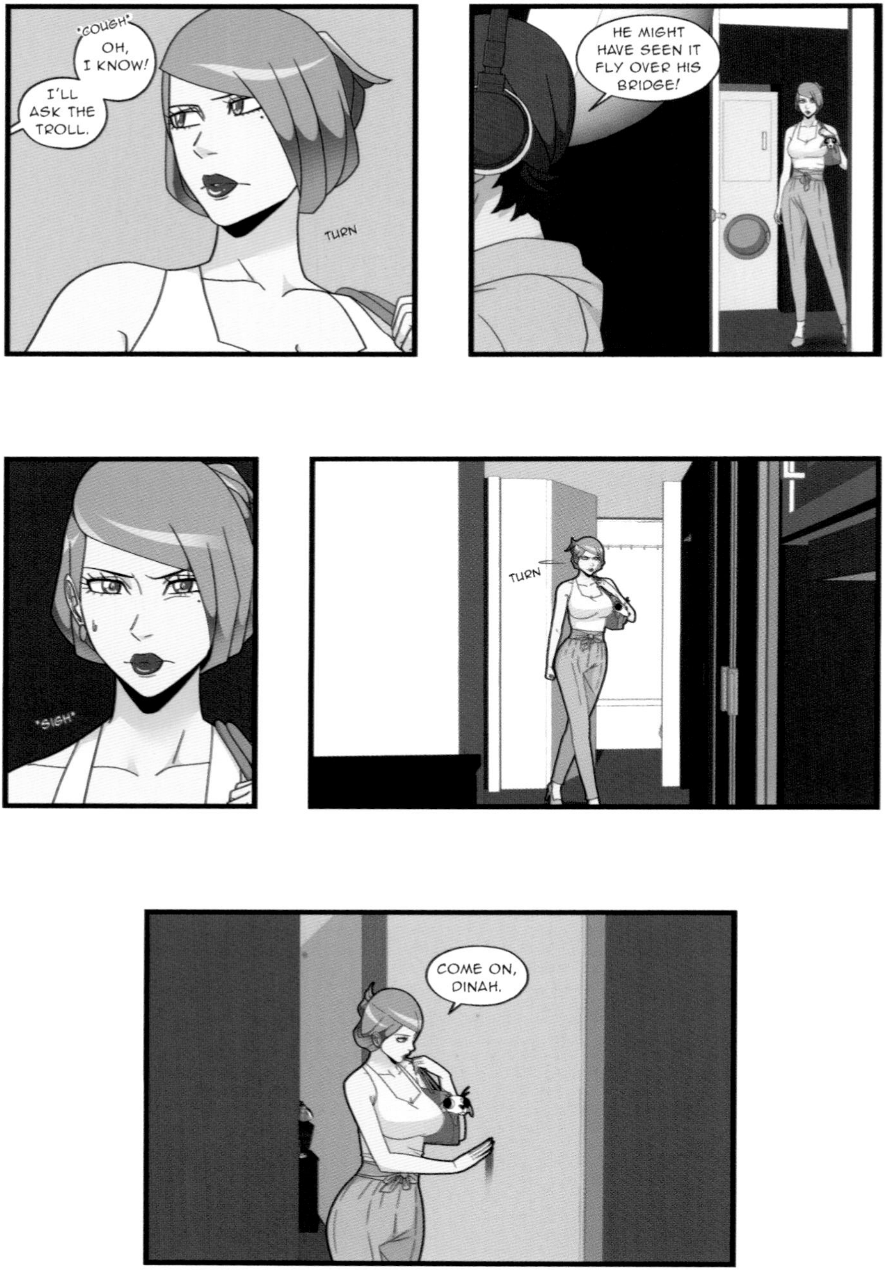
COUGH
OH, I KNOW!
I'LL ASK THE TROLL.
TURN
HE MIGHT HAVE SEEN IT FLY OVER HIS BRIDGE!
SIGH
TURN
COME ON, DINAH.

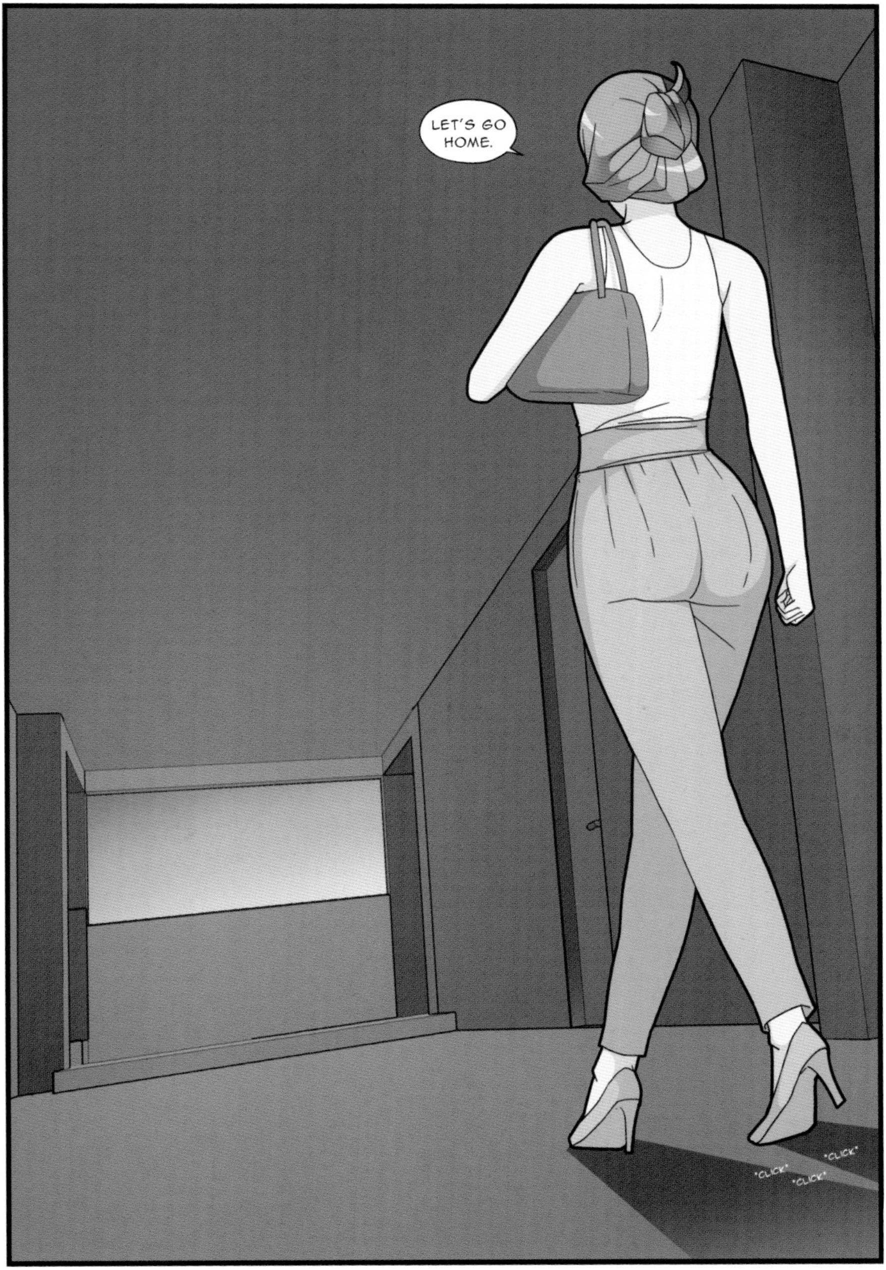
LET'S GO HOME.
CLICK
CLICK
CLICK

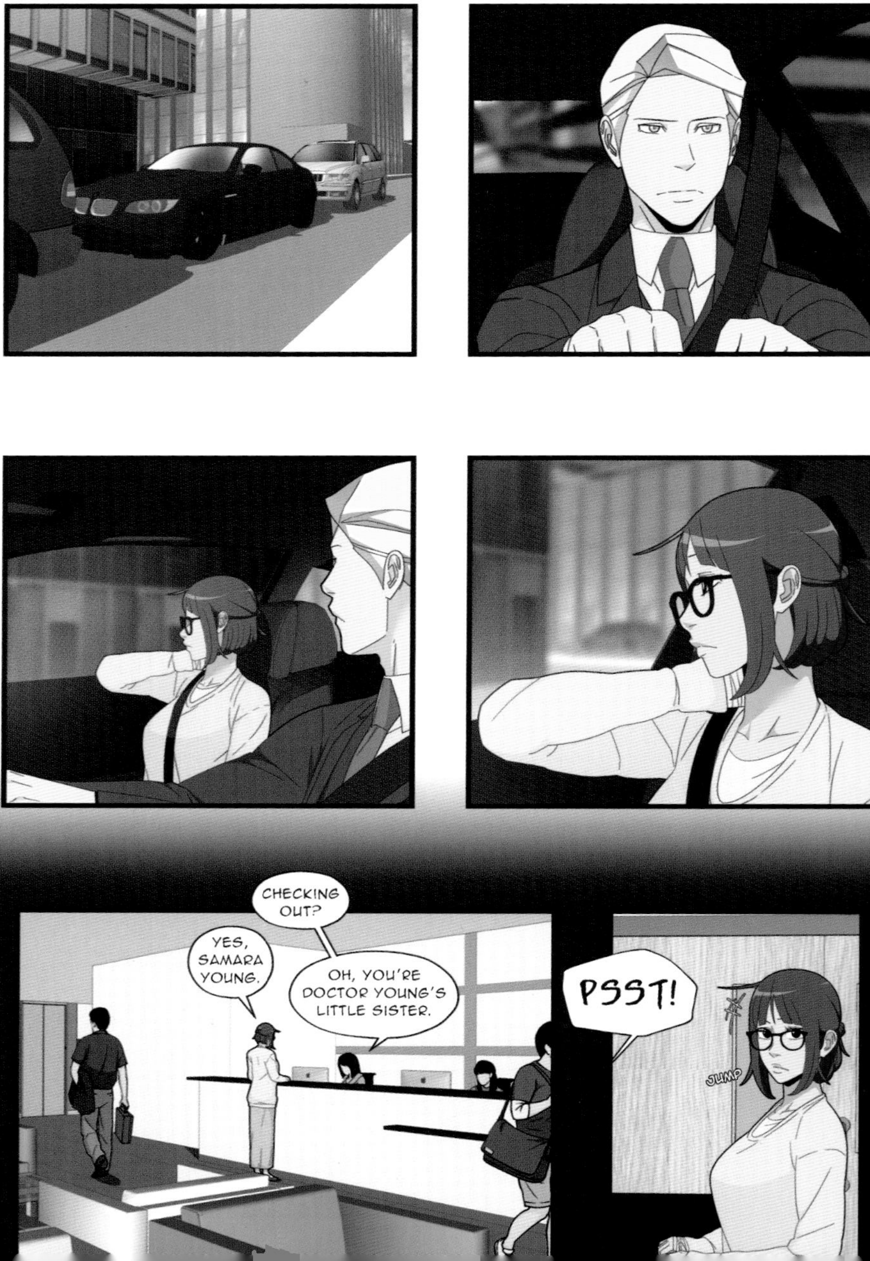
YES, SAMARA YOUNG.
CHECKING OUT?
OH, YOU'RE DOCTOR YOUNG'S LITTLE SISTER.
PSST!
JUMP

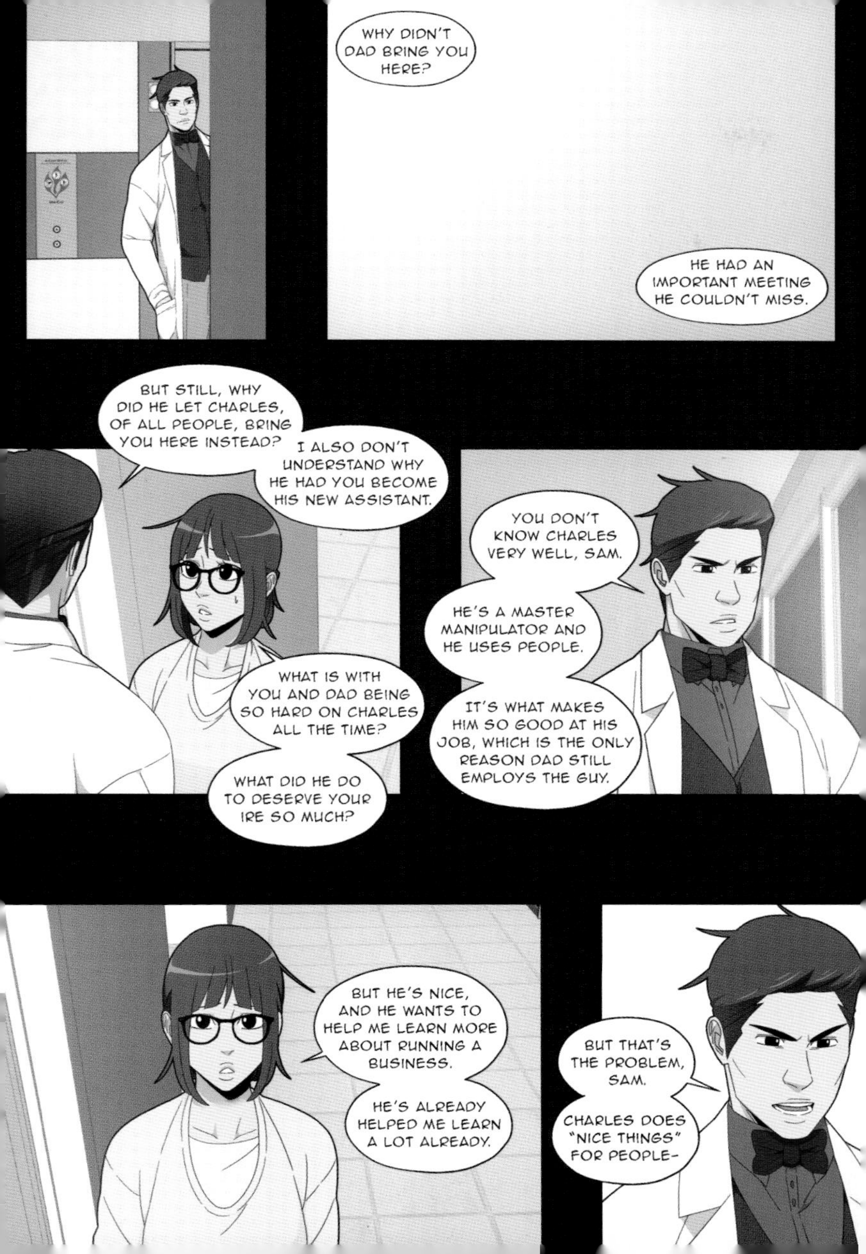
WHY DIDN'T DAD BRING YOU HERE?
HE HAD AN IMPORTANT MEETING HE COULDN'T MISS.
BUT STILL, WHY DID HE LET CHARLES, OF ALL PEOPLE, BRING YOU HERE INSTEAD?
I ALSO DON'T UNDERSTAND WHY HE HAD YOU BECOME HIS NEW ASSISTANT.
WHAT IS WITH YOU AND DAD BEING SO HARD ON CHARLES ALL THE TIME?
WHAT DID HE DO TO DESERVE YOUR IRE SO MUCH?
YOU DON'T KNOW CHARLES VERY WELL, SAM.
HE'S A MASTER MANIPULATOR AND HE USES PEOPLE.
IT'S WHAT MAKES HIM SO GOOD AT HIS JOB, WHICH IS THE ONLY REASON DAD STILL EMPLOYS THE GUY.
BUT HE'S NICE, AND HE WANTS TO HELP ME LEARN MORE ABOUT RUNNING A BUSINESS.
HE'S ALREADY HELPED ME LEARN A LOT ALREADY.
BUT THAT'S THE PROBLEM, SAM.
CHARLES DOES "NICE THINGS" FOR PEOPLE-

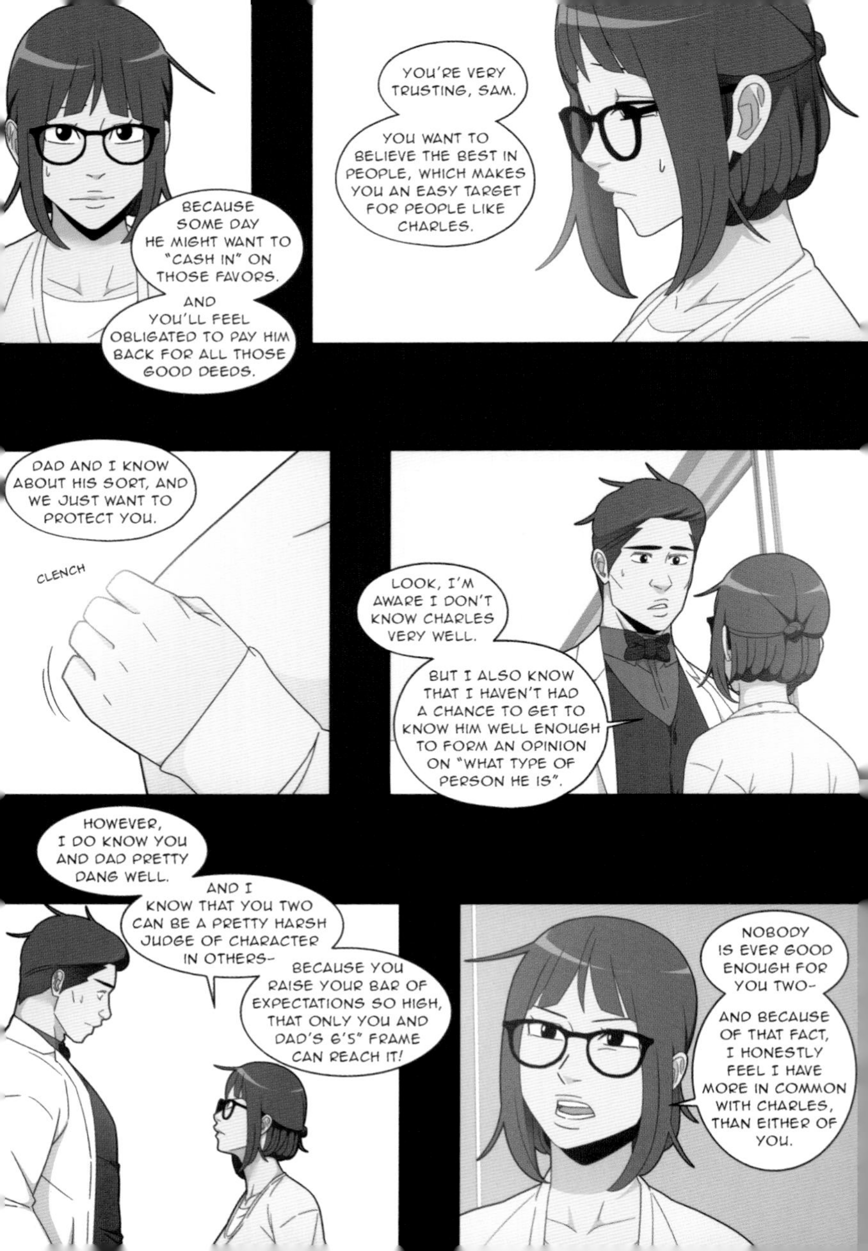
BECAUSE SOME DAY HE MIGHT WANT TO "CASH IN" ON THOSE FAVORS.
AND YOU'LL FEEL OBLIGATED TO PAY HIM BACK FOR ALL THOSE GOOD DEEDS.
YOU'RE VERY TRUSTING, SAM.
YOU WANT TO BELIEVE THE BEST IN PEOPLE, WHICH MAKES YOU AN EASY TARGET FOR PEOPLE LIKE CHARLES.
DAD AND I KNOW ABOUT HIS SORT, AND WE JUST WANT TO PROTECT YOU.
CLENCH
LOOK, I'M AWARE I DON'T KNOW CHARLES VERY WELL.
BUT I ALSO KNOW THAT I HAVEN'T HAD A CHANCE TO GET TO KNOW HIM WELL ENOUGH TO FORM AN OPINION ON "WHAT TYPE OF PERSON HE IS".
HOWEVER, I DO KNOW YOU AND DAD PRETTY DANG WELL.
AND I KNOW THAT YOU TWO CAN BE A PRETTY HARSH JUDGE OF CHARACTER IN OTHERS-
BECAUSE YOU RAISE YOUR BAR OF EXPECTATIONS SO HIGH, THAT ONLY YOU AND DAD'S 6'5" FRAME CAN REACH IT!
NOBODY IS EVER GOOD ENOUGH FOR YOU TWO-
AND BECAUSE OF THAT FACT, I HONESTLY FEEL I HAVE MORE IN COMMON WITH CHARLES, THAN EITHER OF YOU.

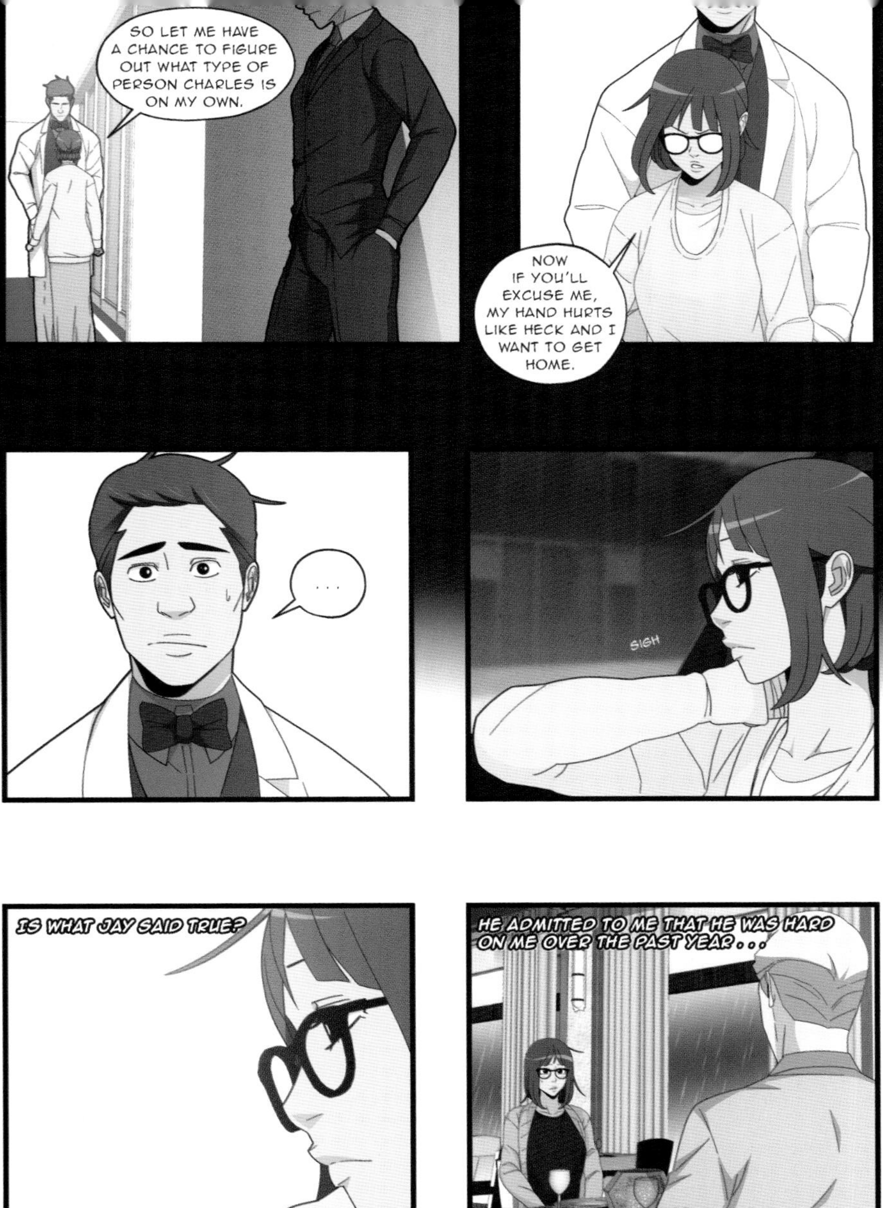
SO LET ME HAVE A CHANCE TO FIGURE OUT WHAT TYPE OF PERSON CHARLES IS ON MY OWN.
NOW IF YOU'LL EXCUSE ME, MY HAND HURTS LIKE HECK AND I WANT TO GET HOME.
. . .
SIGH
IS WHAT JAY SAID TRUE?
DOES CHARLES REALLY USE AND MANIPULATE PEOPLE?
HE ADMITTED TO ME THAT HE WAS HARD ON ME OVER THE PAST YEAR . . .
SO HE COULD PUSH ME INTO BEING A MORE CAPABLE CEO.

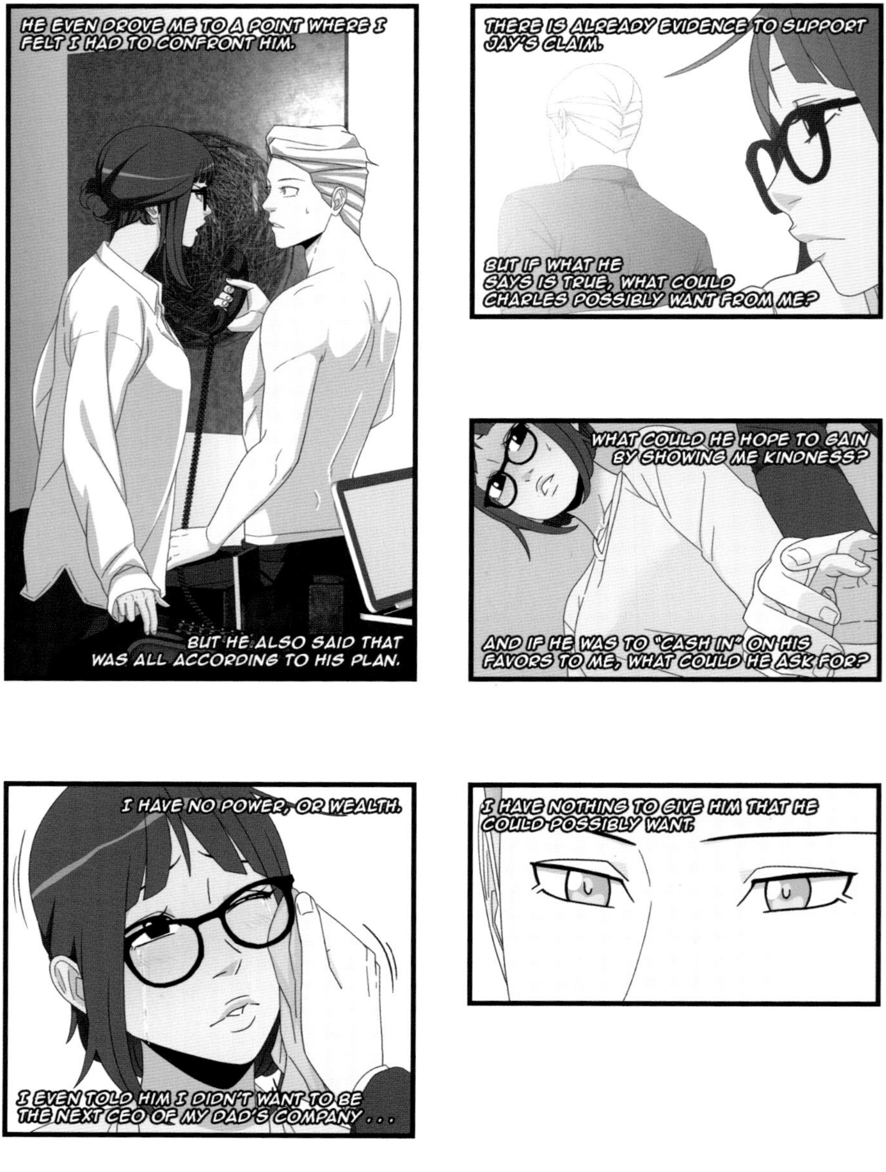
HE EVEN DROVE ME TO A POINT WHERE I FELT I HAD TO CONFRONT HIM.
BUT HE ALSO SAID THAT WAS ALL ACCORDING TO HIS PLAN.
THERE IS ALREADY EVIDENCE TO SUPPORT JAY'S CLAIM.
BUT IF WHAT HE SAYS IS TRUE, WHAT COULD CHARLES POSSIBLY WANT FROM ME?
WHAT COULD HE HOPE TO GAIN BY SHOWING ME KINDNESS?
AND IF HE WAS TO "CASH IN" ON HIS FAVORS TO ME, WHAT COULD HE ASK FOR?
I HAVE NO POWER, OR WEALTH.
I EVEN TOLD HIM I DIDN'T WANT TO BE THE NEXT CEO OF MY DAD'S COMPANY . . .
I HAVE NOTHING TO GIVE HIM THAT HE COULD POSSIBLY WANT.

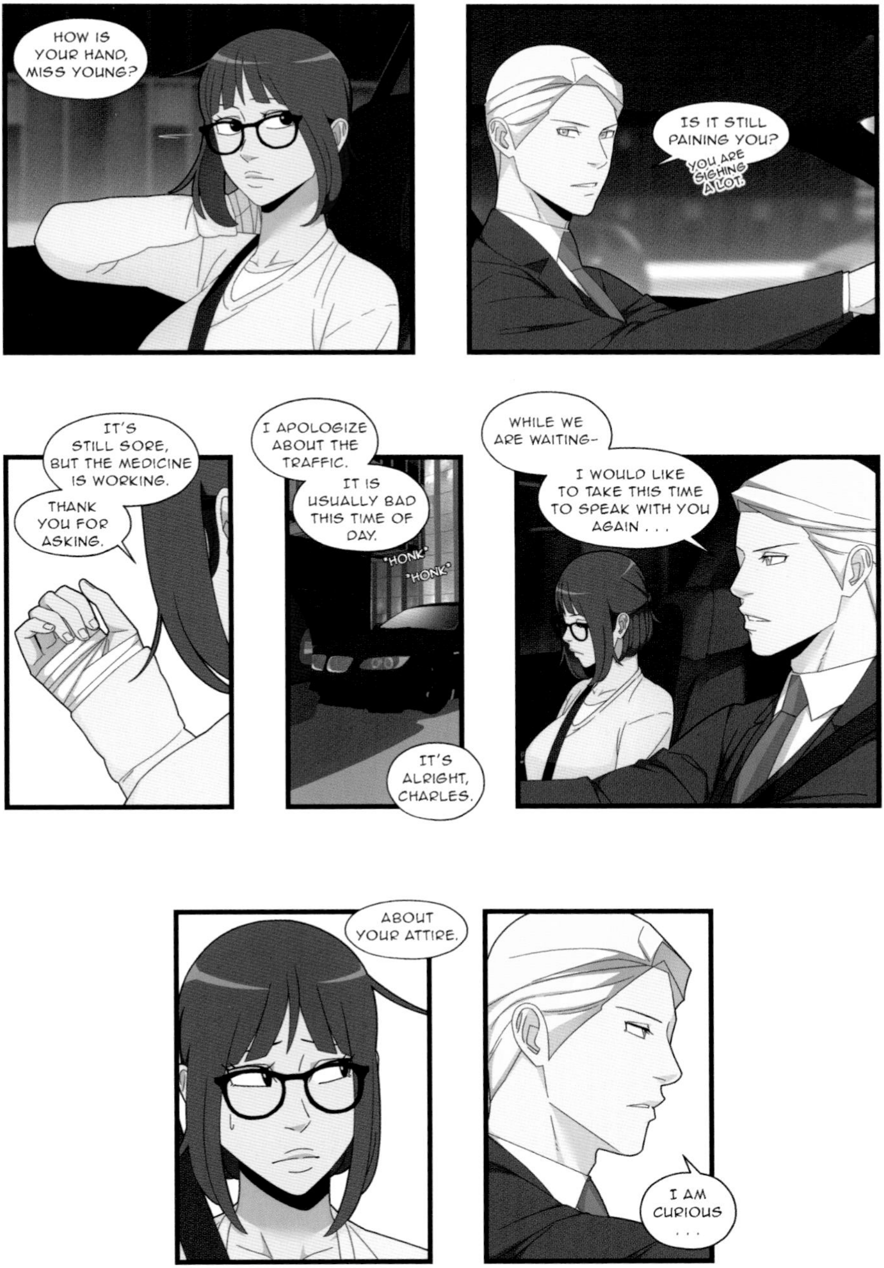
HOW IS YOUR HAND, MISS YOUNG?
IS IT STILL PAINING YOU?
YOU ARE SIGHING A LOT.
IT'S STILL SORE, BUT THE MEDICINE IS WORKING.
THANK YOU FOR ASKING.
I APOLOGIZE ABOUT THE TRAFFIC.
IT IS USUALLY BAD THIS TIME OF DAY.
HONK
HONK
IT'S ALRIGHT, CHARLES.
WHILE WE ARE WAITING-
I WOULD LIKE TO TAKE THIS TIME TO SPEAK WITH YOU AGAIN . . .
ABOUT YOUR ATTIRE.
I AM CURIOUS . . .

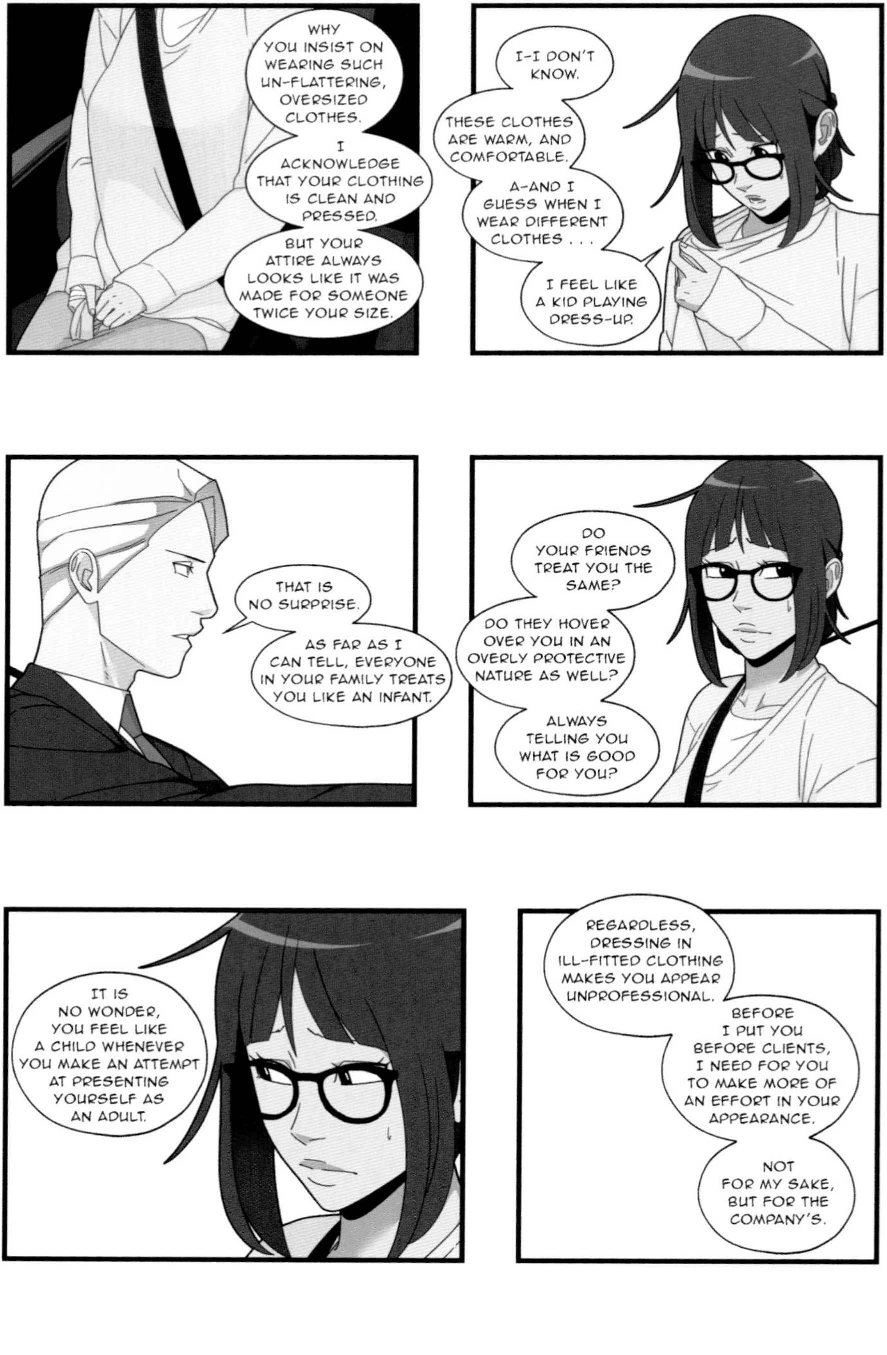
WHY YOU INSIST ON WEARING SUCH UN-FLATTERING, OVERSIZED CLOTHES.
I ACKNOWLEDGE THAT YOUR CLOTHING IS CLEAN AND PRESSED.
BUT YOUR ATTIRE ALWAYS LOOKS LIKE IT WAS MADE FOR SOMEONE TWICE YOUR SIZE.
I-I DON'T KNOW.
THESE CLOTHES ARE WARM, AND COMFORTABLE.
A-AND I GUESS WHEN I WEAR DIFFERENT CLOTHES . . .
I FEEL LIKE A KID PLAYING DRESS-UP.
THAT IS NO SURPRISE.
AS FAR AS I CAN TELL, EVERYONE IN YOUR FAMILY TREATS YOU LIKE AN INFANT.
DO YOUR FRIENDS TREAT YOU THE SAME?
DO THEY HOVER OVER YOU IN AN OVERLY PROTECTIVE NATURE AS WELL?
ALWAYS TELLING YOU WHAT IS GOOD FOR YOU?
IT IS NO WONDER, YOU FEEL LIKE A CHILD WHENEVER YOU MAKE AN ATTEMPT AT PRESENTING YOURSELF AS AN ADULT.
REGARDLESS, DRESSING IN ILL-FITTED CLOTHING MAKES YOU APPEAR UNPROFESSIONAL.
BEFORE I PUT YOU BEFORE CLIENTS, I NEED FOR YOU TO MAKE MORE OF AN EFFORT IN YOUR APPEARANCE.
NOT FOR MY SAKE, BUT FOR THE COMPANY'S.

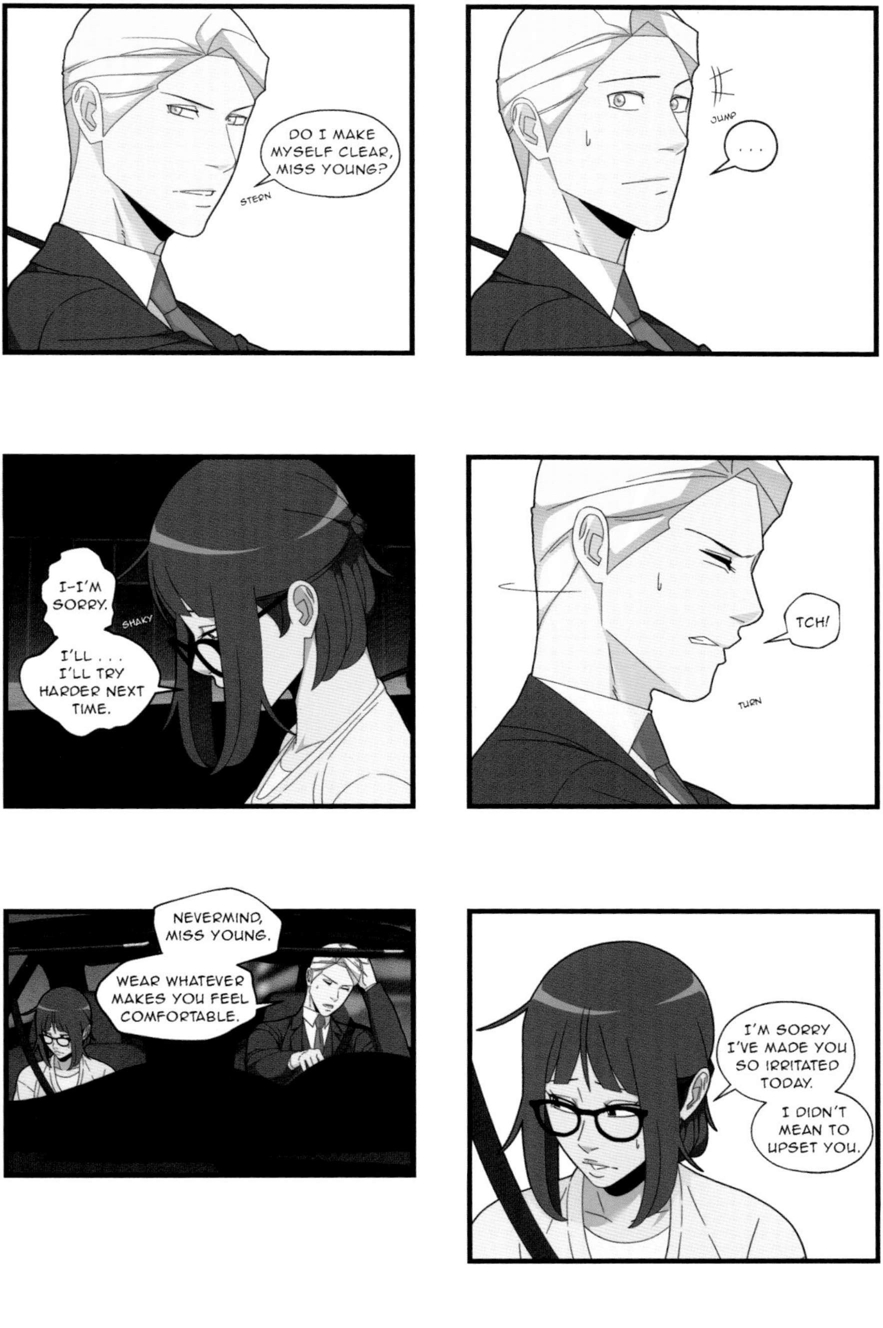
DO I MAKE MYSELF CLEAR, MISS YOUNG?
STERN
JUMP
. . .
I-I'M SORRY.
SHAKY
I'LL . . . I'LL TRY HARDER NEXT TIME.
TCH!
TURN
NEVERMIND, MISS YOUNG.
WEAR WHATEVER MAKES YOU FEEL COMFORTABLE.
I'M SORRY I'VE MADE YOU SO IRRITATED TODAY.
I DIDN'T MEAN TO UPSET YOU.

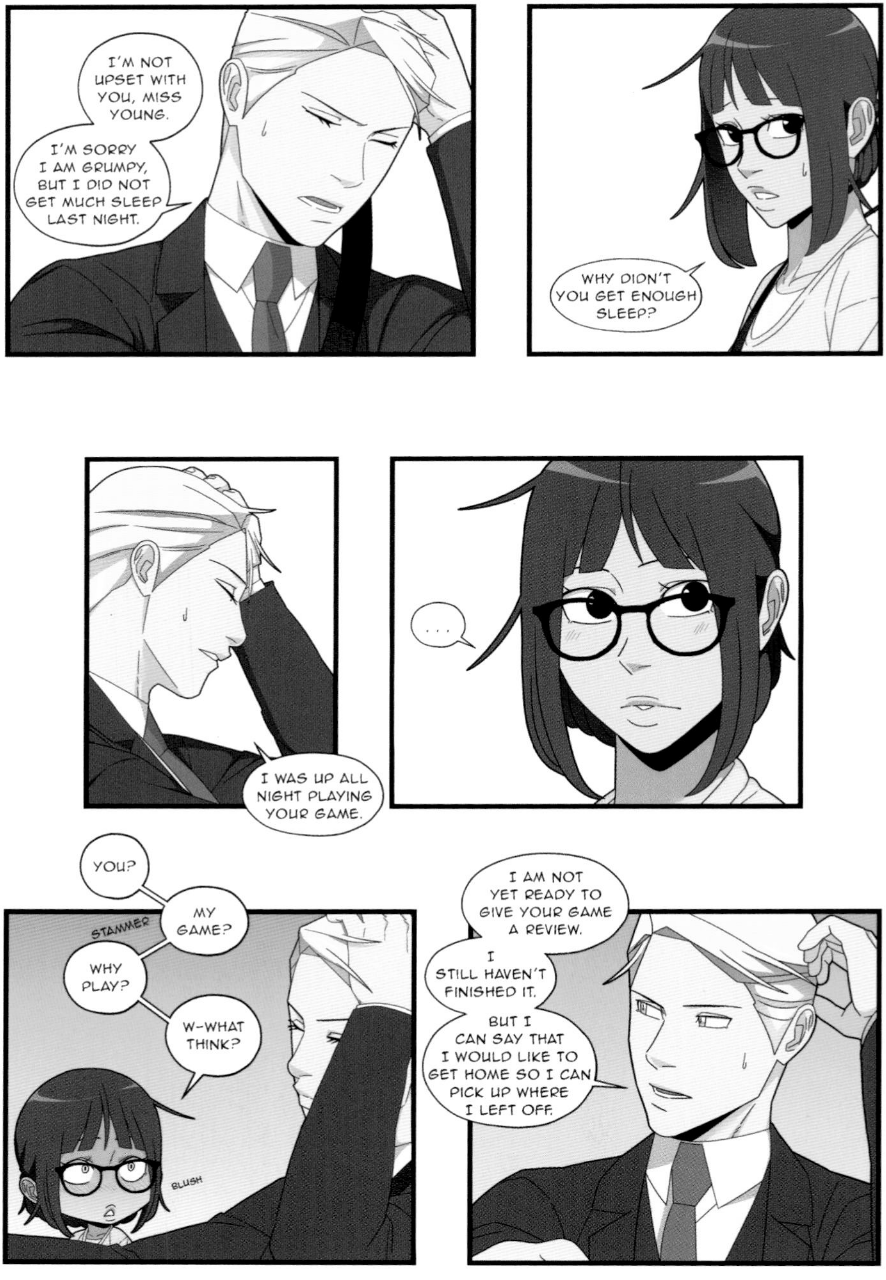
I'M NOT UPSET WITH YOU, MISS YOUNG.
I'M SORRY I AM GRUMPY, BUT I DID NOT GET MUCH SLEEP LAST NIGHT.
WHY DIDN'T YOU GET ENOUGH SLEEP?
I WAS UP ALL NIGHT PLAYING YOUR GAME.
. . .
YOU?
MY GAME?
STAMMER
WHY PLAY?
W-WHAT THINK?
BLUSH
I AM NOT YET READY TO GIVE YOUR GAME A REVIEW.
I STILL HAVEN'T FINISHED IT.
BUT I CAN SAY THAT I WOULD LIKE TO GET HOME SO I CAN PICK UP WHERE I LEFT OFF.

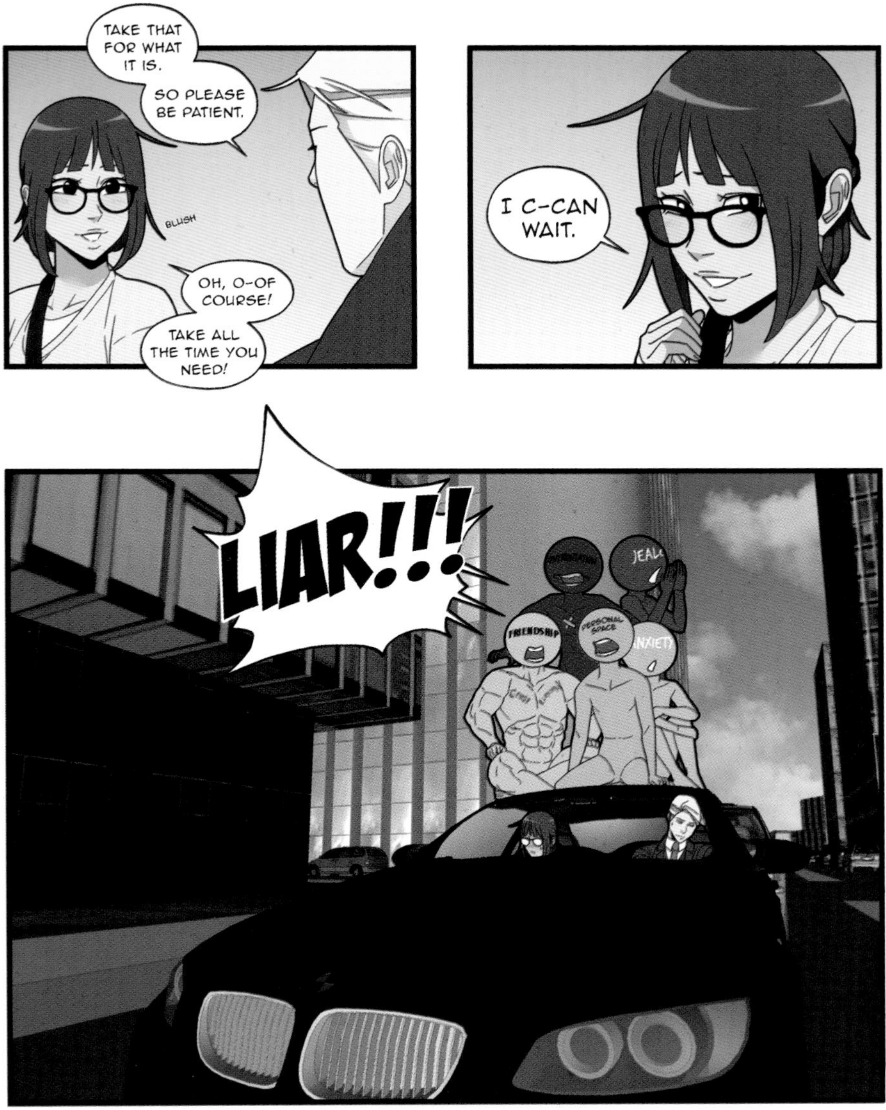
TAKE THAT FOR WHAT IT IS.
SO PLEASE BE PATIENT.
BLUSH
OH, O-OF COURSE!
TAKE ALL THE TIME YOU NEED!
I C-CAN WAIT.
LIAR!!!
FRIENDSHIP
PERSONAL SPACE

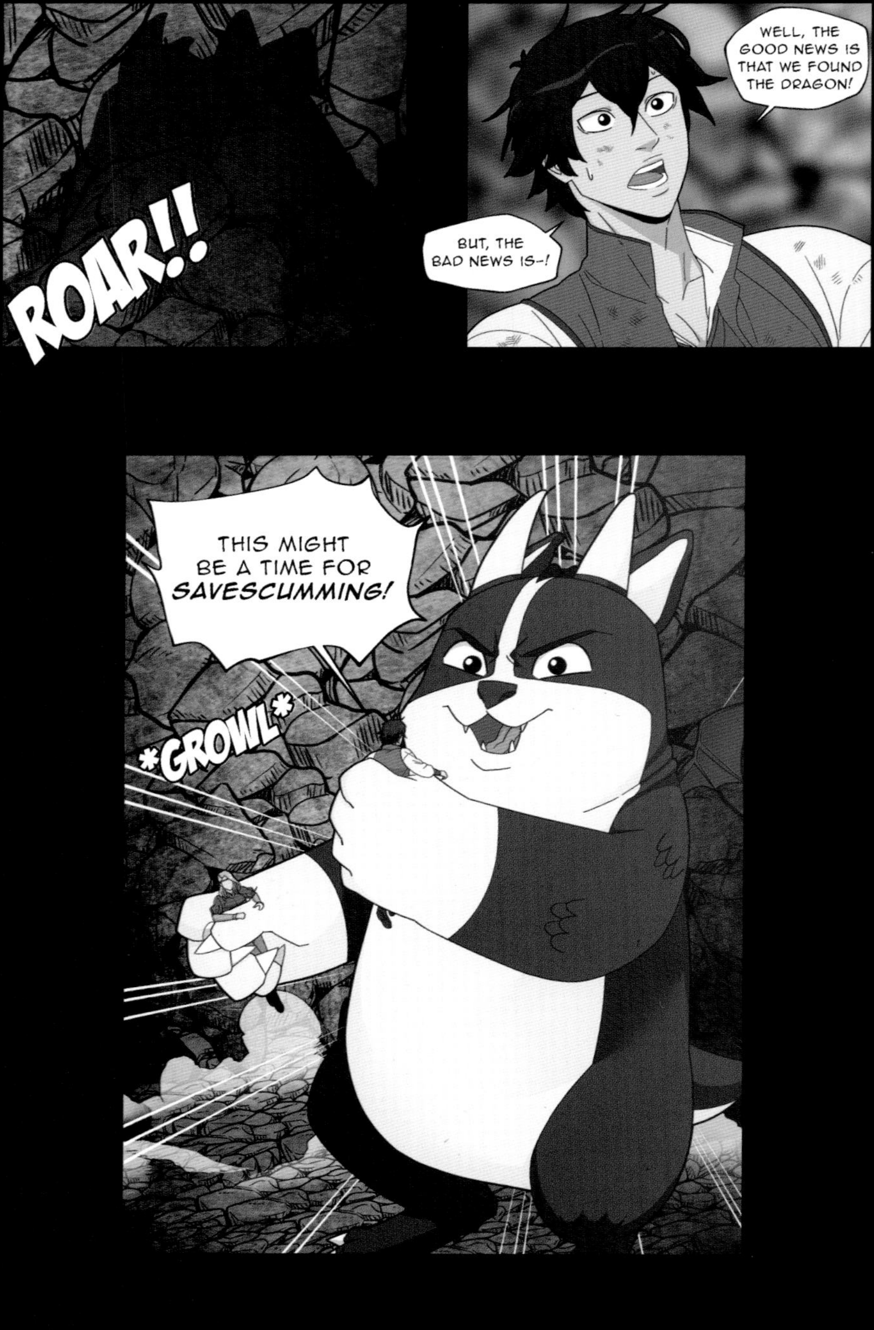
ROAR!!
WELL, THE GOOD NEWS IS THAT WE FOUND THE DRAGON!
BUT, THE BAD NEWS IS--!
THIS MIGHT BE A TIME FOR SAVESCUMMING!
GROWL

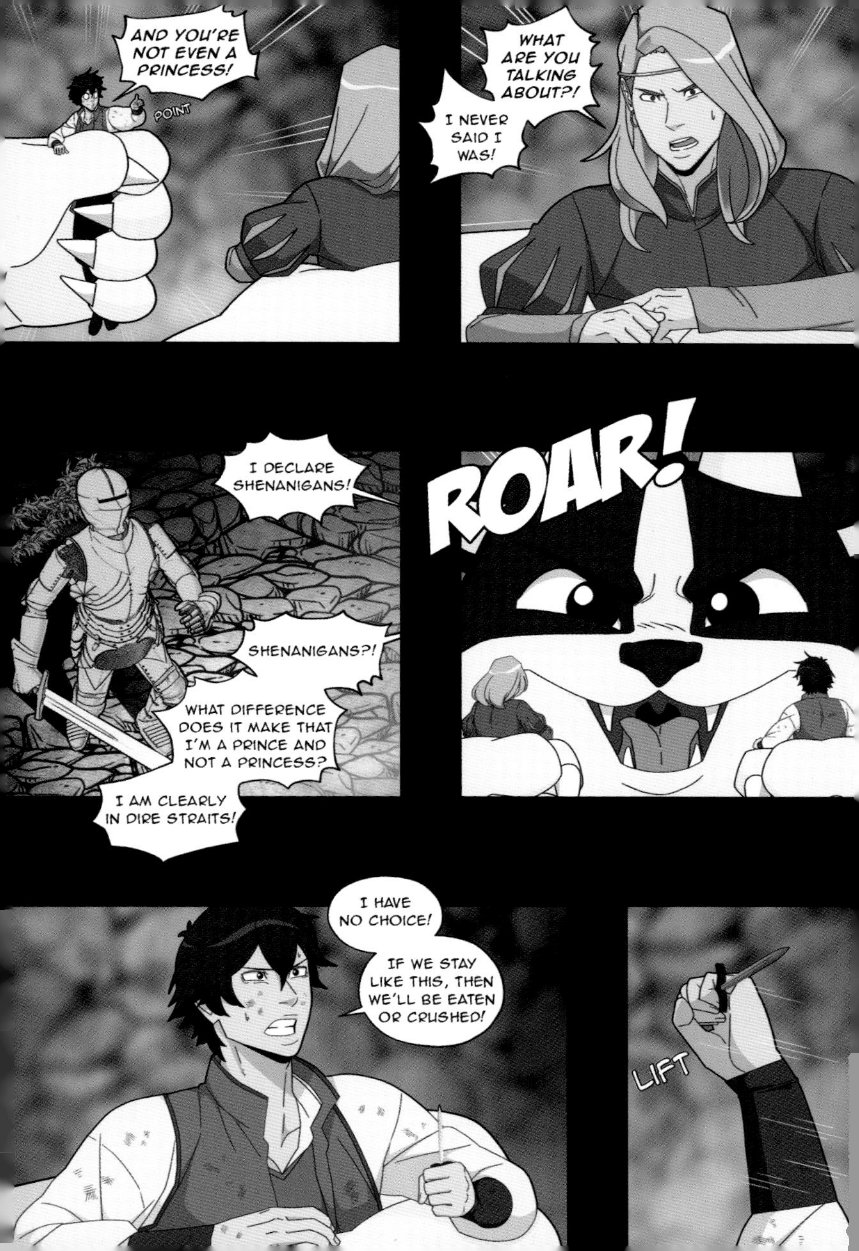
AND YOU'RE NOT EVEN A PRINCESS!
POINT
WHAT ARE YOU TALKING ABOUT?!
I NEVER SAID I WAS!
I DECLARE SHENANIGANS!
SHENANIGANS?!
WHAT DIFFERENCE DOES IT MAKE THAT I'M A PRINCE AND NOT A PRINCESS?
I AM CLEARLY IN DIRE STRAITS!
ROAR!
I HAVE NO CHOICE!
IF WE STAY LIKE THIS, THEN WE'LL BE EATEN OR CRUSHED!
LIFT

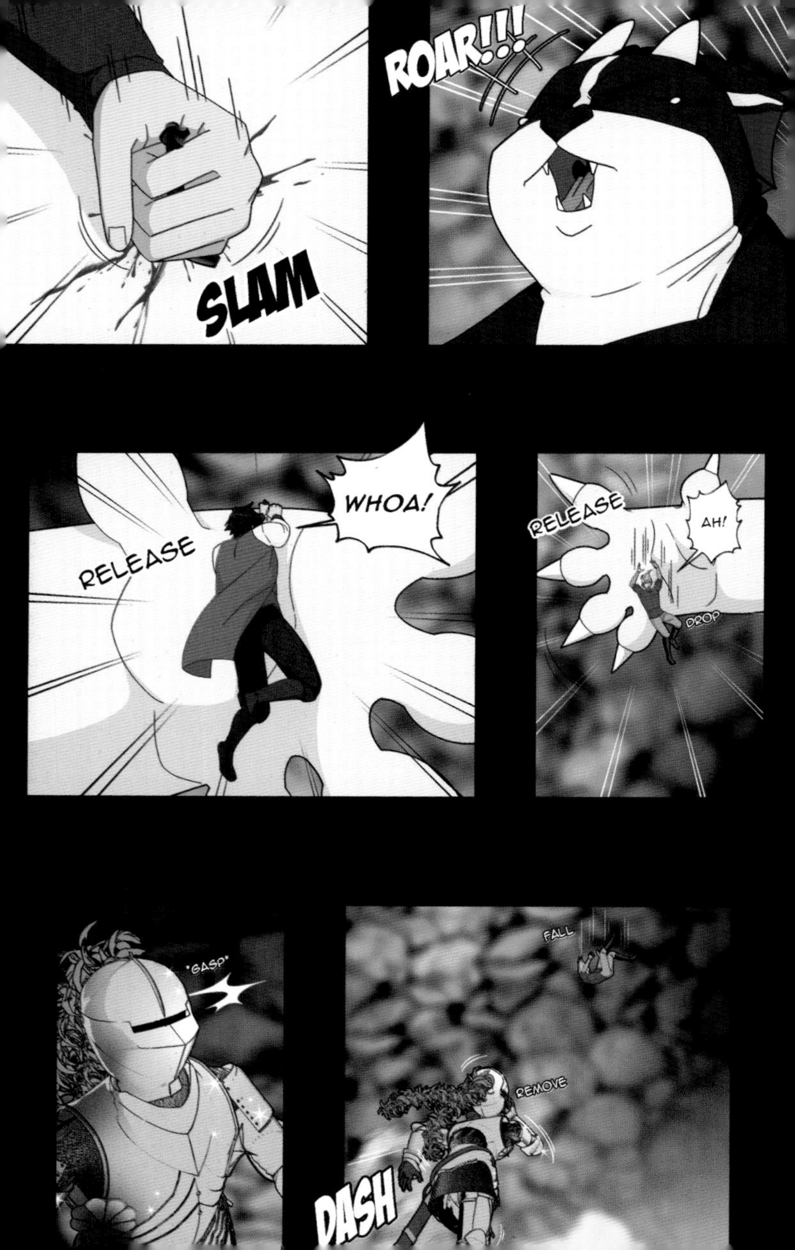
SLAM
ROAR!!!
RELEASE
WHOA!
RELEASE
AH!
DROP
GASP
FALL
REMOVE
DASH

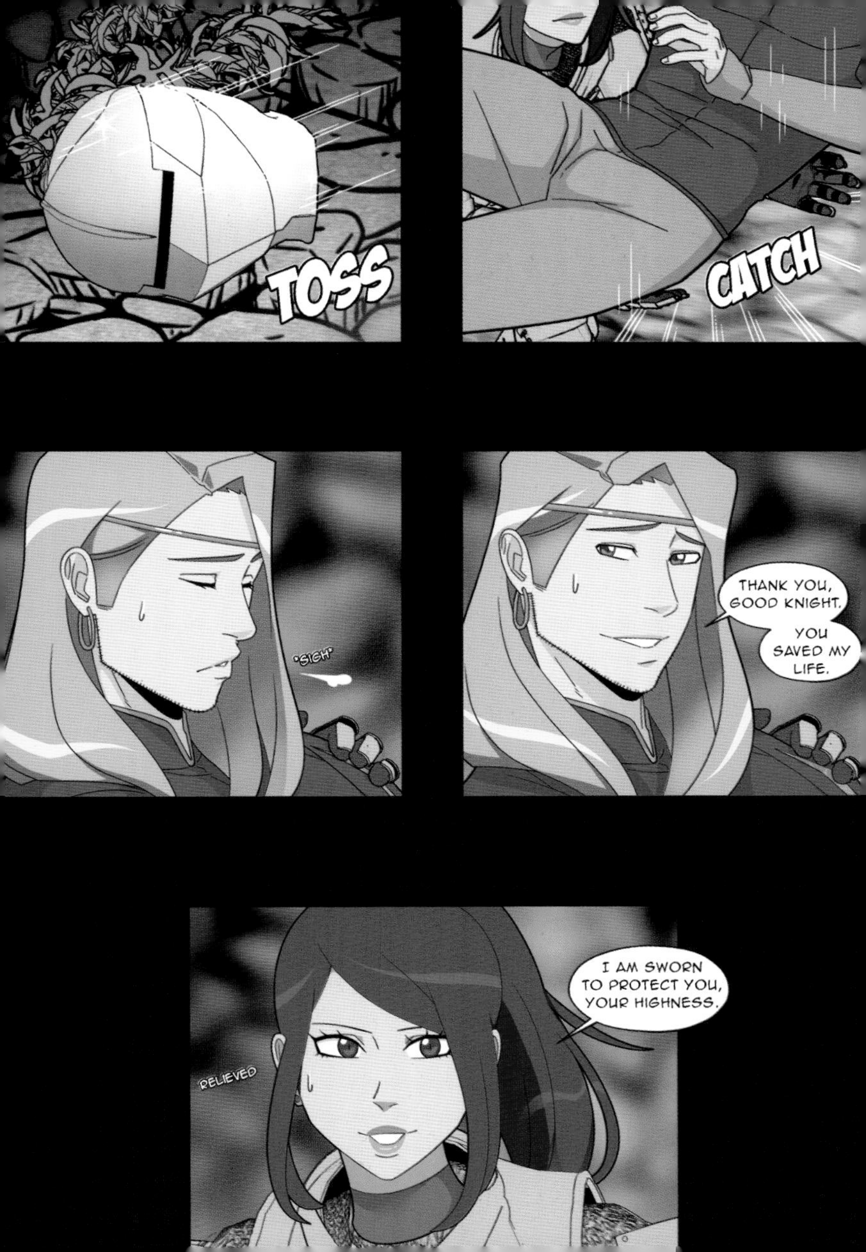
TOSS
CATCH
SIGH
THANK YOU, GOOD KNIGHT.
YOU SAVED MY LIFE.
RELIEVED
I AM SWORN TO PROTECT YOU, YOUR HIGHNESS.

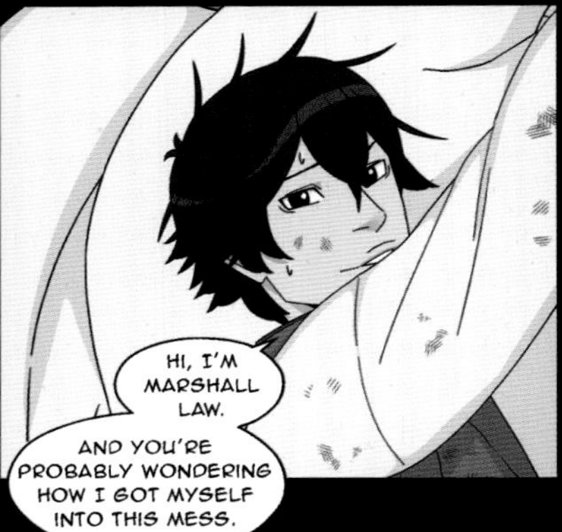
HI, I'M MARSHALL LAW.
AND YOU'RE PROBABLY WONDERING HOW I GOT MYSELF INTO THIS MESS.
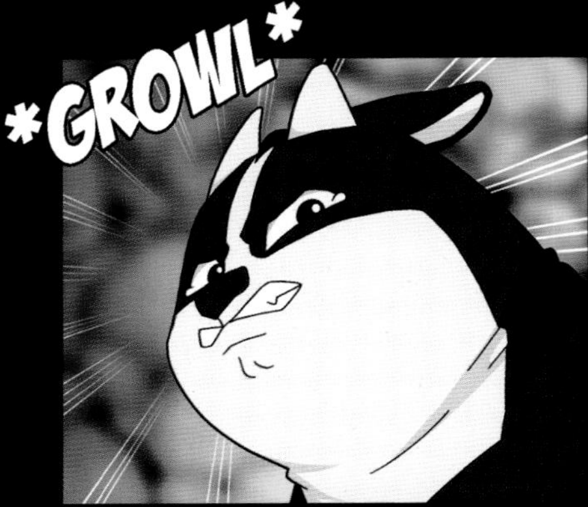
GROWL
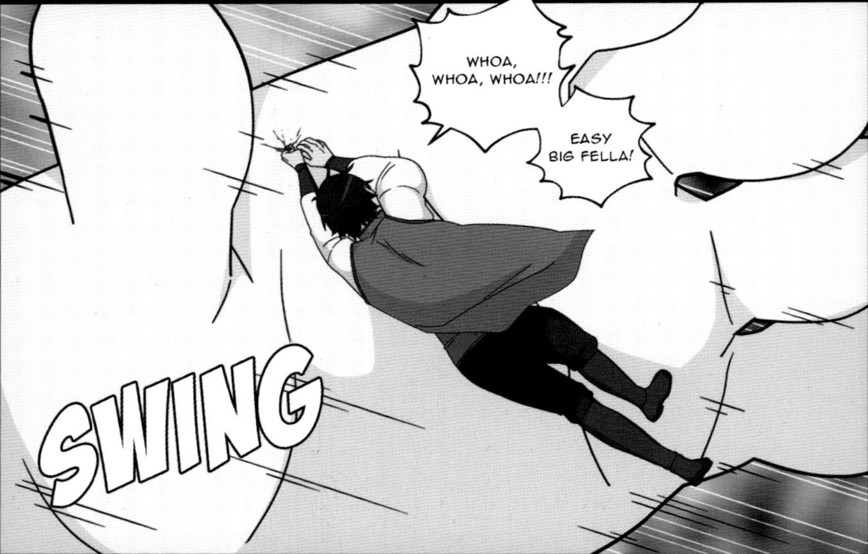
WHOA, WHOA, WHOA!!!
EASY BIG FELLA!
SWING

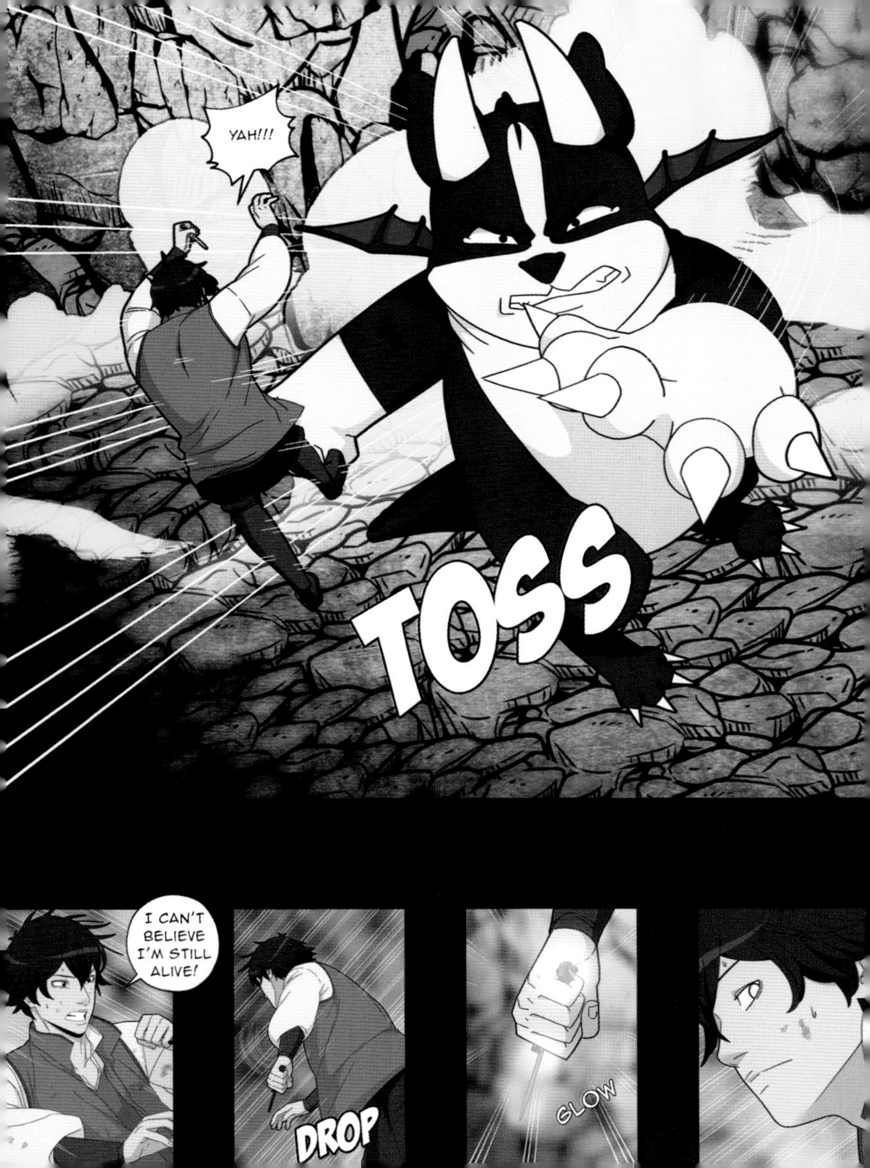
YAH!!!
TOSS
I CAN'T BELIEVE I'M STILL ALIVE!
DROP
GLOW

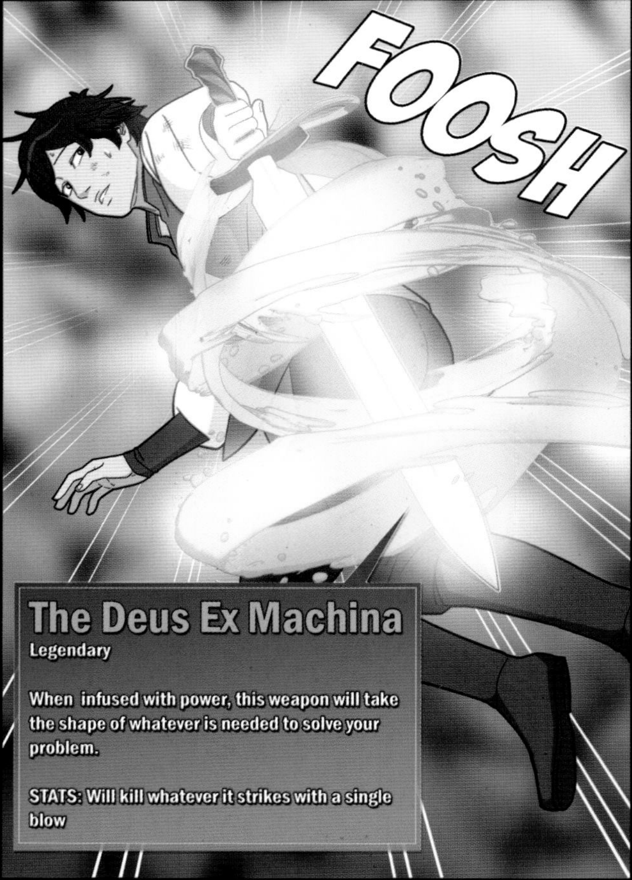
FOOSH
The Deus Ex Machina
Legendary
When infused with power, this weapon will take the shape of whatever is needed to solve your problem.
STATS: Will kill whatever it strikes with a single blow

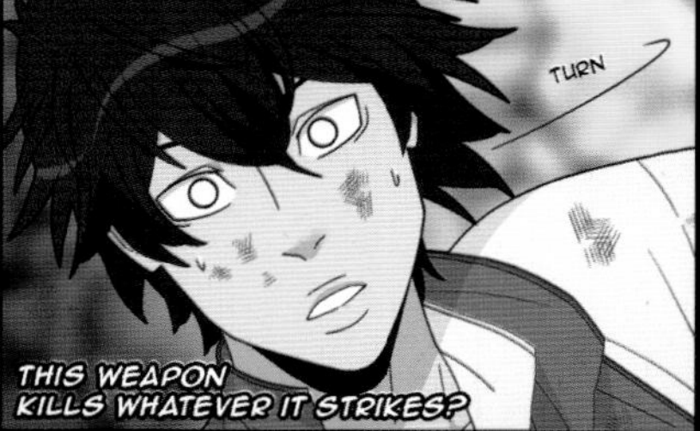
TURN
THIS WEAPON KILLS WHATEVER IT STRIKES?

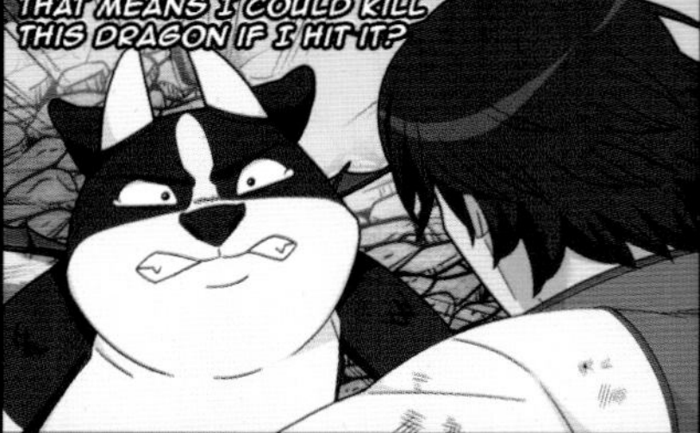
THAT MEANS I COULD KILL THIS DRAGON IF I HIT IT?

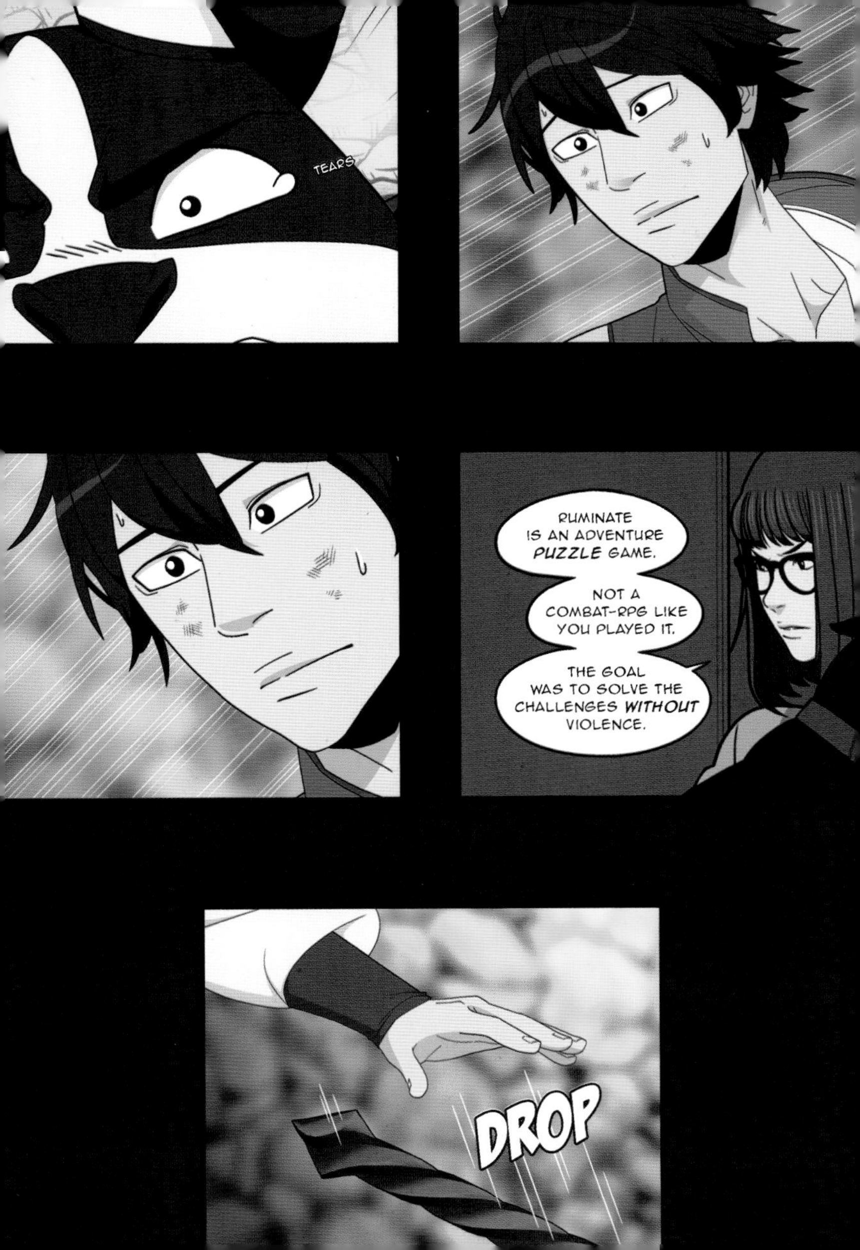
TEARS
RUMINATE IS AN ADVENTURE PUZZLE GAME.
NOT A COMBAT-RPG LIKE YOU PLAYED IT.
THE GOAL WAS TO SOLVE THE CHALLENGES WITHOUT VIOLENCE.
DROP

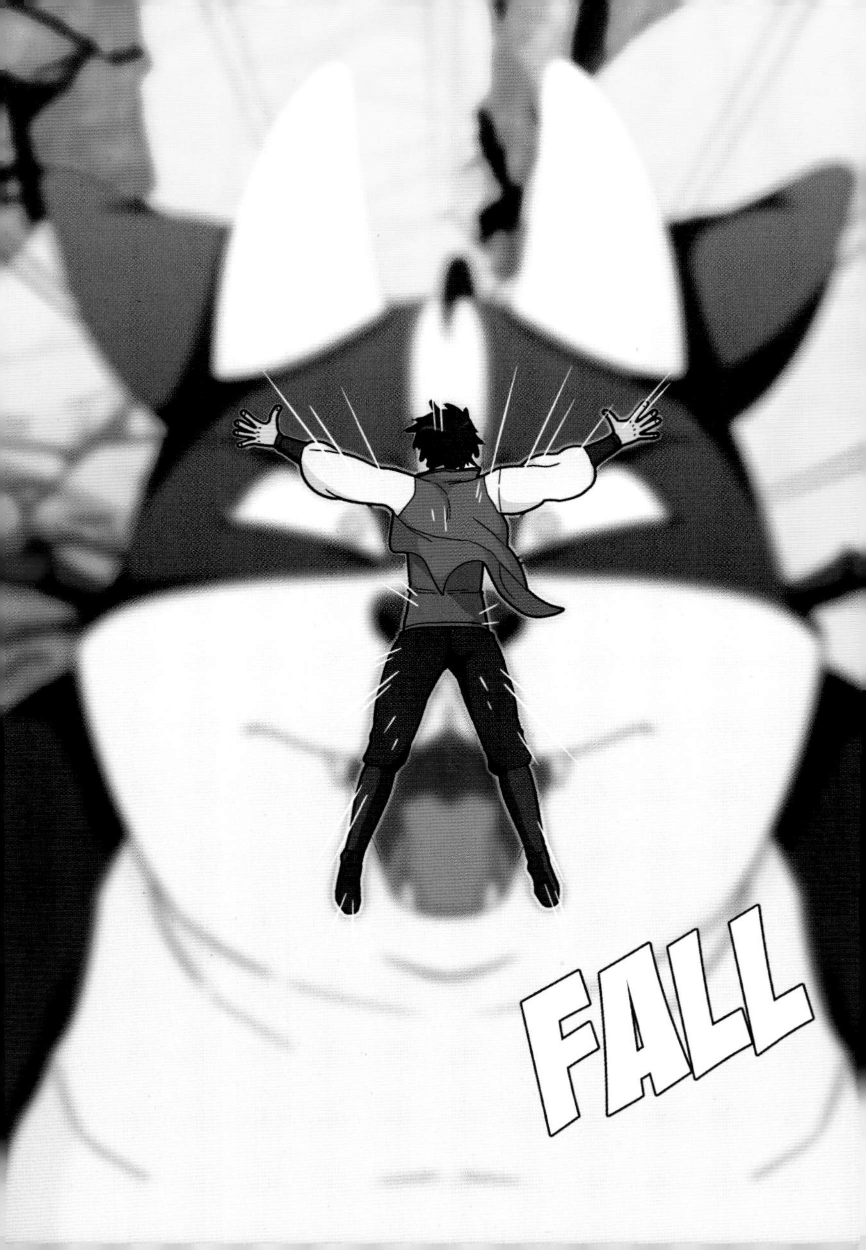
FALL

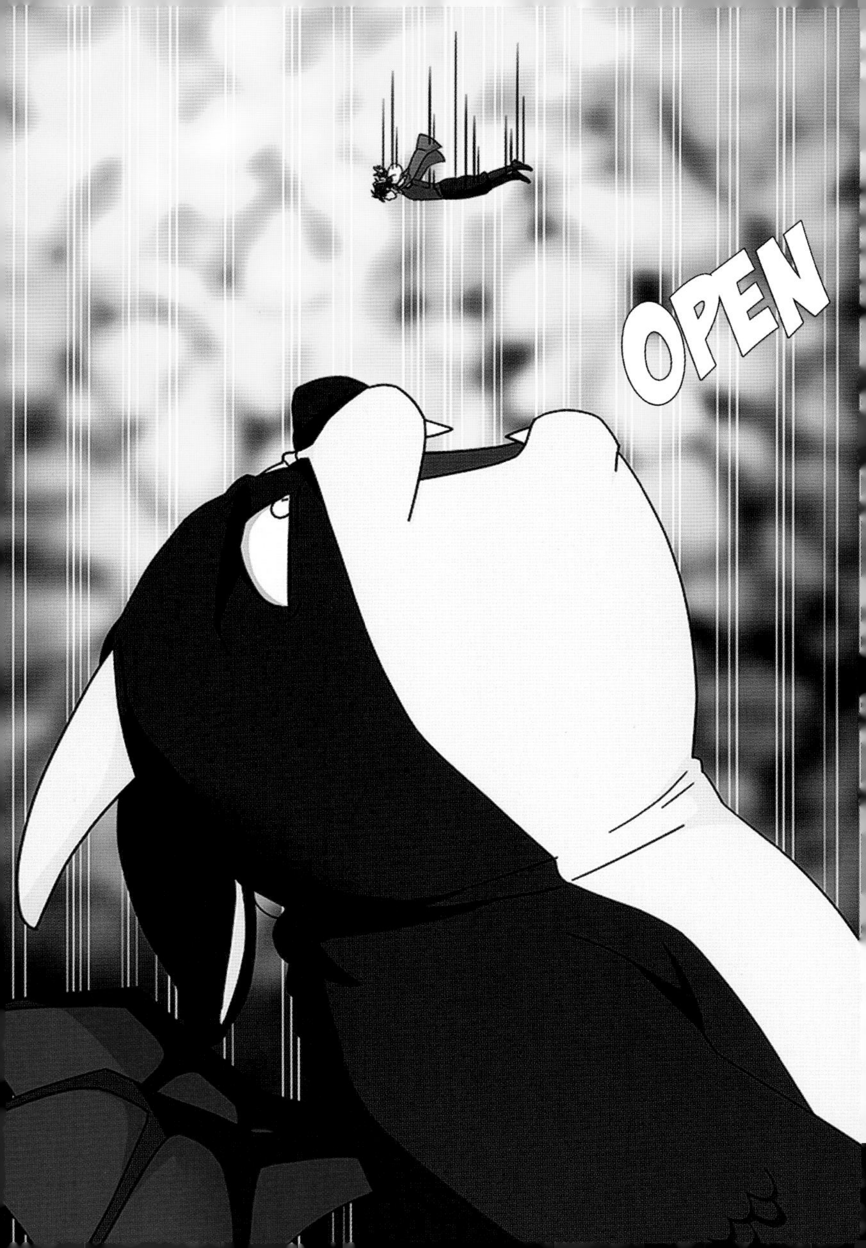
OPEN

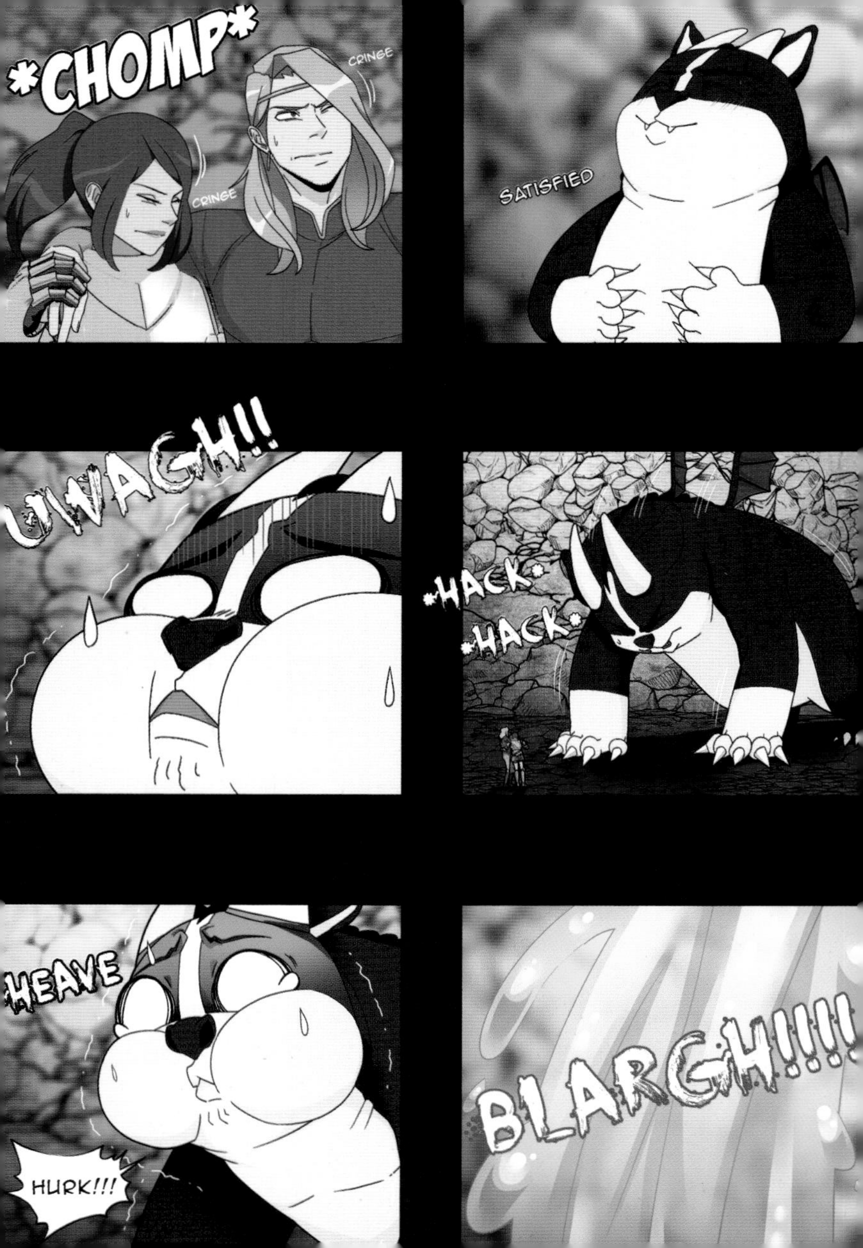
CHOMP
CRINGE
CRINGE
SATISFIED
UWAGH!!
HACK
HACK
HEAVE
HURK!!!
BLARGH!!!!

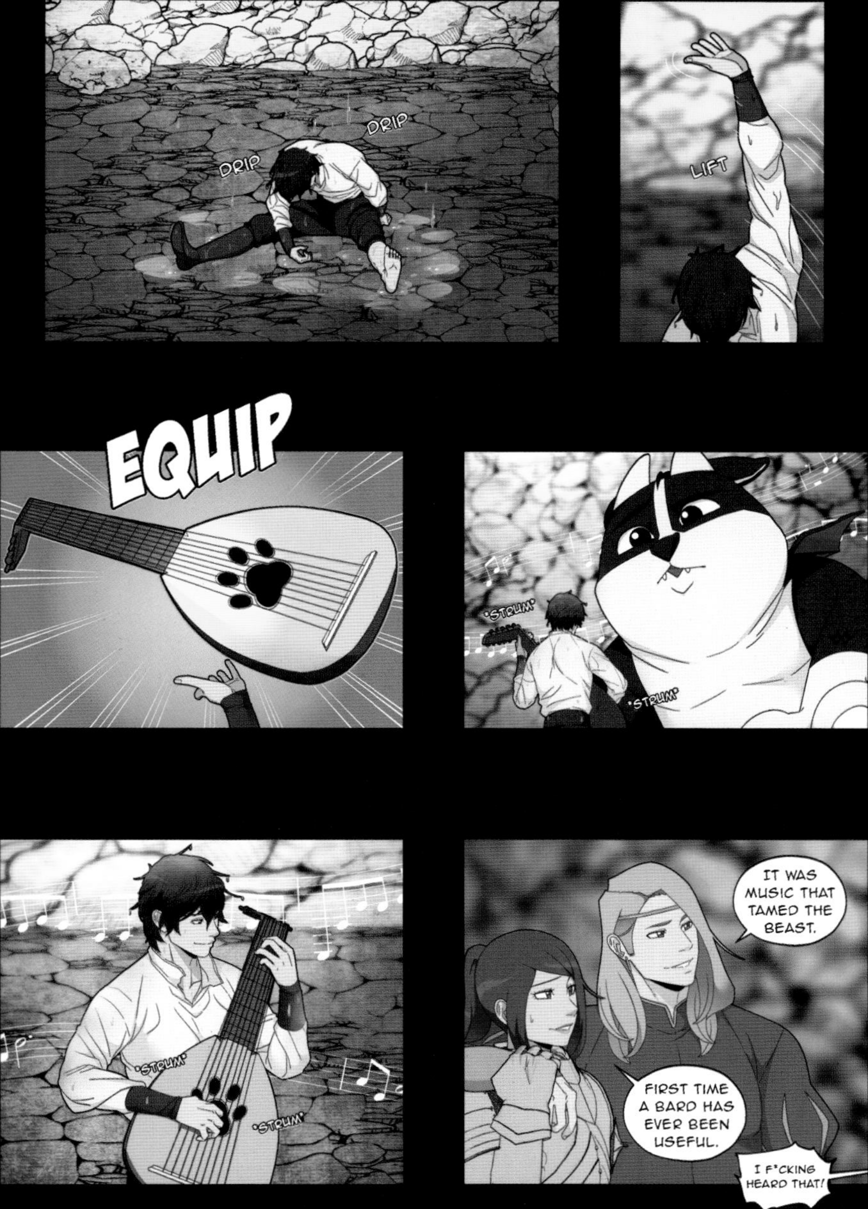
DRIP
DRIP
LIFT
EQUIP
STRUM
STRUM
STRUM
STRUM
IT WAS MUSIC THAT TAMED THE BEAST.
FIRST TIME A BARD HAS EVER BEEN USEFUL.
I F*CKING HEARD THAT!

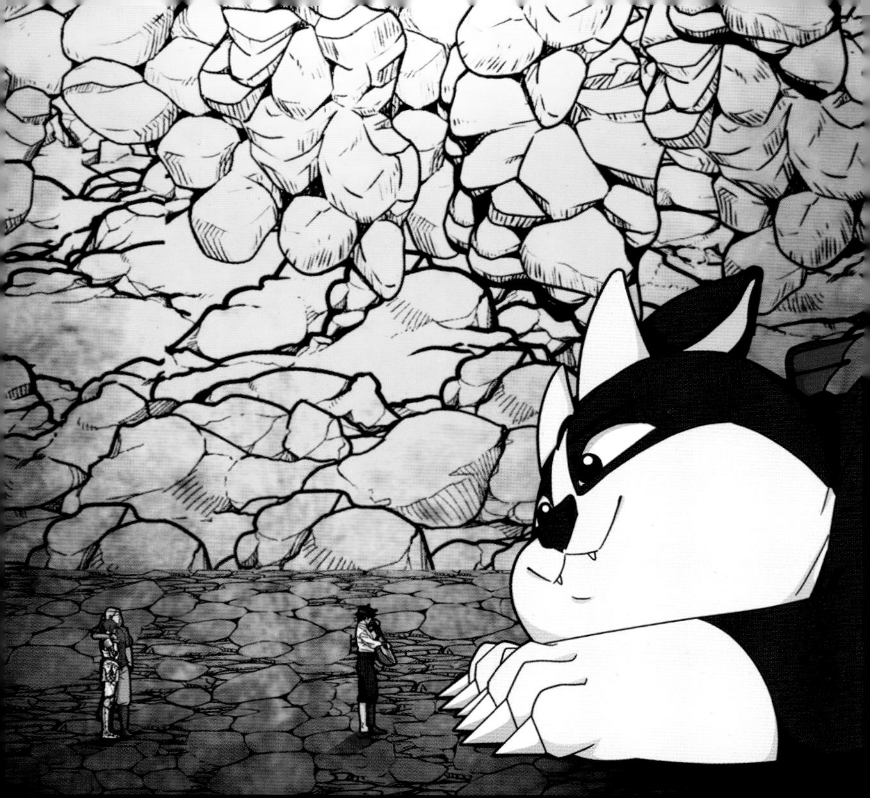
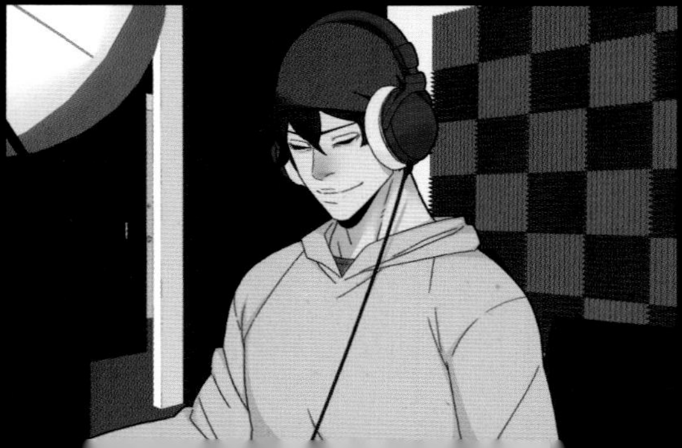

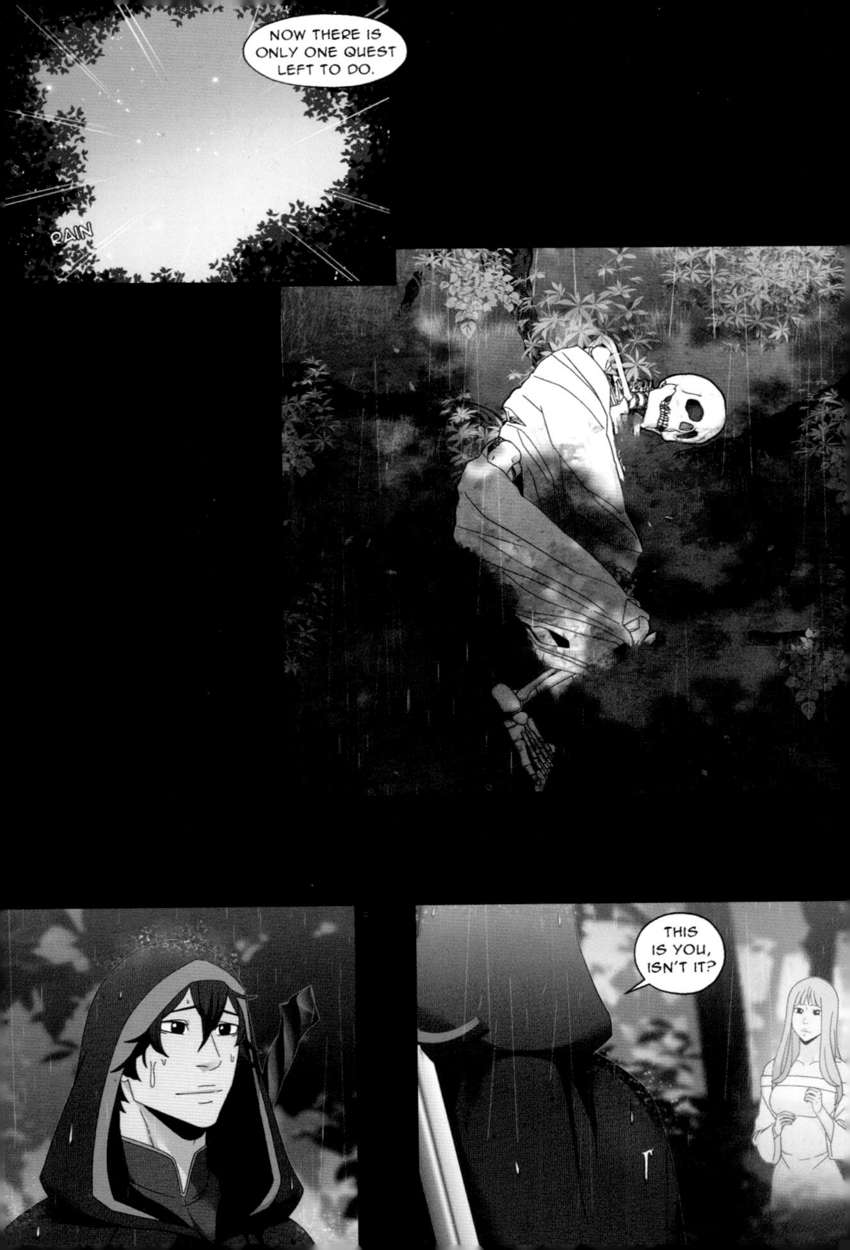
NOW THERE IS ONLY ONE QUEST LEFT TO DO.
RAIN
THIS IS YOU, ISN'T IT?

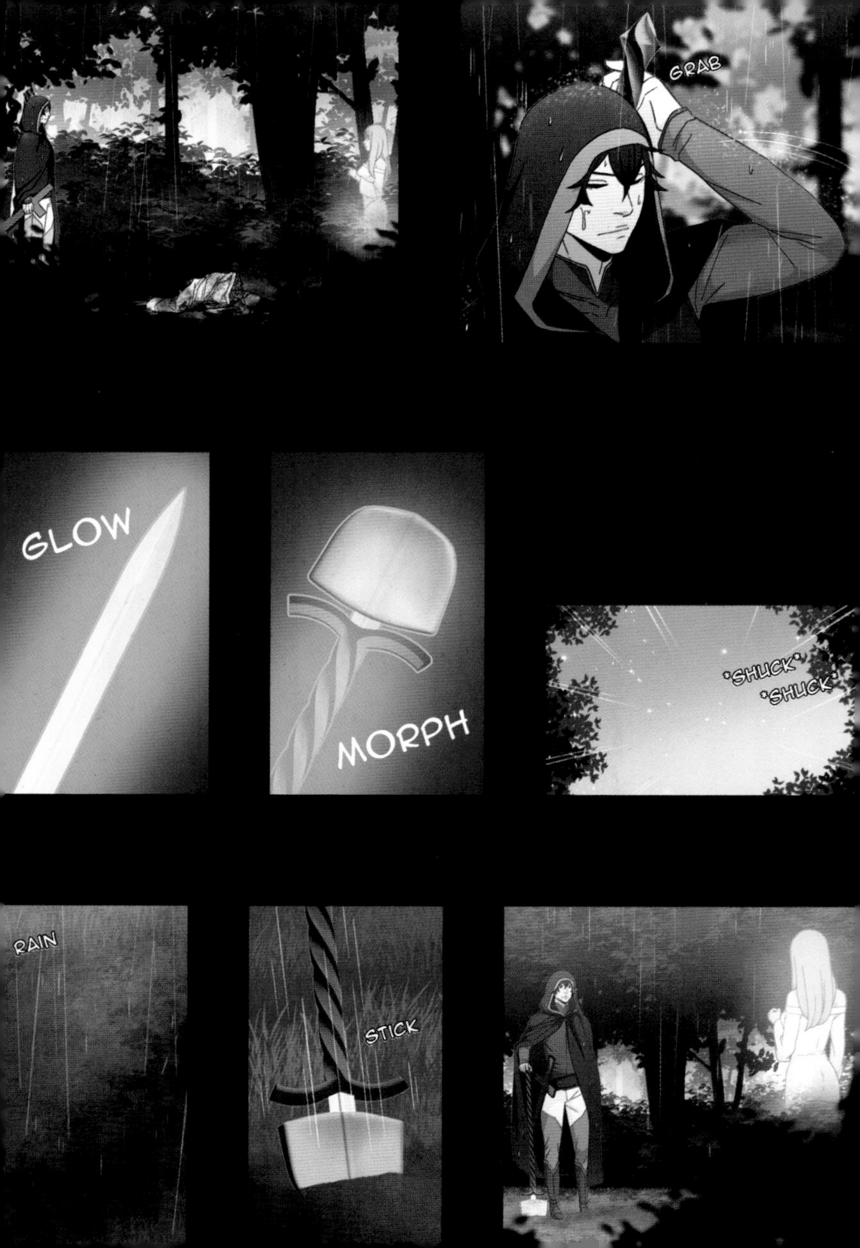
GRAB
GLOW
MORPH
SHUCK
SHUCK
RAIN
STICK

I BURIED YOUR REMAINS.

BUT IT'S NOT ENOUGH, IS IT?

I MUST BE MISSING SOMETHING.

NONE OF THE NPCS KNOW ANYTHING ABOUT A "GHOST IN THE WOODS."

I CAN'T EVEN CHECK A WALKTHROUGH AS THERE HASN'T BEEN ONE MADE FOR THIS GAME YET.

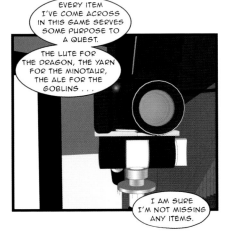

EVERY ITEM I'VE COME ACROSS IN THIS GAME SERVES SOME PURPOSE TO A QUEST.

THE LUTE FOR THE DRAGON, THE YARN FOR THE MINOTAUR, THE ALE FOR THE GOBLINS . . .

I AM SURE I'M NOT MISSING ANY ITEMS.

WAIT.

RUSTLE

YOU WERE NEVER A SWORD, WERE YOU?

LIFT

BUT ME, BEING A MURDERHOBO, JUST ASSUMED YOU WERE A WEAPON.

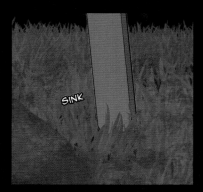

SINK

KNEEL

BOW

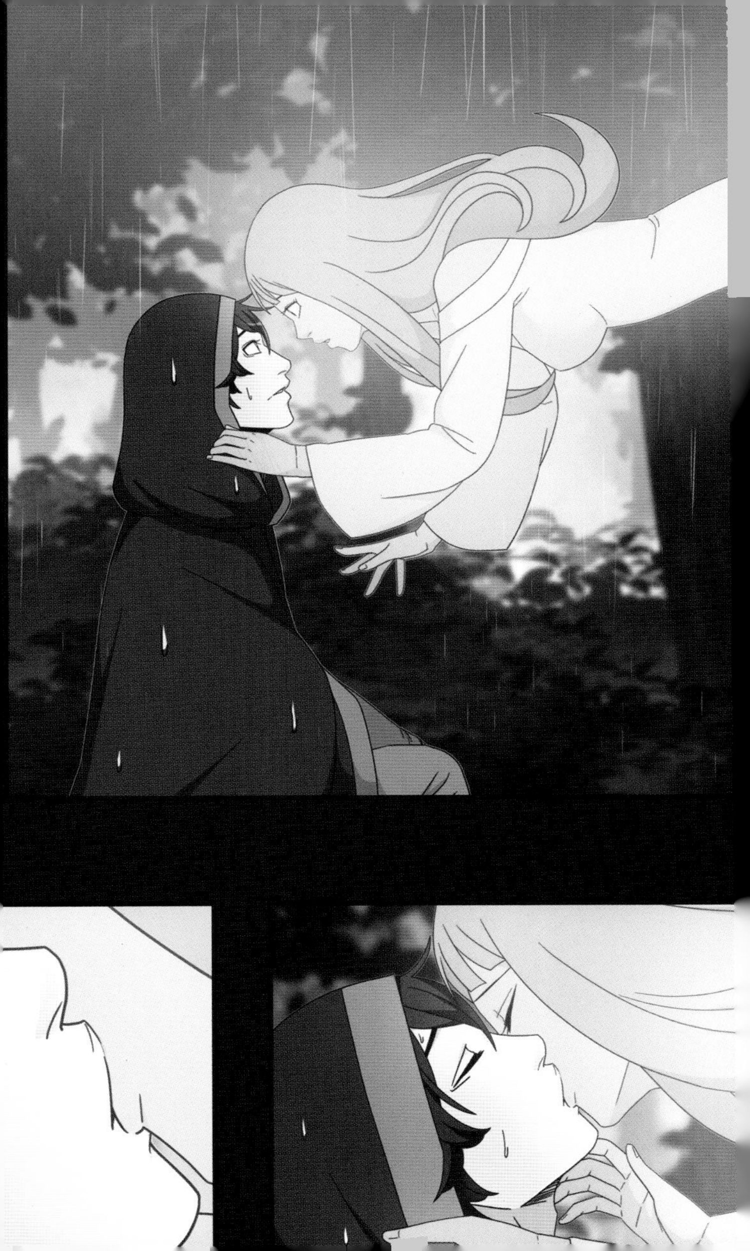

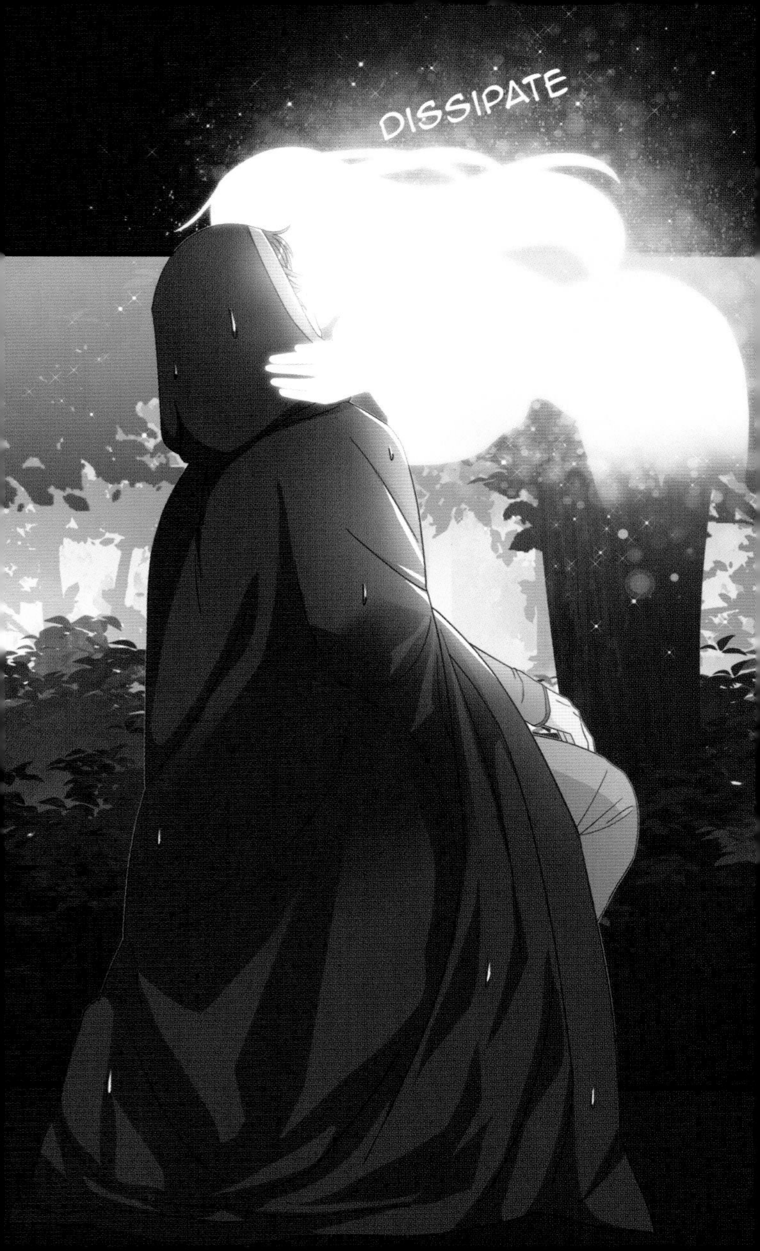
DISSIPATE

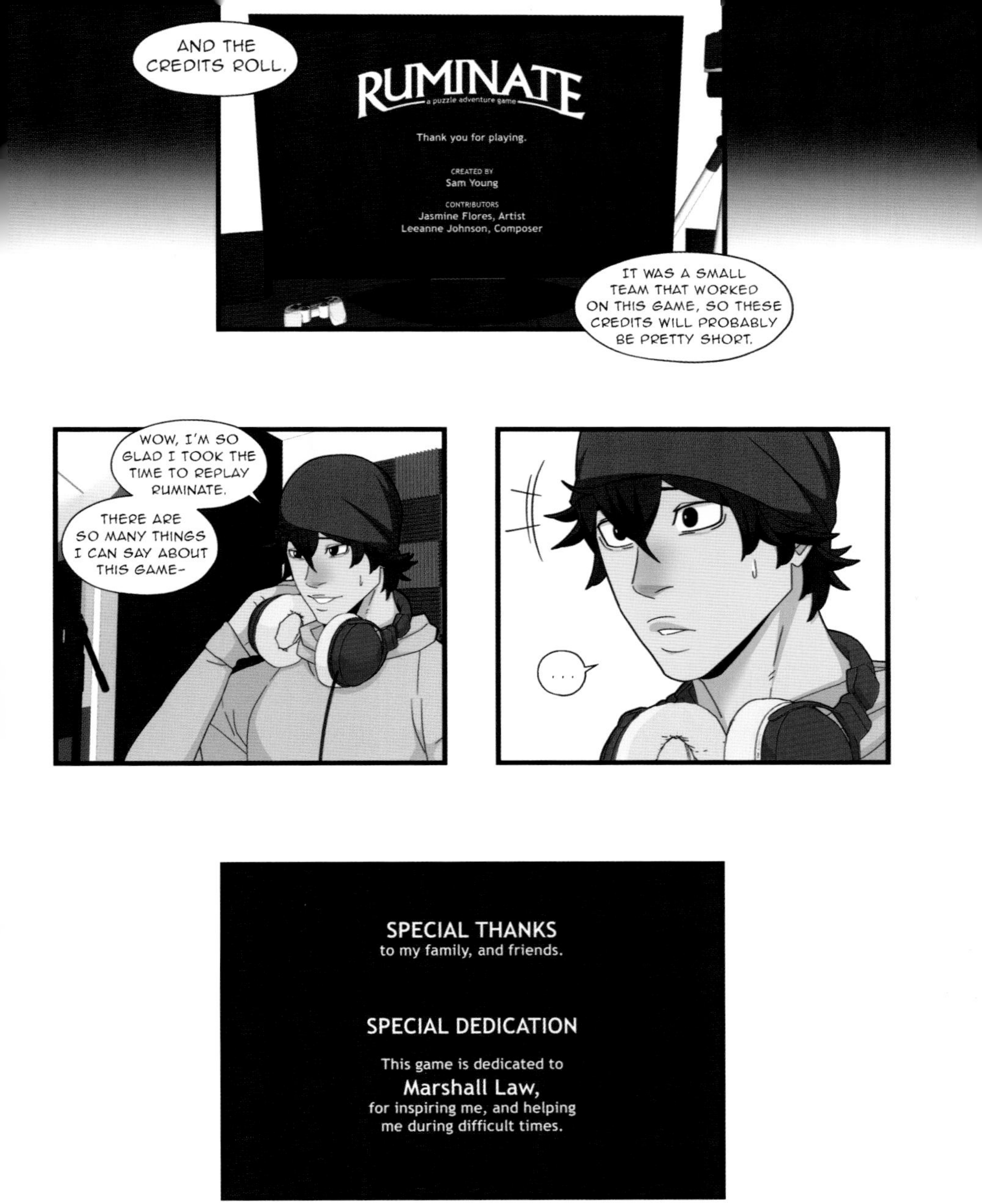
AND THE CREDITS ROLL.
RUMINATE
a puzzle adventure game
Thank you for playing.
CREATED BY
Sam Young
CONTRIBUTORS
Jasmine Flores, Artist
Leeanne Johnson, Composer
IT WAS A SMALL TEAM THAT WORKED ON THIS GAME, SO THESE CREDITS WILL PROBABLY BE PRETTY SHORT.
WOW, I'M SO GLAD I TOOK THE TIME TO REPLAY RUMINATE.
THERE ARE SO MANY THINGS I CAN SAY ABOUT THIS GAME-
...
SPECIAL THANKS
to my family, and friends.
SPECIAL DEDICATION
This game is dedicated to
Marshall Law,
for inspiring me, and helping me during difficult times.

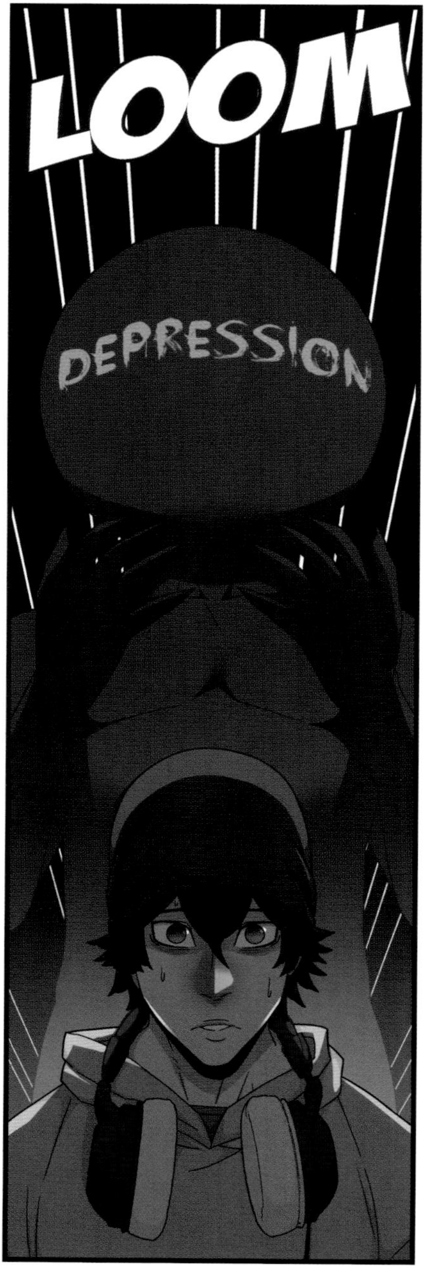
LOOM
DEPRESSION

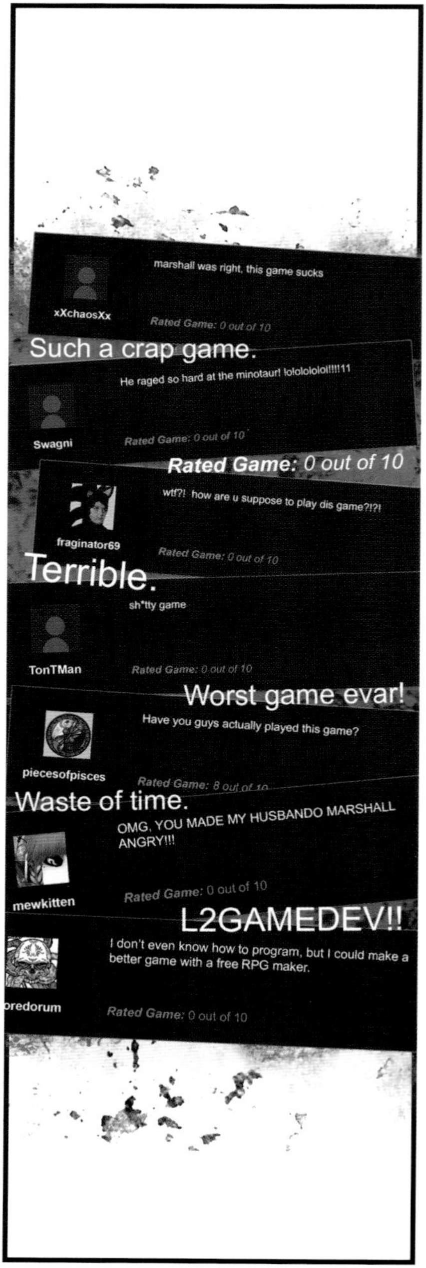
marshall was right, this game sucks
xXchaosXx
Rated Game: 0 out of 10
Such a crap game.
He raged so hard at the minotaur! lolololol!!!!11
Swagni
Rated Game: 0 out of 10
Rated Game: 0 out of 10
wtf?! how are u suppose to play dis game?!?!
fraginator69
Rated Game: 0 out of 10
Terrible.
sh*tty game
TonTMan
Rated Game: 0 out of 10
Worst game evar!
Have you guys actually played this game?
piecesofpisces
Waste of time.
OMG, YOU MADE MY HUSBANDO MARSHALL ANGRY!!!
mewkitten
Rated Game: 0 out of 10
L2GAMEDEV!!
I don't even know how to program, but I could make a better game with a free RPG maker.
Rated Game: 0 out of 10

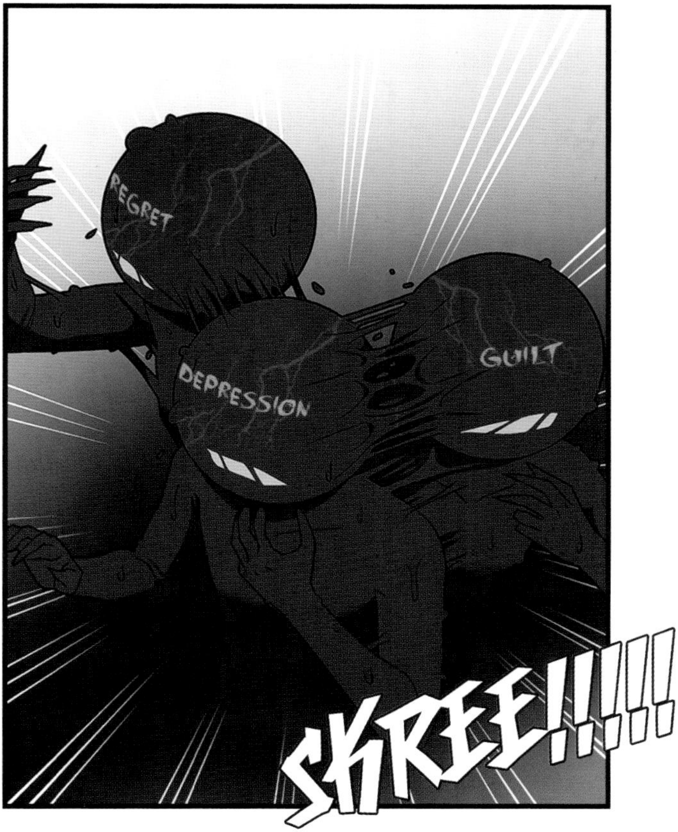
REGRET
DEPRESSION
GUILT
SKREE!!!!!!
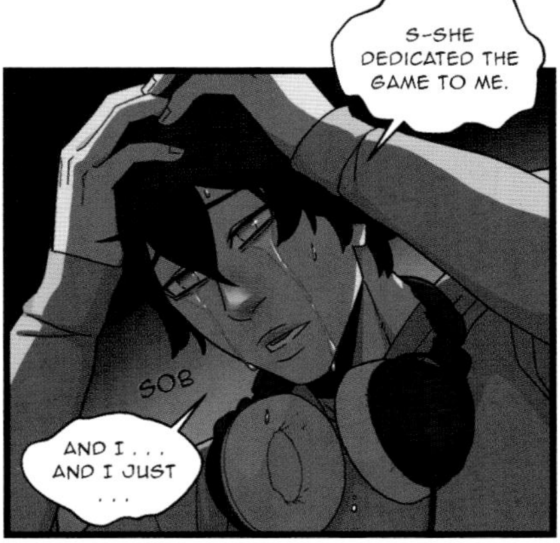
S-SHE DEDICATED THE GAME TO ME.
SOB
AND I . . . AND I JUST . . .

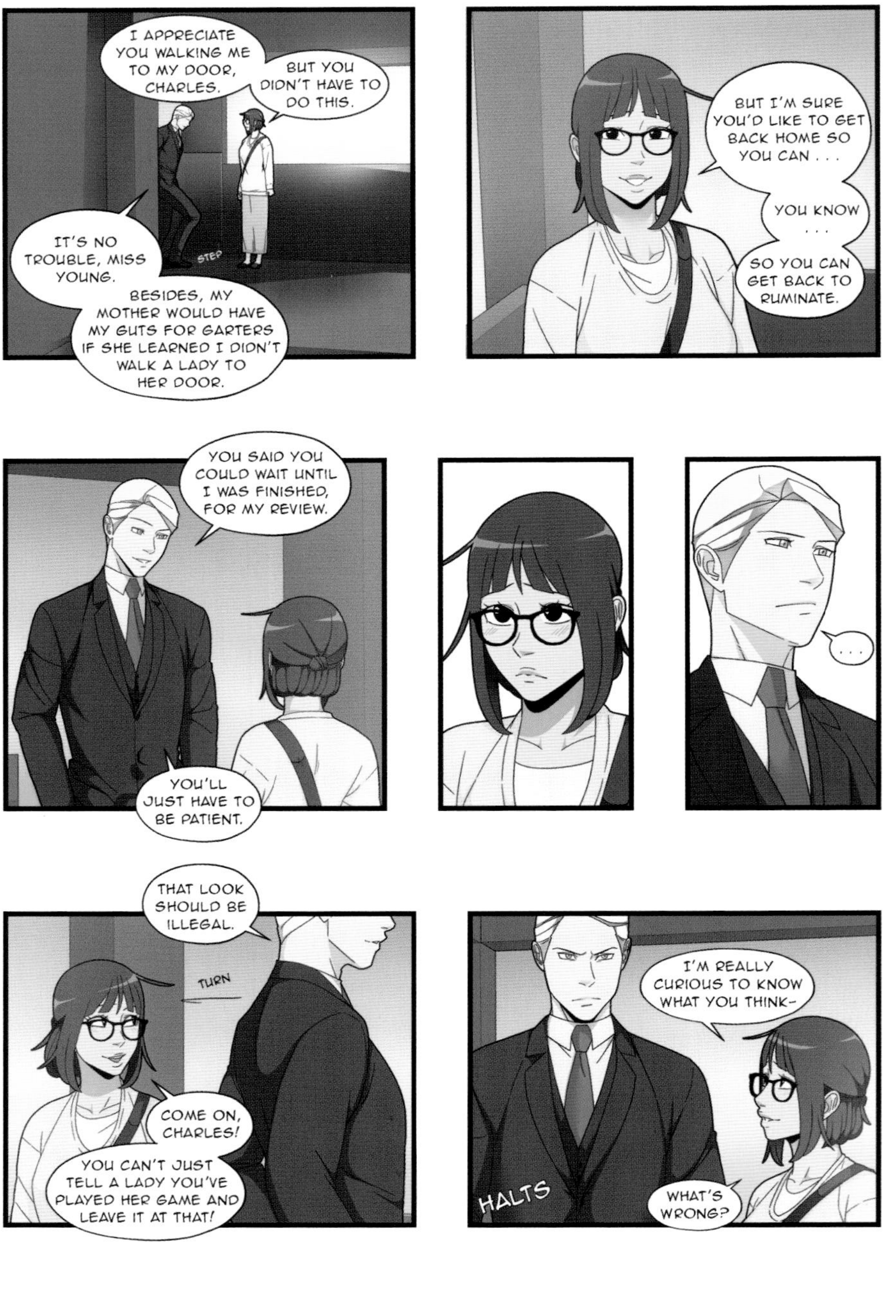
I APPRECIATE YOU WALKING ME TO MY DOOR, CHARLES.
BUT YOU DIDN'T HAVE TO DO THIS.
STEP
IT'S NO TROUBLE, MISS YOUNG.
BESIDES, MY MOTHER WOULD HAVE MY GUTS FOR GARTERS IF SHE LEARNED I DIDN'T WALK A LADY TO HER DOOR.
BUT I'M SURE YOU'D LIKE TO GET BACK HOME SO YOU CAN . . .
YOU KNOW . . .
SO YOU CAN GET BACK TO RUMINATE.
YOU SAID YOU COULD WAIT UNTIL I WAS FINISHED, FOR MY REVIEW.
YOU'LL JUST HAVE TO BE PATIENT.
. . .
THAT LOOK SHOULD BE ILLEGAL.
TURN
COME ON, CHARLES!
YOU CAN'T JUST TELL A LADY YOU'VE PLAYED HER GAME AND LEAVE IT AT THAT!
I'M REALLY CURIOUS TO KNOW WHAT YOU THINK-
HALTS
WHAT'S WRONG?

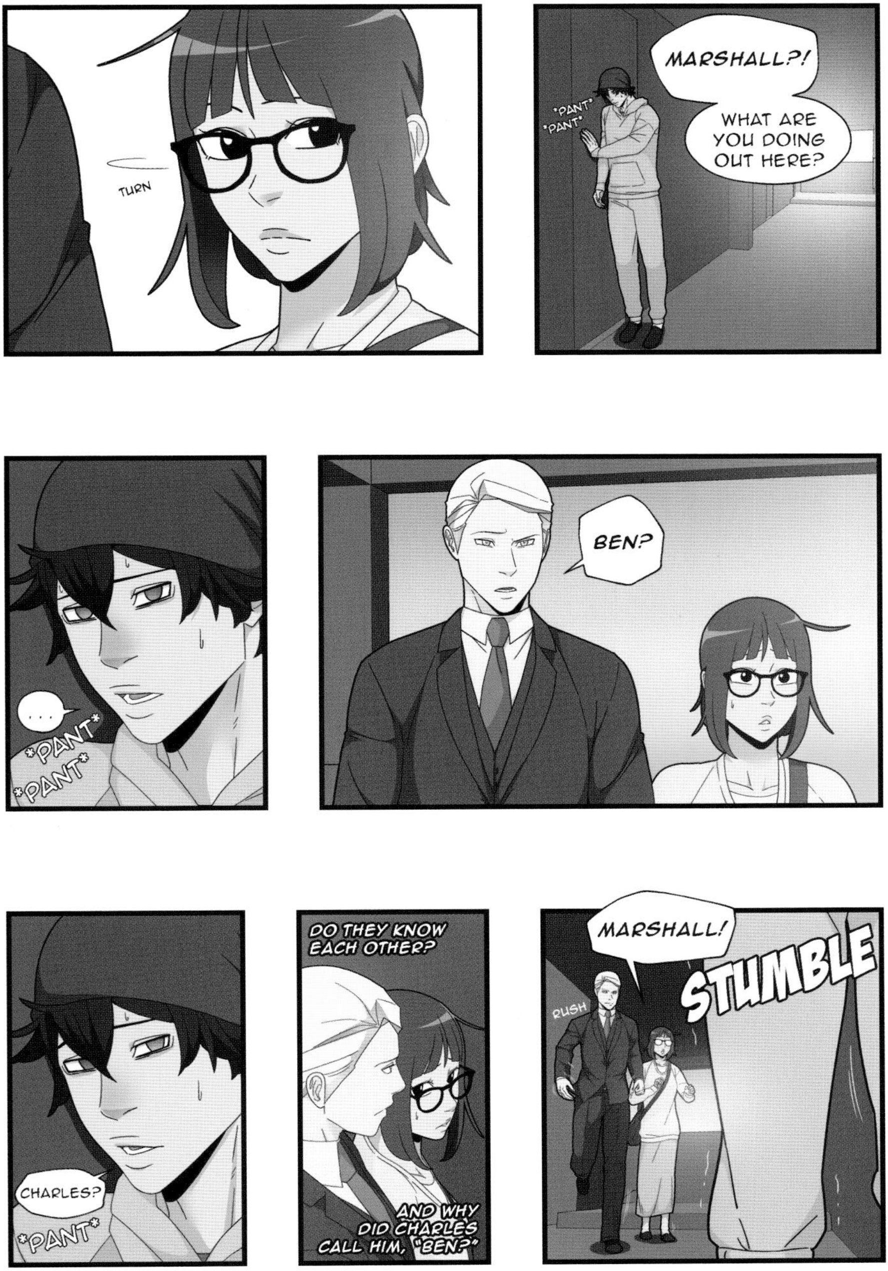
TURN
MARSHALL?!
WHAT ARE YOU DOING OUT HERE?
PANT
PANT
...
PANT
PANT
BEN?
CHARLES?
PANT
DO THEY KNOW EACH OTHER?
AND WHY DID CHARLES CALL HIM, "BEN?"
MARSHALL!
RUSH
STUMBLE

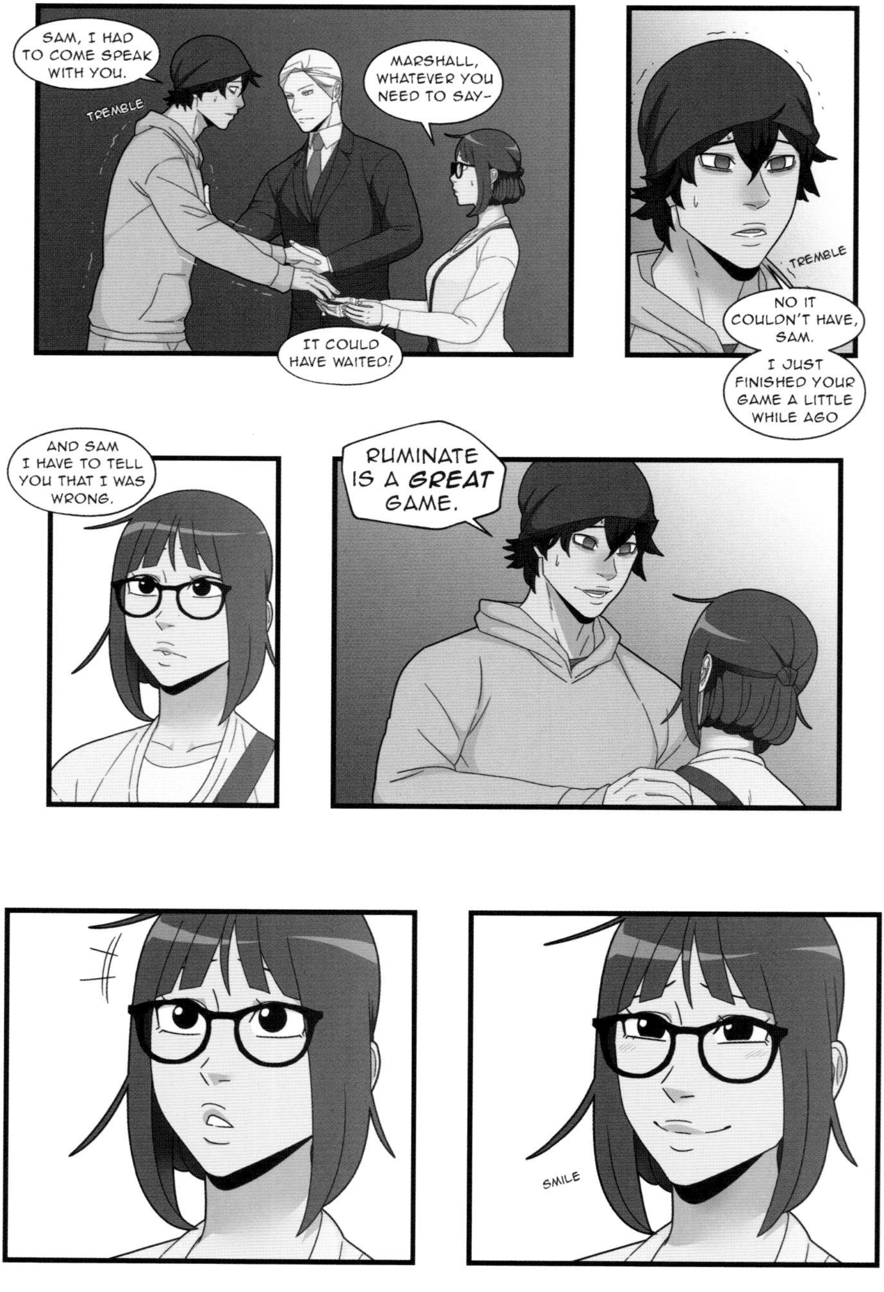
SAM, I HAD TO COME SPEAK WITH YOU.
TREMBLE
MARSHALL, WHATEVER YOU NEED TO SAY-
IT COULD HAVE WAITED!
TREMBLE
NO IT COULDN'T HAVE, SAM.
I JUST FINISHED YOUR GAME A LITTLE WHILE AGO
AND SAM I HAVE TO TELL YOU THAT I WAS WRONG.
RUMINATE IS A GREAT GAME.
SMILE

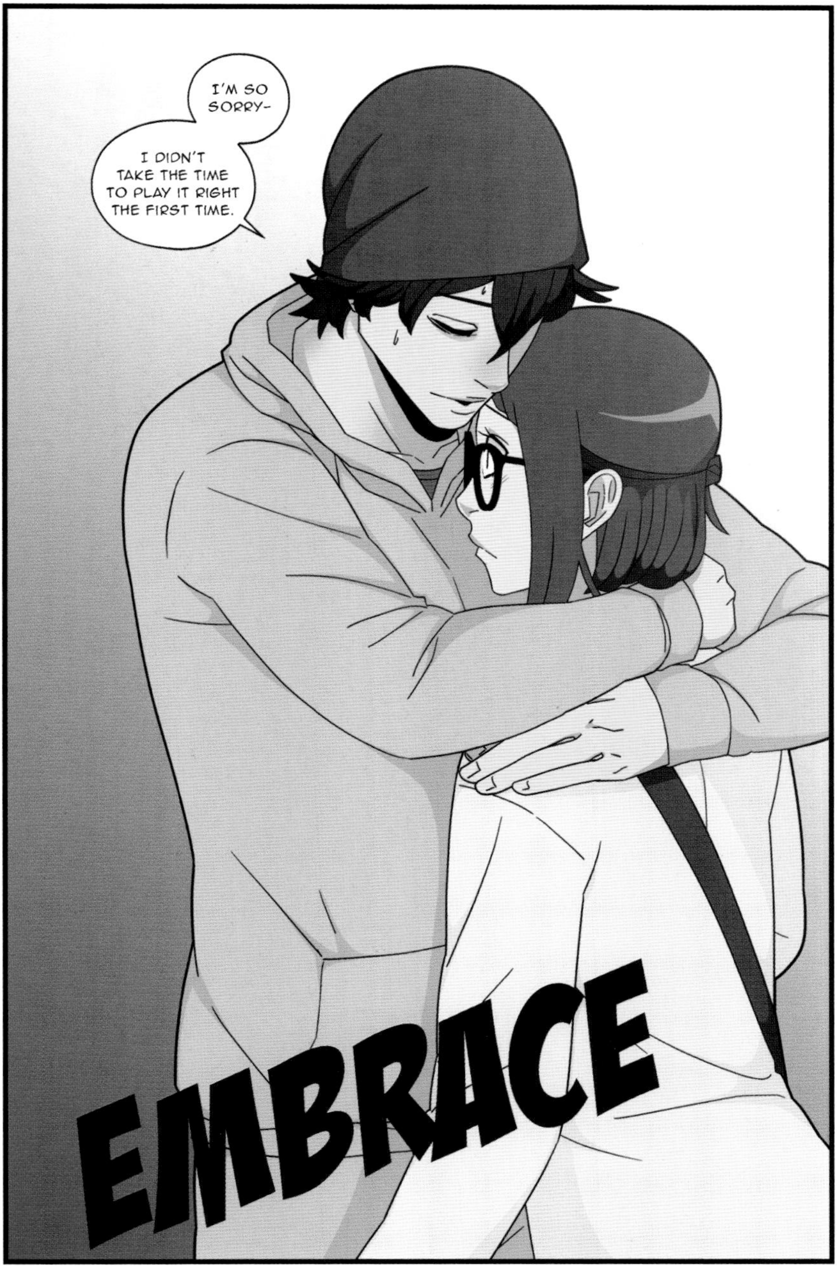
I'M SO SORRY-
I DIDN'T TAKE THE TIME TO PLAY IT RIGHT THE FIRST TIME.
EMBRACE

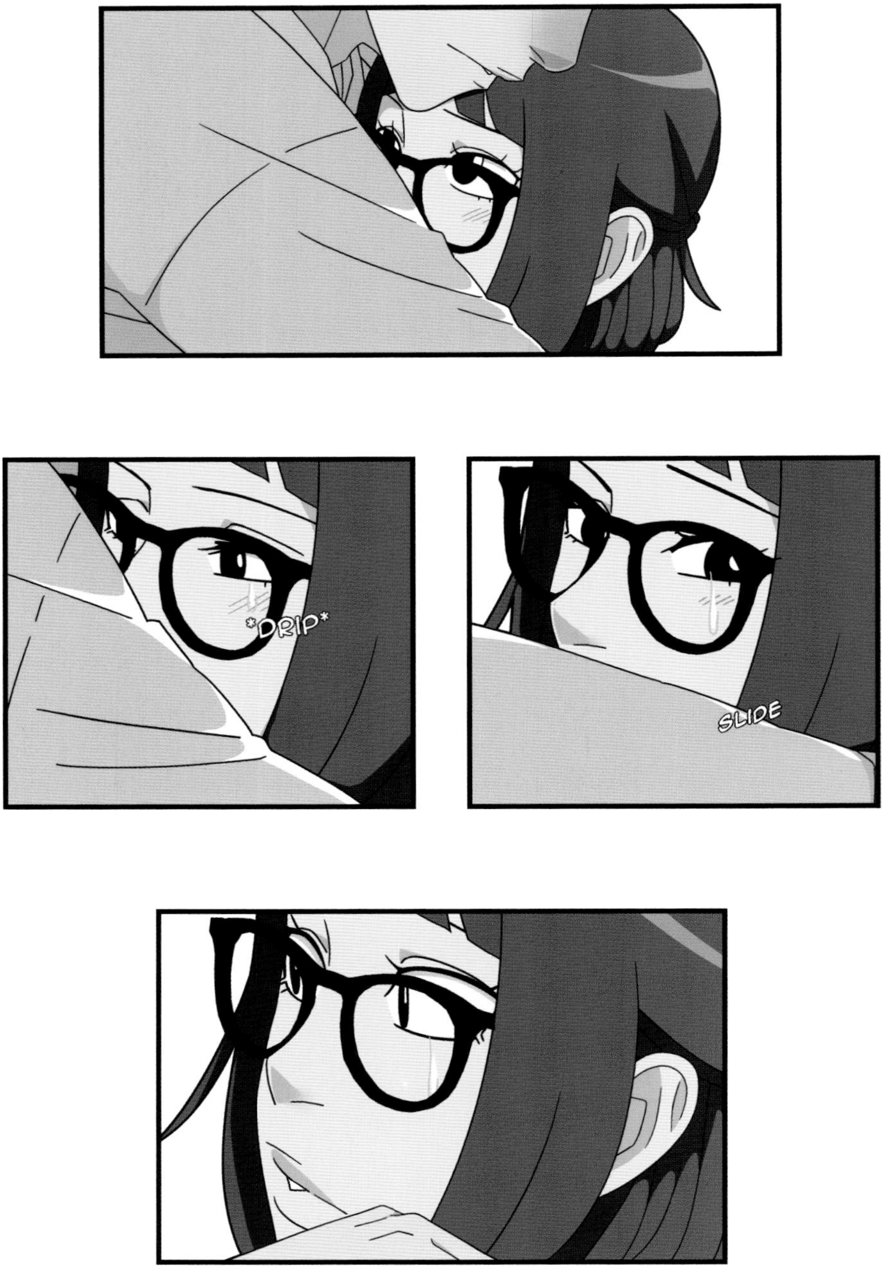
DRIP
SLIDE

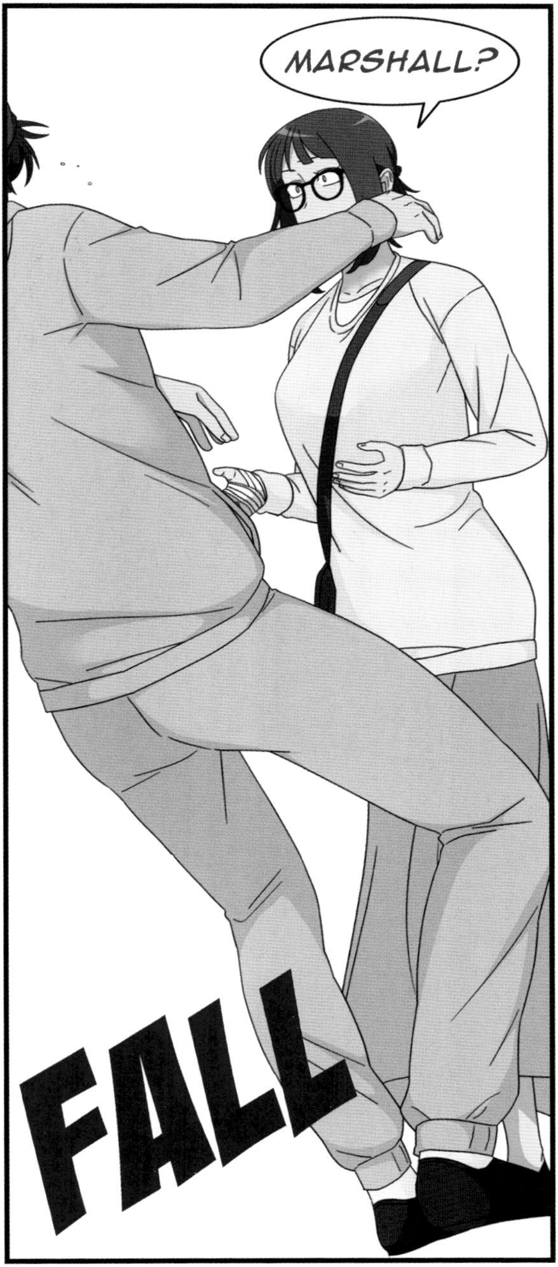
MARSHALL?
FALL

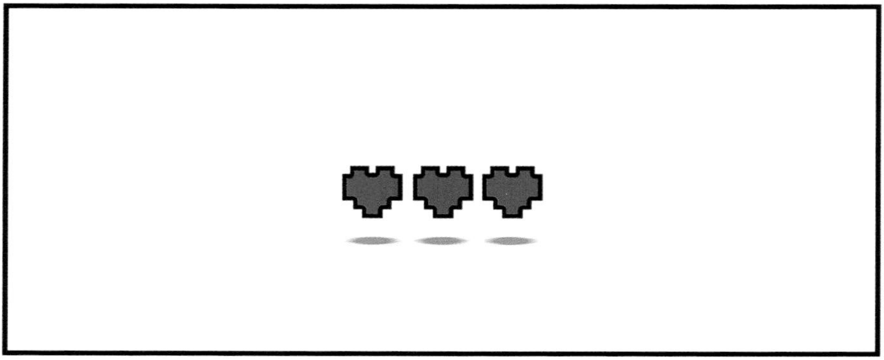
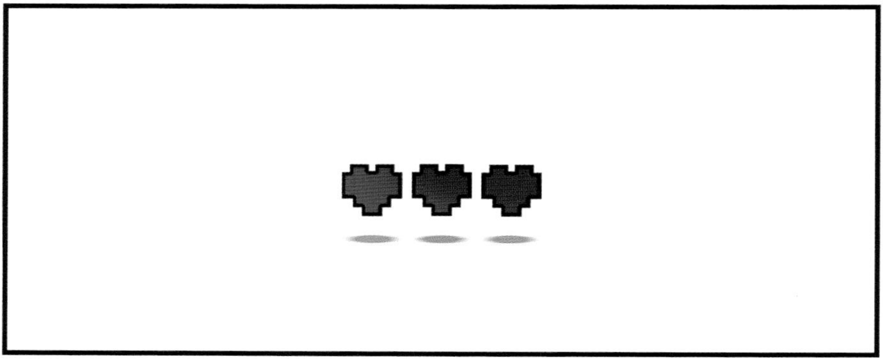
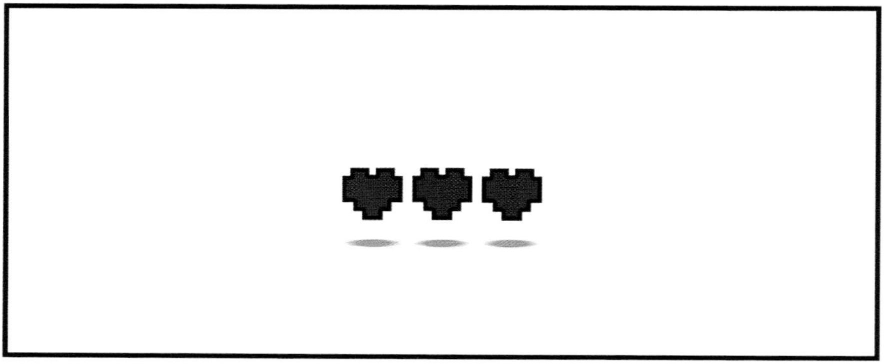

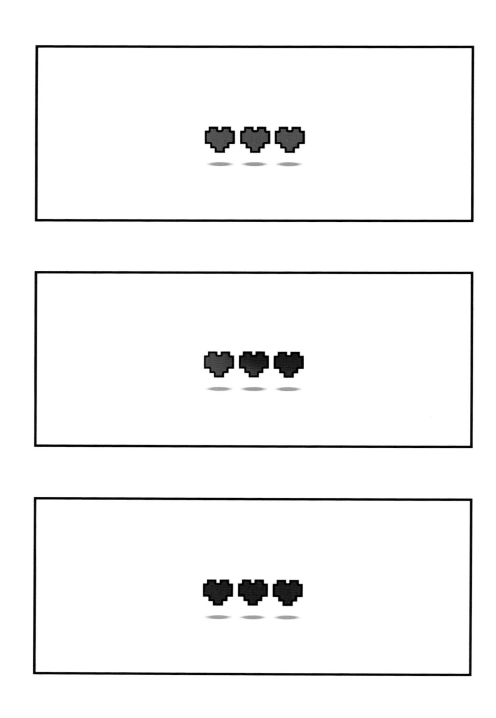

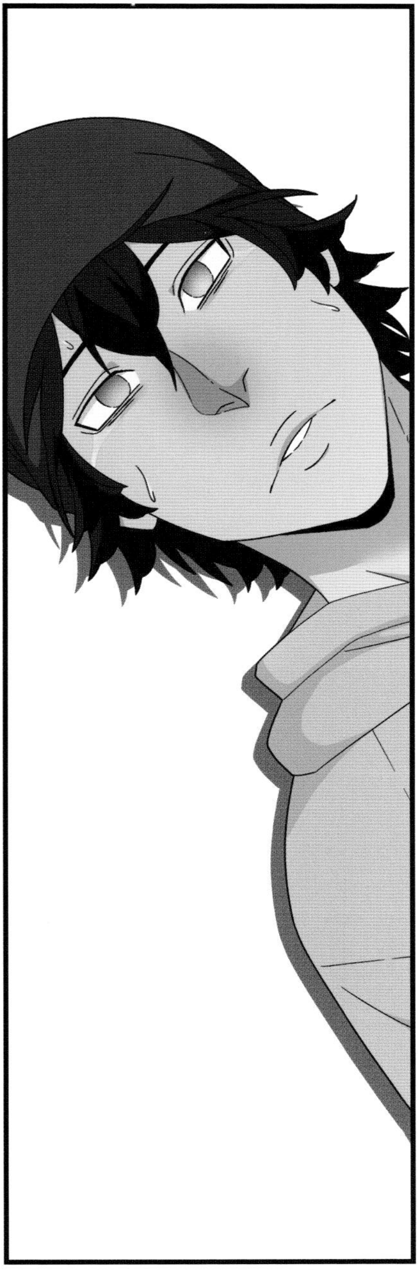

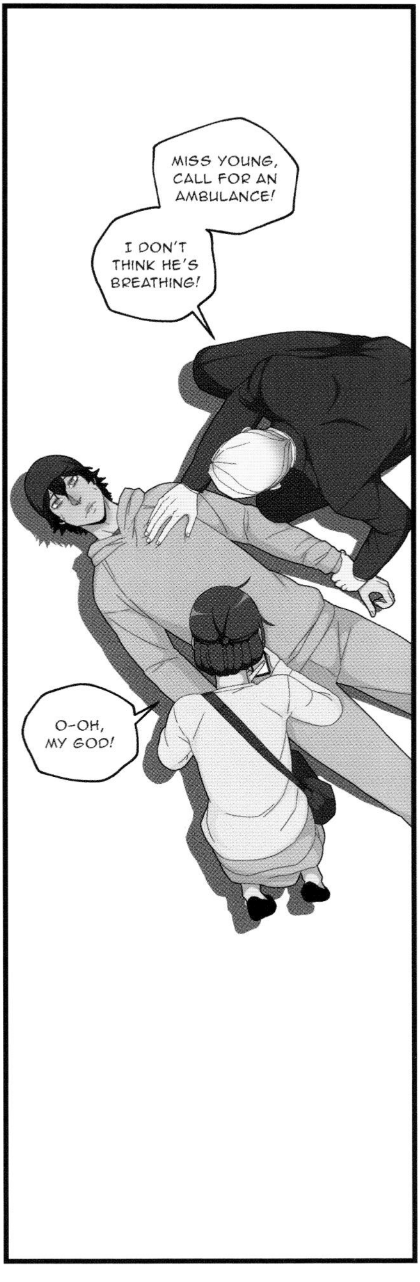
MISS YOUNG, CALL FOR AN AMBULANCE!
I DON'T THINK HE'S BREATHING!
O-OH, MY GOD!

End of Season One

[CONTINUE?]

13TheAce, A Small Evergreen Tree, A. Steagall, A.M.Johnson, Aarin Dreyer, Aaron, Aaron Blank Cameron, Aaron Caldwell, Abbey, Abbigail Dupree, Abby Hi, Abel Padilla, Abigail Calva, Abigail McFall, Adam, Adam Eaton, Adam Hallers, Adam Meyers, Adan, Addicted2pjs, Adele Khor, Adelina Milano, Adiya Zak, Adriana Niño, Adriane Ruzak, Adrianne Cavaioli, Adrienne, Adrienne Bross, Adrienne Nicole, Adrienne Sames, Adventurer Dusk, Aeri, Aeri Fuller, AGC, Agrothia, Ahnikka Hamilton, Aimee, Aimee, Aimee Zagorski, Ainhoa Inza, Ainsley Wells, Aira Nicole Calderon, Airadea, Aisha Lewis, AJ Lopez III, Akkiarn, Alana McC, Alayna, Albert Hehr IV, Aleasha, Aleece, Alesa Netzley, Alessia Curti, Aletua, Alex, Alex, Alex Campbell, Alex Carpenter, Alex Garcia, Alex Hinchcliff, Alex Johnson, Alex Johnson, Alex Koza, Alex Layman, Alex Loader, Alex MacCumber, Alex Oh, Alex Perkins, Alex Ramirez, Alex Riggs, Alex Schroeder, Alex Weglarz, Alexa, Alexa Anders, Alexa Ugarte, Alexander Bystedt, Alexander Chhen, Alexander Hale, Alexander J Orandello, Alexander Nicholas Adams, Alexandra, Alexandra Blasi, Alexandra Cenni, Alexandra Elizabeth, Alexandra Espino, Alexandra Kristina Anastasia Ash, Alexandra Martinez, Alexandra Perreault, Alexandra Roque, Alexandra Specht, Alexandria Adams, Alexandria Molzahn, AlexGC, Alexia Ha, Alexis, Alexis Cannariato, Alexis Farabaugh, Alexis Hawk, Alexx, Alexzandria Steiner, Ali, Ali, Alias, Alice Gao, Alicia, Alicia A, Alicia De Fonte, Alicia Eilers, Alicia Haggland, Alicia Newton, Alicia Trejo, Alicia Vaughn, Alicorne137, alira coffman, Alisha, Alisha Allison, Alisha Walton, Alison, Alison, Alison Benowitz, Alison Bishop, Alison Ponce, Alisone McDonald, Alizarin Crimson, Allex Kirkland, Allie, Allie Cook, Allie Sweeney, Allison Curtis, Allison Flores, Allison Hartwig, Allison Helms, Allison M, Allison Welliver, Allison Wright, Alloette, Ally Berger, Allyson Fyfe, Allyson Gangl, Allyssa Streeper, Alma Jordan, Alora, Alpacas_pls, alpgirl, Alva Claussen, Alyssa, Alyssa Aguirre, Alyssa Cruz-Uribe, Alyssa Evans, Alyssa Flores, Alyssa Galvas, Alyssa Johnson, Alyssa Munoz, Alyssa Ramdeo, Alyssa Sanchez, Alyssa Sherry, Alyssa Staten, Alysse, AMA1, Amanda, Amanda, amanda, Amanda, Amanda, Amanda, Amanda Alianell, Amanda Allen, Amanda Berns, Amanda Brackin, Amanda Calderon, Amanda Cattin-Ford, Amanda Chafee, Amanda Chamberlin, Amanda Chipman, Amanda Crabtree, Amanda Cramer, Amanda Dorian, Amanda Dowling, Amanda Edwards, Amanda Gagne, Amanda Griggs, Amanda Hiltermann, Amanda Johnson, Amanda kercher, Amanda Koolis, Amanda Lococo, Amanda McNamee, Amanda Nappier, Amanda Peterson, Amanda R, Amanda Reagan, Amanda Rhodus, Amanda Rice, Amanda Stickles, Amanda Trower, Amandine H, Amaya Ruszala, Amber, Amber, Amber Beardsley, Amber Campbell, Amber Feltes, Amber Harover, Amber Hittman, Amber Poole, Amber Solvarion, Amber Venema, Amber Walton, Amberlina Joy, Amberly, Amelia, Amelia Gilmer, Amethyst Greye Adams, Amity T, Amoned, Amorette Groen, amtoka, Amy, Amy, amy, Amy, Amy, Amy Barrieau, Amy Bartel, Amy Brabenec, Amy C. G., Amy Coulson, Amy D., Amy Kiger, Amy Linsamouth, Amy Pearce, Amy Villa, Amy Woodall, Amy Zavala, Amy Zerwas, Amyee Korich, Ana c mendoza, Ana Cartamil, Ana Gavilán, Ana Leguillou, Ana Mendoza, Ana O, Anahi Villanueva, Analisa, Ananda Fryer, Anastasia, Anastasia Apple, Andrea, Andrea, Andrea, Andrea Braddy, Andrea Chapman, Andrea F., Andrea Highland, Andreane Brousseau, Andreeal, Andrew "Andrizo" Paulus, Andrew & Jeni Balch, Andrew Brouwer, Andrew Hales, Andrew Kerr, Andrew P, Andrina San Nicolas, Andromeda Taylor, Andy Grass, Andy Maene, Ane Buch, Anessa Halcyon, Angel, Angel, Angel Huynh Ky, Angel Kimmi, Angela Benes, Angela Birmingham, Angela Darveau, Angela LC, Angela Lim, Angela Nail, Angela Rodriguez, Angela Stiles- Walker, Angelica Martinez, Angelica Rosas, Angelina N Mai, Angelique Tucker, Angellica Lara, Angelo Porcu, Angelz Jameson, Angie S, Angie Tidwell, Angie Venturi, Angram09@gmail.com, Angrydwarfaxe, Anhmye Tran, Anibel, Anita Catherine Christensen, Anjelica K., Anjy Delaney, Ann Sellers, Anna, Anna field, Anna Joy, Anna Lee, Anna Marek, Anna N, Anna

Piaia, Anna Van Zuuk, Annabelle Ramos, Annablood, Anne, Anne, Anne Duncan, Anne Hatch, Anne mehlsen, Annette Bowen, Annie Huber, Annika, Annika, Anny Bilet, AnOwlfulPun, Anthony, Anthony K, Anthony T. Carter, Antoine STAELENS, Antoinette Sturniolo, Anton Ooms, Antonia Lopez, Anya P., April, April Koehler, Apurva Desai, Aracely Peñailillo, Araithya, Araña Rose, Arcane Bibliophile, archibwik, Arec Rain, Aretsuya, Argent, Ari & E, Aria Capella, Ariana, Arianna DB, Ariel, Ariel, Ariel, Ariele, Arielle Cushing, Arielle S. Smart, Arielle Time Burstein, Ariqua Furse, Arivelle Carowyn, Arne Seelisch, Arthur, Artie, artificial.ermine@protonmail.com, Artiphyss, artsywithabby, Arturo Garcia, Asha, Ashen, Asher McClure, Ashlee Smith, Ashlei Collins, Ashleigh, Ashleigh Britain, Ashleigh. A, Ashley, Ashley, Ashley Baker, Ashley Boehm, Ashley Demont, Ashley freer, Ashley Gilbert, Ashley Heimbach, Ashley Hollingsworth, Ashley Lemon, Ashley Pancho, Ashley Polhamus, Ashley Pope, Ashley Rawlins, Ashley Robinson, Ashley Rose, Ashley Super, Ashley Taylor, Ashley York, Ashley Youngbeck, Ashlynn Anderson, Ashton, Ashton Potts, ashycoe, Aspen, ATenshi, Athena, Atlas Lee-Reid, Aubrey Kimball, Audra Eaket, Audrey Lerebours, Audrey Mae, Audrey Morin, Audriana Baker, Aurora, Aurora Harvey, Aurora Newcomb, Aury, Austin Barnwell, Austin Durkin, Austin Hernandez, Austin Hicks, Austy Martinez, Autumn Geiger, Autumn Graybill, Autumn Kaviak, Autumn Place, Ava Belles, Ava Lem, AvaruusPupu, Avery, Avery The Awesome, Avital Elizabeth, Aviv survivor priel, Avivana, Ayaka Yoshida, Ayame Suzaku, Ayanna C, Ayanni C.H. Cooper, Azzure Sky

B

badger, Badwolf, Bailey H, Bailey Kennedy, BanditofNerdia, Barbara Kasad, Barton Perkins, Beagle, Beanie Bee, Becca, Becca, Becca Lawrence, Becca Willy, Becky McCrory, Becky Spann, Becky Taylor, Behorn, Bekka, Belinda Zandrama Björklund, Bella Shadow, Ben, Ben B., Benjamin Flood, Benoit Yan Larose, Bensckull, Benson Chen, Bernadette Joseco, Beruchachu, Beth, Beth Coll, Beth Diamond, Beth Garretson, Beth Workman, Bethany, Bethany Fetters, Bethany Robinson-Banks, Bethany Souza, Bev Vazquez, Beverly Quock, BFish, Bianca, Bianca Hudson, Bill Hohm, Billy Muggelberg, Blair, Blair Edwards, Blee Chua, BluexBlossomx3, Bob Cahill, Bobby-Jo Toulouse, BobdaBoops, bookmonkey, Booshort, Boovov, Brad B, Brad Wilson, Braden Fraser, Bradley Happel, Brandi Curry, Brandi Hine, Brandi Lynch, Brandon, Brandon, Brandon Au, Brandon Freeberg, Brandon Rittue, Brandy Gordon, Brandy Kraemer, Brandy Lawton, Brandy Sumner, Brandy Tiller, Braylon Woods, Bre Perkins, Breahna Jordan, Breezy, Bren, Brent Lynn, Brett Bennett, Bri (GoldandGore), Bri1559, Brian, Brian Calhoon, Brian Jones, Brian Patterson, Brian Tumbleston, Briana Cropper, Briana Firth, Briana Serjeant, Briana Urrutia, Brianna Bertrand, Brianna Bloomer, Brianna Cowles, Brianna Page, Brianna Staats, Brianna Steiner, Brianna Welch, Brianne Swailes, Briar, Brice Coquereau, Bridget McElroy, Bridgette, Brie & Marcus, Brii Gonzales, brina, Brit W., Britney, Britni Moritz, Brittania Foster, Brittany Brannen, Brittany h, Brittany Hanly, Brittany Liane Basham, Brittany Maple, Brittany McCall, Brittany Molenda, Brittany Stormoen, Brittany Torres, Brittney Franklin, Brittney Nichols, Brokenjoker1821, Brooke tichy, Bruno, Bruno Torres, Bryan Yu, Bryce Brendel, Bunbearry, bunnimation, Bussy Carla

C

C A I L Y N, C Fair, C. Raine Eisner, Cahl, Cailynn Szabo, Cait, Caithlin Chilton, Caitlen Zettwoch, Caitlin Byrne, Caitlin Dowling, Caitlin Foster, Caitlin Judge, Caitlin Pollastro, Caitlin Rosberg, Caitlin Stenberg, Caitlyn, Caitlyn Roberts, Caitlyn Warren, CaitriaJade, Caity, Calandra Moore, Caleb, Calie, Calie Benke, CALLIS, Camélie Groleau, Cameron Bratz, Cameron Hallman, Cameron Hasty, Cameron Herbert, Camilla Rose, Camille Macdonald, Candice Blume, Candice Smart, candysaur, CannonX88, Cap'nBrik, Carene Dani, Carey Stevens, Cari, Cari Simmons, Carla Carran, Carla Santellano, Carleana Dunn, Carley Lehman-Monak, Carlos Pérez Alonso,

Carmen, Carmen Quain, Carol, Carol Suckerpunch, Carol Wise, Carol Yuen, Carola mathysen, Carolina, Carolina Flores, Carolina Garcia, Caroline A. Robbins, Caroline Belter, Caroline James, Caroline Smith, Caroline_63Tiam, Carolyn Hanley McEllen, Carolyn Jernigan, Carolyn Tetley, Carolynn Sullivan, Carrow Brow, Cas Soulier, Casey Acree, Casey Jane, Casidy Giles, Casper Lambert, Cassandra, Cassandra Cheatham, Cassandra Kaiser, Cassandra Musselman, Cassandra Peter, Cassandra Scott, Cassie Hug, Cassie Morgan, Cassie Neubauer, Cassie Wheeler/Josh Wheeler, cassy foxtail, Cat, Cat Herndon, Cat Pope, Cat Spargo, Cat W, Catherine Contreras, Catherine Kattus, Catherine Levesque, Catherine Russomanno, Catherine Tepper, Catherine Weygant, CatherineHG, Cathlynn Shagonaby, Cathy Chang, Cayla Harms, Cayman Adams, Celeste, Céline BADYKA, Chad_Bonkers, Chandra O, Chandra Stewart, Chantal, Chantel Early, ChaoticAstronaut, Charis Lavoie, Charisma, Charisse Lantaya, Charity zeiger, Charlene Templeman, Charles Pierce Jr, Charles Wallace, Charlie, Charline, Charlotte, Charlotte Tamplin, Charlotte Whatling, Chase Ballard, Chase Horan, Cheezo, Chelsea, Chelsea, Chelsea, Chelsea, Chelsea Cruz, Chelsea Linn, Chelsea Marie M. Cruz, Chelsea Mechan, Chelsea Zhao, Chelsie Roman, Chelsy Zelasko, Cherita Smith, Chesh, Chess Pargeter, Cheyenne, Cheyenne Hawk, Cheyenne Hill, Chezahbelle, Chi Darby, Chianna, Chloe Granberry, Chloe Murphy, Chmii, ChocoBibis, ChocoMellowBunbun, Chris, Chris, Chris Breneman, Chris Cruz, Chris Maynard, Chris Peterman, Chrissy Linfoot, Chrissy Nickel, Christa Fuller, Christel Cervantez, Christi Chenger, Christi Mills, Christian, Christian Boughton, Christian Byrnes, Christie Straw, Christin Little, Christina, Christina, Christina Baril, Christina Esquibel, Christina Gale, Christina Hawley, Christina Miskey, Christina Sanchez, Christina Shackelford, Christina Stitt, Christine Bell, Christine Dunn, Christine La, Christine Ng, Christine Scheu, Christoph "Sicarius" Licht, Christopher, Christopher Alden Hawkins, Christopher Brinlee, Christopher Frost, Christopher J Brennan, Christopher Silva, Christy Dyer, Ciana Konyha, Ciara Prats, Ciara Ychaaq, Cindy, Cindy Robles, Cindy Vertefeuille, cinnaminnt, Claire, Claire Dack, Claire Goldman, Claire Marchal, Claire Murray, Clara Rector, Clare Hernon, Clarissa, Claudia Guanes, Claudia Quintana, Clayton Orman, Clémence Méallier, Clémence Nogrix, Clementine Stowe-Daniel, Cleo Maranski, Cleo Runge, CloClogs, Cnordvall1975, Cody Bland, Colby Hamilton, ColonelMike737, colorfulKati, Colten Flaherty, Conan64ds, Connor Birch, Connor Elam, Cori, Cori Tallent, Corinne Schneider, Corinne Staten JD, Corsair, Courtney, Courtney, Courtney Paul, Courtney Pritchard, Courtney Rabena, Courtney Sinclair, CreatorOfKaos, Cristel, Cristen Allen, CROIZIER, Crystal, Crystal Cepeda, Crystal Herron, Crystal Kramer, Crystal Moon, Crystal Rogers, Crystel Hillman, Crystle, Cuppa, cyle rogers, Cymba, Cympai, Cyndie Chin, Cynthia Fueyo, Cynthia Kay Wright, Cynthia Zelmore, cynthialey, Cyntia, Cytoleone

D

D DeSimone, D.Rail, Dahrah, Daisuke Kazamatsuri, Dakota Brown, Dale Brimhall, Damalis, Damia Dondar'rion, Damion and Cathy Gilzean, Dan Ezzy, Dan Manion, dan_eyer, Dana, Dana C. Morgan, Dana Lopez W, Dana Novak, Dana Prebis, Dana Walsh, Dani Japhet, Dani Ross, Dani White, Danial Hussain, Danica Dempsey, Daniel, Daniel Campbell, Daniel Cellini, Daniel Gilmartin, Daniel Hovater, Daniel Lin, Daniel Neville, Daniel Schmidt, Daniel Schosser, Daniela, Daniela Grob, Daniela Sinner, Daniella Ilyayeva, Danielle Bost, Danielle Cohen, Danielle Emmons, Danielle Harman, Danielle Key, Danielle Perry, Danielle Roth, Danielle Schetter, Danielle St. Oegger, Danielle Tank, Danielle Torres, Danielle Wiedmann, Danielle Williamson, Danitza Lopez, Dany G., Daphne Bonneau, Daphnie j, Darian Mullen, Darla, Darlene Troop, Daryll Collado, Dasani Thompson, Dasha, Dave Aragon, Dave Thomas, David Baker-Austin, David Chuhay, David Clough, David Codd, David Horton, David L Kinney, David Lucas, David Matsui, David Powers, David Tai, Dawn, Dawn Davis, Dawn Garrison, Dawn Schwartz, Daydreamvalentine, Dayne, Dayra, Dazman717, De Jionette Norton, Deadbeccaning, Dean, Deanna Austin, Deanna Campos, DeathGoddessEver, Debraliz, Decary Audrey, Deefisch89, Delia, Demi, Demifrench,

Denise, Denise Ambriz, Denise Dillashaw, Denise Santos, Derek Kinhofer, Derek Webb, deron wan, DerrickF, Désirée Kozich, Desiree Whitney, Destinee Brock, Devi Turner, Devon Sklair, Dez Makowski, Diam, Diana, Diana, Diana Chow, Diana Godinez, Diana Penalba, Diana Turmenne, Diane Goodyk, Diane Smith, Dillon, Dinsy Johns, DJ Hightopp, Djcat_Meow, Dmessengah, Domini Gee, Dominica Rollins, Dominik Pansi, MSc, Dominika Bazyl, Dominique Cepeda, Donald Yarbro, Donia, Donna Manalo, Doomdon28, Dorota, Dorothy Corirossi and Curtis Watson, Douglas Keech, DraconianBriana, Dres, DresdenQ, Drew McPhail, Duck-e Ponce, Dustin Carr, Dustin Gottmann, Dyer's Woad, Dylan, Dylan Gibbons, Dylan Pucilowski, Dylan Schaefer, Dylan Shofner

E

Eboni Chube, Eclipse McLeod, Eddie, Edgar Paez, Edie Fel, Edward C Torres, Edward Jager, Edward M Lomeli III, EfratXLoki, Ekaya Williams, Elaine Galang, Elaine M. Cassell, Elamonster, Eleanor Michalski, Elena Zanconato, Eleonore, ElfyTheRinger, Eli Carter, Elias Rosner, Elijah Higgins, Eliott Bonds, Elisa "sca" Desmetz, Elisa Hossfeld, Elisabeth D'Albero, Elisabeth Joy Bender, Elisabeth Steinkress, Elise Chom, Elisha, Elisha, Elisha C., Elizabeth, Elizabeth, Elizabeth, Elizabeth Barrington, Elizabeth Bougie, Elizabeth Chalikyan, Elizabeth Dille, Elizabeth Garcia, Elizabeth H., Elizabeth Killingsworth, Elizabeth Kneeskern, Elizabeth Lehmkuhl, Elizabeth Lopez Corrales, Elizabeth Lyddiatt, Elizabeth Moore, Elizabeth O'Donnell, Elizabeth Overland, Elizabeth Pauza, Elizabeth Sauvageau, Ella, Elle Borland, Ellen, Ellen Adams, Ellena Murgu, Ellie Brick, Elllundril, Elyott, Elyse Ashcraft, Elz Hernández, Emanuelle Avila Rodriguez, Emelissa Padilla, Emi London, Emil, Emilia Louis, Emilie Witt, Emily, Emily, Emily, Emily, Emily Barger, Emily Bishop, Emily Bostrom, Emily Green, Emily Gunn, Emily Hall, Emily Holmes, Emily Karr, Emily Kelsey, Emily Marsh, Emily Maylish, Emily Noonan, Emily Parent, Emily Rivera, Emily Schroen, Emily Smith, Emily T., Emily Teague, Emma, Emma Haller, Emma Lozey, Emma McSween, Emma Olsson, Emma Roberts, Emma southall, Emmanuelle, Emmy, EPISCESGIRL85, Eric, Eric, Eric Chan, Eric Chang, Eric Tank, eric yost, Erica Andreen, Erica Chase, Erica Cobb, Erica Lanphear, Erica McCulloch, Erica Oakley, Erica Pruitt, Erica Rodriguez, Erica Schwoerer, EricaMA90, Erik Gutierrez, Erik Kendall, Erika Newman, Erin, Erin Beyrooty, Erin Collins, Erin K., Erin Popov, Erin Urffer, Erin Ziegler, Erynn Wells, Eshani Perera, Esmeralda, Esmeralda T Oliva, EstaMujer, Estarry, Eszter, Eva Franco, Eva Lai, Evan and Breanna Reynolds, Evan Baker, Evan K, Evan Miller, Eve Ngo, Evilloki, Evilnursealice

F

fallenangelkirimi, familiar-refrain, Fantasy_Girl_974, Fawn Carlson, Faysal, Feliza, Fen Rooks, Ferosthefox, Flare18, Fliva23, Florence Verreault, Florine Chan Li, Flower And, Fluffy, Fluffybuddy1, Fofawari, Forrest Eclipse, Forrest Ream, Francis, Francis Limoges, Frank Neumann, Frankie, frankieswiggs, Franklin Prue, Franziska Lunardi, Frédérique Blais, Fredrik Arvidsson, Furied Fate,

G

Gabby Parker, Gabriel, Gabriel DaCosta, Gabrielle, Gabrielle Camassar, Gabrielle Cheyenne Collier, Gabrielle Finkbeiner, Gabrielle Nowakowski, Gabrielle Spicer, Gaëlle forgeot, Gail McCormick, Galadreal, Gamefreakgeek, GamerWitchJ, Gangariar, Ganrokh, Garin Dangler, garret, Garrett McGiffert, Gary kromer jr, Gem, Gemila, Gemma JD Hart, Gene Hendricks, Geneviève Collette, Geneviève Hérard, Genie Frost, Geny Gonzalez, Geoffrey Oyler, Georgia Dyer, Geri-Ann Quinivan, Getselious, Ghessica, Ghostie, Gillian Adam, Gimarie Battle, Gina Collura, Gloria Boggs, Gloria Law, Gloria Montes, goatwarii, Goth Ghoulfriendx, Gothqueen, Grace Eccleston, Grace Grant, Grace Jerrell, Grace Meisel, Gracy, Grant Vanhaitsma,

GrayCatbird, Greelyienne, Greg Levick, Gregory Wirtjes, Gretchen Villella, Guejazi Navarrete, gunslingerpro, Gwendolyn, Gwyndolyn Heitman

H

Haenah Kim, Hailey, Hailey, Hailey Gleisner, Hailey Moon, Hailley Brune, Haircraft Kristen, Haley Batchelor, Haley Kilgore, HalfSize, Hallie Bonet, Hannah Chesser, Hannah Elmore, Hannah Freeto, Hannah Hess, Hannah J, Hannah Johnson, Hannah Kamphuis, Hannah Kneuss, Hannah M. Behrens, Hannah Thrush, Hannah Vary, Hannah Witt, Harminnie Berger, Hayden, Haylee, Hayley Austin, Hayley Orten, Heather, Heather Back, Heather Bezanson, Heather Corder, Heather Hayden, Heather Long, Heather Nathanson, Heather Pirie, Heather Rohr, Heather Sounik, Heather Williams, heatherhira, Heaven Sulflow, HeavensArcher, Hector A. Vazquez Flores, Heidi, Heidi Mangold, Helene ROUX, Hellsbells, Helouise, heymissvickie, Hiesse, Hiiryu, Hikari Kaze, Hilary, Hilary, Hollie Bittrick, Holly, holly dobbs, Holly Ellison, Holly M, Holly Snyder, Hollykins, Honeybunny, Hugo Dahl, Hugues Schils, HuntedAngel

I

Iaine MacKay, Ian Clark, ian moore, Ieshia, Ignacia_MT, Ika, Ilana Ariel, Ilda Rodriguez, illfatedFinch, Imani Youngblood, Indy, Injaeri, inuloved, Irene, IronRequiem, Irving Tejada, Isabella McLaughlin, Isabelle A. Reynolds, Isabelle Murphy, Isaiah Cruz, Isaias Leal Reyes, Isidro Lopez, Isobel Olivia O'Growney, Issy Varga, Ita Fischer, itsGeorgic, Ivan A. Perez, Ivan David Howard (IVATOPIA), Ivonne Reyna, Ivy M Landry, Ivy Rosen, Ixzacil, Iza F, Izzy, Izzy King

J

J, L, & H Entezami, J. Baird, J.M.Fenner, Jaaron Ashdown, Jabra S, Jacie Couture, Jack Cole, Jack Morningstar, Jack Wolfe, Jackelyn Raymundo, Jackie, Jackie Esposito, Jackie Lacy, Jacklynn, Jacob Chartrain, Jacob Mickey, Jacob Smith, Jacqueline Beyrouty, Jacqueline Parchois, Jacqueline Place, Jacquelyn Babich, Jacqui Ouellette, Jade Elizabeth, Jade Sanchez, Jaime Ford, Jaime Jackson, Jaime Vitale, Jaime Whitney, Jaina Headrick, Jakob, Jamee Obradovich, James Daniel Edward Rowlingson, James Elliott, James Ho, James Kirby, Jamie Arsic-Hinman, Jamie Barker, Jamie Farrell, Jamie Kasmiskie, Jamie LaMoreaux, Jamie Sundin, Jaminx, Jane, Jane Walton, Janelle Bukauskas, Janelle Hebert, Janelle Johnson, Janelle Moran Bukauskas, Janet, Janet Kasper, Janice, Janice Pennington, Janucha, Jasef Wisener, Jasmin Aguilera, Jasmine Lee, Jason Crase, Jason Gottweis, Jay Reynolds, Jayderbug Spencer, Jazzy Mills, Jeanna Savoca, Jeff Bandera, Jeff Peterson, jekki, Jen Cliff Harrington, Jen Dennis, Jen Lynn, Jen Martinez, Jenessa Lingard, Jenifer Garcia, Jenifer Gitzen, Jenn Andersen, Jenn L Phillips, jenna gordon, Jenna Raven, Jenni Tang, Jennie Walsh, JennieDubbs, Jennifer, Jennifer, Jennifer Castro, Jennifer De Marco, Jennifer Eldracher, Jennifer Gracin, Jennifer Hubka, Jennifer Lam, Jennifer Lin Freese, Jennifer Mercado, Jennifer Nolan, Jennifer Parks, Jennifer Philburn, Jennifer Plank, Jennifer Schulze, Jennifer Scouras, Jennifer Tao, Jennifer Tran, Jenny C, Jenny cobb, Jenny Kreuzmann, Jenny Yao, JenTheNoobishGeek, Jeremiah Bentley, Jeremiah Eoff, Jeremiah Johnson, Jeremiah Robinson, Jérémy, Jeremy and Kirsten Walters, Jeremy Castillo, Jeremy Moyle, Jeremy Oakes, Jeremy Quickel, Jeremy Vyska, Jerika Snively, Jesi Saige, Jesi Velvetine, Jess, Jess, Jess Borucki, Jess Hendricks-D'Asaro, Jess Sam, Jesse Simonsson, Jesse Smith, Jessi Moss, Jessica, Jessica, Jessica, Jessica, Jessica, Jessica Altmeyer, Jessica Becker, Jessica Blair, Jessica Bohli, Jessica Carrillo, Jessica Carter, Jessica Clamp, Jessica Cooney, Jessica Elizabeth Salinas, Jessica Ernest, Jessica Estrada, Jessica Gamble, Jessica Griffith, Jessica Harrie, Jessica Hippert, Jessica Hocken, Jessica Hoover, Jessica Ignatoski, Jessica Johansen, Jessica Juliano, Jessica M., Jessica Park, Jessica Prince, Jessica

Richards, Jessica Rose, Jessica Simmons, Jessica Sutter, Jessie Eldridge, Jessie Gassen, Jessie Reno, Jessie Sakamoto, Jewel, Jherika Howze, Jill Donahue-Lamb, Jillian Ekenberg, Jillian Muller, Jillian Strazzere, Jimpo01, Jinx, jjpetey, Jo Bro, Jo Carter, Joakim Elofsson, Joanetta Smith, Joanna Peguero, Joanna Pereyda, Jocelin, Jocelyn Mallon, Jocelyne Carrillo, Jodi, Joe Kotanchik, Joe Martinez, Joe Niffen, Joel Cright, Joelle L, Joey Atadero, Joey Watkins, Johanna Pettersson, Johanna Tsai <3, John Abeyta, John Albinsson, John Breslin, John Desmarais, John Mead, John Respeto, John Siegel, John Velazquez, JoJoX, Jomega, Jon Bomarito, Jon Dalle, Jon Darling, Jon Henning Haugland, Jonathan, Jonathan Davis, Jonathan Evans, Jonathan Kane, Jonathan Smith, Jonathan Yao, Joni, Joni Mora, Jonothan Harbourne, Jordan, Jordan, Jordan Campbell, Jordan Devine, Jordan Gisch, Jordan Hall Campbell, Jordan McBrayer, Jordan Penrose, Jordin Baugh, Jörg Sonnenberger, Jose, Josee Hildebrandt, Joseph Hudson, Joseph Prine, Josh K, Josh Lambert, Josh Levenberg, Josh Parr, Joshua A. Torres, Joshua Gerdes, Joshua M Dreher, Joshua Phillips, Joshua Wilusz, Joss, Journee Gautz, Jovs, Joy, Joy Manzo, Joyce Levengood, JPaupst, Judit Martínez, Judith Hall, Judy, Jukeboxpanda, Julia F, Julia Ferreira, Julia Groscost, Julia Litzbarski, Julia Maria Espejo, Julia S., Juliana Knight, Juliana Moraes, Juliann Weidenmoyer, Julianna Frasca, Julianna Manfredo, Julie, Julie DeCarlo, Julie E. Hirata, Julie Scott, Julie TELLIER, Juliet Goyert, Juliet Rosales, Juliette Lansoy, Juliette Nash, Justice, Justin Chmieleski, Justin Flatt, Justin Mercer, Justine Ghosty, JustJonnie, JustLynette, jzengg@gmail.com

K

K Harris, K. Simone Kelly, Kaas, Kacey Collinsworth, Kachina Mabey, Kady Kilmer, Kaela, Kaelie, Kaelyn, Kaerien Yang, Kage CMore, Kaither NoxBlood, Kaitland, Kaitlen, Kaitlin Parr, Kaitlin Schultz, Kaitlyn Adams, Kaitlyn Bolton-Blevins, Kaitlyn G, Kaitlyn Myers, Kaitlyn Wong, Kaity, Kaity Seitz, Kalamithé, Kaleigh Jones, Kales, Kali Murguia, Kali Pettersen, Kalika, Kalyn E. Smith, Kalyn Surls, Kana Rey, Kara, Kara Obosky, Kara Webster, Karen, Karen, Karen Bogard, Karen Broughton, Karen DeStefano, Karen Dobis, Karen Middaugh, Karen Takel, Karen Tobon, Karen Zaragoza, Karin, Karina Grimaldi, Karissa Ramos, Kasey Cooksey, Kaslin Fields, Kat, Kat Combs, Kat Graves, Kat Jennings, Kat Laue, Katariina, Katariina Kurjessuo, Kate Bleyle, Kate Christensen, Kate Jones, Kate Kress, Kate Lyons, Kate Nowack, Kate Orwig, Kate Sickels, Kate Tilton, Kate VanDonge, Katee, Katee Robert, Katelyn Ferrie, Katelyn Gallagher, Katelyn Moore, Katelyn Noyes Lmt, Katelynn Robinson, Kateri Anderson, Katharina G., Katharina Schoeneck, Katherine, Katherine Anne, Katherine Camille Yuri Horikami, Katherine Davis, Katherine Heriford, Katherine Hunt, Katherine Novick, Katherine Paisley, Katherine Wright, Katherine-Ali-Rubio-Long, Kathleen Hickey, Kathleen Lillard, Kathleen Montgomery, Kathleen Rose Muir, Kathleen Sansfacon, Kathryn Brattmiller, Kathy Chester, Kathy Dowdell, Kati, Katie, Katie, Katie, Katie, Katie, Katie Alphenaar, Katie Anderson, Katie Bennett, Katie Fortenbacher, Katie Havird, Katie Holschlag, Katie La Creta, Katie Marie, Katie Muscente, Katie Quinn, Katie Rachowicz, Katie Shainline, Katie Talhelm, Katie W., Katja ;), Katrina, Katrina, Katrina Pettigrew, Katrina Rowley, Kay, Kay Kuever, Kay T., Kay-Ann Barrett, kaydeebee, Kayla, Kayla, Kayla Gibson, Kayla Gilmore, Kayla McPherson, Kayla Oser, kayla pfotenhauer, Kayla S, Kaylan Lee-Kwai, Kaylee, Kaylee Crance, Kaylee May, Kaylee Micu, Kayleigh Wynne Cimino, Kaylin Quinn Espinosa, Kayloni, Kazicle, Kazu, kbozzelli, KDBeckwi36, kdukes2, Keely Jackson-Hoare, Keely Rivers, Keera, Keira, Keith E. Hartman, Kelcey Nicole, Kelci Griffith, Kelley Carpenter, Kelli Rioux, Kelly Cathey, Kelly Croft, Kelly Evans, Kelly Fruge, Kelly John Cooke, Kelly Stacy, Kelly Wallace, Kelsey, kelsey, Kelsey Costa, Kelsey Matheis, Kelsey Reger, Kelsey S, Kelsey S. Hoffman, Kendall Fuller, Kendall Lesperance, Kendallchaos, Kendra Hilse, Kendra Jones, Kendra Kilian, Kendra Maeda, KendragonTheGreat, Kenneth Howell, Kenzie Anderson, Kenzie Sturgill, Keri, Kerry, Keshia, KETEVAN TOPCHISHVILI, Kethry Willow, KETS, Kevin, Kevin Orme, Kevin Serrano, Keyang, Khillynn Thyme, Khue Nong, Kian, Kiana, Kiana Wilkerson, Kiara Rojas, Kiersten

Kozbial, Kih Sarad, Kika, Kiley Helblig, Kim, Kim, Kim Curler, Kim Kline, Kim Kluss, KIM PAO, Kim Phan, Kim Picard-Dufresne, Kim Woo, Kimberley Thouin, Kimberly, Kimberly Bain, Kimberly Chopin, Kimberly Foster, Kimberly Grisham, Kimberly Miller, Kimberly Trant, Kimberly Wilcher, Kimu, Kindra Roberts, Kinsey, Kirah Bruce Tagoe, Kiri H, Kirste Vandergiessen, Kirsten Mulvihill, Kirsti, kirsty tomlin, Kisame, Kit, KitKat V, Kitsunot, Kitty Moritz, Kiwixlove, kkmjyy, Kleenixon, KM, Knight of Words, Kno Problem, Kookie, Kori Gonzalez, KRDiamond, Kreozot, Kri Bartholomew, Kris, Kris DeRhodes, Kris Lisi, Kris Waleisky, Krissy Olson, Krista, Krista Harris, Krista R Shafer-hazlet, Kristan Hardy, Kristen Dettlinger, Kristen Durairaj, Kristen Ferrell, Kristen Haggerty, Kristen Kelly-Aechter, Kristen Russell, Kristen Saunders, Kristen Tennison, Kristie Neises, Kristie Taphouse, Kristin, Kristin Gugino, Kristin Houchin, Kristin Niicole, Kristin Paull, Kristin Peers, Kristin Petroske, Kristina, Kristina, Kristine Nguyen, Kristiné Sharp, Kristopher Atchley, Krystina Stigman, Krystine Sahagun, Kuo, Kuris Khaos, Kye Handy, kyi, Kyle, Kyle Hart, Kyle Pluemer, Kyle Sprowles, Kylee Hall, Kylie Couvelha, Kylie Enten, Kylie Tovine, Kylie-Lynne Bechdel, Kyliee Colyer, KylieKittie, Kylish Renner, Kyndall, Kynnadie Bennett, Kyotaka, Kyrah de Wit

L

L Selina Delgadillo, L Taylor, L.d. MacKrell, Lacey K., Lacey Oscarson, Lacey Sears, Ladarrius Yarbrough, LadyKage, LadyWest, Laerke, LaiaMoon, Lairi86, Laith, Lanise Brown, Larissa Z, Lark Blocher, LaTeeshKnows, LaToya, LaToyia Hanson, Laura, Laura A. Kurtz, Laura Benson, Laura Clark, Laura Ellyson, Laura Flouzat, Laura Joy, Laura Newquist, Laura Repass, Laura Stoops, Laura Vondenhuevel, Lauran Foegen, Laurel McGinley, Lauren, Lauren Bomse, Lauren Hogan, Lauren Lam, Lauren Lennon, Lauren Lloyd, Lauren M Smit, Lauren Poet, Lauren Potts, Lauren Sullivan, Lauren Wilson, Lauretta Lambert, lauriane simon, Laurie M, Lauryn Hill, Layla Rinn, Layna-Boo, Lea, Lea B, Lea Mara, Leah Davis, Leah Rocha, Leah Webber, LeAnn LaFollette, Leann Overby, LearaWolf, Leila Varzideh, Leland Hanna, Leslee Wodrich, Leslie de la Torre, Leslie Guandique, Leslie Smith, Leticia Betteridge, Levi Boggs, Levi Chapin, LexasaurusR3x, Lexi, Lexi Lucy, Lexx, LGlaser, Li Yu, Liam Coballes, Liane Herzog, Libby, Libraryheir, lida_wood, Lieyle Gonzalez, Lilac P., Lili Hodgins, Liliqued, Lillian Bright, Lilly Parreira, Lilo, Lily Lovett, Lily Riehn, Lily Rinehart-Mann, Linda F, Linda Smit, Lindsay D., Lindsay Galbraith, Lindsay Shurtliff, Lindsay Trychta, Lindsey, Lindsey, Lindsey Anne Hunter, Lindsey White, Lindsey Yery, Linh Chau, Linh Tang, Linnea, Lionel Margaka, Liri, Lisa, Lisa, Lisa Bannon, Lisa Bohn, Lisa Clarke, Lisa Czagas, Lisa Lawford, Lisa Ward, LittleLunar, LittleRedBee, Liverius, Livi Seguna, Liz Babcock, Liz Gruenwald, Liz kidd, Liz Kimbrell, Liz S., Lizbeth Rhea, Lizzy Breakwell, Lizzy McIntyre, LJB2145, Lodeme, Logan, Logan Arnone, Lohcan, Lorena Sinaha, Lori Grande, Lori Willis, Lorna Harris, Losty, Lotti Rogers, Lou, Louis Carr, Louise Sidney, Lucas-Ray-Curry, Lucey Snyder, Lucia, Lucia, Lucia Piazza, Lucie M, Lucifer, Lucy Garcia, Luis Garcia, Luiza Bondila, Luke, Luke Shelton, Luli, Luna, Luz Jatip, Luz K., Lydia J Kopsa, Lynée Boackle, Lynnette lavalle, Lyra Hawkins, Lyric Graves, Lyzette Vega

M

M, M Dilling, M_Rashino, Maarten Van Ginhoven, Mackenzie Clem, Mackenzie Lee, Mackenzie Walls, MadCatter (Cat Fleming), Maddy Butcher, Madeleine Alexandra Applegate-Gross, Madeline D, Madeline Delamora, Madeline Szymanski, Madeline Wilson, madelines.2015@gmail.com, MadhattersTwin, Madi, Madi Burley, Madison Kolke, Madison Nicole, Madison Thie, Magda Garza, Magdalena, Magdalena M Kessler, Maggie, Maggie Straub, Makayla, makayla rush, Makenzie Grissom, Maksim Krautsou, Malary Florek, Malia Gonzales, MaLinda Rose, Mallory Hetherington, Mallory Krishna, MamaVia03, ManajuiceLizzy, Mandi, Mandi Gray, Mandy Barnes, Mandy Bauza, Mandy Ing, Mandy Vang, Manel GHARBI, Manic, Manny-i-C, Manon, Manon Schertz, Manon Wofford, Mara, Maranda Hernandez, Marcus Dolce, Marcus

J, Marcus Warchhold, Margaret Brown-Bury, Margaret M, Margaret McMillan, Margaret Rogers, Margherita Monico, Margret Wood, Maria, Maria, Maria Babko, Maria Christina Tiglao, Maria Esmeralda, Maria Fischer, Maria Hutt, Maria Margaret A, Maria Morera, Maria Rivera, Maria Shinn, Mariah Brune, Mariah Griffin, Mariah Martinez, Mariam, Mariam Bertalan, Marianna, Maricela Ramirez, Marie-lou Martel, Marie-Pier Drapeau, Marie.S, Marielle Riveros, Marietta Delene, Marina Kinalone Simonnet, Marion Avalon, Marisa Obregon, Marissa Schwartz, Marjorie Dawson, Mark G, Mark Rice, MarkusW, Marrisa Lynn, MarsBars, Martha Irene Vega Frola, Martha Nussbaum, Martial M, Martika Carrasco, Martin Buschmann Rustan, Mary Beth, Mary Birkhead, Mary Delgado, Mary Elizabeth, Mary Polk, Mary Ragain, Mary Selby, Mary Smith, Mary Viehweg, Mary Wampach, MaryBeth Franklin, matlock0065, Matt, Matt Switzer, Matthew, Matthew Boston, Matthew Miller, maud Melan, Maude Malenfant, Maureen Pauly-Hubbard, Maureen Riehl Albertson, Maxine Lopez, May de la Cruz, May Yan, Mayan Levin, MayB, Mayhem's Muse, Maz, McKayla Gray, McKenna Brutlag, Meagan, Meagan Porter, Meaghan Brassey, mealaXselkie, MechaStitch, Meg, Meg, Meg Myers, Megan, Megan, Megan Bosch, Megan Brennan Limerick, Megan Bush, Megan Campbell, Megan Carl, Megan Elizabeth Johnson, Megan Griffin, Megan Gruginski, Megan Hall, Megan Harper, Megan Laureen, Megan Lewis, Megan May Sass, Megan Reed, Megan Rogers, Megan S. Lauderdale, Megan Schmidt, Megan Van Sickles, Megan Williams, Megann Flowers, Megaroonie, Meghan, Meghan Lloyd, Meghann Eisermann, Megyn MacDougall, Melanie Broggi, Melanie G, Melanie Kuhlman, Melanie Lim, Melena Torretta, Melina Talo, Melinda Adams, Melissa, Melissa, Melissa, Melissa, Melissa, Mélissa, Melissa Arruda, Melissa Etheridge, Melissa Gardner-King, Melissa Johansson, Melissa Porter, Melissa Tatum, Melissa Ward, Melissa Weller, Melissa Williams, MelissaDAnnasun, Mellizard, Melody, MelyannaSanoir, Melyssa Preast, Mercedes Lamb, Mercedes Veronica, Mercier-Krzychacz, Meredith, Meredith M, Meredith Staton, Meredith Summers, Meridith Sotolongo, Mermagonairy, Mia Artiles, Mia Cuk, Mia Jones, Miakim Egglefield, Micah Wege, Micala Dawkins, micayah smith, Michael "Nighteyes" Poulsen Dürr, Michael Cleveland, Michael David Robertson, Michael Diley, Michael Forbes, Michael Goins, Michael Levine, Michael Litterell, Michael Luinge, Michael Roemer, Michael Shunnarah, Michael Tyler, Michael Wall, Michael Woods, Michaela, Michaela Balkus, Michaela E Blow, Michaela Jackson, Michaela Laurencin, Michal Adini, Micheapet, Michele Hope, Michelle, Michelle, Michelle, Michelle Andrea Pang-Oden, Michelle Bonelli, Michelle Coston, Michelle Hamilton, Michelle Huhn, Michelle Kay, Michelle Kern, Michelle Knight, Michelle Lawson, Michelle Maria Bryant, Michelle McAveney, Michelle Mertz, Michelle Oriolo, Michelle Rodriguez, Michelle Steele, Michelle Wendler, MichelleG, MiChera Begano, Michiel D, Mickayla Walsdorf, Mickeal Prince, Mieko Bilz, Miffy Minty, Miguel A Valencia, Miguel Ponce De Leon Jr, Mikaela Benner, Mikaela Matney, Mikaela Wantz, Mikala Champin, Mikayla, Mikayla Alt, Mikayla DeBaker, Mikayla I Johnston, Mike Bachle, Mike Cunningham, Mike Curtis, Mike Wieczorek, Miki Marsala, Mimi Chung, Mindy Regnell, Mink Krone, Minna Mai, Minna Turunen, Minotaar, Minzoku, Mioko, Miranda, Miranda Donnellan, Miranda Marini, Miranda Olson-Inman, Miranda Rollins, Miranda Weavil, Miriam Harries, Miriam Sleight, Mirroredmei, Miss Fats, MissSqueakyTV, Missy, Missy B., Missy Woford, Misty, Misty, Misty Bradley, Misty Jandron, Misty R., MK, Mo Regalado, Molly Wheeler, Monday Megan Schmitt, Monica, Monica Ambrozej, Monica Lopes, Monica Ritz, Monica Wilner, Monique Kirkwood, MoonLitShadowz, Morgan, Morgan McEvoy, Morgan Mosier, Morgan PixieRook Busby, Morgan Robinson, Morgan Strite, Morgane RODRIGUES, Moriah Wrenn-Sandkulla, Morwen Elda, mouselet, Moyochi, Mr Rikkles, MrPippali, MrPlaywright, MsBrinaBell, Muchipanuchi, Muniba Khan, municc, Muriel Michael, Murielle Guénou, muzaiden, My Master, Mykala Kearney, Mylon Elliott, Myra Lopez, Myrisha, Mystique.Pins

N

Nadia, Nadia Hammad, Nadine Kennedy, Nadine Malench, Naida Inoa, NalieRay,

Nancy, Nancy Florence, Nanexxe, Nano DiamondHeart, Naomi "Phoenix Feathers" Wong, Naomi Garcia, Naomi Palmer, Naomi Usher, Natalie, Natalie Laffranchi, Natalie Little, Natalie MacDonald, Natania Nisbet, Natasha Neher, Natashja Gentry, Nathalie DeFelice, Nathalie Rancourt, Nathan, Nathan Howe, Nathan Schwartz, Nathan Smernoff, Nathaniel Luna Stigger, naviolivia, Naytia, Neil James Gibson, Neil Reynolds, NekoRaveWolf, Nelfalot, Nelly R, Nelson J. Alfaro, NeonMuffin, Nerdy_Kinks, Nery Morales, Nessa Bond, Never After, Nicholas Joly, Nicholas Kendall Whittington, Nicholas Stephenson, Nick, Nick Burrill, Nick Clark, Nick Nerdvana, Nick Nesti, Nick Townsend, Nick Williams, Nicki Greene, Nicole, Nicole, Nicole, Nicole, Nicole Bak, Nicole Boks, Nicole Copeland Perez, Nicole Evensen, Nicole Flynn, Nicole Gerth, Nicole Gonzales, Nicole Gonzalez, Nicole McFall, Nicole Mitchell, Nicole Overstreet, Nicole Peterson, Nicole Stanzini, Nicole Taylor, Nicole Tolman, Nicolette Andrews, Nicolette Cooper, Nicolle Stern, Nidoking, Niicky Bee, Nikeesha Gooding, Niki Coppola, Nikki, Nikki Oquendo, NiljaLee, Nimthiriel, Nina mak, Nini Seang, Nirina Hadjicosta, nlg734, Noah, Noah E, Noelle, Noemi, Noemi Aldape, Nohelly Negrete, Norberto Leon, Norma JMB, Nott, Nova Unlimited, Nova Wolf, Nugget, Nyoka Miller

O

Odie Michelle, Ogre328, Oldguygamer, Oliver, Oliver Brink, Olivia, Olivia, Olivia Bacarella, Olivia M., OLIVIA MORTIER, Olyvia Cepeda, Omi, OneBigAssSquid, Or Segal, Ositha, Oswin W, Ouran, Overlyconfused

P

Paige Massingale, Paloma, Pamela Hartwig, Pamela Palumbo, Paola Badia, Paola Cresti, Paradox, Parita Patel, Parker, PathosMachine, Patricia Allen, Patricia Cottrell, Patricia Garcia, Patricia Stewart, Patricia Topp, Patrick Douglas, Patrick Lambert, Patrick Landry, Patrick Millican, Patrick Voight, Paul Diaz, Paul Hendricks, Paul Kobylka, Paul Kramer, Paul Perrotti, Paula Georgescu, Paula M Fama, Pauline Ma, Paweł Kostka, Paweł Wasilewski, Pchełka, Peach Hatt-Beattie, Peaches Nester, Pedro Ezequiel, Peggy Pillers, penguinonstrike, Penny Rubin, Perdire, Peter Ryan, Petra Bartha, phaeley, PhantomFantasy, Pheonix, Philip, Philip Perez, Phoebe, phrevan, Phylicia Newton, Phylicia S., Pierre-Luc Vachon, Pikarumblee, Pilar Swanson, Pinakamataas, PinkL8dy, Pinupcomedian, Piper Nraenog, pj_brady, Popsicle Emperor, Preslee McWhorter, Preston Leftwich, Princess-Melynne Claveria, PrincessBoone, Prisca, Priscila, Priscilla, Priscilla Malerbe, Pueschel Edmonds, Purple Parfait, Purple Piece Games

Q

QCLady, Quarras, Queen Elizardbeth, QueenieNoodle, Quinn Speaker, QuinTalon

R

R San, R. Alexander Spoerer, Rachael, Rachael Houchin, Rachael M Bianco, Rachael Marie Simmonds, Rachael Meilak, Rachel, Rachel Bennett, Rachel Chaffin, Rachel Frandsen, Rachel Gerold, Rachel Hooper, Rachel Kent, Rachel Miller, Rachel Nelligan, Rachel Riley, Rachel Rodriguez, Rachel Sawyer, Rachel Serna, Rachel Sutphin-Kocher, Rachel T, Rachel Underwood, Rachel Vernon, Rachel W., Rachel Wesson, Rachel Wing, Rachel Wolven, Rachelka, RachelLPelfrey, Raine Garcia, Raluca Chirosca, Ramiyah Valentine, Randiman Rogers, Randy Fisher, Raquel, Raquel Hernandez (Rocket_Sprocket), Raul Silva, Raurasaurus, Raven Coit, Rayavous, Rayven Nightfall, Realitie Vittoria Butler, Reanna B, Rebecca, Rebecca, Rebecca Baldus, Rebecca Davis, Rebecca Doyle, Rebecca Gurwah, Rebecca Harkness, Rebecca Hazen, Rebecca Jewell, Rebecca Johnson, Rebecca Leannah, Rebecca Lehman, Rebecca

Olashuk, Rebecca Ramsey, Rebecca Starling, Rebekah, Rebekah Dawn, Rebekah Wolf, reduL, Reece Laabs, Reese+Kyle, Regalia Shady, Regan, Regan Merlenbach, ReiDesu Arts, reika817, reirachiruu, Ren Perry, René Kristensen, René Mackenzie, Rene Roy, Renee, Renee Lynde, Renee Olin, RenegadeNeedle, Renell Decker, Renita Williams, Renzy Sprouse, Repa, Rhozlyn Javier, Rhylie Fyre, Rhys Morgan, Ri Farris, Richard, Richard Bousquet, Richard Godfrey, Richard Theobald, Richard Webb, Richelle Hamment, Richelle Heilmann, Ricki, Ricki Mudd, Riikka Puttonen, Riley, Riley Freeman, Riley Rachelle, Rita Junot, Rivadrea, River Verdin, RJ, Rlaein, Rob Fowler, Rob MacAndrew, Robert Chute, Robert Ellison, Robert McClelen III, Robert Prine, Robert Russell, ROBIN, Robin Grace, Robin Schmitz, Robyn, Robyn Smith, Rochelle Walker, Rockxane Lapointe, Rolf stevns, RoMina Boss, Ronan Pritschet, Rosa, Rosalyn Moistner, Rosamaria Ewing, Rose, Rose, Rose spahr, Rosettarose, Rosmery Banegas, Rowan Minney, Roxan Vasilik, Roxana, Roxann Nunez, Roxanne Powell, RoxyRose, Ruby Nelson, Ruixiao Zuo, RuncibleFox, Rusty B, Ruth Baumann, Ruth Tyler, Ruthenia (Ruth) Dillon, Ryalyn, Ryan Bugbee, Ryan Burbridge, Ryan Coltrain, Ryan Cruz, Ryan Dodge, Ryan Gates, Ryan Horng, Ryan Ikerd, Ryan Morford, RYAN OENTOJO

S

S.L. Johnson, Sabatier Marion, sablec@hotmail.com, Sabra Jones, Sabrena Evanson, Sabrina Dragomir, Sabrina Medhkour, Sabrina Ty, Sadie, Sadie Fitzgerald, Sahara Gonzalez, Saharrah Marrket, Sally Collins, Salume Osakue, Sam, Sam Giles, Sam Loveless, Sam O, Sam Powell, Sam Zimmerman, Samaira Ahmed, Samantha, Samantha Aguilar, Samantha Brown Moore, Samantha Caldwell, SAMANTHA CAPUTO, Samantha Carroll, Samantha Claman, Samantha Clough, samantha cruse, Samantha D, Samantha DeWitt, Samantha Dowling, Samantha Elmer, Samantha Flynn, Samantha Gebbie, Samantha Laine, Samantha Looney, Samantha McBride, Samantha McGuire, Samantha Mendez, Samantha Meyer, Samantha Miller, Samantha Mohr, Samantha Richardson, Samantha Shaw, Samantha Singh, Samantha Wood, Samara Poole, SAMazon Creations, Samma Carder-Wicker, Sammy Jaye, Samuel, Samuel Archambault-Masse, Samuel Bennett, Samuel Urquhart, Samuel Weiss, Sandra Volz, sandrey, Sandy, Sara, Sara, Sara A. McGuire, Sara Adams, Sara Bedard, Sara Buckhammer, Sara Dziubek, sara hadwiger, Sara Keller, Sara Lin, Sara Marie Harrah, Sara McLean, Sara Nelson, Sara Pislaan, Sara Smith, Sara Weimer, Sara Witt, Sarah, Sarah Alvarez, Sarah Ankepr, Sarah Anuszkiewicz, Sarah Ari, Sarah B, Sarah DeLacey, Sarah Doulman, Sarah Elizabeth Koenig, Sarah Elizabeth Lawrence, Sarah Elliott, Sarah Fornoff, Sarah Frederick, Sarah Frisk, Sarah Heverling, Sarah Humphreys, Sarah Johnson, Sarah Jungling, Sarah M Brown, Sarah M Eggleston, Sarah M., Sarah Martineau, Sarah McCormick, Sarah McLean, Sarah Morton, Sarah Nash, Sarah Okura, Sarah Plum, Sarah Rose, Sarah Roudon, Sarah Smith, Sarah Thompson, Sarah von Seggern, Sarah Wingo-Story, Sarahseesthis, Sarai Narvaez, Sarath Vega Gutiérrez, Sarina, Sarina Davis, Sarina Kruse, Sasha L, Satesh Charran, Savannah Remmers, Savannah Singh, SavvyVamp, Sayaka Jane, Saysha Sebren, Scheree Reeves, Schkaka, scifantasy, Scott, Scott Adams, Scott Bates, Scott Boyce, Scott C, Scott Mertens, Scott Nedved, Scott Resseguie, Scribellz, Scrim, Sean, Sean Ewing, Sean F, Sean Fansler, Sean Lawrence, Sean Mayovsky, Séan Michael Milljour, Sean Pierce, Sebastian Groth, Sébastien Cassard, Seffi, seibersays, Selena, Selene Schneider, Selpher, Serena, Serena Marika, Sergio J Tuero, Seth Kropp, Shaina Kannady-Solel, Shanice, Shaniel Bowen, Shannan Strickland, Shannara M S, Shannon & Matt Burke, Shannon Blair, Shannon Buchal, Shannon Collins, Shannon Hamburger, Shannon Marie Collins, Shannon/Melody, Sharifa, Shark_Kitty, Sharlene Gardiner, Sharon, Sharon, Shauna Yuen, Shaunna, Shawn Creese, Shawn M Banks, Shawna Kolb, Shayla Sackinger, Shayné R., Sheena Gotta, Sheila, Shelby Covey, Shelby Llewellyn, Shelby Ray Wood, Shelby Stevens, Sheldon, Shelly Rose Weinryb, Sheree Blanchard, Sheri, Sheridan Barber, Sherry Mock, Shiloh-Rose Meikel, Shiny yih, Shivas_Avatar, Shondel, ShounenHeart, Shy Ruparel, Sida, Sierra and Dillion, Sierra C, Sierra Geiger, Sierra Keith, SilentKnight, Silver, Silvia, Silvia Sgalippa, simon,

Simplicity1511, Simply Radiant, Simplymali, SimplyNobody, Sinead Heffernan, Sintheyah Siyarath, Siobhan Cemper, Skribblz, Sky Stationery Studio, Sloan Gibson, Smileangel, Smurk, Sofia, Sofia R, Solveig, Solveig Nelson, Soma, SombrioFe, Sondra Bakke, Sonia Beaulieu, Sonia Brugger, Sonia Lai, Sonia Minta-Mae Hartley, Sonia Rebai, Sonja Richardson, Sonya Schultz, Soobie Mennym, Sophia J Robinson, Sophie Bowden, Sophie Gigl, Sophie Paquet, Spicymiso, Spockrocket, SqueeAsaur, St0rmyski3s, Stacey-Ann Sterling, Stacia Orange Tafoya, Stacy Bowers, Stacy Juan, Star, Star Joens, Starry, Stefani, Stefani Soares, Stefanie, Stefanie Day, Stelmine, Stephanie, Stephanie Barnett, Stephanie Bayani, Stephanie Dion, Stephanie Flinders, Stephanie Graham, Stephanie Jackson, Stephanie Jepson Klonowski, Stephanie JS Steenstra, Stephanie L. Cone, Stephanie L. Johnson, Stephanie L. Salas, Stephanie Leal, Stephanie Morris, Stephanie Renee Trull, Stephanie Tanada, Stephanie Wallace, Stephanie Wood, Stephanie Zars, Stephen Farrell, Stephen Keltz, Stephen Schwindt, Stephleda, Steve Dong, Steve Rosa, Steven Harbron, Stevie_05, Suki, Sulyn, Summer Coffey, SummerRose100, Sunny, supjfos, Susan, Susan G., Susan Lam, Susan Perez, Suzanna Au, Suzanna Greer, Suzanna Stenger, Swati, Swiftfox_reign, Sybille Hauser-Raspe, Sydney Sallows, SylaRaza, Sylvano Tumelero, Sylvia Alesia

T

T B., T-Minus 10, T.j. Stacey, Tabby Butcher, Tabetha Aldridge, Tabitha, Tabitha Arment, Tabitha Forman, Taelor, Tahnia, Tal De La Rosa, Tal Meloche, tallerfar, tallulah, Tamara Funck, Tammy Lo, Tanja Hummel, TANNA, Tanner Herrmann, Tanya Charron, Tanya Hunter, Taryn Bell, Taryn Stewart, Tasha Bogan, Tasha Burdette, Tatiana MacGregor, Tatiana Pujkis, Tatianna Forget, TatyanaAlexander, Tay, Taylor, Taylor, Taylor Bobrich, Taylor Cox, Taylor Kiechlin, Taylor Lackey, Taylor Noles, Taylor O'Donnell, Taylor Quinley, Taylor Reitmeier, Taylor Smith, Teairra Starks, Tegra Shepherd, Teisha, telanthar, Telia Phillips, Teresa Chappell, Terri Renaud, terrukallan, TES, Tess Serendipity Sterling, TexasJV4, Thaddeus Nowak, Thalya, The Combs, The Creative Fund by BackerKit, The Robot Wolf, The Waffle, The5am1am, TheDoctor19901, TheLazyPanduh, TheMainRed, Theora LaBarge, TheyPaints, Thien Nguyen, This_Anne, thomas, Thomas Bryant, Thomas Burgess, Thomas Mecklenburg (Highlander), Thomas Meyer, Thomas Pine, Thu Ha Le, Tiana K Langer Arroyave, Tiara Scribner, Tiarra L., Tibor Oo, Tiffani Gunter, Tiffany, Tiffany, Tiffany "Vengeance" M., Tiffany Adams, Tiffany Coward, Tiffany Duquette, Tiffany Horton, Tiffany Isselhardt, Tiffany Jenna Farley, Tiffany L, Tiffany Roberts, Tiffany Sun, Tiffany Tullos, Tiffany Zabrina Henderson, Tim, Tim Bowes, Timothy Hansmann, Tina, Tina "MrsRedWych" Kennedy-Sabri, Tina Bryant, Tina Cochran, Tissysbaby, Tobias Rieper, Todd Waddell, Tom Carter, Toni Bausman, Toni Lynn Spath, Toni Taylor-Satterfield, Tony, Tori, Tori Johnwatson Sneden-Mansir, Tori_K, Torikita, Torri Davios, Tracey DeVoe, Tracey Elser, Traci Hofer, Tracie Beth Lucas, Tracy, Tracy Boyette, Tracy C, Tracy Levesque, Travera, Trevor Landon, Trevor O'Brien, Trevor Sthen, Trinity, Trinity Corsetti, Trinity87, Trinket, Trishna, Tristan Davolt, Tullia Yu, TurtleDuck48, Tuula, Tylar Bright, Tyler, Tyler Anthony Edwards, Tyler Bunn, Tyler Cummings, Tyler Potter, Tyler Will Davidson, Tyler Wydendorf

U

Ulinda Minatel, UmbraVGG, Urbandruid2112, UwU Francia Mariby UwU

V

Valda793, ValeLux, Valemunate, Valentina Dowdy, Valeria Garza, Valerie Brazzale-Russell, Valerie Owenby, Valisa Aho, Vanessa, Vanessa Ayotte Gravel, Vanessa Blacow, Vanessa Garcia, Vanessa Gonzalez, VasaiM, Vashti, Vergia Farrow, Vero A, VertuHonagan, Vesenia Lindsey, Vianney Tansia, Vicente Gonzalez, Vicki, Vickie_ Martinezz, Victendo64, Victorbjorn, Victoria, Victoria, Victoria, Victoria Dwyer,

Victoria Ferrell, Victoria Green-Pinelli, Victoria Hirons, Victoria Lin, Victoria MacEntee, Victoria Phongpaew, Victoria Rietz, Victoria Rojas, Videl50million, Vietanh Tran, Vikki Regan, Vil, vince bayless, Vincent Mak, Vindhler, Virginia Montserrat Argüelles Santoni, Viridiana, Visa Diep, Vivi.T, Vivian, Vivian Liu, Vivian Santamaria, Viviana Ferreyra

W

WahZahXin, Walter Griffiths, Waouhhh, Wendy, Wendy, Wendy Briggs, Werysek11, Whitney, WhyIsGamora, Wild Gambit, Willem, William Hernândez, William marshall, William T. Thrasher, William Tseng, William Yap, Willscotty, Winter Corbeau, Wissall Homayun, WolfDragoness, Wolxies

X

Xenia Silva, Xiara A.

Y

Yanette, Yang, Yasha Akume, Yasmin Medina, Yates Gregg, YD95, Yeng-Ching Lee, Yesenia Grisales, Yesenia Sheridan, Yibo Bodi, Yolanda Míguez, Yuki, Yume_Cross, Yunina, Yuuga, Yvonne Martinez

Z

Zach, Zach, Zachary Borup, Zaide Jiwani, ZBrook, Ze-Friend-Zone, Zearan, Zephram Wolf, Zoe Bagal, Zoe Hanks, Zoe Ngai, Zuni Aurora Vargas Catalan, ZuzzleQT